W9-AFF-164

continued . . .

"Albert threads through the story her wide-ranging knowledge of plants and herbals. Her ability to use historical research to realize settings and characterizations that ring true should appeal to those seeking a simpler life, one in which there seems to be time to share a story or a slice of pie and write up frugal homemaking tips for the club's newspaper column." —*Booklist*

"As always in any [of] Susan Wittig Albert's series, including this one, the reader feels transplanted in time and place as the meticulous interwoven tidbits bring to life late 1930. Dizzy Lizzy and her eccentric Darlings want to insure that the Day Chicago Dies is not in Sweet Home Alabama." —*The Mystery Gazette*

"Well researched." —*Kirkus Reviews*

The Darling Dahlias and the Cucumber Tree

"Cozy fans will be delighted to learn that the prolific Albert—known for her clever puzzles, engaging characters, love of nature, and outstanding historic research—is debuting yet another exceptional series." —*Booklist* (starred review)

"[Albert] hits all the right notes in this series debut. The plot's believable, the Southern color brims with authenticity, and the characters are charmingly and realistically drawn . . . *The Darling Dahlias and the Cucumber Tree* blooms with success, and here's hoping the ladies have many more opportunities to dig into crime." —*Richmond Times-Dispatch*

"A small Southern town blooms into life in Albert's nostalgic first in a new Depression-era mystery series . . . Albert combines great period detail with sure-footed sleuthing that should satisfy fans and attract new ones." —*Publishers Weekly*

"The author of the popular China Bayles Mysteries brings a small Southern town to life and vividly captures an era and culture—the Depression, segregation, class differences, the role of women in the South—with authentic period details. Her book fairly sizzles with the strength of the women of Darling." —*Library Journal*

THE
DARLING DAHLIAS
AND THE
TEXAS STAR

Susan Wittig Albert

BERKLEY PRIME CRIME, NEW YORK

THE BERKLEY PUBLISHING GROUP
Published by the Penguin Group
Penguin Group (USA) LLC
375 Hudson Street, New York, New York 10014

USA • Canada • UK • Ireland • Australia • New Zealand • India • South Africa • China

penguin.com

A Penguin Random House Company

THE DARLING DAHLIAS AND THE TEXAS STAR

A Berkley Prime Crime Book / published by arrangement with the author

Berkley Prime Crime Books are published by The Berkley Publishing Group.
BERKLEY® PRIME CRIME and the PRIME CRIME logo are trademarks of
Penguin Group (USA) LLC.

For information, address: The Berkley Publishing Group,
a division of Penguin Group (USA) LLC,
375 Hudson Street, New York, New York 10014.

ISBN: 978-0-425-26059-3

PUBLISHING HISTORY
Berkley Prime Crime hardcover edition / September 2013
Berkley Prime Crime mass-market edition / September 2014

PRINTED IN THE UNITED STATES OF AMERICA

10 9 8 7 6 5 4 3 2 1

Cover illustration and logo © by Brandon Dorman.
Cover design by Judith Lagerman.
Interior text design by Tiffany Estreicher.

For Lucille, Pearl, Mildred, and Josephine,
four sisters who made the best of even the worst of times.

Author's Note

The Darling Dahlias and the Texas Star takes place in the summer of 1932. Across the United States, it has already been a year of extreme highs and abysmal lows. More than 13 million Americans have lost their jobs since 1929, and in that same period, more than 10,000 banks have failed—at a time when there is not yet any unemployment or depositors' insurance. The Dow Jones Industrial Average has dropped to 41.22, down 340 points from its bull market high of 381.17 on September 3, 1929.

Looking to the future, the Republicans have nominated President Herbert ("Brother, Can You Spare a Dime?") Hoover for a second term, while the Democrats have selected Franklin Delano ("Happy Days Are Here Again") Roosevelt. Hoping to collect the compensation already due for past service, the Bonus Army of 20,000 Great War veterans has marched on Washington, D.C., and it will take General Douglas MacArthur, an infantry regiment, a cavalry regiment, and six tanks to oust them. It is also the year of the Lindbergh baby kidnapping, of cigar-smoking Bonnie and gun-toting Clyde, and dust storms that turn the sky over the Great Plains, as Aunt Hetty Little would say, as black as the inside of a dog.

Nineteen thirty-two is a year when everything seems to move slower than molasses. The Gross National Product has fallen 43 percent since 1929, and the unemployed and homeless are mired in a Slough of Despond. But it's also a year when things go faster and farther than ever before—a time of exciting achievements. Jimmy Doolittle flies his Gee Bee Model R-1 aircraft into the record books with a speed of 296 miles per hour, and Amelia Earhart pilots her Lockheed Vega 5B (which she affectionately calls "Old Bessie, the fire horse") from Newfoundland to Ireland in 14 hours and 56 minutes—the first woman to fly solo nonstop across the Atlantic. Not satisfied with that record, she flies from Los Angeles to Newark in just over 19 hours, the first woman to fly solo nonstop across the United States.

When I began this mystery series, I thought it might be difficult to write about the Depression, because . . . well, lots of people were depressed. But as I've dug deeper into the newspapers, magazine articles, interviews, and letters of the time, I've learned that while people saw very clearly the difficulty they were in, they resisted giving in to their heartaches and fears. In my family, my mother always told me, "Folks just put their heads down and kept on keeping on." Hard times, yes, and people in our family didn't have one nickel to rub against another. Or, as Mom wryly put it, "We darned the darns in our stockings and then, gol-darn it, we darned 'em again." But they worked hard, found fun where they could, and met often overwhelming challenges with courage, determination, and a deep awareness that almost everybody was in the same leaky boat.

And throughout my research, it is the women who have impressed me the most, the women who made do or did without, shared what they had with those who had less, and smiled as hard as they could to cover their tears.

That is the spirit I want to celebrate in these books about the Darling Dahlias.

I hope you find their stories as heartening as I do.

Thanks to Deborah Winegarten, whose wide acquaintance with the life and times of Pancho Barnes and other early women pilots (and her wonderful collection of books!) gave me a wealth of ideas. Thanks to Nancy Lee McDaniel, for volunteering to help out on the Darling switchboard. And special thanks to my husband, Bill Albert, who, among his many other talents, has flown small airplanes. He suggested some nefarious ways they might be sabotaged.

A note about language. To write about the people of the rural South in the 1930s requires the use of terms that may be offensive to some readers—especially "colored," "colored folk," and "Negro" when they are used to refer to African Americans. Thank you for understanding that I mean no offense.

Susan Wittig Albert
Bertram, Texas

July 30, 1932
The Darling Dahlias Clubhouse and Gardens
302 Camellia Street
Darling, Alabama

Dear Reader,

This is getting to be quite a habit—having books written about our garden club, that is. And a very pleasant habit, too, we must say!

But we're not one bit surprised that Mrs. Albert has decided to write another book about us, because every flower has a story to tell. And the story of the Texas Star (that would be Hibiscus coccineus, according to Miss Rogers, who is such a stickler when it comes to Latin names) is more sensational than most. Who could have guessed that the Texas Star herself, Miss Lily Dare—the fastest woman on earth, faster even than Amelia Earhart!—would have chosen our little town to show off her Dare Devils Flying Circus. Or that Miss Dare might be the object of so much envy and hate because of the way she lived her life and . . .

But then, we'd better not say any more about that, because we might steal Mrs. Albert's thunder and we certainly wouldn't want to do that. Of course, we were understandably uneasy about a story that involves the secret shenanigans of the husband of one of our very own members. We don't like to embarrass people we care about. So we sat down and had a serious discussion with Mrs. Albert about whether she ought to write this particular story or go find something else to write about.

But as Mrs. Albert herself is fond of saying, a little truth never hurt anybody very much, except where it ought to. And since everybody in town already knew all there was to know about the situation by the time the Dare Devils flew away, we decided that it was a story that ought to be told. We understand that this husband—whose name you will learn later in this book—has apologized to all concerned and promises to behave himself from now on. (We also hope that all our Darling husbands will profit from seeing his transgressions written up in a book and think twice before they stray too far from the straight and narrow.)

In our garden club, we all love flowers. But we have also planted a big vegetable garden. It is true that flowers are comfort food for the soul. But a big plate of green beans and fatback, stewed okra with tomatoes, buttered corn on the cob, and potato salad can go a long way to comfort a body, especially these days, when jobs and money are scarce as hens' teeth and everybody's got something to worry about.

And yes, it's a sad fact but true: there is just too much grief and too many crooks and cheaters in this world. (We're not naming any names—we'll leave that to Mrs. Albert.) But we agree with a French fellow named Marcel Proust, who wrote, "Let us be grateful to people who make us happy; they are the charming gardeners who make our souls blossom." So if you'll excuse us, we'll pay attention to being happy and hope that our souls will bloom.

And just to make sure, we'll plant a few pretty flowers along with the beans and okra.

Sincerely yours,
Elizabeth Lacy, President
Ophelia Snow, Vice President & Secretary
Verna Tidwell, Treasurer

The Darling Dahlias Club Roster, July 1932

CLUB OFFICERS

Elizabeth Lacy, club president. Garden columnist for the Darling *Dispatch* and secretary to Mr. Moseley, attorney-at-law.

Ophelia Snow, club vice-president and secretary. Linotype operator and sometime reporter at the Darling *Dispatch*. Wife of Darling's mayor, Jed Snow.

Verna Tidwell, club treasurer. Acting Cypress County treasurer, manages the Cypress County Probate Clerk's office.

Myra May Mosswell, communications chairwoman. Co-owner of the Darling Telephone Exchange and the Darling Diner. Lives with Violet Sims and Violet's baby girl, Cupcake, in the flat over the diner.

CLUB MEMBERS

Earlynne Biddle, a rose fancier. Married to Henry Biddle, the manager at the Coca-Cola bottling plant.

Bessie Bloodworth, proprietor of Magnolia Manor, a boardinghouse for genteel ladies.

Fannie Champaign, proprietor of Champaign's Darling Chapeaux. Sweet on Charlie Dickens, editor and publisher of the Darling *Dispatch*.

Mrs. George E. Pickett (Voleen) Johnson, president of the Darling Ladies Guild, specializes in pure white flowers. Married to the owner of the Darling Savings and Trust Bank.

Mildred Kilgore, married to Roger Kilgore, the owner of Kilgore Motors. The Kilgores have a big house near the ninth green of the Cypress Country Club, where Mildred grows camellias.

Aunt Hetty Little, gladiola lover, town matriarch, and senior member of the club. A "regular Miss Marple" who knows all the Darling secrets.

Lucy Murphy, grows vegetables and peaches on a small farm on the Jericho Road. Married to Ralph Murphy, who works on the railroad.

Miss Dorothy Rogers, darling's librarian. Knows the Latin name of every plant and insists that everyone else does, too. Resident of Magnolia Manor.

Beulah Trivette, artistically talented lover of cabbage roses and other exuberant flowers. Owns Beulah's Beauty Bower, where all the Dahlias go to get beautiful.

Alice Ann Walker, grows iris and daylilies. Her disabled husband, Arnold, tends the family vegetable garden. Cashier at the Darling Savings and Trust Bank.

ONE

Liz Lacy Is in Charge

Monday Evening, July 11, 1932

"Well, it's almost all over," Mildred Kilgore said in her slow Southern drawl. She sat down at the table in the Dahlias' clubhouse kitchen. "I don't mind saying that I, for one, am glad."

Aunt Hetty Little came to the table with a pitcher of cold lemonade and began to fill the four glasses on the table. "All over?" She chuckled wryly. "Why, bless your heart, child, it's just *begun!*"

Mildred was nearly forty, but Aunt Hetty was no spring chicken and felt qualified to call everyone "child," especially when they were talking about presidential elections. At eighty, her memory of presidents went back to Abraham Lincoln, although she had only been able to cast her vote since Mr. Harding, twelve years before. "Can't blame the mess in Washington on us women," she liked to say. "That place was a mess long before we got the vote."

"The nominating conventions are just the beginning,"

Elizabeth Lacy said, agreeing with Aunt Hetty. She put her Dahlias' club notebook on the table and sat down, taking a deep breath. The kitchen door was open and the sweet scent of honeysuckle filled the room, along with the evening song of a perky Carolina wren, perched in the catalpa tree just outside the window. "It's a long time to the elections, although Mr. Moseley says he's pretty sure that—"

"We all know what Mr. Moseley says, Liz," Verna Tidwell put in dryly. She took a chair on the opposite side of the table. "He's been angling for months to get that fellow Roosevelt on the ticket. I sure hope he doesn't regret it. We all know Hoover. Nobody knows what FDR will do."

Verna was tall and thin, with narrow lips, an olive complexion, and dark, searching eyes under unplucked (and thoroughly unfashionable) brows. She didn't pay much attention to fashionable dressing, either. She had come to the meeting straight from her office in the Cypress County courthouse and was still dressed in her working clothes: a plain white cotton short-sleeved blouse and a belted navy gabardine skirt. But what Verna might lack in conventional prettiness, she more than made up for in smarts, which was why Lizzy Lacy liked her so much.

Lizzy reached for one of the pecan jumbles, an old-fashioned cookie that Aunt Hetty had brought. The previous week, the Democrats had nominated Franklin D. Roosevelt, the governor of New York, on the fourth ballot, after a floor fight that just about wore all the delegates out. At least, that was according to the story in the Darling *Dispatch*. What Lizzy herself knew about politics wouldn't fill a peanut shell. But for over a year, Mr. Moseley (her boss and the most prominent lawyer in Darling) had been working like a stubborn mule for Roosevelt, and she tried to keep up with what he was doing. She and Verna and several of their friends had got together in the diner after closing on Saturday night to listen to Mr. Roosevelt's acceptance speech on the radio. The governor had actually chartered an airplane and flown all the way from Albany to Chicago to speak to the convention delegates. An airplane! That was a first for any presidential candidate.

Lizzy wasn't sure how she felt about Governor Roosevelt. He had talked about the federal government's responsibility to help people who needed to find work. But he'd been pretty vague about what he intended to do, except for promising a "new deal," whatever that was. Some people thought they could guess, based on his plans for an old-age pension and unemployment insurance, which he had tried to push through the New York state legislature. But nobody knew for sure.

Lizzy was the kind of person who always liked to know as much as she could about what was going on, so she had asked Mr. Moseley for an explanation. But even he didn't know what a "new deal" was, at least, not specifically.

"It's something the Brain Trust cooked up," he said. When she asked what a "brain trust" was, he'd just laughed. "You might call it a kitchen cabinet," he replied, which left her even more mystified—until he had handed her the third volume of James Parton's *Life of Andrew Jackson.* A scrap of paper marked page 338, where she read about the men who were "supposed to have most of the president's ear and confidence." The kitchen cabinet, she imagined, got together over cigars and coffee (or something stronger) to cook up policy.

Aunt Hetty finished filling the lemonade glasses. "Mr. Moseley is doin' more than just angling," she observed wryly. "I read in the *Dispatch* that he's organizing a group called Darling for FDR."

"Roger is getting some supporters together to campaign for President Hoover," Mildred said in an offhanded tone. She was wearing a new white tucked and pleated cotton shirtwaist dress—her golfing costume. The outfit looked very snazzy, Lizzy thought with a quick stab of envy. The Kilgores had plenty of money, and Mildred—who was plump and rather plain—went to New York to buy her clothes. She always looked like something out of *Vogue*, while the rest of them made do with the out-of-date clothes in their closets. Or, in the case of Verna, a gabardine skirt that was a little shiny in the seat.

"But we're afraid it'll be an uphill fight for Mr. Hoover," Mildred added ruefully. "Here in Darling, anyway."

That was probably true, Lizzy thought. Mildred and her husband, Roger Kilgore (the owner of the only automobile dealership in town) had cheered when Hoover and his vice president, Charles Curtis, were renominated at the Republican convention in Chicago in June, on a "balanced budget" platform. Back in 1928, the Republicans had coasted into the White House on a wave of economic prosperity and a booming stock market. But that was before Black Tuesday, when the bottom fell out of the market, the banks began to fail, and people lost their jobs. The Crash wasn't President Hoover's fault, of course. But in Darling and around the country, his administration was being blamed for not doing anything to ease the miserable situation. People were ready for a change.

"You're right about that uphill fight, Mildred," Verna said with an ironic lift to her eyebrow. "People might not know Mr. Roosevelt from Adam's house cat, but lots of folks are ready to cast their vote for good old A.B.H."

"A.B.H.?" Aunt Hetty sat down at the table. "Never heard of him. Who's he?"

"Anybody but Hoover," Verna replied. "I predict it'll be Roosevelt in a landslide."

Aunt Hetty chortled, and even Mildred had to laugh.

But the Dahlias hadn't given up their evening to discuss politics. Lizzy opened her notebook, picked up her pencil, and cleared her throat.

"Okay, everybody. We're here to go over the last-minute planning for next weekend's festival. There's plenty to do, so let's get started."

Darling's clubs and organizations took turns coordinating the annual Watermelon Festival, which would be held over the coming weekend at the Cypress County Fairgrounds, just outside of town. This year, it was the Dahlias' turn to coordinate the event and make sure that things ran as smoothly as possible—which was usually *not* very smoothly, since the unexpected had a way of cropping up, well, unexpectedly.

Take last year, for instance, when the Masonic Lodge was in charge of the festival. A trio of Mr. Burley's milk goats unexpectedly escaped from their pen in the livestock pavilion and nipped off all the blossoms in the Dahlias' flower booth. Somebody kicked a tent peg loose and the Ladies Club tent collapsed on the unsuspecting (and newly shampooed and set) head of Voleen Johnson, wife of Mr. George E. Pickett Johnson, the owner of the Darling Savings and Trust Bank. The Eastern Star's hot dog stand ran out of hot dogs halfway through the event. The Chamber of Commerce popcorn machine caught fire. And Mrs. Peabody fell off the stage in the act of awarding the 1931 Darling Baby award to Mrs. Starks' little Bluebelle. Bluebelle, whom Mrs. Peabody was holding at the time, was unharmed. Mrs. Peabody broke her nose.

But the worst happened when the motor on the Ferris

wheel burned out, leaving a dozen juvenile Darlingians stranded some thirty feet above the ground. This was not a serious problem for the strandees, of course. They were thrilled by every delicious minute of their extended ride, especially since they could look down and see everybody pointing excitedly up at them and yelling at them to be brave.

But their mothers were hysterical, and with good reason, for it took two hours for the Darling Volunteer Fire Department to get their youngsters down from their precarious perch. The Ferris wheel motor turned out to be unfixable. The merry-go-round quit shortly thereafter, so that was the end of the carnival rides. The Darling children, who had been saving their hard-earned pennies for months, were inconsolable.

It was the Odd Fellows who had booked the broken-down carnival, so the Ferris wheel problem was rightly their responsibility. But the Masonic Lodge was in charge of the festival and the fine finger of scorn was mostly pointed at them. It was months before they lived down the disgrace. Lizzy was determined that the Dahlias were going to do a better job. As the Dahlias' president, she wasn't about to let the club's sterling reputation be besmirched by a few unexpected incidents. She was even more determined, because she knew that this would be the most exciting festival ever. This year, the festival was going to feature a special, never-been-done-before event that had the whole town buzzing.

Well. Now that we've come this far in our story, it's time to pause for a few words about the Darling Dahlias. The club was founded in the mid-1920s by Mrs. Dahlia Blackstone, who died after wearing herself out in decades of community service and left her small white frame cottage at 302 Camellia Street to the town's garden club. The club promptly renamed itself the Darling Dahlias in honor of this generous lady and committed itself to the beautification of Darling, one blossom at a time.

With the cottage, the Dahlias inherited almost an acre of once-beautiful flower gardens, as well as a half-acre vegetable garden in the adjoining lot. The yard in front of the cottage was planted with wisteria, azaleas, Mrs. Blackstone's prize hydrangeas, and the old-fashioned wiegelas that came from her mother—an everyday-pretty Southern front yard that people admired as they drove down Camellia Street.

But it was the garden behind the house that people liked to talk about. It had once been truly spectacular, sweeping down a sloping, velvety green lawn toward a stately cucumber magnolia, a clump of woods, and a small, clear spring smothered in ferns, bog iris, and pitcher plants. The borders and beds were rich in roses and camellias, iris, stokesia, hibiscus, and dozens of different lilies—along with a rainbow of brightly colored annuals. It was so beautiful that it had been written up in the Selma *Times-Journal*, the Montgomery *Advertiser*, and in newspapers as far away as North Carolina.

In Mrs. Blackstone's declining years, however, the garden had gotten the best of her. Left to fend for themselves, the plants grew rowdy and rumpled and dreadfully tousled—because gardens don't just *grow*, of course; they require looking after. When the gardener isn't around to pay the right kind of attention, plants have a tendency to wander off in whatever way they prefer, putting out a bud here and a branch there and dropping seeds (or extending roots) into their neighbors' bed. Without the gardener, a garden quickly becomes a disorderly, unruly place.

As a result, when the Dahlias inherited Mrs. Blackstone's garden, it was no longer as tidy as it was when Mrs.

Blackstone could put on her garden gloves and get out there every day. The ladies had to arm themselves with rakes and hoes and trowels and clippers and set about restoring the necessary botanical order—which they did, although the job took the entire summer and most of the following autumn. Now, although there was always plenty of weeding, trimming, pruning, and even planting to be done, the Dahlias were pretty much ready to rest on their laurels as far as their "show" garden was concerned.

But then (as if they hadn't already worked hard enough) Lizzy and the other club officers decided that it would be smart to use the vacant lot next to the clubhouse to grow vegetables. Times were hard, and people needed beans and okra and corn and tomatoes even more than they needed roses and camellias and gladiolas—although as Aunt Hetty Little liked to point out, a life without a few glads is a very sad life indeed. The Dahlias sold their vegetables, cheaply, at the Saturday farmers' market on the square. And what they didn't sell, they gave away to people who were hard up for cash—including some of their very own Dahlias who were having a tough time making ends meet.

So they hired old Mr. Norris and his bay gelding, Racer, to plow up Mrs. Blackstone's empty lot, where they planted snap peas, corn, green beans, collards, Swiss chard, okra, Southern peas (purple hull was the hands-down favorite), tomatoes, peppers, eggplants, squash, cantaloupes, cucumbers, and sweet potatoes. This month, the garden was yielding its summer produce in great abundance. They would be selling it at their booth at the Watermelon Festival, with Aunt Hetty Little in charge. They planned to use the money to buy a pressure cooker and a case of Mason jars with new lids and rings. That way, they could can up the vegetables and give them to the Darling Family Food Pantry.

"How's the work coming, Aunt Hetty?" Lizzy asked. "Do you need any extra help?"

"Not if all the Dahlias show up for work on Friday afternoon," Aunt Hetty said. She might be eighty years old, but she was well-organized and had a reputation for getting things done. "The Kentucky Wonders really took off and there are a *lot* of green beans to pick. There'll be several bushels of sweet corn, as well as tomatoes, okra, eggplants, and squash—not to mention the watermelons. Lucy Murphy volunteered to load it all into that old Buick of Ralph's and cart it off to the fairgrounds. Ralph has been laid up with a bad back, but if he's able, Lucy volunteered him to set up shelves in the tent for our boxes and baskets and such."

Everybody had to chuckle at that, for they all knew that, in spite of being young and pretty, Lucy wore the pants in the Murphy family. Bad back or not, Ralph would be setting up the shelves—and his two teenaged sons (by the first Mrs. Murphy) would be lending him a hand. The second Mrs. Murphy would see to it or know the reason why.

"I'll ask Myra May to call the members and remind them of the picking party on Friday afternoon," Lizzy said, making a note. Myra May and her friend Violet Sims owned the Darling Diner and were half owners of the Darling Telephone Exchange (with Whitey Whitworth, who owned the other half). Myra May was the communications chairwoman for the club, and whenever there was telephoning to do, she took care of it. Since many of the members were on party lines, a few calls went a long way toward bringing everyone up to date.

"I ran into Bessie Bloodworth at Mann's Mercantile this morning," Mildred put in. She sipped her lemonade. "She said she made an extra dozen half-pint jars of strawberry jam just for our booth. She'll bring them on Saturday morning."

"Oh, wonderful!" Aunt Hetty exclaimed. "People are crazy for Bessie's strawberry jam." She made a note on her notepad. "Does anybody know whether Obadiah Carlson has got enough watermelons to give us some?" Every year, the Watermelon Festival offered all the free watermelon that festival-goers could eat. It was Aunt Hetty's job to round up the watermelons.

"I saw him at the courthouse yesterday and he said he'd bring a couple dozen," Lizzy replied. "And Alice Ann says her Arnold has a wagonload for us, if somebody'll come and get them."

"Mr. Norris told me he'd bring a wheelbarrow full," Verna chimed in. "His patch is in the field behind my house. He's got some good-looking melons." She grinned. "He was out there last night with his shotgun, threatening to pepper the backsides of a couple young kids he caught raiding."

"If they'll just wait a few days, they'll get all the watermelon they want for free," Aunt Hetty said tartly, adding Obadiah Carlson, Arnold Walker, and Mr. Norris to her watermelon list. "Everybody, if you hear about any more contributions, please let me know. One thing's for sure, we don't want to run out. That would be almost as bad as running out of hot dogs." She scowled. "Or the Ferris wheel breaking down again."

"Neither of which is going to happen as long as the Dahlias are in charge," Lizzy said, but with greater conviction than she felt. For some reason—or for no reason at all, she didn't know which—she was apprehensive about the festival. Something always happened, like Mrs. Peabody's broken nose. What would it be *this* year?

She pushed away the worry. "Now, let's go down this list

of chores. Aunt Hetty, you're done." She put a checkmark by the first item. "I'm doing publicity. I guess you've all seen the articles in the *Dispatch*." Lizzy was the right person for this job, since she wrote a garden column for the Darling newspaper and found it easy to write up the publicity for the festival. "I've also sent announcements to the *Monroe Journal* and the Mobile *Register*," she added.

Mobile was two hours away by car, but city folks might like to make a day of it at a country festival—especially with this year's big attraction. In addition, Charlie Dickens, the *Dispatch* editor and proprietor of the town's printing shop, had printed up fifty fliers announcing the festival and Lizzie paid Old Zeke fifty cents to put them up all over town and out at the Dance Barn on Briarwood Road, and the Watering Hole. Because of the *very* special event, they were hoping to attract the biggest crowd ever.

"Verna, what about you?" Lizzy asked, going to the next item. "Have you made the arrangements for the tents?"

Verna was responsible for making sure that the tents and booths were set up and ready for their occupants. She also had to manage the tickets, and supervise the volunteers who cleaned up the fairgrounds after the weekend was over. Altogether, this was a big job, but Verna was the acting county treasurer, the first woman ever to hold that position in Cypress County. She was good at getting things done because she was the one who knew where the bodies were buried. She didn't have to say one single word: she just looked at people with those dark, searching eyes of hers and they decided they'd better do whatever they were supposed to do, right *now*.

"The tents are supposed to arrive on Wednesday afternoon by train," Verna said, "from the rental agency in Mobile that supplied them last time. The guys from the Masonic Lodge are setting them up on Friday morning. The

Chamber of Commerce will be manning the ticket booth, starting Friday evening. I think we're all set."

Lizzy made another checkmark. "Mildred, you're next. What's up with the Odd Fellows? I truly hope they haven't booked the same carnival they brought in last year."

"Amen to that," Aunt Hetty said fervently.

"They wouldn't dare," Verna said in a dark tone.

"They didn't," Mildred said. "They've booked an outfit called Tinker's Traveling Carnival. The hard times have driven a lot of the smaller carnivals out of business. But they finally located Tinker's, and they hope it will work out."

"Tinker's Traveling Carnival." Lizzy made a note. "When are they getting in?"

"Thursday night, on the railroad," Mildred replied. "They'll set up on Friday and open in time for the Family Fun Night Friday evening." She looked around the table. "And yes, there will be a Ferris wheel, which the Odd Fellows guarantee will *not* break down."

Verna chuckled. "Can the Odd Fellows put that in writing?"

Mildred ignored her. "There will also be a merry-go-round, a pedal-car ride for the kiddies, and games for everybody—shooting gallery, high-striker, baseball throw, coin toss, and darts. Oh, and the usual cotton candy and hot buttered popcorn machines."

Aunt Hetty shook her head. "Lots of ways for young people to spend money they don't have, just for a little fun."

"But people *need* fun," Mildred protested. "Especially these days, when everybody is worrying about something." She sighed heavily.

Lizzy doubted that Mildred had anything to worry about. She and Roger lived a picture-perfect life. They had a beautiful house, a lovely young daughter, and financial security. But now that she thought about it, Lizzie believed that Mildred had been looking a bit wan and worried for the past couple of weeks, as if something serious was bothering her. This was unusual for Mildred, who was usually a happy-go-lucky, carefree person.

"People don't short themselves where fun is concerned," Verna put in. "Mr. Greer says movie attendance is better than ever." Don Greer and his wife Charlotte ran the Palace Theater on the courthouse square. Even though it cost a quarter to see a movie, it was one of the most popular places in town. "He says people would rather skip a meal than miss the latest Gable or Garbo," she added.

"Well, people won't have to skip a meal to come to the festival," Lizzy said. "Admission is only fifteen cents, and that includes free watermelon. Of course, there's another dollar a car for the air show, and the airplane rides cost a penny a pound per passenger. But people who don't have a dollar to get onto the airstrip can watch from the fairgrounds."

At the mention of the air show, everybody brightened. The Darling Lions Club usually sponsored an exhibition golf tournament the same weekend as the Watermelon Festival. But it was hard to entice competitive golfers to Darling and attendance at the tournament had been declining. So this year, the Lions had decided to try something different, in the hope of drawing people from as far away as Mobile and Montgomery.

The new and very exciting event was Lily Dare's Dare Devils, featuring the gorgeous Texas Star herself, Miss Lily Dare, and her partner, handsome Rex Hart, "King of the Air."

When the announcement was made a few months before, the people of Darling could scarcely believe their good luck.

Miss Dare was one of the most famous female pilots in the country, almost as famous as Amelia Earhart. Airplanes seemed to be on everybody's mind these days. Just two months before, Miss Earhart had flown solo from Newfoundland to Ireland in 14 hours and 56 minutes—the first woman and only the second person to fly alone across the Atlantic. The first was Colonel Lindbergh, of course, just five years before, in 1927. Miss Earhart looked so much like him—the same cool, direct gaze, the same wide forehead and freckled nose, the same shyly engaging grin—that the newspapers had taken to calling her Lady Lindy.

And just like Lady Lindy, Lily Dare had caught the attention of the public. Everybody in the country had read about the Texas Star and seen photographs of this beautiful, exotic-looking woman dressed in her trademark flying costume: white leather helmet, goggles, and white flying suit with a long, flowing red scarf looped around her neck. Known as the "fastest woman in the world," she had participated in all the major women's long-distance air competitions and flown as a stunt pilot in the dogfighting scenes of Howard Hughes' famous war movie, *Hell's Angels*. What's more, she was a founding member of The Ninety-Nines, an association of pioneer women trying to fly high in a man's world. It hardly seemed possible that a nationally famous female pilot was actually bringing her flying circus to Darling, which was definitely not the biggest small town in the state of Alabama.

But in fact, this glamorous, exciting woman *was* coming to Darling! And as everybody in town knew by now, she probably wouldn't be coming if it hadn't been for Mildred Kilgore's husband Roger, who was president of the local Lions. Roger had met the Texas Star a couple of years before when she put on an aerobatic show at a national Lions Club convention in San Antonio, Texas. It was said that Roger—a silver-tongued charmer with a strong resemblance to the new screen sensation, Clark Gable—had *sweet-talked* Miss Dare into bringing her Dare Devils to the Watermelon Festival. That's what the men were saying at Bob's Barbershop, anyway, punctuating their remarks with knowing nods and sly winks. This was according to Lizzy's boyfriend, Grady Alexander. Lizzy hadn't believed it, though. The idea seemed so ridiculous. Why, Roger and Mildred had been married for nearly fifteen years! Everybody said they were a perfect couple.

Miss Dare was due to land her airplane, which was also called the Texas Star, on the grassy airstrip just west of the fairgrounds on Thursday morning, with other members of the team flying in later that day. The fun was scheduled to start on Thursday evening, with a special showing of the movie *Hell's Angels* at the Palace Theater, which Miss Dare was expected to attend. On Friday, there would be airplane rides for anybody who could pay a penny per pound of his own weight for twenty minutes aloft—or *her* own weight, if any woman was brave enough to hop in that plane. And on Saturday afternoon, there would be an air show with Lily Dare and Rex Hart.

But the Texas Star and the King of the Air weren't the only attractions. A well-known aerialist, stuntwoman Angel Flame, would also perform, doing headstands, wing-walking, wingdancing, and other high-flying acrobatics. She would also execute her incredible "Dive of Death," a free fall from an altitude of 10,000 feet. At the last moment, just when everyone thought she must surely perish in her plunge, she would open a parachute. And then of course, there was the field show, with a magic act for the kids, a car crash, and a clown.

LILY DARE, THE TEXAS STAR
& THE DARE DEVILS
FLYING CIRCUS!
Darling Airfield. Fri. & Sat. July 15–16
Friday
Airplane Rides All Day, a Penny a Pound!
SATURDAY AIR SHOW
Admission: $1 Per Carload
(Load 'Em Up, Folks—No Limit on # Per Car)
Single Admission: 35 Cents

PROGRAM

9 a.m.–12 p.m. Airplane rides.

2:30 p.m. Miss Lily Dare, the Texas Star, will perform a stunning aerial ballet of loops, tail spins, whip tails, barrel rolls, upside-down flying and other thrilling stunts.

3 p.m. Dare Devil Angel Flame will perform incredible wingwalking acrobatics 1000s of feet in the air while you hold your breath.

3:30 p.m. Rex Hart, King of the Air, will perform more aerial stunts in his C3R Stearman, ending with his famous dead-stick landing. You'll be gasping every minute! You won't believe your EYES!

4:00 p.m. Special on-field show. Drawing for a free airplane ride. Magic show for the kids and a Pony Express Race! This will WOW you—worth the price of admission all by itself! (Remember, just a buck for your flivver, fully loaded!)

4:30 p.m. Incredible Dive of Death! Parachute jump by Angel Flame, holding a smoking flare in each hand. She will land on a MATTRESS provided by Mann's Mercantile in Darling!

5:30 p.m. Grand Finale! Aerial dogfight between the Texas Star and the King of the Air, as performed in the films *Hell's Angels* and *Dawn Patrol!* Ends with a skywriting flourish!

Purchase a new or used car from Kilgore Motors
by Sat. July 16 and get a free airplane ride!

And if this weren't enough excitement, there was also going to be a party, a fancy black-tie affair given by Mildred and Roger Kilgore, who had a reputation for giving the best parties in the entire town of Darling. At the party, the Dahlias planned to present Miss Dare with a beautiful Texas Star hibiscus: *Hibiscus coccineus*, according to Miss Dorothy Rogers. The hibiscus, which had a gaudy red blossom, would be planted in the garden at the Dahlias clubhouse, with a plaque honoring Miss Dare's visit. And because the Dare Devil Flying Circus was coming to Darling at the invitation of Roger Kilgore, Mildred had invited Miss Dare and Miss Flame to stay at the Kilgore home. (Mr. Hart and the rest of the team would be staying with the airplanes, at the airstrip.)

With a frown, Lizzy looked down at her list, wondering if she had reminded Aunt Hetty about the plant. "Aunt Hetty, did I ask you to pot up the Texas Star for the presentation?"

"The *Hibiscus coccineus*, you mean," Verna and Mildred said, almost in unison.

"The Texas Star," said Aunt Hetty firmly. She refused to use Latin names. "Puttin' on the dog," she called it—acting as if you were special because you knew a few words that nobody else knew (or could spell), in a language that had been dead since Hector was a pup. "Yes, you asked me, child. And yes, I potted it up, so it's all ready for you to hand it over to the guest of honor. I promised Mildred I'd bring it over to her house before the party." She gave Lizzy a kind look. "Now, you stop worryin' so, Liz. You're nervous as a long-tailed cat in a room full of rockin' chairs."

"I can't help it." Lizzy sighed. "I'm a natural worrier. And there's so much to keep track of!" She felt that formless apprehension again, the uneasy conviction that with so much going on, something very serious was sure to go wrong—

and this time, the finger of scorn would be pointed at the Dahlias. She looked down at her list again. "Mildred, do you need any volunteers to help you with the party?"

Mildred considered. "Myra May and Euphoria, from the diner, are catering the food. I've lined up two colored girls from Darling Academy to serve at the buffet, and a couple of boys to set up dining tables and chairs in the garden. Thanks for asking, Liz, but I think it's all pretty well organized." With a delicate laugh, she added, "We'll be serving sparkling punch, of course—and a little something extra for those who like to imbibe. Roger has charge of that, naturally." She leaned forward and spoke in a conspiratorial whisper. "He usually tells our guests to bring their own corkscrew."

Verna snorted into her lemonade. Aunt Hetty chuckled. She might be a little old-fashioned, but she had never believed, as she put it, in "prohibitin' what comes natural. And there's nothin' more natural on God's green earth than good corn whiskey."

"Mmmm," Lizzy murmured. Alabama had been officially dry since 1915, and the Volstead Act had taken effect, nationally, in 1919. But Lizzy had noticed that in Darling, there seemed to be even more booze after Prohibition than there had been when Alabama was wet. Judging from what she read in the newspapers, this seemed to be true across the country, too. At a time when ordinary folks were out of work and desperate, moonshiners and bootleggers were big business everywhere. They made sure that anyone who wanted to have a drink could get a bottle or two—even in the South, which, as Will Rogers joked, would keep on voting dry as long as there was anybody sober enough to stagger to the polls.

"Well, then." Mildred sat back in her chair. "The party is all taken care of, the Odd Fellows are in charge of the carnival, and the air show promises to be a thrilling event. Lizzy has everything under control. And I, for one, intend to sit back, relax, and just have a good time."

"Oh, yeah?" Verna raised a cynical eyebrow. "It's been my experience, Mildred, that when everything seems to be under control, that's just the time when it *isn't*. When everything just plain goes to hell in a handbasket."

Lizzy shuddered. "Don't say that, Verna." She looked back down at her list, which seemed to have grown longer and more complicated in just the past few minutes. "I can't bear to think of it." Or of that shapeless apprehension that was lurking at the back of her mind.

"Oh, but it's true," Aunt Hetty said wisely. She patted Lizzy's hand again. "You have got to stop trying to make everything turn out exactly the way you think it ought to, child. If you don't, you'll be crazy as a bedbug."

Afterward, Lizzy wished that she had paid more attention to Aunt Hetty. But if she had known everything that was going to go wrong before the Watermelon Festival even opened, she might have thrown in the towel at that moment and canceled the whole entire weekend.

TWO

Myra May Is in Trouble

Myra May Mosswell reached up and switched off the Philco radio on the shelf behind the counter in the Darling Diner. "In a Shanty in Old Shanty Town," performed by Ted Lewis and his band, had been at the top of the charts for several weeks and it seemed like WODX, down in Mobile, was playing it every fifteen minutes or so. Every time she heard it, she wondered just what kind of silly fool would actually be ready to give up his palace and go back to that old tumbledown shack next to the railroad track, even if his silver-crowned queen—presumably his mother—was waiting for him. And what kind of man who lived like a king would let his gray-haired old mother live in a little old shack with a roof that slanted down to the ground? It didn't make a lick of sense.

Myra May herself had been lucky enough *not* to grow up in a shanty. Her daddy had been a prosperous Darling doctor and they had lived in a very nice house. Her mother, Ina Ray, had died when Myra May wasn't any bigger than a minute—and she hadn't died at home, either. She had been taken sick on a visit to her parents in Montgomery, where she was buried. Myra May had never even seen her mother's grave.

Dr. Mosswell, who felt his young wife's loss very keenly, adamantly refused to speak of her, so Myra May had no secondhand recollections of her mother to comfort her. Nothing except for the gold-framed photograph she kept on the dresser upstairs, a striking young woman in the lacy white shirtwaist and ankle-length gored skirt of the prewar era, holding her baby girl in her arms. Every time Myra May looked at the photograph, she felt an aching emptiness in her heart. Her life would have been so different if her mother had lived to love her, laugh with her, and take care of her. Instead . . .

Instead, Myra May had been brought up like a very proper young Southern lady by her very prim and proper Aunt Belle (whom Myra May irreverently called Auntie Bellum). In spite of this smothery upbringing, she certainly knew what a shanty looked like and smelled like, because there were plenty of them on the other side of the L&N railroad tracks. She also knew that every person of her acquaintance—that is, every man, woman, and child in Darling—would a darn sight rather live in a palace, although in these hard times, they would be happy if they had electricity and indoor plumbing and the rent paid up for the next month.

Myra May glanced around, checking to be sure that everything was in order. It was a half hour past closing time on a Monday evening, and the front door was securely locked. The diner's lights were off, except for the flickering red neon Coca-Cola sign on the wall over the Dr Pepper clock, which cast moving red shadows across the oilcloth-covered tables. The red-checked curtains had been pulled neatly across the lower half of the front window, the red and gray linoleum was swept clean (and mopped, where Mr. Musgrove, from the hardware store next door, had dropped the catsup bottle), and the red-topped, chrome-plated counter stools were wiped and stowed neatly under the long red linoleum-topped counter. Behind the counter, the coffee urn was waiting for its next-day job. And on the other side of the pass-through window to the kitchen, the cookstove top was clean and ready for Myra May to start the bacon and eggs and fried potatoes at six the next morning, and for Euphoria to come in at nine and start baking her Pie of the Day. Since tomorrow was Tuesday, that would be peanut butter meringue pie, which was a favorite among the noon crowd.

Myra May sighed. That is, *if* Euphoria came in tomorrow, which she might not. She had taken off her apron and gone home sick after this morning's breakfast—at least, that's what she'd said, although she didn't look sick to Myra May. Which left Myra May, Violet, and Earlynne Biddle's boy Bennie to handle the noon crowd *and* the supper crowd by themselves. Again.

At the back of the diner, the door to the telephone exchange was open and Myra May could hear the low murmur of Nancy Lee McDaniel's voice as she worked the switchboard. There was a cot with a pillow and a blanket back there, so Nancy Lee or Rona Jean Hancock or Henrietta Conrad—whoever was on overnight duty—could catch forty winks between calls. All three were light sleepers, which was good, because they had to wake up fast when somebody rang the switchboard. After midnight, calls were usually emergencies, either for Doc Roberts (somebody having a baby or one of the old folks sick) or for Sheriff Roy Burns (somebody getting liquored up and using his neighbor's cow for target practice). And just last Friday, Nancy

Lee had fielded a call for Chief Pete Tate of the Darling Volunteer Fire Department. Mr. Looper's barn was on fire. Resourcefully, Nancy Lee had remembered that Friday night was Chief Tate's poker night and had overheard (on the exchange, where else?) that this week's game was in the back room at Musgrove's Hardware. The chief got the word and Mr. Looper's barn was saved.

Past the open door to the telephone exchange were the stairs that led up to the flat that Myra May shared with her friend and co-owner, Violet Sims, and their little girl, Cupcake, the sweetheart of Darling. At this very moment, Myra May could hear Violet's light footsteps over her head as she moved around, putting Cupcake to bed and getting ready to settle down to some needlework (she liked to embroider little things for the baby) or a library book before bedtime. Violet was one of Miss Rogers' most devoted customers at the Darling Library. She liked to improve her mind.

Myra May took off her apron and hung it on the peg beside the door to the exchange. She was well aware that their upstairs flat was not a luxury penthouse and the diner was by no means the Ritz. That distinction belonged to the Old Alabama Hotel, on the other side of the courthouse square, where guests sat down to dining tables that were all gussied up with white tablecloths, damask napkins, tall candles, and crystal bowls of flowers. And while they enjoyed their tomato frappe, asparagus vinaigrette, filet mignon wrapped in bacon, and maple nut sundae, they could listen to Maude LeVaughn playing tasteful dinner music on the rosewood square grand piano in the hotel lobby. Everybody said that it was all just as elegant as the finest Mobile hotel.

The Old Alabama, however, had recently raised the cost of a meal from seventy-five cents to a dollar, which generally limited the clientele to traveling gentlemen who had come to Darling on an expense account—and there weren't too many of them, these days. Most Darlingians couldn't fork over four bits a plate for dinner, even if it did come with flowers, candles, and Maude LeVaughn at the piano.

On the other hand, almost everybody could afford a meal at the Darling Diner. The tables were covered in oil-cloth; the paper napkins stood up proud in a shiny metal holder with red Bakelite salt and pepper shakers on either side; and instead of Maude LeVaughn's keyboard rhapsodies, the Philco behind the counter was likely to be reporting the current price of pork bellies and soybeans or playing Ted Lewis and his "In a Shanty in Old Shanty Town."

But you could get a plate of fried chicken, meat loaf, or liver and onions, along with sides of boiled cabbage or green beans or okra with fatback and onions, or potato salad and sliced fresh tomatoes, plus all the coffee you could drink. This would set you back just thirty cents, plus ten cents if you wanted a piece of pie—a generous piece, one-sixth of a whole pie instead of the measly one-eighth served over at the hotel.

There were plenty in town who preferred the diner, and not because it was cheap, either. It was on account of Euphoria Hoyt, the colored cook who had come as part of the deal when Myra May and Violet bought the diner and half of the Darling Telephone Exchange from old Mrs. Hooper a couple of years before, and who was famous all across southern Alabama. Euphoria was known not just for her crispy, crusty fried chicken, but also for her pies, especially the ones with meringue on top, which stood up in tantalizing bronzed peaks and swirls and curls all over their chocolate or lemon or banana cream filling. In fact, Euphoria's reputation was a more important drawing card at the Darling Diner than candles and flowers and Mrs. LeVaughn's piano music at the Old Alabama Hotel.

But there was a drawback. Euphoria might be one of the best cooks in southern Alabama, but she was also queen of the kitchen, ruler of the roost, and sovereign of the skillet, all rolled into one—and she knew it. She made sure that Myra May and Violet and even Earlynne Biddle's boy knew it, too. And lately, she had begun acting on her queenhood, coming in late or going home early, at her royal pleasure.

In fact, today was the third time in the past seven days that Euphoria had taken off her apron and headed out the door, leaving Violet to make the biscuits and Myra May to fry the chicken and bake the meat loaf. The two previous times, Euphoria had shown up right on time the next morning, tying on her apron just as if nothing out of the ordinary had happened the day before. But even though Myra May knew she should sit down and have a serious heart-to-heart with Euphoria about this deplorable behavior, she just couldn't stiffen herself to the task. Her heart quailed within her. She lacked the courage. While Myra May was tough about a great many things, she was a scaredy-cat when it came to dealing with Euphoria.

And with good reason. If Myra May got feisty about the need to show up and leave on the dot, Euphoria might just up and quit. And that would be a catastrophe, especially since they had agreed to cater the garden party at the Kilgores' on Friday night. Thirty couples, plus special guests. Myra May wasn't sure that she and Violet could handle the job alone, without Euphoria.

Without Euphoria. Myra May pushed this thought away with a shiver. But the burden of worry was like a twenty-pound sack of cornmeal grits on her shoulder as she said good night to Nancy Lee and turned away to climb the stairs. The more she thought about it, the more she feared that they were going to have to find another cook. But where on earth could they find somebody whose fried chicken and meringue pies could hold a candle to Euphoria's? Not in Darling, that was for darn sure.

Myra May was not going to carry that worry into the flat she shared with Violet and Cupcake, however. When they first bought the diner and agreed to share the upstairs apartment, Violet had made a very strict rule. Except in the case of a dire emergency, like a fire or food poisoning among the customers, they would leave the diner's business downstairs in the diner and spend their evenings together talking about anything else.

Now, if you happened to glance at Violet's pretty face, petite figure, and frilly, feminine dresses, you likely would never guess that this young woman had a spine of steel. She also had a very definite way of explaining just how things ought to be done, although she always sweetened it up here and there with a winning smile and "honey" or "darlin'" delivered with a charming Southern accent. Violet might be slight and frilly, but she could work as hard and as long as any man, and at the end of the day, she'd look just as cool and unruffled as she had that morning.

Myra May, on the other hand, had never been anybody's idea of pretty—or sweet, either. She had a square jaw, a determined mouth, and a long history of tomboy ways. As a girl, she insisted on wearing overalls to play, like the boys in her class at school, and refused ribbons, ruffles, and Mary Janes. No matter how often Auntie Bellum attacked her dark brown hair with the curling iron, it still hung limp and straight—until her friend Beulah scissored it off in a bob that was cool and easy, and that was the end of the curling iron forever. It was the end of dresses, too, for Myra May had taken to wearing trousers, which suited her much better. Poor Aunt Belle (dead now some dozen years) had despaired of her awkward, gawky niece ever finding a husband who would tolerate her straight-shooting, pull-no-punches way of meeting the world.

After high school, Myra May went away to the University of Alabama, where she majored in Domestic Science, minored in Education, and figured out that she lacked the patience to be a teacher and tell kids what to do—or the inclination to marry somebody who would tell *her* what to do. After college, she came back to Darling to take care of her ailing father. After his death, she got a job managing the kitchen at the Old Alabama and then (with Violet) bought the Darling Diner, demonstrating that her bachelor's degree in Domestic Science had not been a complete waste of time and money after all.

Myra May was on the third step when Nancy Lee called out from the switchboard. "Oh, Miz Mosswell, somebody's askin' for you. Do you want to talk to her down here at the board or would you druther I wait and ring you when you get upstairs?"

Myra May turned around and went back down. "Down here," she said, picking up the other headset and sitting at the switchboard next to Nancy Lee. "If you ring upstairs, it'll wake Cupcake."

"Well, we sure wouldn't want to bother that sweet little thing," Nancy Lee said, and plugged her in.

Myra May put on the headset. "Hello," she said.

There was a breathy pause.

"Hello," Myra May repeated. "Who is this?"

"This is . . . Raylene Riggs," a soft female voice said. "Am I speakin' to Miz Mosswell?"

"Yep, that's me," Myra May said curtly. "Myra May Mosswell." By now she was suspecting that this was some sort of sales call. Well, she knew how to handle that. She'd make it short and not-so-sweet. "Just what is it you're wanting, Miz Riggs?"

Clearing her throat, the caller spoke hesitantly. "Well, I . . . I'm stayin' with some friends just now, over here in Monroeville." Some twenty miles to the east, Monroeville was the county seat of Monroe County. "Years ago—years and *years* ago, really—I used to come over to Darlin' to visit. I always thought it was a right pretty little town, the kind of place I'd like to live. I'm lookin' to settle down now, after travelin' around all over, and I—"

"Excuse me," Myra May broke in. "It sounds to me like you're lookin' for Mr. Manning. That would be Mr. Joe Lee Manning, Junior. He handles real estate, and last I heard he had a whole long list of houses for sale or rent." A long, sad list, most of them bank foreclosures, sitting silent and empty. She reached for the switchboard plug that would connect the caller to Mr. Manning. "It's a little on the late side, but I can ring him for you. I'm sure he won't mind." He wouldn't, either. Joe Lee Manning would drag himself out of bed at any hour to unload one of those vacant houses.

"Oh, no, ma'am, I'm sorry," Raylene Riggs said quickly. "I am not lookin' for a *house*, at least, not yet. Maybe later I will, after I've landed a job." She cleared her throat apologetically. "That's actually what I'm lookin' for. A job."

Myra May was nearly out of patience. Didn't this woman know *anything?* "Well, then, you want to pick up a copy of the Darling *Dispatch*. If there's any jobs to be had in this town, that's where you'll find them." Lots of luck, she thought ironically. Job openings in Darling were few and far between. Anybody who had one hung on to it like grim death.

"But I'm not lookin' for just any old job." The woman pulled in her breath. "What I mean to say is that I hear your cook is quittin'. There at the diner, I mean. That's why I'm callin', Miz Mosswell. I am a real good cook with lots of experience. I thought I might could—"

"I don't know where you heard that," Myra May snapped. "About our cook, I mean."

"A . . . friend of mine happened to hear it," Raylene Riggs said, almost apologetically. "He says that Euphoria is a real good cook and he'll truly miss her fried chicken. But he thinks my meat loaf is even better than hers and my meringue pies—"

Myra May cut her off again. "She didn't actually quit— she just took off a little early one day. So you tell your friend he can rest easy about his fried chicken. We are not in need of a cook." *I hope,* she added silently, thinking of Friday night's party. *Oh, lord, lord, I hope.*

There was a moment's pause. Then, "Well, I guess I must've heard wrong. My friend also works with Miz Euphoria's oldest boy, Chauncy, at the depot here in Monroeville, you see. Chauncy happened to mention that his mama and her sister, Jubilation, have decided to set themselves up in business, in one of those little joints over in Maysville."

Myra May gulped a breath. She knew for a fact that Euphoria had a sister named Jubilation and that her son Chauncy unloaded freight at the railroad depot over in Monroeville. Maysville was the colored section of Darling, on the east side of the railroad tracks, and several juke joints there were known to serve very good food. Altogether, the story had the ring of truth. Myra May shivered. Was it possible that Euphoria's recent irregularities were inspired by a plan to strike off on her own?

But she didn't want to let on what she was thinking. She steadied herself and said, cautiously, "Well, I don't know anything at all about that, Miz Riggs. Far as I know, we've still got us a cook. A real good one, at that."

"It sounds like Chauncy was misrememberin'," Raylene Riggs replied hesitantly, "or else he maybe didn't have all the facts." She wasn't making any effort to disguise the disappointment in her voice. "But I wonder—well, how 'bout if I just give you the phone number, here at this place where I'm stayin'? That way, you can call me if things don't turn out the way you think. I'm available now, in case you find out that you need help right away." Without waiting for Myra May to answer, she rattled off a telephone number.

Myra May reached for a pencil. "What was that again?" she asked, reminding herself to be polite. After all, the woman was only looking for a job, like lots of other out-of-work, out-of-luck people these days. Anybody who heard about a possible opening was smart to jump on it lickety-split, since there were bound to be a couple dozen folks in line before the day was an hour older. She wrote down the number the woman had given her.

"Thanks," she said. "I don't think we'll need anybody, but if we do, we'll let you know."

"That's all I'm askin'," the woman said. She added, with what Myra May thought was an odd, lingering reluctance, "It's been real nice talkin' to you, Miz Mosswell." A breath, and then, with greater—and more puzzling—intensity. "Just *real* nice. I appreciate it."

"Same here," Myra May replied uneasily, and broke the connection. Next to her at the switchboard, Nancy Lee shifted in her chair. Myra May noticed that she had not unplugged her switchboard jack, which meant that she'd been listening in—not usually allowed, but she would've overheard Myra May's half of the conversation anyway.

Nancy Lee gave her a look over her glasses. "I couldn't help hearin' what you were saying about Euphoria," she remarked. "I was over to the post office this afternoon when Old Zeke came in. I heard him tellin' Mr. Stevens that Euphoria and Jubilation are goin' to work for shares in the Red Dog, that juke joint over in Maysville. They're fixin' to start cookin' there this week. I figured Zeke was talkin' about Jubilation cookin' full time and Euphoria nights and Sundays, but maybe——" A caller's buzz interrupted her. When she plugged in the call, she turned back to Myra May. "Sorry I'm not a better cook, or I'd be glad to help out. My Daddy Lee says all I'm good for is makin' chick'ry coffee." Nancy Lee had grown up in New Orleans, where chickory coffee was a favorite.

Myra May sighed, said good night, and went upstairs, feeling like that sack on her shoulder was another twenty pounds heavier. It was a warm July night, and the windows were open to the buzzy song of the cicadas in the trees and the sweetly scented nighttime breeze. Wearing her old pink flowered cotton sleeping chemise, Violet was sitting in her favorite chair with a book—the library copy of Edna Ferber's *Cimarron*—and idly fanning herself with a black-bordered cardboard fan from Noonan's Funeral Home while she read.

She looked up and closed the book on her finger to mark her place. "There's a pitcher of cold tea in the icebox. Everything okay downstairs?"

"Not exactly," Myra May replied glumly, thinking that what she had just heard constituted an emergency and thereby permitted her to break Violet's rule. She went to the icebox and took out the frosty glass pitcher. "We got a phone call from some woman over in Monroeville who heard that Euphoria and Jubilation are going to cook at a juke over on the other side of the tracks. Specifically, at the Red Dog, was what Nancy Lee heard Old Zeke tell the postmaster. Zeke said they're working for shares in the business. They're going to be part owners."

There were several jukes in Maysville, but the Red Dog was the most popular. It showcased traveling blues musicians like Son House and Lead Belly, who always brought in a crowd when they came to town. Myra May suspected that if Euphoria and Jubilation were cooking there, the Red Dog would soon be as popular for its food as it was for its music.

"Well, if that don't beat all," Violet said, laying her book aside. "It makes a lot of sense, though—and it's better for Euphoria. Why should she work for us when she can work for herself? More power to her, I have to say."

"You're right," Myra May said, sinking into her favorite chair, across from Violet. "But I wish she would've told us what she was planning. I guess when she comes in tomorrow morning, I have to ask her straight out if this is true or not. I'd rather know for sure than stand around worrying whether it's actually going to happen. Or when." She shivered. "I sure hope she'll stay for the weekend, anyway. We could probably handle the Kilgores' party without her, but it would be pretty tough."

Violet pulled up her legs and propped her chin on her knees. She looked worried. "Euphoria is going to be a tough act to follow. You got any ideas who we can get to replace her?"

"Ophelia Snow's maid, Florabelle, has a sister who does good fried chicken," Myra May said. "I had some at the Snows' picnic last summer. I could ask Ophelia to find out if she's available. Or—" She paused, sipping her cold tea. "There's that woman who called tonight looking for a job—Raylene Riggs, her name is. She says she's a real good cook. Experienced."

"That's what they all say," Violet replied pertly. "But it usually turns out that they're good at one thing or another but not good at both. The thing about Euphoria is that her pies are every bit as good as her fried chicken—and her catfish is the best I've ever tasted. We might check this woman out, though. If it turns out that Euphoria is fixing to quit, we could invite her in to cook one day. Give her a tryout. Florabelle's sister, too." She paused, cocking her head. "Actually, we might run an ad in the *Dispatch* asking folks to audition, the way they do for dancers and actors and such."

"Now, there's an idea," Myra May said, snapping her fingers. "If we're trying out cooks, we could get the customers to tell us who they like best. Maybe the auditions can even tide us over until we find a replacement for Euphoria—*if* we have to." She paused, adding hopefully, "But it might not be true, this rumor about her quitting, I mean. Maybe it's just talk. You know how people are."

Violet considered this. "Well, I'm thinking that even if she says she's staying on, it wouldn't be a bad idea to let her know we're looking for a backup. The way it is now, we are at her mercy. What do you think?"

"Agree a hundred percent," Myra May said definitively. "I'll talk to her first thing in the morning."

"Good luck," Violet said, picking up her book again.

"You bet," Myra May muttered, under her breath.

It took her a long time to fall asleep that night, and when she did, she dreamed of going into the diner kitchen and finding it silent and the kitchen range stone cold, while customers were lined up outside the front door and around the block, waving signs and shouting in unison, "We want Euphoria! We want Euphoria!"

Myra May woke up in a cold sweat. She lay there for a long time, thinking how much she hated to be at the mercy of a cook who couldn't be counted on, no matter how talented she might be when it came to fried chicken and chocolate pie.

THREE

Looking for a Cook

When Tuesday morning came and Myra May and Violet went downstairs to start the biscuits for the breakfast crowd, there was no Euphoria. She failed to show up to cook the noon dinner, too, so Myra May wound up repeating the Monday special, which was meat loaf. Sticking several pans of meat loaf into the oven was easier than standing over three or four skillets of frying chicken and turning the pieces every few minutes. Violet fried catfish and made coleslaw. Sissy Dunlap (the daughter of Mr. Dunlap, who owned the Five and Dime) came in to help with the serving and the cleanup, and Bennie Biddle helped, too. But between cooking and managing the counter, Myra May and Violet were as "busy as a stump-tailed cow in fly season," as Mr. Greer (from the Palace Theater) put it. And all the while, Myra May was worrying about the coming weekend and the Kilgores' party. How were they going to manage?

As soon after lunch as she could get away, Myra May went next door to the office of the Darling *Dispatch*, where she stood at the counter and filled out an advertising form for auditions for the Darling Diner cook's position. Every applicant would be required to fry chicken, catfish, and liver and onions, as well as make a meat loaf, cook beans and greens, and bake biscuits and pies. The "audition" would be an on-the-job test that would also show how well the person worked under pressure. She didn't put all of this in the ad, though, since she was being charged by the word.

Charlie Dickens, the *Dispatch* editor, was sitting at his desk, frowning about something. He had just picked up the candlestick telephone when he looked up and saw Myra May. He put the phone down, pushed back his chair, and came to the counter. He wore a rumpled white shirt with the sleeves rolled up, red suspenders, and a green celluloid eyeshade.

Charlie had grown up in Darling, but he had left when he was young, soldiered in France in the Great War, hoofed it through Europe and the Balkans, then became a reporter for the Cleveland *Plain Dealer,* the *Baltimore Sun*, and the Fort Worth *Star-Telegram*. His nomadic experiences had given him a slantwise, skeptical view of settled, small-town life. In fact, it was such an un-Darlingian view that most folks figured he stayed only because—given the depressing economic effects of the Depression—he couldn't afford to leave. This was just about right, as Charlie might tell you if you happened to ask him when he'd been helping himself from the bottle of Mickey LeDoux's bootleg corn whiskey he kept in the bottom drawer of his desk. When he was sober, he'd just say it was none of your damn business.

"So what's this?" Charlie asked in an ironic tone, looking down at the ad copy Myra May handed him. "Auditions at the diner? You and Violet planning to add some supper-time entertainment?" He tipped his eyeshade back with his thumb. "Some hootchy-kootchy? A sword-swallowing act?" He seemed to find this amusing.

Myra May explained the predicament they were in and what they wanted to do, and Charlie pursed his lips. "Maybe you better put 'cooking' in front of 'auditions,'" he said. "To get your meaning across." When Myra May nodded, he penciled the word in, then turned and shouted, "Ophelia! Hey, Ophelia. I got an ad for you. And a story."

While Myra May was writing out her ad, the Linotype machine had been clunking slowly away at the back of the big room. It stopped, and the woman who had been operating it slid out of her seat and made her way through the maze of type cases and makeup tables to the front counter. People (mostly men) sometimes said that a woman didn't have the kind of muscle a Linotype operator needed to pull the casting lever, but that was a lot of hooey, according to Ophelia Snow, who had been pulling that lever for over a year.

"If I can wrestle Jed's wet denim overalls through the crank wringer on that antique washing machine of mine," she liked to tell her friends, "I can wrestle that Linotype. It takes about the same amount of muscle."

"Hi, Myra May," Ophelia said, tucking her brown hair back under her blue kerchief. Ophelia worked full time as the *Dispatch*'s advertising and subscription manager, Linotype operator, and society reporter, assigned to cover clubs and civic organizations. (Charlie handled what he laughingly called the "city desk.") Married to Jed Snow, the owner of Snow's Farm Supply and the mayor of Darling, Ophelia had never planned to "work out," as the Darling matrons disdainfully put it, for she considered taking care of her husband and two children job enough. But she had gotten in over her head the previous year when she bought a smart living room suite on Sears' time-payment plan and needed to find the money to make the monthly payments. She couldn't ask her husband because too many of the farmers were behind on their seed and equipment bills at the Farm Supply. And while being mayor of Darling allowed Jed to swagger around with his thumbs hooked in his suspenders, looking important, it didn't pay one red cent in salary.

In fact, scarce as jobs were, Ophelia counted herself lucky that she happened to come into the *Dispatch* office the same afternoon that Mr. Dickens was trying to figure out how to replace Zipper Haydon, who was retiring from several decades at the *Dispatch*. (It was surely time, for Mr. Haydon was old enough to remember when the rabble of Union soldiers had ripped their way through Darling in the last days of the War for Southern Independence.) Mr. Dickens needed somebody who could type and correct copy, operate the Linotype, get to work on time and sober—and do it all for ten dollars a week. Ophelia could type sixty words a minute, spell like a dictionary, never touched a drop on principle, and thought ten dollars sounded like the pot of gold at the end of the rainbow. Jed had sulked when he first learned that she was going to work, but he quit complaining when he saw the extra money coming in.

Charlie handed Ophelia Myra May's ad. "The girls are gonna audition cooks for the diner—like a chorus line or something. Might be a story in it. You write something up, we'll run it on the local page for Friday."

"Audition *cooks*?" Ophelia glanced in surprise at the ad. "What happened to Euphoria?"

Myra May explained again. "A story would be swell," she added enthusiastically. "It would get a lot more attention than an ad." As an afterthought, she said, "Violet wondered if Florabelle's sister might like to try out."

Ophelia frowned. "Wisteria—that's her name—would be great for fried chicken. Her biscuits are middling. But

I'm telling you as a friend that you'd be disappointed in her piecrust. You'd have to find somebody else to bake pies."

"That might not be a bad idea," Myra May said thoughtfully. "A different pie cook, I mean. That way, we wouldn't have all our eggs in one basket, so to speak." She sighed, thinking of the party. They'd had their eggs in Euphoria's basket, and now they were smashed, all over the floor. How in the world could they handle that party?

The door opened, and the three of them turned to see Elizabeth Lacy, one of Myra May's best friends. She was slender and summery in a pink print silk crepe dress with organdy ruffles at the neck and arms. Her brown hair was cut short, parted on one side, and fell in soft waves on either side of her heart-shaped face. She looked like Loretta Young, who was featured on a recent cover of *Movie Classic* magazine.

Liz wasn't just pretty, but warm and caring, as well. She worked as a secretary and legal clerk in the law office of Moseley and Moseley, upstairs over the *Dispatch*. And even if she didn't always get the credit due her, most Darlingians knew that Mr. Moseley couldn't manage without her. She handled the paperwork, met the filing deadlines, and kept the office running during her boss's frequent absences. People said that the only thing she couldn't do was appear for him in court. Old Judge McHenry couldn't see very well, but he'd know the difference between Liz and Mr. Moseley right off.

"It's Tuesday, so here's Mr. Moseley's legal advertisements," Liz said, handing Charlie a typed page. She looked from Myra May to Ophelia. "What's this?" she asked, laughing lightly. "A meeting of the Dahlias' officers—and you didn't invite me?" Ophelia was the vice president and secretary, and Myra May was the communications chairwoman. Liz, of course, was the president.

"Auditions," Ophelia said. "At the diner." She held up

Myra May's ad, which required Myra May to tell her story one more time.

"I'm sorry you've lost Euphoria," Liz said. She tilted her head to one side, considering. "Mrs. Alexander is letting her cook go. Pearly is a good hand with pies and biscuits, and Grady says she definitely has to find another job. You could give her a try."

Grady Alexander, the Cypress County agriculture agent, was Liz's boyfriend. Just the month before, his father had died when the M&R locomotive he was driving derailed at the river crossing. Myra May had heard that his mother had to cut back on expenses.

Liz paused, then qualified her recommendation. "Pearly's meat loaf is only so-so, though. And I wouldn't recommend her pies, especially her meringue. It's weepy."

Charlie snorted. "Lord deliver us from weepy meringues."

Myra May pressed her lips together, thinking that hard times for some folks—like poor Mrs. Alexander, who had not only lost her husband but her husband's paycheck— meant hard times for even more folks. "Euphoria is one of a kind," she said with a sigh. "It might take two, maybe three, to replace her."

"Well, look at it this way," Ophelia said in a practical tone. "You get yourself seven cooks to come in and audition, you've got free cooking for a week."

Charlie looked down his nose at Ophelia. "Free advertis-in', too, if Ophelia gets right on that story." He turned to Liz. "I was just reaching for the phone to call you when Myra May came in with her ad."

"What's up?" Liz asked.

"It's the Dare Devils," he replied. "The air show."

Liz looked apprehensive. "Uh-oh. What about it? Don't tell me that something's gone wrong!"

"Maybe yes, maybe no," Charlie said in a deliberate,

matter-of-fact tone. "But since you're in charge of the festival, I think you ought to know how things stand. I just got off the line with Lily Dare. She called because I'm supposed to interview her when she flies in, for the story we're running. But there's been some trouble. They did an air show down in Pensacola last weekend. Seems there was a problem with Miss Dare's plane." He pulled his eyebrows together. "She thinks it was sabotage."

"Sabotage," Ophelia echoed blankly. "Why, who would do a thing like that?"

"Sabotage!" Myra May's eyes widened. "That sounds serious."

"Sabotage?" Liz asked uncertainly. "What kind of sabotage?"

Charlie shrugged. "How should I know what kind of sabotage? I'm just repeating what Miss Dare told me. The bottom line is that the plane needs a new propeller, which has to come from St. Louis. Nobody's just real sure when it'll arrive. She said she'd call as soon as she had any news."

"Rats," Myra May said expressively, and Ophelia groaned.

"Oh, dear." Liz's voice was low and anxious. "There's no chance the show will be canceled, is there?"

"Dunno," Charlie said. "But it didn't sound too good."

"I sincerely hope they don't cancel," Myra May said, pursing her lips. "If they do, Darling is going to be very disappointed."

"I hope not, too," Ophelia said fervently. "This air show is the biggest thing that's ever happened in this town." She paused. "I guess I'd better tell Jed. He's vice president of the Lions Club, you know. And Roger Kilgore will have to be told, of course. He's the one who arranged all this—and he's got that special promotion going on. If you buy a car, you get a free airplane ride." She turned to Liz. "Maybe you ought to let Mildred know, too, Liz. Miss Dare is supposed to be the guest of honor at her party. And she's staying at their house."

"Yes, I think I'd better," Liz said slowly. "Although I hate to bother her before we know anything for sure. Mildred seems to have had a lot on her mind lately."

"Then maybe you should wait until Charlie hears back from Miss Dare," Myra May said. She was torn. She hoped that the Kilgores' party wouldn't be canceled, since she and Violet were counting on the extra money. But if they couldn't find another cook, they'd be in serious trouble.

"I'm afraid not," Liz said reluctantly. "Once Jed and Roger know, Mildred is going to find out. So I'd better tell her."

Myra May went to the door. "I've got to get back to the diner, girls. Violet's in the kitchen all by herself." Over her shoulder, she added, "Ophelia, if you want to write that story about our auditions, you just come on over. And Liz, you be sure to let me know if you need help with the festival."

"You could call all the Dahlias and let them know about Friday afternoon," Liz said. "The garden is producing like crazy and we need to get stuff picked and toted over to the fairgrounds. Everybody has to pitch in."

"I'll do the calls this afternoon," Myra May promised. Most of the Dahlias were on party lines. It took only two or three phone calls to reach the entire membership.

Ophelia reached under the counter for her notebook. "I finished my work on the Linotype," she told Charlie. "I might as well go on over to the diner with Myra May and get this story now, before you start the layout for the local page."

Charlie fished in his pocket. "You could bring me a piece of pie when you come back," he said, handing a dime to

Ophelia. "Chocolate, if they've got any left." He added a nickel. "And coffee. Black."

"Yes, boss," Ophelia said wryly, and they all laughed.

By this time, Myra May was feeling much more optimistic about finding a replacement for Euphoria. While Ophelia interviewed Violet for the newspaper story, she phoned up Raylene Riggs in Monroeville, who said she'd be glad to get somebody to drive her over so she could demonstrate her cooking skills.

And after Ophelia had finished the interview and returned to the *Dispatch* office with Charlie's pie and coffee, Myra May and Violet agreed that if Euphoria decided she wanted to come back and cook at the diner, they would tell her they were sorry and wish her good luck in her new cooking career at the Red Dog.

Unless, of course, she agreed to come back and cook for the Kilgores' party, in which case they would be very glad to see her.

FOUR

Charlie Dickens Has a Story to Tell

Lizzy was about to follow Myra May and Ophelia as they went out the door. But she stopped when Charlie put out his hand and said, in a lower voice, "Hang on a shake, will you, Liz?" When the others had closed the door behind them, he turned back to her, his expression grave.

"I didn't tell the full story just now. There's more about this business with Lily Dare."

"More what?" Lizzy asked. Her earlier apprehension about the upcoming festival—her worry that something was bound to go seriously wrong—was returning with a vengeance. Only this time, it had a sharper focus: the air show, and Miss Dare. "What is it, Charlie? What's happened?"

Charlie reached into his shirt pocket, pulled out a crumpled pack of Lucky Strikes, and fished out a cigarette. "It's not so much about what's happened." He opened a book of matches, snapped one with his thumbnail, and lit his Lucky. "It's about what *might* happen. Take it from me, Liz. Lily Dare spells trouble. Serious trouble." He motioned with his head. "Come around to my desk and let's sit down for a minute."

"Trouble?" Lizzy went around the end of the counter. "You're talking about the airplane sabotage?"

"That, among other things. Lily has a way of . . . well, of making enemies. Plenty of them." He sat down at his cluttered wooden desk and pushed a straight-back chair toward her with his foot.

"I guess I'm not surprised," Lizzy said, sitting down. "You can't become famous as the 'fastest woman in the world' without wounding a few egos. She's got to be highly competitive, which likely doesn't sit well with a lot of men. And judging from the photos I've seen, she's beautiful. She's glamorous. Most women probably envy her." She sighed and made an honest confession. "I do—although I'm not sure I'd be very comfortable taking the risks she must take every single day."

Charlie pulled on his cigarette. "You're right about both, Liz. She's competitive. And she's certainly beautiful. It's a potent combination. But she's . . . well, she's a schemer." He shifted uncomfortably. "And pretty is as pretty does, as my mother used to say. By that definition, Lily certainly wouldn't win any beauty contests."

"A schemer?" Lizzy asked, puzzled. "You must know her, then."

She studied Charlie. She liked him and respected his opinions, partly because (like Mr. Moseley) he had a wider view of the world than most Darlingians. He'd been to more places, Europe, even, and Baltimore and Cleveland. He had more experience. Still, she was surprised that he knew the Texas Star. It seemed almost too coincidental. But maybe it wasn't a coincidence.

"Maybe you had something to do with the fact that she decided to come to Darling," she guessed.

"Nope. Roger Kilgore did that all on his own hook." Charlie looked away, frowning. "I offered to put in a word with her, if that would help. But he said she had already agreed."

"I see," Lizzy said thoughtfully, wondering at Charlie's evident discomfort. "Well, however it happened, everybody's really excited about her coming." She paused, then said again, "I suppose you know her."

He caught her glance and held it for a moment, as if he were trying to decide how much to tell her. Then he answered, slowly, "I met her when I was working as a reporter at the Fort Worth *Star-Telegram*. Her name wasn't Lily Dare—not then. It was Henrietta Foote."

"I see." Lizzy suppressed a smile. Henrietta Foote's Flying Circus—it didn't have quite the right appeal.

Charlie nodded. "At the time, she had a big, fancy ranch house on three thousand acres of Texas rangeland west of town. That's where she gave her parties. And when I say parties, I mean *parties*." He picked up an empty Hires root beer bottle and tapped his cigarette ash into it. "Henrietta's friends from the West Coast—Hollywood types, mostly—would fly their own planes in for a weeks-long, round-the-clock open-door, open-bar party. Her bar was stocked like a San Antonio bawdyhouse. There was enough offshore rum, bathtub gin, and south-of-the-border tequila to keep her pals drunk as skunks for a month. And she had a big swimming pool where everybody skinny-dipped whenever the spirit moved them—which it did, very often."

"Oh, my," Lizzy said weakly. She had never been to a party like that, of course, but she had read about them. The magazines on the rack over at Lima's Drugstore—*Hollywood Life* and *Silver Screen* and such—were full of stories about the sensational goings-on at such parties.

Charlie eyed her, judging her response, then went on. "Some years ago, a guy—Pete Rickerts—died when he flipped his plane when he was landing on the airstrip on her ranch. It was a dangerous strip, too short and full of potholes. Her pilot friends had been telling her so, and warned her to do something about it before somebody got hurt. She laughed at them. She said *she* didn't have any trouble landing there. It was a test of flying skill, she said. After Rickerts died, she went out and made a dozen landings, touch-and-gos, just to prove it could be done."

He gave her a level, questioning look. Lizzy thought she should say something but she couldn't think what to say, other than, *Is that why she calls herself a Dare Devil?* But she couldn't make herself say it.

"Well." He tapped his fingers on the scarred top of his desk. "You can bet your sweet life that Rickerts' pals weren't too happy about the way she was showing off." He stopped and gave that some thought, then said, as if to himself, "Could be that something like that was behind what happened in Pensacola. The sabotage, I mean. Somebody trying to get even."

By now, Lizzy was both intrigued and troubled. She wasn't a risk-taker herself. She was by nature a cautious person, and anyway, you didn't get many opportunities to practice taking chances in Darling, where nothing much ever happened. Still, she admired gutsy women, and Henrietta Foote wouldn't have become Lily Dare if she wasn't willing to take chances. But Charlie's story about Rickerts' death made it sound as if the Texas Star didn't have much concern for the safety of others.

"You were there, I guess," she hazarded. "At the parties, I mean."

"I was. We were . . . friends, you might say." Charlie gave a dry chuckle. "While it lasted. Her *friendships* never last very long."

Hearing his tone, Lizzy's curiosity mounted. What kind of friends had they been? she wondered. Charlie wasn't a handsome prince, by any stretch of the imagination. But he had a certain cynical charm, a wide experience, and a sharp intellect, which made him attractive to some women—to Fannie Champaign, at least.

Fannie, the newest member of the Dahlias, owned Champaign's Darling Chapeaux, on the other side of the square, and employed Lizzy's mother to help her make hats. (The job, Lizzy felt, was a miracle, since it kept her mother busy and out of Lizzy's hair.) Several months ago, Fannie and Charlie had become an item, at least in the minds of the Darling ladies. They were frequently seen at picnics and church suppers together and at the movies on Saturday nights. And the last time Lizzy got a shampoo and set at Beulah Trivette's Beauty Bower, she had heard from Bessie Bloodworth (who was getting her hair permed in Beulah's electric perm machine) that Fannie was expecting a marriage proposal. That bit of gossip had disturbed Lizzy, because Charlie Dickens did not seem to her to be the marrying kind. She sincerely hoped that Fannie wasn't about to get her heart broken.

But she could understand why certain women found Charlie appealing, and she guessed that an adventuresome woman like Lily Dare might be more to his taste than quiet, sweet-natured Fannie Champaign. Had Charlie and the Texas Star been . . . lovers, once upon a time?

It wasn't a question that Lizzy could ask, of course. Instead, she ventured, "You said Miss Dare *had* a ranch. Past tense. She doesn't live there anymore?"

"Henrietta—Lily, that is—is a big spender." Charlie's tone was matter-of-fact. "She married oil money, and when her husband died—he was nearly thirty years older and drowned in his bathtub—she got it all, every cent. There were people who thought that the drowning was a bit too convenient, and her stepsons were furious at being cut out of their father's will. Still, the lawyers told them there was nothing they could do about it. Lily was rolling in dough, at least for a while. But the Crash hit her like a ton of bricks. She lost the ranch to the bank. And her record-breaking airplane—her Travel Air Speedwing, which cost her a cool thirteen grand—was repossessed. She started the circus to make some money. I doubt that it's been a big financial success."

Lizzy was struck into silence by the weight of the story. At last she managed a question, then another. "Her airplane was repossessed? Then what—I mean, she's flying *something*, isn't she?"

"She's flying a Jenny." He stubbed out his cigarette in the ashtray.

"A Jenny? What's that?"

"A Curtiss JN-4. It's the plane most barnstormers fly. It's a bi-wing and stable at low airspeeds, which makes it ideal for stunt flying and aerobatics. But believe you me, it's nothing like the Travel Air. That's the plane she flew when she set the woman's speed record back in 1930. It had a Wright J-6-7 engine and racing wings. The fastest plane ever designed, at that time. And nobody could figure out what made it go fast. Was it the engine? The wings, the cowling—what? The specs were so secret that the press dubbed it the 'Mystery Ship.'" He stubbed out his cigarette, hard. "Lily Dare flew that plane faster than anybody, faster than Amelia Earhart, even, at 197.6 miles per hour."

"Amazing," Lizzy murmured. "Almost 200 miles an hour! It's hard to imagine anybody going that fast." What was just as amazing, she thought, was Charlie Dickens' enthusiasm. Normally, the man was as cool as a cucumber. Obviously, Lily Dare, whatever her faults and failings, had a place in his heart. Was Miss Dare's visit likely to rekindle Charlie's former feelings for her? What effect would this have on his relationship with Fannie?

Charlie's grin was crooked. "Of course, that record has already been broken, numerous times. Lily loves to fly fast, but closed-course racing—where the speed can be clocked and the records set—is too predictable and repetitive for her. She refuses to fly in circles, even if it means giving up her main claim to fame."

"I see," Lizzy replied thoughtfully. She could understand that, and the knowledge made her like Lily a little more. She herself wouldn't enjoy setting speed records if it meant flying in a circle, hour after hour, like a yo-yo at the end of a string. Where was the fun and adventure in that? But if she listened between the lines, Charlie seemed to be saying something else.

"What you're telling me," she said slowly, "is that Miss Dare isn't the big star that people in Darling think she is. She's not the fastest woman on earth."

"Well, she may not hold the current speed record, but she's still a star. She flew for Howard Hughes as a stunt pilot in *Hell's Angels*, and followed that up with Howard Hawks' *The Dawn Patrol*." He fished in his pocket for another Lucky, lit it, and blew out the match. "Of course, she was flying as a stand-in. The fans think the leading man was in that cockpit." He chuckled wryly. "The anonymous Miss Lily Dare. Unsung star of the silver screen."

"Gosh," Lizzy breathed. She preferred romantic comedies, especially now that most of them were talkies. But Grady was a big fan of adventure movies and they saw every one that came to town. "*The Dawn Patrol*? Wasn't that the one with Douglas Fairbanks, Jr.? Miss Dare was in it?"

"That's right," Charlie said. He pursed his lips. "From what I heard, Lily and the dashing Douglas played quite a few scenes together—off the set, that is. After hours."

Lizzie imagined she heard jealousy in his voice. "But I thought Douglas Fairbanks was married to Joan Crawford," she ventured. Was Lily Dare the kind of woman who fooled around with another woman's husband? Then she thought of what Grady had told her about the barbershop gossip about Roger Kilgore and Lily Dare. Could it possibly be true?

"Don't be so naïve, Liz," Charlie said with an ironic laugh. "A little thing like a wedding ring never stops Lily Dare." His voice hardened. "When something's off-limits, it just adds to her fun."

Now, Lizzie knew for certain that Charlie was jealous. So there *had* been something between him and Miss Dare! Was he still carrying a torch for her? How did she feel about him? What did this mean for Fannie? But she couldn't ask those questions.

Charlie broke the silence. "When she can get work," he went on after a moment, "she still flies stunts for the movies. But times are tough. Up until the last couple of years, the studios were paying good money for stunt pilots. Fifty dollars for a single spin. A hundred for flying upside down. Once, Lily agreed to crash an airplane into a tree—she got twelve hundred dollars for it." He blew out a stream of blue smoke. "But she never does that stuff for the money. She does it for the thrills. The riskier the better, as far as Lily

Dare is concerned. She burns the candle at both ends, as they say."

Lizzy was still trying to figure out why Charlie was telling her all this. "I guess I don't quite understand," she said. "If stunt flying is what Miss Dare loves to do, does it matter that she sometimes—?" She hesitated, trying to find a way to say it, then settled for the word Charlie himself had used. "That she's a schemer?"

"Sure, it matters," Charlie said, leaning back in his chair. "Take this sabotage business, for instance. Lily didn't tell me what was behind it. In fact, she was deliberately secretive. But I got the impression that Rex Hart is somehow involved."

"Rex Hart? But he's her partner, isn't he?"

Charlie nodded. "They got together fairly recently, I understand. But that's just an impression, so don't quote me. Anyway, there have been several threats—or sabotage attempts, or something."

"What kind of threats?"

"She didn't say." Charlie's voice dropped. "Of course, Lily would never admit to being afraid of anything or anybody. The Texas Star likes to pretend that danger is her middle name. But I know her well enough to know that she's scared." His voice dropped even lower. "I can't tell you what she's afraid of, but she's *scared*."

Lizzy paused, considering. "Of course, there's danger and there's *danger*," she said thoughtfully. "Miss Dare is probably a lot more comfortable with the danger she's trained herself to handle. Danger in the air is something she knows how to deal with. Danger on the ground is something else altogether."

"That's it exactly, Liz," Charlie said. "You've put your finger on it. And whether she thinks she's the one who's in danger or whether it's somebody else, I don't know." He leaned forward. "But I do know this, Liz. We have to be on the lookout for trouble while she's here. And I think you can help."

"Me? But I don't—"

Charlie interrupted her. "Look. I intend to hang around the airstrip as much as I can and keep an eye on her plane, make sure there's no repetition of that sabotage. I understand that Lily and that aerialist—Angel Flame, she calls herself—are staying with the Kilgores while they're here in Darling. And you and Mildred Kilgore are friends." He gave her a raised-eyebrow look. "True?"

Lizzy nodded slowly. Yes, they were friends, although she and Mildred didn't see much of each other outside the Dahlias' meetings these days. The Kilgores lived practically next door to the golf course. They belonged to what Lizzy thought of as Darling's "high society."

Charlie was going on. "So I thought maybe you could keep an eye on things at the Kilgore place. While Miss Dare is staying there, I mean."

Keep an eye on things? "I don't know how I can do that, Charlie." Lizzy paused, wondering if she should tell him about the awkward corner she had backed herself into—about her date for the party—and then decided against it. "I'm a guest at the party Friday night. The only reason I'm there is to present the plant—the Texas Star—that the Dahlias are giving to Miss Dare. Most of the time, I'm not invited to country club parties."

Charlie was silent for a moment. Then he sighed. "I see. Well, there's probably nothing you can do, then." He looked embarrassed. "Oh, hell," he muttered. "I guess I shouldn't have opened my big mouth. Sorry I bothered you with this, Liz."

Lizzy reached out and put her hand on his arm. "Oh, don't

be sorry!" she exclaimed. "I'm glad you told me. Maybe I can think of some way to help." She hesitated. "Would it be okay if I shared some of what you've told me with Mildred? I wouldn't say anything about your knowing Miss Dare, of course. But I can at least alert her to the possibility of trouble. And if I talk to her, maybe I can figure out how to be of more help."

Charlie pulled his brows together. "Well, I don't know—"

"And in a way," Lizzy broke in, "now that I know there might be a problem, I feel sort of obligated to tell Mildred." She was being truthful. "I mean, it really doesn't seem right to let her go into this situation blind, so to speak. After all, it's her house." *And her husband,* she thought, but didn't say.

Charlie considered that for a moment, then nodded. "Yeah. Yeah, that sounds right, Liz. Go ahead and talk to Mildred Kilgore, although I'd appreciate it if you kept me out of it as much as possible. I'll have a little talk with Lily when she flies in. *If* she flies in," he amended. "If they can't get that airplane in the air, the show's likely to be canceled. And you can forget everything you heard just now. In fact, I wish you would."

"Oh, I hope not," Lizzy exclaimed. "That it's canceled, I mean. Everybody would be so disappointed."

Charlie shook his head. "I don't know, Liz," he said ominously. "I have the feeling it might be better if it were."

The door opened and Lizzy and Charlie looked up. It was Ophelia, carrying two pieces of pie and two cups of coffee.

"Gee, Liz," she said, as she came around the corner. "If I'd known you were still here, I would have brought pie and coffee for you, too."

"On my way upstairs," Lizzy said, and got up. "Thanks,

Charlie," she said, and put her hand on his shoulder. "I'll let you know what happens."

"Yeah," Charlie replied. "Good luck." To Ophelia, he said, "What kind of pie did you bring me? Chocolate, I hope."

"Raisin was all they had," Ophelia replied apologetically.

"Dang," Charlie muttered. "I miss Euphoria already."

FIVE

Lizzy Spills the Beans

Lizzy climbed the outside stairs to the Moseley law office and let herself in. Mr. Moseley had gone to Montgomery on business and wasn't expected back until the following week, so the office was empty and all hers, which suited Lizzy just fine, because she wanted time to think.

From one angle, her talk with Charlie Dickens had been a real eye-opener. She'd had no idea about Charlie's relationships with women in the past, and this glimpse into his life revealed a web of intriguing mysteries. It was, she thought, like opening a friend's photograph album somewhere in the middle and trying to connect the random snapshots on the page to the real person sitting in front of you.

From another angle, the talk had been troubling, and she sat down at her desk to mull over what she ought to do. She really should speak to Mildred Kilgore—but should she be direct or beat around the bush? Should she telephone, or would it be better to have a face-to-face talk? And what, if anything, should she say to poor Fannie Champaign to prepare her for what might be a great shock, if Lily Dare reignited Charlie Dickens' old torch? It wasn't in Lizzy's nature to meddle in other people's business, and some of Mr. Moseley's cases had shown her the unfortunate outcomes to which meddling could lead. So these were serious questions.

Lizzy took a deep breath and looked around the office. The dusty old rooms had their own special character, with their creaky wooden floors and wood-paneled walls hung with certificates and diplomas and the gilt-framed oil portraits of the three senior Mr. Moseleys—Mr. Benton Moseley's great grandfather, his grandfather, and his father, all now deceased. The junior Mr. Moseley refused to sit for his portrait. "All traditions have to come to an end sometime," he said. "And I am putting a stake through the heart of this one right now. Anybody wants to know what I look like, they can by God take a gander at my *face,* not at my portrait."

But still, Lizzy loved the paintings, as much as she loved the sepia prints of maps of Cypress County and the old framed documents and the floor-to-ceiling shelves of law books and the fact that the office door was always open during working hours. When she first came to work here, it had seemed to her that the books and the documents and the dignified wood-paneled walls and—yes, even the open door—symbolized justice itself: stable and established and reliable and trustworthy and readily available to anybody who needed it. And if she needed another reminder of justice, there was the Cypress County courthouse right across the street, a beautiful redbrick building, foursquare and sturdy and solid, with white trim and a white-painted dome with a clock and a bell that rang out the hours with such regularity that you could set your mantel clock by it and so loud and clear that everybody in town could hear it, even when the doors and windows were shut.

In the past few years, though, Lizzy had begun to feel that her ideal of justice and the law might be a bit naïve and unsophisticated, for the more she saw of the law, the more elusive *justice* seemed. There were too many cases where the rich got all the "justice" they wanted and the poor got none at all, even though Mr. Moseley did the very best he could to get a fair hearing under the law for every one of his clients, rich and poor. And then there were the colored folks over in Maysville, who were most in danger of getting the short end of the stick, as Mr. Moseley put it when he was frustrated with a case. What kind of justice did they get?

In fact, justice was beginning to seem to Lizzy a lot like that shiny brass balance scale that sat on the shelf behind Mr. Moseley's big walnut desk. It had two small metal pans that were supposed to balance against one another, both of them equal. But there was something wrong with the scale's mechanism, so that no matter how carefully it was adjusted, one side always hung lower than the other. Lizzy didn't like to think of it, but that was the way justice seemed to operate these days. It tipped in the direction of the people who had money and influence and power, and the rest . . . well, they came up short.

But Lizzy wasn't thinking about justice today. She was thinking about what Charlie Dickens had told her about Lily Dare, the sabotaged airplane, and the possibility that the air show might be canceled. Of course, the Watermelon Festival would go on, with or without Miss Dare and her Dare Devils. There would be plenty of fun for everybody, especially for the young folks, who would enjoy the carnival rides and cotton candy and free watermelons.

But the air show—well, that was something people were looking forward to. It was the brightest spot in an otherwise pretty dismal summer, what with Ozzie Sherman cutting back on the hours his men worked at the Pine Creek saw-mill, and the Coca-Cola bottling plant laying off one full shift, and Cypress County reducing the size of the road repair crews. If Dad was out of work and the family couldn't afford the buck it cost to watch the air show from the field, they could pay fifteen cents apiece for tickets to the Water-melon Festival and watch the show from the fairgrounds. They wouldn't get to see the clown or the magic show or the head-on car crash, but they could see the airplanes and the wingwalker. If that was canceled, there'd be dozens of dis-appointed dads, moms, and kids.

Lizzy thought for a moment more, then reached for the telephone. What she had to tell Mildred was important, and she could say it without mentioning anything about Lily Dare and Roger Kilgore. She would call and be sure that Mildred would be home this evening, then ride her bike out there after work and have a little talk with her friend.

During her lunch hour on Wednesdays, Lizzy usually treated herself to a shampoo and set at the Beauty Bower over on Dauphin Street, just a couple of blocks from the office. The Bower was owned and operated by fellow Dahlia Beulah Trivette and located in the enclosed back porch of her house, where her devoted husband Hank had installed two shampoo sinks, two barber chairs, and two big wall mirrors in front of the chairs. Hank also put in an electric hot water heater, which meant that Beulah and her helper, Bettina Higgens, wouldn't have to pour hot water for sham-poos out of teakettles and pitchers, with the potential for somebody to get scalded.

In addition to the hot water heater, Hank had recently

installed another innovation for his wife: a new electric permanent wave machine. Well, it wasn't new, it was used, but the condition was "like new" and the price was right. Aunt Hetty Little had sniffed at the contraption and said it looked like a "flock of black caterpillars dangling from a buzzard's nest." But as far as Beulah was concerned, it turned the trick. With that magic machine, she could make any woman beautiful.

Beulah loved everything that was beautiful but especially adored big, floppy pink cabbage roses and had wallpapered the Bower's walls with them. In fact, pink was her very favorite color, so she painted the floor a beautiful shade of pink and spattered yellow, gray, and blue paint all over it, much to the amazement of her older customers, who had never seen so unusual a thing as a deliberately paint-spattered floor, let alone one that started out pink. ("A *pink* floor," Mrs. George E. Pickett Johnson had sniffed. "I don't know what this world is coming to.") After the floor was spattered, the walls were covered with roses, and the furnishings installed, Beulah hung her beautiful gilt-framed degree from the Montgomery College of Cosmetology on the wall where everyone could see it and declared that the Beauty Bower was open for business.

Beulah had chosen to practice the art of making women beautiful, in part because she herself had been gifted with physical beauty and wanted to share it. Her blond hair was loosely curled and artistically lightened and she had a glorious complexion and a generous mouth with dimples that deepened when she smiled. She also had an enviable figure. (That is, the Darling women envied her figure, while the Darling men envied her husband.)

And as an artist, Beulah was truly gifted, especially where hair was concerned. She kept informed about the latest hair styles by studying photographs of starlets in the

Hollywood magazines. She worked astonishing miracles with the curling iron, even on the most uncooperative hair. And while coloring hair was considered daring, Beulah dared to do it, offering any shade that any client (she never called her customers "customers") might desire, from the palest peroxide platinum of Jean Harlow to Myrna Loy's gorgeous russet-red. These talents had earned her a special spot in the hearts of Darling ladies, and especially in the hearts of her sister Dahlias, who were as eager for beauty as anybody else.

Indeed, as Lizzy walked in just after noon that Wednesday for her regular appointment, she saw that two other Dahlias were there before her. Aunt Hetty Little was just leaving, her old black handbag over her arm, her snowy white hair faintly blued and beautifully waved. And Fannie Champaign had her head in the shampoo sink, where Bettina was giving her a vigorous shampoo and scalp massage.

"I'm glad I ran into you, Liz," Aunt Hetty said. "I stopped over at the Dahlias' vegetable garden this morning to see how it's coming along. We're going to have more snap beans and sweet corn than you can shake a stick at. Did you remember to ask Myra May to call the Dahlias and remind them about the pickin' party on Friday afternoon?"

"I sure did," Lizzy said, and added fervently, "I hope we'll have plenty of help getting everything to our booth." With all the other problems involved with the festival, she didn't need another worry.

"We've got more watermelons than we banked on, too," Aunt Hetty added. "Obadiah Carlson said he's bringin' a wagonload. Says he can't sell 'em so he might as well give 'em away. And he might have more by Sat'iddy afternoon."

"A wagonload!" Lizzy's eyes widened. "That's a *lot* of watermelons, on top of what's already promised."

"My sentiments exactly." Aunt Hetty paused, frowning.

"It's got me wonderin' if there's such a thing as too many watermelons."

"Never!" Beulah declared, bustling into the beauty parlor from her kitchen with a fresh pitcher of lemonade. She liked her clients to think of coming to the Bower as though they were coming to a party (which most of them did), and always served cookies or cupcakes with drinks. "We can never have too many watermelons at the Watermelon Festival—and if we do, why, we'll just give 'em to people to take home. Folks'll love us for it." She gave them a dazzling smile.

"Beulah, dear," Aunt Hetty said, "you are always so danged *cheerful.* Makes my teeth hurt just to see you smile." She glanced at Lizzy. "I dug up that Texas Star and put it into a pretty pot so you can give it to Miss Dare at the party Friday night."

"Thanks for taking care of that," Lizzy said gratefully. Aunt Hetty might be twice as old as the rest of them, but she could always be counted on to do what she promised. And she could outlast them all in the garden.

"I'll be ready to shampoo you in a few minutes, Liz," Beulah said, waving good-bye to Aunt Hetty. She put the lemonade on a small table, beside a plate of cookies. "You just take a seat while I go check on Spoonie." Spoonie was Beulah's little girl. "She's out back playing with her chicken."

Lizzy sat down in a chair beside the shampoo sinks, where Bettina was applying a conditioner to Fannie's hair and scalp. Commercial hair conditioners had gotten so pricey, Beulah said, that she'd started mixing up her own, from eggs (produced by her backyard chickens), Johnson's Baby Oil (lightly scented, just twelve cents a bottle at Lima's Drugstore), and warm water. If you wanted this extra-special conditioning, Beulah added a nickel to the price of the shampoo.

Fannie was already wearing Beulah's homemade facial mask, whipped up from grated cucumbers (peeled, of course), mixed with buttermilk and a spoonful of cream from the top of the milk bottle. It was only a nickel, too—and even better, Beulah's clients said, than Frances Denney's facial cream, which cost almost six dollars for a teensy tiny jar. Beulah herself said she was thinking of going into business with her own cosmetic line, which she could sell right there at the Beauty Bower.

"There now, Miz Fannie," Bettina said, rinsing her hands. "You just lie in that chair and relax and think beautiful thoughts, and then I'll rinse you off."

Bettina herself was no beauty. When she came to work for Beulah, she wasn't even pretty. Her dark brown hair was thin and limp, she was as skinny as a flagpole, and flat as a board. She hadn't been to beauty school, either. But Beulah (who always saw the beauty in everybody) spotted Bettina's hidden talent with a comb and scissors and gave her a chance to put it to work. Under Beulah's generous guidance (and with a few beauty tips here and there), Bettina was blossoming. She even had a beau, Lizzy had heard—Alice Ann Walker's brother Lester.

Lizzy glanced at Fannie, her head still in the sink. "Getting all prettied up for the Kilgores' party Friday night?" she asked. "From everything I hear, it's going to be quite an occasion."

Lizzy had always admired Fannie's lovely complexion and light brown hair, which was short and softly curled. It was an attractive complement to the hats Fannie wore as an advertisement for Champaign's Darling Chapeaux, the only milliner's shop in Darling. If you admired the hat she was wearing, she would encourage you to try it on, to see if it looked good on you. If you liked it, she'd sell it to you right off her head, with a ten or fifteen percent discount because it was "gently worn." And since every one of Fannie's hats was an original, you didn't have to be afraid that you'd end up in church on Sunday morning, sitting right next to (or right behind) the very same identical hat.

"The party?" Fannie asked. The mask completely covered her face and she wore a cucumber slice over each eye. She lifted one now to see who she was talking to. "Oh, hi, Liz. No, I wasn't thinking about the party. I just like to look nice for Mr. Dickens." Her voice softened. "He's coming for supper tomorrow night. Wednesdays are our regular nights, you know."

"Is that right?" Lizzy murmured, uncomfortable now. Should she spill the beans to Fannie, and let her know that one of Charlie's old friends—a former lover, it seemed likely—was going to be in town this weekend? Or should she keep what she knew to herself and let Fannie discover whatever there was to discover? Of course, she didn't like to interfere, but at the same time she hated to see Fannie build up her hopes. It was a difficult subject to get into, though. If she was going to give Fannie a hint of what was brewing, she'd have to have an opening.

There had always been something of a mystery about Fannie Champaign—where she had come from and why she had chosen their town as a place to live and set up her hat shop. Her hats were very attractive, but it was clear to anyone with eyes to see that she wasn't selling a lot of them to the local ladies, maybe because the local ladies didn't have a lot of money to buy hats—or maybe because Fannie's hats had too much big-city style and made the Darling ladies (only a few of whom kept up with the latest style in hats) uncomfortable.

And Lizzy had her own questions. Fannie had once told her that her sister had a millinery shop in Miami and a cousin had a shop in Atlanta, so she was able to send her hats there for sale. But even that couldn't bring in very much, Lizzy thought. Hats couldn't fetch that much of a price, could they? So where was she getting the money to pay the rent on her shop and apartment and buy groceries and the stylish clothing she liked to wear?

Lizzy wasn't the only one who wondered about Fannie Champaign, of course. Some of the Darling ladies—Leona Ruth Adcock, for instance, the biggest snoop in town—had made it a point to try to find out about her. To no avail, however. Fannie kept her business to herself and turned away with a polite smile from the (sometimes impolite) questions asked by nosey parkers like Leona Ruth. But no doubt their curiosity about Fannie was one reason why people were watching and wondering about her and Charlie Dickens.

Lizzy didn't know Fannie any better than did Leona Ruth or the others. But she had found her to be such a sweet, modest person that she couldn't help but like her— and besides, Fannie had given her mother a job making hats when no other work would have suited. So Lizzy felt as if she owed her a debt.

Fannie smiled again, as if to herself. "I don't know if you've heard this, Liz," she said softly, "but Mr. Dickens and I have been seeing quite a lot of one another lately."

"I've heard something to that effect," Lizzy said reluctantly, thinking that Fannie sounded like a schoolgirl with a crush.

Fannie folded her hands across her midriff. "We go out sometimes—to a movie or a social event. But I like it best when he comes over to my apartment for supper. I make something easy, jambalaya or stewed chicken and dumplings, and we play pinochle and sometimes dominoes and listen to the radio." She sighed happily. "He pretends to be a crusty old journalist who has seen too much of the world and is tired of all of it. But underneath that tough veneer, he's a very sweet man."

"Mr. Dickens has definitely been around," Lizzy agreed. Maybe this was the opening she was looking for. "I'm always surprised when he tells me about the places he's been and the people he's known. Why, just take Miss Dare, for instance. The Texas Star," she added, just in case Fannie didn't remember who Miss Dare was.

"The female pilot?" Fannie asked. "The one who's doing the air show this weekend?" She raised her head and peeled off one of the cucumber rounds so she could look at Lizzy. "Mr. Dickens *knows* her?"

"Oh, yes." Lizzy chuckled uneasily, wondering if she would regret opening this subject with Fannie. "I understand that they're . . . old friends." She didn't intend for the last two words to have such a significant emphasis, but they certainly came out sounding that way, as if she meant to suggest something more than a friendship.

"Old friends," Fannie repeated slowly, replacing the cucumber slice and putting her head back down. "He . . . told you this?"

"Yes," Lizzy said. "We were talking about the air show, and he started telling me about Miss Dare. He seems to be excited about seeing her again. He knew her when he was working at the newspaper in Fort Worth. I gather that they developed a rather . . . close friendship."

"I see," Fannie said quietly, chewing on one corner of her lip. "Well, I don't suppose that's a huge surprise. Mr. Dickens has worked and lived and traveled in lots of places. He must have . . . friends all over the world."

"Yes," Lizzy said. "I suppose he does."

"I have been very foolish," Fannie said, again as if to herself, speaking so low that Lizzy could barely hear her. "How could I have been so foolish?"

Lizzy knew she wasn't expected to answer, but she felt like apologizing for having spilled the beans. Obviously, Fannie was very badly hurt by what she had heard. She was enormously relieved when Beulah came hurrying back into the beauty shop.

"Sorry, Liz," Beulah apologized. "Spoonie had to be rescued. She loves to play with her pet chicken, but that old rooster has spurs like knives and Spoonie's afraid of him. I had to pen him up, and he's the dickens to catch." She picked up a towel. "Now, then, we're doing a shampoo and set today? Or do you want a trim, too?"

"Just a shampoo and set," Lizzy said. As she sat down in the shampoo chair and leaned back so that Beulah could wash her hair, she was beginning to feel distinctly uncomfortable about what she had said to Fannie.

Had she done the right thing by tipping her off to Charlie's relationship to Lily Dare?

Or should she better have kept her mouth shut and let Fannie find out for herself?

SIX

"I Have to Stop Her!"

Lizzy was still turning these questions over in her mind as she went back to the office. But what was done was done and there was no help for it. All she could do was hope she hadn't caused Fannie too much grief and go on about the usual work of the office on a day when Mr. Moseley was out of town. She was also thinking ahead to the evening, when she had promised to talk to Mildred Kilgore, who lived near the Cypress Country Club on the southern outskirts of town.

Lizzy didn't own a car. Until a year or so ago, she had been saving to buy a used one. But instead, she had handed over the money to Mr. Johnson at the Darling Savings and Trust, to keep him from foreclosing on her mother's house.

Now, to somebody who didn't know the full story, using her hard-earned car money to save her mother's house from foreclosure might have seemed like a generous and unselfish act. Lizzy, however, knew that the opposite was true. She was very selfish, at least where her mother was concerned. If she hadn't done this, her mother would have moved in with *her*. She and her cat, Daffodil, lived all by themselves in a beautiful little house that was just big enough for the two of them. There simply wasn't room for her mother, who always seemed to take up more than her share of space and who (to make things worse) was constantly telling her daughter what to do, how to dress, and who to marry: Grady Alexander, of course.

Besides, as Lizzy often reminded herself, she didn't really need to own a car. She could always borrow Grady's blue Ford or Myra May's old Chevy touring car when she had to drive over to Monroeville or (less often) down to Mobile. And Darling was a small town. She lived close enough to walk to the office, and she could ride her bicycle anywhere else she wanted to go.

"We never sit down to supper before eight in the summer, so you just come on out whenever you get off work," Mildred had said over the phone. So after Lizzy closed the law office for the afternoon, she hurried home, grabbed a quick peanut butter and jelly sandwich, and changed into a pair of khaki slacks and a green plaid blouse. Then she climbed on the old blue Elgin bicycle she had ridden since her sophomore year in high school and biked all the way south on Robert E. Lee to Cypress Avenue, then turned off Cypress onto Country Club Drive.

The evening was warm and humid and the air was as heavy as a hot, wet blanket. But Lizzy was riding through a pretty part of town so she was distracted from the heat by the summer flowers blooming in people's front yards. In Lizzy's opinion, all of Darling was pretty. Some of it wasn't, of course, but Lizzy understood that not everybody had the time, the money, or the inclination to keep a place looking good—and pretty wasn't everything. In her view, her little town was a fine place to live, with friendly residents, mild winters, and a long gardening season. She smiled a little as she rode down the shady streets lined with beautiful magnolias and live oaks. She thought back over Darling's history and reflected that the original settlers—Mr. Darling and his wife and children—would be utterly amazed if they could see the town today, with its impressive brick courthouse, its well-kept streets, and its up-to-the-minute electrical and telephone systems.

The town had come a long way since it was established (more or less accidentally) by Joseph P. Darling. Some 125 years before, he was on his way from Virginia with his wife, five children, two slaves, two milk cows, three old hens and a rooster, a team of oxen, and a horse. He was aiming to start a plantation somewhere along the Mississippi River and make a lot of money growing cotton.

But Mrs. Darling had had enough. She put her foot down. "I am not ridin' another mile in this blessed wagon, Mr. Darling," she declared resolutely. "If you want your cookin' and your washin' done reg'lar, this is where you'll find it. You can go on if you want, but the lit'le uns and me are not stirrin' another step." She is said to have added, "And we are keepin' the chickens and the red cow—you can take the old black cow. She's dry, anyway."

Mr. Darling looked around and saw that the gently rolling hills were covered with longleaf and loblolly pines, and that there were sweet gum and tulip trees growing in the creek and river bottoms, along with sycamore and magnolia and sassafras and pecan. There was wild game on the land and fish in the nearby Alabama River, and Andrew Jackson had already evicted the Creek Nation (which Lizzy had always thought was very cruel and unjust) so there was nobody to tell him that the land already belonged to somebody else. All told, Mr. Darling figured, this was a pretty good place—as good as he was likely to find anywhere. And anyway, he liked to eat every day and wear a clean shirt on Sundays and was mightily fond of Mrs. Darling and their little Darlings.

So he built a big log cabin for his family and a very little log cabin for his slaves and a fair-sized log barn for the milk cows. Then he built a log hut and nailed a painted sign over the door: *Darling General Store.* Mr. Darling's cousin followed him out from Virginia and built the Darling saw mill on Pine Creek. Another Darling cousin built the Darling grist mill just upstream, so that people could get their corn ground for corn pone. Then they planted cotton, and when their cotton fields began producing, they built a cotton gin and a cottonseed oil mill. Traffic on the nearby Alabama River began to build, with steamboats plying a weekly route between Montgomery and Mobile, stopping at plantations along the way to drop off supplies and pick up bales of cotton and other produce.

But things began to change. The War (always spoken of in Darling with a capital W) put an end to slavery, thereby putting an end to the plantation system and substituting sharecropping instead. The Louisville & Nashville railroad, which by the 1800s ran from Kentucky all the way to the Gulf of Mexico, put an end to the steamboats, since trains were cheaper to operate than paddle wheelers, ran on time, and almost never blew up or hit a snag. Then the boll weevil came along and put a crimp in cotton.

But by that time, the Darling city fathers had built a twenty-mile railroad spur connecting Darling to Monroeville and the L&N, and farmers and timber merchants could get their beef, poultry, and lumber to markets around the state, which made them—some of them, anyway—wealthy. The wealthier farmers and merchants got together and bought a large piece of land from the Little family. On it, they built the Cypress Country Club and Championship

Golf Course, and then they bought property and built houses as close to the golf course as they could get. It was exclusive, and they liked that.

Lizzy was thinking about all this as she swung off Country Club Drive and into the Kilgores' circular driveway. Mildred and Roger lived with their young daughter, Melody, in a large plantation-style white house a short walk from the ninth green. As Lizzy rode up, she saw that Mildred's car—a snazzy-looking 1932 blue Dodge Roadster with chrome wheels—was parked in front of the house. She gave it an envious glance. Mildred's father's money had set Roger up in the Dodge dealership, and Roger thought that letting his wife drive the latest model was good advertising.

Lizzy leaned her bike against the wrought-iron fence, went up on the impressive plantation-style portico, and rang the brass doorbell. The door was opened by Mildred's colored maid, Ollie Rose, dressed in a black uniform, spotless white apron, and perky white cap. Mildred had kitchen help, as well. The Kilgores were among the few Darlingians who could still afford to keep full-time servants.

Lizzy followed Ollie Rose through the big house to the back veranda. There, Mildred was stretched out on a cushioned chaise longue, a pitcher of cold lemonade and two glasses on the glass-topped table, beside a large crystal bowl filled with plump, pillowy purple and blue hydrangeas.

From the veranda, Lizzy could look out across Mildred's camellia garden. It was planted around a rustic pergola and a native stone fountain, with a greenhouse off to one side. Lizzy knew that Mildred had spent a lot of money on her garden, and if there was a camellia anywhere in the world that she didn't have, she would pay any price to get it. What's more, she had a gardener who worked three days a week—full time during the annual December Home and

Garden Tour. Many of her camellias were in bloom then, and people came from as far away as Montgomery to admire their spectacular beauty.

Lizzy's own garden was filled with pass-along plants that hadn't cost her a red cent. But she could not really begrudge Mildred her garden or her gardener—or, for that matter, her stylish clothes or her big house and servants. Mildred had inherited a sizeable fortune from her father (one of those who had grown wealthy planting cotton) and Roger was a respectable Darling businessman. How the Kilgores chose to spend their money, Lizzy always told herself, was no business of hers.

But her friendship with Mildred (which went all the way back to elementary school) was sometimes complicated by a few uncomfortable feelings of . . . well, envy. Lizzy wasn't jealous of Mildred's money and easy life, exactly. But she had to admit that every so often she felt a few sharp prickles of resentment. It usually happened when Mildred went out of her way to tell her about a Mediterranean cruise that she and Roger were planning or some extravagant trip they had taken to New York or Chicago or San Francisco.

There hadn't been much of that kind of talk lately, however. Mildred and Roger didn't seem to travel together as much as they had in the past. But Mildred's splendid camellias were a sight to behold, and Lizzy could never in the world bring herself to criticize somebody who spent her money on flowers.

As Lizzy came up behind Mildred, she saw that her friend was reading a letter. Mildred glanced up, saw Lizzy, and hastily slipped the letter between the pages of a book that was open on her lap, her cheeks flushing a dull red. A plump, rather plain-looking woman, she had a too-high forehead, a too-long nose, and a receding chin. But she made up for her plainness by choosing expensive, smart-looking clothes and wearing them with panache. This evening, she was dressed in a yellow-and-red flowered cotton sundress with a flared skirt and perky bunny-ear straps that tied over her bare shoulders.

"My gracious, Elizabeth Lacy," she said in her usual Southern drawl. She closed her book with a solid thump. "Just *look* at you. You are sweatin' like a field hand and your face is as red as a firecracker. You walked all the way here?"

"Rode my bike," Liz said, wiping the sweat off her cheeks with her forearm.

"Serves you right, then," Mildred said in a scolding tone. "All you had to do was ask and I would've driven over and picked you up. It is just too hot to go riding that bicycle of yours all over creation." She looked down at her book as if to make sure that the letter wasn't visible. Then she reached over and picked up the pitcher of lemonade. "You need to sit down and cool yourself off."

Mildred was sometimes sharp and critical, but it was just her way. Lizzy knew she didn't mean it. She accepted the frosty glass of tart-sweet lemonade and settled back gratefully into a comfortable chair, wondering how to work her way around to the subject she had come to discuss.

But Mildred took charge of the conversation. "Are you all set for the party? I suppose you'll be coming with Grady, but you can tell that man from me that he *has* to wear a dinner jacket, or he will be turned away at the door. And what are you wearin'?" She was talking faster and more nervously than usual.

Without waiting for an answer to her question, she added, "I swear, Liz, I have just about worked my fingers to the bone getting ready for this party. I sent Melody off to stay with her aunt for the entire week. I just could not bear to have her underfoot. And of course Roger has not been one bit of help." She spread out her fingers to indicate how bony they had become, and her diamond wedding and engagement rings glittered. "I am goin' to be a complete wreck by Friday night. I have told myself that this will be the biggest and best party of the season. I will allow *nothing* to go wrong. Not one little-bitty thing."

If Mildred's fingers were worked to the bone, Lizzy thought, they didn't show it. But of course she didn't say so. Stalling for time (she still hadn't decided the best way to get around to the reason for her visit), she countered with her own question. "What are you going to wear, Mildred?"

Mildred brightened. "Oh, thank you for askin', Liz. I have the most *marvelous* new dress! It is emerald green silk, with a beaded bodice and shoes to match. I bought it at Bergdorf Goodman, on Fifth Avenue, especially for the party." Her voice sounded tinny and she swallowed. "What did you say you're wearing, Liz? Don't forget—you'll be in the spotlight. As the Dahlias' president, you are presentin' the Texas Star to Miss Dare."

Lizzy thought that Mildred spoke the last two words as if they were distasteful, but she only said, "It's not a Texas Star. It's a *Hibiscus coccineus.*" They both laughed. "I'm wearing my gray silk," she added, and sighed, feeling briefly envious of Mildred's Bergdorf Goodman dress. "It's the only halfway decent thing I own."

Actually, the dress was rather pretty, the soft fabric cut on the bias and draped across the bodice and hip to show her slim figure to advantage. With it, she usually wore her grandmother's antique silver earrings and the silver bracelet Grady had given her, back when he could afford things like that. She wore the dress often, but since she wasn't usually invited to country club parties, it ought to do for this one.

"To answer your other question," she went on, "no, I'm not coming with Grady."

"You're not?" Mildred raised both eyebrows. "Well, then, who *are* you comin' with, Liz?"

"Nobody," Lizzy said with a sigh. "I'm coming by myself. I'm afraid it's my own fault," she added ruefully.

"There's got to be a story behind this," Mildred said.

There *was* a story—and it was indeed Lizzy's fault, for *two* men had asked to take her to the party.

One was Grady, of course, her more-or-less-steady boyfriend for the past three years, who fully expected her to marry him. Both her mother and Grady's mother expected it, too. In fact, the last time Lizzy and Grady had gone to his mother's house for Sunday dinner, Mrs. Alexander had casually commented that now that Mr. Alexander was gone, she was just rattling around in the big old place and that after the wedding, there was not a reason in the world they couldn't come and live with *her.* Grady had said he thought this was a good idea—until Lizzy said she definitely didn't.

The other was Mr. Moseley.

"Mr. Moseley asked to take you to the party!" Mildred sat forward, her eyes widening in surprise. "Mr. Benton Moseley, your *boss?* I must say, Liz, he's quite a prize! Why in the world aren't you comin' with *him,* then? You couldn't have been fool enough to turn him down. Could you?"

"Not exactly," Lizzy said.

She sighed and went on with her tale. The problem was that over the past year, Grady had begun to take her pretty much for granted. He more or less assumed that they would go to the party together in the same way he assumed they'd get married and have three children and that Lizzy would give up her job and stay home to take care of them, just as his mother had done. So he hadn't bothered to invite her. In fact, he hadn't even mentioned the party, which led Lizzy to wonder whether he had been invited. For all she knew,

Mildred was inviting (besides the Kilgores' country club friends) only the Dahlias, and inviting them only because of the plant they were presenting to Miss Dare.

"Well, of course Grady was invited," Mildred put in crossly. "I wrote the invitation myself."

"I wish I'd known that," Lizzy said. It was truly awkward, because *she* had been invited and because a properly brought up Southern girl did not ask a man to take her out, even a man whose mother was expecting to be her mother-in-law. Lizzy was very modern in some ways. She loved earning her own paycheck and living in her own house, she smoked occasionally, she drank when she felt like it (no matter that booze was illegal), and she didn't mind necking in the front seat of Grady's blue Ford, even going a little farther than necking when they were both in the mood.

But she was old-fashioned in other ways, and not wanting to ask a man—even Grady Alexander—to go to a party with her was one of them. Even more, she was irritated by the fact that Grady was taking her for granted, not just as his date for the Kilgores' party but as his soon-to-be spouse—although she had not agreed to be either one.

And then, while she was mulling over these admittedly contradictory feelings, she found an entirely unexpected note on her desk the morning after Mr. Moseley had left for the Democratic convention in Chicago. The note, written in Mr. Moseley's strong, sprawling hand, asked if Lizzy would go with him to the Kilgores' party. He had been invited, of course, since he belonged to the country club.

Mildred blinked. "My goodness gracious, Liz. You must have been surprised."

"Could've knocked me over with a feather," Lizzy confessed. She had been so stunned that she had sat at her desk for a full five minutes, looking down at Mr. Moseley's invitation and wondering what to do.

Not many of her friends knew it (certainly not Grady), but Benton Moseley held a special place in Lizzy's heart. He was sweet and very good-looking, and when she had first gone to work for him and his father, she was smitten. He was just out of law school, bright and full of Southern charm. He had never been more than courteous and polite, but Lizzy (who had read too many dime-novel romances in which beautiful but penniless young women married wealthy and handsome young gentlemen and lived happily ever after) managed to conjure up endless fantasies about him. It was a serious crush and—unfortunately—a durable one. In fact, she continued to carry her secret torch right up to the point where Mr. Moseley had gotten himself married to a beautiful blond debutante from a wealthy Birmingham family.

The marriage had not lasted long: just long enough to allow Lizzy to outgrow her adolescent crush and feel only a quiet, respectful warmth for Mr. Moseley and a genuine regret for the failure of his marriage. But as it happened, on the morning she found his invitation, she was feeling deeply annoyed at Grady. So when Mr. Moseley telephoned a little later to pick up his messages, she had told him she would be delighted to go to the Kilgores' party with him.

"That's swell, Liz," he had said, and she heard the pleasure in his deep, resonant voice. "I'm looking forward to it."

"So am I," she said, and found to her dismay that it was true. She really was looking forward to going to Mildred's party with Mr. Moseley. And *he* had never seen her in that lovely gray dress.

"Then why aren't you coming with him?" Mildred demanded. "Did he change his mind? Did *you*?"

"Well . . ." Lizzy said. Not twenty minutes after she had happily accepted Mr. Moseley's invitation, Grady had stopped by the office to tell her that he had just learned that the Kilgores' party was "black tie" and wanted to know what that meant. When she told him, he was pained.

"A *dinner jacket*!" he growled. "Good grief, Liz. I haven't worn a dinner jacket since college."

"I don't doubt that." Lizzy glanced at his working clothes: a blue cotton shirt with the sleeves rolled high on tanned, strong arms, twill wash pants, a sweat-stained felt fedora pushed to the back of his head, boots caked with barnyard mud. If it weren't for that rakish fedora, he might have been a cowboy in one of Tom Mix's Western movies. "You're not exactly the black tie type, Grady."

"Damn right. I don't even know if my old jacket will fit." He sighed, a heavy, put-upon sigh. "I suppose you'll be all dolled up. Do I need to buy you a corsage or something?" He paused, considering. "Say, how about if I pick you some lilies of the valley? My mother has some blooming beside her front porch. They'd look kinda nice on that gray dress of yours."

"You don't have to do that, Grady," Lizzy had said in her sweetest voice. "Mr. Moseley will take care of it."

"Mr. Moseley?" Grady scowled. He pulled down the corners of his mouth. "What the devil has Bent Moseley got to do with your flowers?"

"Why, he's taking me to the party," Lizzy replied lightly. "You didn't say a word about it. So when Mr. Moseley asked, I said I'd be glad to go with—"

Grady stood up so fast that he knocked the chair over. "You are going to the Kilgores' party with Benton Moseley?" he roared. When Lizzy said yes, she was, he said, well, that beat all he'd ever heard. He stomped out of the office, slamming the door so hard that Mr. Moseley's great-grandfather tilted to one side on the wall.

All Lizzy could do was stare at the closed door. Grady

had occasionally displayed spurts of jealousy, but never anything like this volcanic eruption. Seeing his reaction, she began to feel guilty. She hadn't really wanted to make him jealous—had she?

"Well, if you ask me, Mr. Grady Alexander got just what he deserved," Mildred remarked tartly. "The two of you aren't engaged, at least not so far as I've heard. He should never have assumed." She frowned. "But what about Mr. Moseley? *He* asked you—why aren't you coming with him?"

"Because," Lizzy said. Last week, when Mr. Moseley got back from helping to put Governor Roosevelt at the top of the Democratic ticket, he had told her that he had to break their date. He'd been called to Montgomery on a case that was being heard in state court there and would have to stay the whole weekend. "I'll call Roger and tell him I won't be there.

"I am so very sorry, Liz," he said penitently. "I was looking forward to it. I'll think of a way to make it up to you. Maybe we could go to—"

"Oh, don't, please," Lizzy had replied. "It's all right, Mr. Moseley. I don't mind one bit. I know there are things you have to do."

And while she couldn't help feeling disappointed, it really *was* all right. Going out with Mr. Moseley might have been a memorable experience, but it wasn't the best idea in the world.

"Not the best idea in the world is right," Mildred said flatly. "What would you do if Mr. Moseley wanted to kiss you? One thing leads to another, you know." Her voice took on an oddly bitter edge. "It could be dangerous, Liz. There's no telling where it would end. In a scandal, probably."

Lizzy stared at her in some surprise, thinking that in all the years she had known Mildred Kilgore, she had never heard her friend use such a darkly judgmental tone. Mildred made it sound as if going to a party with Mr. Moseley meant that they would end up in bed together—and Lizzy knew that was definitely *not* going to happen. A little harmless flirting was one thing, especially if it made Grady appreciate her a little more. Sex was quite another. She was saving herself for marriage—or trying to, anyway, although that was sometimes a challenge, especially because Grady wasn't very cooperative. She opened her mouth to correct this wrong impression, but Mildred was going on.

"I'm sorry you have to come to the party alone, Liz. If I could think of somebody to fix you up with, I would. But we're a little short of single men these days." She paused, raising one eyebrow. "Or maybe you should let Grady know that you're available again."

"I don't think so," Lizzy said, remembering the way Grady's mouth had twisted like a knotted rope and how hard he had slammed the door. That had been several days ago and she hadn't heard a word from him since. He was sulking.

"Anyhow," she added, "a date might get in the way."

"In the way of what?" Mildred asked.

Lizzy put down her glass. It was time to spell out the reason for her visit. "Charlie Dickens had a call from Miss Dare this afternoon."

"Oh, *that* woman." There was no mistaking it this time. Mildred sounded as if she found the two words as distasteful as spoiled sauerkraut. "What did *she* want?"

Now Lizzy really was puzzled. Something was going on here—something involving Miss Dare. But what it was, she had no idea. So she only said, "It looks like we might have a bit of a problem, Mildred."

Then, for the next few minutes, she gave Mildred a thoroughly edited version of what Charlie had told her, omitting any mention of a personal relationship between the editor of the *Dispatch* and the Texas Star—or between the Texas Star and anybody else. And especially not Roger Kilgore.

Mildred was staring at her, eyes narrowed, an unreadable expression on her face. "Lily Dare's airplane was sabotaged?" she said. "Does that mean that somebody tried to *kill* her?"

The question stopped Lizzy. She had thought of the sabotage merely as a way of causing trouble for the flying circus, a nuisance kind of thing, nothing else. She hadn't thought of it as an attempt on Lily Dare's life. But now that Mildred raised the question—

She shivered. "Gosh, Mildred, I just don't know. I guess if somebody was tampering with her plane, she could have been killed. And Charlie says he thinks she's scared. He believes that she might be in danger—while she's here, I mean. That's why he asked me to help."

"In danger." Mildred's eyes narrowed. "Well, I have to say I'm not surprised. If that woman is in the habit of behaving the way she did at the Lions Club convention in San Antonio, she probably has quite a few enemies following her around. I—"

She stopped, pressing her lips together, as if she had said more than she meant to say.

San Antonio, Lizzy thought. That was where Roger had first met Miss Dare, wasn't it? All of a sudden, everything clicked into place. Mildred (who wasn't the prettiest peach on the tree) was jealous of Lily Dare (who was). And while Lizzy didn't like to think about it, Mildred's worries might well be justified. She remembered Grady's report of the gossip at Bob's Barbershop. And Charlie Dickens' remark that a little thing like a wedding ring wouldn't stop the Texas Star from fooling around if she wanted to. Miss Dare might have been tempted with Roger Kilgore in the same way that (according to Charlie) she had been tempted with Douglas Fairbanks.

Lizzy felt as if she had just stepped into a tangle of poisonous snakes, but of course this was all conjecture, and (as Mr. Moseley liked to say) an ounce of facts always outweighed a ton of speculation. She took a deep breath and hurried on.

"Charlie says he's going to hang around the airfield over the weekend. He's worried that there might be another attempt at sabotage. But he knew that you've invited Miss Dare to be your guest, so he thought—"

She paused, uncomfortably aware that she had gotten to the tricky part. "He suggested that I might try to keep an eye on things here—at your house, I mean. In case somebody tried something."

"Tried something?" Mildred asked, frowning.

"Tried to . . . oh, I don't know. Cause trouble, I suppose." Lizzy took a breath. "I told him I was planning to be here just for the party. But as I was riding over just now, it occurred to me that maybe there might be another possibility. Of course, it's just an idea, and maybe you won't like it, but—"

"What did you have in mind?" Mildred asked, cutting Lizzy short.

Feeling awkward, Lizzy cleared her throat. "Well, I thought maybe I could sleep over on Friday and Saturday nights. If you have room, that is," she added hastily. "I don't want to impose or upset any of your plans. And I certainly don't want to invite myself as a houseguest if I'm not—"

"Oh, don't be silly," Mildred interrupted brusquely. "Of course you wouldn't be imposing, Liz. Actually, I think it's a good idea. I certainly wouldn't want any trouble while she's here."

She paused, tapping her manicured fingernail on the

arm of her chaise longue. "Yes, I'm sure we can manage. I'm putting Miss Dare"—she said the two words with a distinct distaste—"in the yellow room at the top of the stairs. I was planning to put Miss Flame in the pink room, adjacent to Miss Dare's, with a connecting door. But you could sleep in the pink room and Miss Flame could have the blue room across the hall. I understand that Mr. Hart will be staying at the airfield."

"That would be perfect," Lizzy said, relieved. "I'll let Charlie know. Thank you." She was a little surprised that Mildred was so willing to let her stay—it was, after all, an unusual request. But perhaps her friend had her own personal reasons for being so accommodating. If she was really jealous of Roger and didn't want him to spend time alone with Miss Dare over the weekend, she might welcome the idea that Lizzy was sleeping in the next room.

"Please don't thank me," Mildred said in a dry, ironic tone. "I certainly wouldn't want anything to happen to Miss Dare while she was under *my* roof. She's such a celebrity." She leaned forward, speaking more seriously. "That sabotage business—you don't really think there's any real threat, do you?"

"I don't know what to think," Lizzy confessed. "I don't know any of the details, although Charlie did say that Miss Dare was afraid." She smiled slightly. "He made it sound rather melodramatic."

"Miss Dare is a melodramatic woman," Mildred replied.

"You've met her, then?" Lizzy asked curiously.

"No," Mildred said darkly, "but I—" She seemed on the verge of saying more, then stopped and waved her hand. "That's . . . that's just my impression. And it's entirely possible that she's making up that business about the sabotage, you know. It could be her way of getting attention. And guaranteeing publicity, of course. She seems to be quite adept at that."

"I suppose you could be right," Lizzy admitted. "But Charlie Dickens isn't the sort of man who would be taken in by somebody's melodrama."

Not to mention, she thought to herself, *that he seems to know Lily Dare pretty well. If anybody would suspect her motives, Charlie the Skeptic would be the one.* She frowned. *On the other hand, maybe not. The two of them had obviously been close at one point. Maybe that made it more likely he would be taken in. Oh, why did people have to be so* complicated*!*

Mildred put her lemonade glass on the table and lowered her voice. "Now that we're talking about this, I have something to ask you, Liz, as a friend. But I need you to keep it confidential. *Very* confidential."

"Of course," Lizzy said.

Mildred looked over her shoulder as if she thought that one of the servants might be listening. She spoke in a half-whisper that Lizzy had to strain to hear. "Did Mr. Dickens happen to mention . . . my husband? In connection with Miss Dare, that is."

"Mention Roger?" Suspicions confirmed, Lizzy spoke hesitantly. "Well, he said that Roger could take the credit for bringing her here—something like that." It was true. Everything else was her own conjecture. "Why?"

"Oh, no special reason," Mildred replied hurriedly. Then she bit her lip and looked away, and Lizzy saw from her face how desperately unhappy and troubled she was. "Actually, there is a reason, Liz. I wouldn't have said anything, but . . . Well, the truth is that I received a terribly disturbing letter, full of the most awful kind of accusations. Not that I believe a single word of it, of course, but—"

Her glance went to the book beside her on the chaise longue, and Lizzy understood. She had been reading that letter when Lizzy arrived. No wonder she was nervous and on edge. Poor Mildred. Something like that could be *poi-sonous.*

"I am so sorry, Mildred," Lizzy said, very honestly. "The accusations—they're about Roger and Miss Dare?"

"How did you know?" Mildred's brown eyes flooded with tears but she didn't wait for an answer. "Yes. The letter claims that they have been seen together. Not here in Darling, of course. But elsewhere. In different places."

"Who wrote the letter?" Lizzy asked.

"It wasn't signed." Mildred wiped her eyes with the back of her hand. "The envelope was postmarked in Atlanta, but there was no return address. Ordinarily, I wouldn't believe anything that somebody put in an anonymous letter, but . . ."

"But what?" Lizzy prompted gently.

"But whoever wrote it knew that Roger was in Orlando on a business trip a couple of months ago, and in Baton Rouge the month before that. He—or she, the handwriting looked like a woman's—said that Lily Dare was in both cities, too. At the same time." She bit off the words as if they tasted bitter. "At the same hotel."

"Oh, dear," Lizzy said. Instinctively, she reached out and took Mildred's hand. The fingers felt cold and fragile, and Lizzy could feel them trembling.

Mildred took a deep breath. "So even after I got the first letter a couple of weeks ago, I just laughed it off. I tried to deny it, you see. I just couldn't . . . I couldn't believe that Roger would do such an underhanded thing."

"The *first* letter?" So there had been two. "What did it say?"

"I can't remember exactly." Mildred lowered her head. "I . . . I burned it. I thought it was all a pack of lies."

Lizzy couldn't help thinking that it hadn't been a good

idea to burn the letter, but it wouldn't do any good to say so. "You changed your mind, though?" she asked tentatively. "You think it's true?"

"I know it's true," Mildred said bleakly. "This time, the person who wrote it sent a photograph." She picked up the book, opened it, and took out the letter that Lizzy had seen her slip between the pages. A photograph spilled out, and she handed it to Lizzy. "Here. You can see for yourself how beautiful she is. And sexy." She took a deep breath and blew it out, explosively. "God, how I *hate* that woman. And to think that she'll be sleeping under my roof this weekend!"

The photograph showed a man and a woman seated together at a table in what looked like an outdoor café. It was clear that they were more than just friends: they were holding hands and their heads were close together. All Lizzy could see was their profiles, but she recognized Roger Kilgore's dark hair and strong, regular features. She recognized the woman, too, from the publicity photos that had appeared in the Darling *Dispatch*. She was stylish, slender, and generously endowed. She was sexy. She was Lily Dare.

Lizzy handed it back. "I am so sorry," she said again. "This must be terribly difficult for you. Have you . . . have you spoken to Roger about it?"

"No," Mildred said miserably. "I can't. I'm afraid if I do, it might bring everything crashing down. I love him, Lizzy. I love him desperately, and I don't want to lose him. When you came, I was sitting here hoping that I could think of a way to make him see how she's *using* him."

"Using him?" Lizzy asked.

"Well, of course! That's what the letter says, anyway. Here. Read it for yourself." She thrust the letter into Lizzy's reluctant hands.

The letter was written in a distinctive back-slanting hand, in purple ink on a dusty-pink paper. It was not dated.

Dear Mrs. Kilgore,

I'm sorry to write you again, but I think you should know that your husband is still seeing Miss Dare. This picture was taken in New Orleans and it proves what I'm saying. It would be one thing if she loved him from the heart, but she doesn't. She doesn't love any of the men who think she does and who give her money to support her expensive habits. They're just saps and suckers that she uses, then throws away when she's done, like a piece of trash. Like Pete Rickerts, who crashed his airplane because he was so crazy in love with her. She is a terrible person who goes around destroying marriages, tricking men into giving her money, and making a mess out of innocent people's lives. She must be stopped. If you love your husband, you'll do whatever it takes to protect him from her. And do it before she wrecks his life—and yours and your little girl's.

> *With all best wishes,*
> *Your Friend*

Lizzy went back and reread the sentence about Pete Rickerts, remembering that he was the pilot who had died on Miss Dare's ranch. Had he been one of Miss Dare's lovers? Had he crashed his plane on purpose?

She felt the skin prickling between her shoulder blades. *"She must be stopped." Stopped how? Who's going to stop her?*

She folded the letter and handed it back. "What . . . what do you think it means, Mildred?"

Mildred didn't answer Lizzy's question. She put the letter back in her book, her mouth hardening. After a moment, she said, "Obviously, the woman has no soul. She has made a mess out of many lives. The lives of many innocent children, like my little Melody."

By this time, Lizzy could hardly think of anything to

say. Her conjectures had been redeemed by the facts, as Mr. Moseley would say, but she felt no satisfaction. She managed, "But maybe it's not as bad as you think, Mildred. Maybe—"

But Mildred wasn't listening. "I'm sure Roger believes that he is very special to her. But he is obviously just the next man in a long line of . . . of *suckers*." Mildred's words were like acid. "He must be in love with her—or think he is—or he wouldn't be behaving the way he is. I can't tell him that she's using him to get whatever she wants—love, admiration, money—"

"Money?" Lizzy asked sharply. "You mean, there's money involved?"

"Is there *ever*," Mildred said, with a bitter little laugh. "The first letter claimed that Roger was writing checks to her out of his business accounts, using the name Lily A. Star." She gave a sarcastic laugh. "Lily Dare, the Texas Star. If she was trying to hide what she was doing, she didn't try very hard. Even a dummy could get that one."

Lizzy frowned, wondering how the letter writer knew about the checks. It had to be someone close enough to Miss Dare to know where her money was coming from. But maybe—

"That's an easy claim to make," Lizzy said, and asked the question she knew Mr. Moseley would ask in this circumstance. "Is there any evidence? Do you know whether it's true?"

Mildred pressed her lips together to keep them from quivering. "Yes," she said, lowering her head. "I waited until he was out of the office one day and went through the ledger. In the last six months, he wrote three checks to Lily A. Star, for a total of nine hundred dollars. I have the canceled checks."

Lizzy flinched. Nine hundred dollars was a lot of money,

especially these days. And Mildred had known this for a while. No wonder she had been looking wan and worried.

Mildred's voice was choked but the words came out in an explosive rush, as if they had been bottled up for too long and the speaker felt a terrible pressure, a push to get them out in the open air, once and for all.

"The dealership is in a terrible situation these days, Liz. Nobody's got the money to buy anything, and months go past when not a single cent comes in—not even the money that's owed on time payments, thousands and thousands of dollars. Roger has had to lay off poor Freddie Mann in the repair department and Duffy Peters from sales, and both of them with wives and children at home. I helped Roger get that dealership started with the money I inherited from Daddy, and I've been using it to support this house and the hired help. But if things keep up as they are, there'll soon be nothing left of Daddy's money, and what we'll do when it's gone, I have no idea. Just no *idea*!"

"Oh, Mildred, I'm so sorry," Lizzy began, but Mildred had gulped a breath and was going on, her voice ragged and desperate, out of control.

"And now I find out that he's been writing checks to her out of the dealership bank accounts. I have to stop that horrible woman, Liz. I simply *have* to, or I'll lose it all! This house, the business, my husband—they're all I have!" Her voice thinned to a wail, like a trapped animal. "When they're gone, there'll be nothing left of me. Nothing!"

Lizzy stared at her, suddenly thinking that perhaps the big plantation-style house and the servants and the chrome-trimmed roadster and the stunning collection of camellias and, yes, even Roger and Melody—they were all one and the very same thing to Mildred, and all of them like the Bergdorf Goodman dress she'd bought for the party and the other expensive clothes she wore. They were ways of covering up and disguising an emptiness inside. But perhaps she was overreacting. Maybe it wasn't like that at all. Maybe—

"Yoo-hoo," a high, light voice called. "Oh, Mildred, Liz, it's me!"

A gate at the back of the garden had opened and Aunt Hetty Little was coming down the path toward the house. She wore a flowered print dress and carried a pot containing the *Hibiscus coccineus*, the plant that Liz was supposed to present to the Texas Star at the party.

"Oh, dear," Mildred said, very low. "If it isn't old Aunt Nosy." She sighed heavily. "Sorry. I don't mean to complain. Aunt Hetty is a sweet old thing, and rather pitifully lonely. I just wish she didn't live quite so *close*."

In the early 1920s, the Cypress Country Club and the properties on Country Club Drive had been carved out of the large Little cotton plantation, which at one time was one of the most beautiful and substantial plantations in the area. The Little plantation house had burned down the year before President Wilson dragged the country into the Great War, and all the servants had been let go. Since then, Aunt Hetty—the last surviving Little—lived by herself in a cottage on the other side of Mildred's back garden hedge. She was a congenial neighbor, although (as Mildred frequently complained) an irritatingly nosy one, who liked to know everything that was going on.

Mildred turned to Lizzy. "Now that she's here, Liz, we can't talk anymore. I'm sure I've said far too much, anyway—about those letters, and about everyone else. You must promise me not to say anything to anybody about them."

"I promise," Lizzy said. "Not a single word. To anyone."

She didn't imagine that she might come to regret that promise—and to break it.

SEVEN

Some Unexpected Magic

By the noon hour on Wednesday, Myra May and Violet were feeling the pinch at the Darling Diner. Ophelia's story and the ad for cooking auditions would run in Thursday's *Dispatch*. But that wasn't helping them get through the middle of the week. Business had fallen off dramatically as the news got around that Euphoria had abandoned the diner for the Red Dog. ("Like a rat from a sinkin' ship," Mr. Mann had been heard to mutter.) And the regular customers were beginning to grumble.

"Meat loaf *again*?" Mr. Musgrove from the hardware store asked. "Didn't we have it yestiddy? And the day before?" Suspiciously, he poked his food with his fork. "This ain't left over, is it?"

"No, it's not left over," Myra May snapped. She turned down the volume on the Chicago farm commodities market report on the radio and picked up the flyswatter. She had to admit that the meat loaf wasn't her best. She'd been rushed when she made it and she was pretty sure she'd left out the salt. But she wasn't about to tell Mr. Musgrove *that*.

"There's liver and onions," she added crossly. She whacked a fly on the counter. "You could've ordered that, if you didn't want the meat loaf."

A few seats down the counter, Mr. Dunlap from the Five and Dime spoke up. "It's good liver and onions, Myra May. The liver's maybe a mite overcooked, but it's tasty." He glanced over his shoulder at the empty tables. "I'm surprised you ain't got more traffic today."

"It's still early," Myra May replied defensively, hanging up the flyswatter and giving the counter a swipe with her cloth. "They'll be along."

But it wasn't *that* early. The tables should have been filled by now, with secretaries from the county offices in the courthouse, clerks from Mann's Mercantile, and the men from the repair shop at Kilgore's Dodge dealership. Obviously, news of Euphoria's defection was making the rounds. Of course, people didn't have a lot of choices when it came to eating out in Darling. But they could be going home for the noon meal, or packing a sandwich. Or going across the tracks to the Red Dog.

"Don't like liver and onions," Mr. Musgrove said morosely. "My mother pushed it down my throat when I wuz a kid. Ain't been able to stand it since."

J.D., Mr. Musgrove's scrawny, grizzle-cheeked helper, was sitting next to his boss at the counter. He pointed up at the blackboard that advertised the diner's weekly specials. "I wanna know what happened to our fried chicken, Myra May. Ain't we supposed to have fried chicken and chocolate pie on Wednesdays?" He peered nearsightedly at the glass-door cabinet where the pies were usually kept. "I don't see no pies, neither. We ain't got no chocolate pie for dessert today?"

J.D. was known around town for his ill temper and bad manners, but that didn't soothe Myra May's raw unhappiness.

"What happened to the fried chicken," she said in a chilly tone, "is that we're one pair of hands short in the kitchen. It takes longer to dress and cut up a chicken and fry it than it takes to make a meat loaf. And what happened to the chocolate pie is that Euphoria isn't around to bake it." She picked up an eraser and wiped off the blackboard. "Until we get ourselves some more help, I am suspending the specials. You'll get what we got and be glad of it— unless, of course, you want to walk across the square to the Old Alabama. Or up to Miz Meeks' place, over by the rail yard. I reckon she'd be glad to set a place for you."

Mrs. Meeks ran a boardinghouse for the single men who worked at the sawmill and on the railroad. If there was room at her table, you could get chicken and dumplings or a bowl of Mrs. Meeks' okra gumbo, plus a big chunk of hot corn bread and all the coffee you could drink. What's more, Mrs. Meeks had dropped her price to a quarter, which was a nickel cheaper than a meal at the diner. The trouble was (and everybody knew it) that the railroad and sawmill workers who boarded there got first dibs on the food. You could sit down with the second shift but you ran the risk of getting small helpings, depending on how many there were at the table, and you had to eat fast, because there might be a third shift waiting to sit down. And of course women wouldn't be comfortable there, watching those men put their faces to their plates and slurp up Mrs. Meeks' gumbo.

Rubbing his mostly bald head, Mr. Musgrove gave Myra May's suggestion a moment of serious consideration, then said mildly, "Reckon I'll skip Miz Meeks'. And four bits for that hotel dinner is too pricey for me." He picked up his fork. "Sorry if I made you sore, Myra May. This meat loaf is every bit as good as it was yestiddy."

J.D. chortled sourly. "'Every bit as good as it was yestiddy.' That's a sharp 'un, Marvin."

"J.D., you're as growly as some old treed black bear," Mr. Dunlap said. "You shoulda had the liver and onions. And the apple crumble wa'n't bad, neither, although I gotta say I'd rather have pie." He held up his cup. "Myra May, pour me another cup of coffee, would you?"

Myra May had made apple crumble instead of pie because it took less time to make the topping than to roll out and trim up a pie shell, and time was what they were short of right now. As she picked up the coffeepot, she heard the tinny roar and hiccup of Buddy Norris' Indian Ace motorcycle. A moment later, Buddy pushed open the front screen door and swaggered in, his holstered revolver slung from one hip, a wooden baton and a shiny pair of handcuffs from the other.

Buddy was Darling's deputy sheriff and—for all his youthful arrogance, derring-do, and reckless driving—a first-class law-enforcement officer. A few years back, Buddy had gotten the deputy's job by ordering a how-to book on scientific detective work from the Institute of Applied Sciences in Chicago, Illinois. He had taught himself how to take fingerprints and make what he called "crime scene" photographs, which was a lot more than Sheriff Roy Burns—now in his sixties and finishing up his fourth term of office—could do. When elections came around again next year, everybody said that Buddy was likely to give the sheriff a run for his money. The only thing that would save old Roy from getting de-elected was the secret dirt he had surreptitiously compiled on several important Darlingians. But it would do the trick. His people would get out the vote, for sure, and the sheriff would keep his job.

"Hey, Deppity," J.D. said, raising his fork. "You're just in time for meat loaf."

"Meat loaf?" Buddy frowned as he pulled off his leather motorcycle helmet and goggles. He was dressed in his usual khaki uniform, with lace-up brown leather motorcycle boots he'd gotten from the Sears catalog. "Today's Wednesday, ain't it? I've been lookin' forward all mornin' to havin' me some good ol' fried chicken." He sat down next to J.D. "Hey, Myra May. I'll take the special."

"Meat loaf for Deputy Norris," Myra May yelled over her shoulder to Violet in the kitchen. She took a bottle of orange Nehi out of the ice cooler and popped the top with the beer opener she kept hanging from a string. Buddy liked orange soda with his meal.

"Aw, shucks," Buddy said, and turned down his mouth. "And here I had my heart set on fried chicken." He took a pack of Chesterfields out of his uniform pocket. "Why, I said to the sheriff as I was leavin', 'Roy, it's Wednesday. I'm goin' over to the diner and get me some of that good fried chicken.'" He scraped a match against his boot heel and lit his cigarette, and Myra May slid a metal ashtray across the counter to him.

J.D. leaned over to Buddy and growled, "When I finish up this here meat loaf, I might just go 'cross the tracks to the Red Dog. Euphoria and Jubilation are cookin' over there." He smacked his lips. "Bet they'd be glad to fry me up some chicken." He said it just loud enough for Myra May to hear.

Myra May, who couldn't decide whether she was being teased, folded her arms and replied with a frosty sarcasm, "Well, now, J.D., you just go on and do that. But you might want to take Buddy here with you. I hear the Red Dog can be rough, and you're just a little guy."

Mr. Musgrove threw back his head and laughed heartily. "Yeah, sure, J.D. I'd like to see you go over to the Red Dog. 'Cept if you did, you might not come back and I'd have to hire me a new helper." He held out his empty cup. "I'll have another cup of that java, Myra May." He raised his voice. "And don't you worry yore purty head none 'bout losing customers. We'll stick by you 'til you get yourself a new cook. Won't we, Buddy?"

"Reckon we will," Buddy said, pulling on his cigarette. He swigged his Nehi, his prominent Adam's apple bobbing, and gave Myra May a disarming smile. "Reckon we ain't got much choice."

"Speak for yore selfs," J.D. said grumpily. "You wise guys'll change yore tune when you come in tomorrow with yore heart set on the Thursday pot roast and there ain't nothin' but fried green tomato sandwiches."

Violet, who believed in good customer relations, stuck her head through the kitchen pass-through and spoke up. "J.D., honey, Billie Bob just brought in a string of fresh catfish, already cleaned. We've got it on tonight's supper menu, but I can fry some up real fast for you, if you feel you haven't had yourself enough to eat."

J.D. fished in his pocket and pulled out some change. "Don't reckon I will," he muttered grumpily, counting it. "I ain't got me but eighteen cents, and I don't figger you're givin' it away."

"Wish we could," Violet said regretfully. She smiled at Buddy. "Same goes for you, Buddy. You want a plate of catfish instead of the meat loaf?"

Buddy brightened. "You'd fry up that catfish, Violet? Just for me? Why, that would be swell." Buddy had had a mad crush on Violet ever since she arrived in Darling. He'd once said he'd lay down his life for her and her little Cupcake, and Myra May thought he probably would.

Mr. Dunlap spoke up. "Myra May, don't you pay J.D. no never mind. He's got rocks in his head. You just do the best you can. Like Marvin says, we'll stand by you 'til you get a new cook." He paused, adding judiciously, "That's gonna be sometime soon, ain't it?"

"Soon as we can," Myra May said, and managed a smile. Deep down, though, she was desperately worried. The Red Dog might be a little rough for the likes of Marvin Musgrove and Mr. Dunlap. But the guys from Kilgore's repair shop and the pool room down the street wouldn't mind going over to Maysville if they thought they'd find a plate of Euphoria's fried chicken waiting for them on the other side of the tracks.

Anxiously, she looked up at the clock. Twelve thirty. She had expected Raylene Riggs to come in early this morning and try out for Euphoria's job, but the woman had telephoned and said she was still trying to get a ride over from Monroeville. She didn't know when she was going to make it, or if she could. And it might be Saturday before they got any response to the article and the ad in the Darling *Dispatch*. The Watermelon Festival crowd would be in town by that time, and there was the Kilgores' party to deal with. Myra May swallowed down her panic. She and Violet had been in tight spots before. Surely they could weather this one. But it wasn't going to be easy.

And then, as if she had been waiting just outside for Myra May to think about her, the screen door opened and a woman stepped inside. She was tall, about the height of Myra May, with heavy dark brows, a firm mouth and chin, and auburn hair streaked with gray, cut short and snugged around her ears. She was dressed in a blue cotton dress with a white eyelet V-collar and white patent belt and white low-heeled shoes and carried a canvas bag and a leather purse over her arm. She marched straight up to the end of the counter and spoke to Myra May in a businesslike voice softened by a Southern drawl.

"Miz Mosswell? I'm Raylene Riggs. We talked on the

phone. I'm here to try out for the cook's job." She held up the bag with a smile. "Brought my apron," she added, "and a few special little things—like chocolate for fudge cake— that I wasn't sure you'd have on hand. I'm just real sorry I couldn't get here earlier. Mr. Clinton didn't want to leave until he had a full load."

Mr. Clinton drove an old red Ford that served as a taxi between Darling and Monroeville. It was cheap (only fifteen cents one way, while the train was a quarter) and convenient. But you had to wait until he got enough passengers, which could be an hour or so. And sometimes you might have to ride with a crate of live chickens or a lapful of somebody's dog.

At Mrs. Riggs' announcement, there was a sudden silence in the diner. Four men's heads swiveled for a look. Under his breath, Buddy Norris uttered two words, in a low, crooning voice: "Fudge cake."

Myra May lifted the hinged countertop that served as a gate. "Glad you could make it, Miz Riggs," she said cordially. "You just come right straight to the kitchen. The lunch crowd is just starting to show up. You can get started right away."

"How's your fried chicken?" J.D. growled, as Mrs. Riggs went past him on the other side of the counter.

"You can ignore J.D.," Myra May said, low. "He's mad because of the meat loaf."

But Mrs. Riggs had already turned to him. Her smile softened her firm mouth and transformed her rather plain face. "Well, you'll have to be the judge, Mr. Jay-dee, but folks tell me that my fried chicken is pretty good. What they seem to like best, though, is my pies." Her brown eyes were fixed on him. "My sweet potato meringue pie, for instance."

J.D.'s mouth fell open and he stared at her. "Sweet potato

meringue pie!" he said, almost incredulously. "My sainted aunt Mamie used to make the *best* sweet potato meringue pie I ever tasted. She put coconut in it." He closed his eyes. "I ain't had pie that good since she died."

"Why, isn't that a coincidence?" Mrs. Riggs replied with a husky laugh. She lowered her voice to a seductive whisper. "It just so happens that I brought some coconut with me, too. That pie is always so much better with a half cup of coconut—but it should be toasted just a little. Did your aunt Mamie ever put toasted coconut into her pie?"

Still staring and nearly overcome with emotion, J.D. could only nod. "I would give just about anything in the world for a taste of that pie," he managed at last. "With some toasted coconut."

"Sounds right to me," Myra May said, and gave him a look that said, plain as day, *Put that in your pipe and smoke it, J.D.*

Mrs. Riggs straightened. "Well, if you'll be a little patient, I think we can fix you up," she said with another smile, and followed Myra May. At the kitchen door, she turned and gave J.D. a wink.

"It was like magic," Myra May said later that night. She and Violet were finally able to sit down in their upstairs flat with glasses of cold iced tea and two small pieces of a fudge cake so rich it was almost like a double chocolate brownie and delectable beyond belief. "I swear, she charmed that spiteful old J.D. right down out of his tree. And that was even *before* he tasted her sweet potato meringue pie."

Smiling, Violet cuddled a sleepy Cupcake up against her. "And did you see the look on Buddy Norris' face when he took the first bite of that fudge cake? He said it was just like his mother's." She shook her head, marveling. "What

Raylene did in the kitchen today was nothing short of magical. Honestly, Myra May—I wouldn't have believed it if I hadn't seen it with my very own eyes. She cut up three chickens and fried them, fried up that big mess of catfish, put together a huge bowl of potato salad, cooked vegetables, baked three sweet potato pies, and made that fudge cake."

"Yeah." Myra May chuckled. "I thought Euphoria was lightning fast, but compared to Raylene, she was about as slow as a turtle on a cold December morning."

Mrs. Riggs had insisted on being called Raylene from the minute she put her apron on. She said it made her nervous when people called her "Mrs." when she was cooking. "I always think they're talking to somebody else and I'm looking over my shoulder to see who it is," she said with a little laugh. "So you just call me Raylene and I'll be easy in my mind."

"If you ask me, Raylene's fried catfish was even better than Euphoria's," Myra May went on energetically. "And I just can't get over her vegetables. Collard greens cooked with mustard sauce. Rosemary—*rosemary*—with roasted tomatoes, potatoes, and bacon! And garlic and red pepper in the okra! Did you *ever*?" She rolled her eyes.

"Amazing," Violet agreed. "There's no getting around it, Euphoria was definitely a top-notch down-home cook. But with Raylene, those plain old everyday vegetables taste like they came from a fancy gourmet restaurant. She makes it seem so easy, too. It looks like all she has to do is wave her magic wand and *abracadabra*, there it is. And what in the world do you suppose is in that special seasoning she brought to use for the fried chicken? I've never tasted anything quite like it."

"Neither have I," Myra May replied. "No doubt about it. She is an extremely talented cook." She frowned a little. "I can't quite believe that she wants to come to work for us. I keep asking myself *why.*"

By the end of the afternoon, word of Raylene Riggs' audition as a replacement for Euphoria had rippled around town the way gossip does in Darling, starting at one end of town and ending up at the other, getting somewhat magnified along the way. The evening crowd was bigger than it had been for some time, and definitely curious. J.D. returned for supper, in order to judge Miz Riggs' fried chicken and see for himself if she was the cook she claimed to be. If there was any doubt in his mind, though, it was completely dispelled when he got a mouthful of her sweet potato and toasted coconut meringue pie. It was even better, he swore, than his sainted aunt Mamie's, and he vowed to tell everybody he knew that the diner had a *swell* new cook who was (incredibly) even better than Euphoria.

And it wasn't just the speed and quality of Raylene's cooking that recommended her. In the kitchen, Raylene was easy to get along with and willing to listen—a far cry from Euphoria, who was queen of the cook stove and ruler of the roost, and made darn sure that everybody knew it. Toward the end of the supper hour, Raylene even took off her apron and left the kitchen to visit with the diners at their tables, asking people what they thought of this dish or that, just as if they were all old friends at a church social or a school reunion. The customers might have found this a little strange, but they seemed to like it.

In fact, Edna Fay Roberts (Doc Roberts' wife and Charlie Dickens' sister) had come up to Myra May after supper and said, "You know, Miz Riggs seems so familiar to me, Myra May. I could swear that I have run into that woman somewhere before. Is she from around here?"

"She hasn't said," Myra May replied.

Indeed, Raylene Riggs was something of a mystery woman, which to Myra May seemed very strange. She was friendly and outgoing, but she didn't seem eager to answer any personal questions, such as where she came from and whether she had a family and how long she might be thinking of staying in the area. She did say that if she got the job in the diner, she would start looking right away for a cheap place to live in Darling, since she couldn't depend on Mr. Clinton to get her to work on time. She was afraid that transportation could be a problem.

By the time they closed up that night, it was too late for Mr. Clinton's taxi. So Myra May left Violet to close the diner and drove Raylene back to Monroeville in Big Bertha, her old green canvas-topped 1920 Chevy touring car. Once Bertha got cranked up and running, she was pretty reliable. But she never went anywhere very fast, so the thirty-minute drive had given Raylene time to ask quite a few questions about Darling, and about Myra May, as well. She wanted to know who Myra May's mama was, and when she heard that she was dead and that Myra May had been raised as a proper Southern girl by her aunt Belle, she let out a long, sympathetic sigh and murmured, "You poor thing." Then she asked about Myra May's daddy (who had been dead some three years now), and how it had happened that she and Violet had purchased the diner together, and whether Myra May wanted to stay in Darling or live somewhere else. Myra May answered as fully as she could, if only to oblige Raylene to do the same.

But that strategy failed abysmally. When Myra May tossed out a few questions of her own—Where was she from? Did she have any children? How long did she think she might stay in the area?—Raylene sidestepped them as deftly as if she were playing dodgeball. It was obvious that the woman intended to remain a mystery.

And when they got to Monroeville, she instructed Myra May to drop her off on a corner not far from the square, saying that since it was such a pretty night and she wasn't the least bit tired, she would walk the rest of the way home. Myra May was deeply curious, but short of parking Big Bertha and following Raylene on foot through the darkness, there wasn't any way to know where she was staying. When she had time, she'd get the Monroeville switchboard—maybe Marybelle Ralston, who was on duty during the morning hours—to tell her whose telephone number she called from. Marybelle would know.

"Far as I'm concerned, we can hire her right now," Violet said positively. "If you want, though, we can go ahead and audition anybody else who applies. It would be a good idea to have a list of people who are available if one of us gets sick or wants to take the day off. I've never been very happy with just Euphoria in the kitchen. We were too dependent on her."

"I agree," Myra May said, "although I wish Raylene weren't so mysterious. I have a lot of questions."

"Me, too," Violet said. "But her private life is *her* business, isn't it? As long as she does her job, that's all we need to know."

"You're right, I guess," Myra May replied. "Anyway, I told her what we could pay. She said she'd come for that, as long as we agreed that it was just a starting salary." In a lower voice, she added, "I still don't understand why such a talented and obviously experienced cook would want to work for what little we can afford to pay. She could go *anywhere*, even these days."

"Well, when word gets around about her talent, the customers will start flocking in," Violet said. She stood up, holding Cupcake in her arms. "When that happens, we can give her a raise." With a smile, she looked down at the baby's sleeping face, sweetly damp in the heat of the evening. "Come and help me put the baby to bed."

"I told her that you and I would talk it over and phone her first thing in the morning," Myra May said, getting up to follow Violet into Cupcake's corner of their small bedroom. "She says she's available to start right away, which means that she can help cook for the Kilgores' party. Which is a huge load off my mind," she added. "She has some ideas for the menu, too. Good ideas—things we wouldn't have thought of. Things we can afford."

She stood next to Violet as they both bent over the crib, covering Cupcake with a cotton sheet and smoothing back the little girl's damp strawberry blond curls. She slipped her arm around Violet's shoulders and gave her a quick hug. She was suffused with a warm rush of affection for the two of them and with the feeling that their little family was absolutely complete and that everything she loved was right here in this room. What more could she possibly want?

Well, maybe one thing, she thought. Raylene's questions had reminded her of how much she missed having a mother when she was growing up—a real mother, her *own* mother, not Auntie Bellum, dear as she was. It would be wonderful if her very own mother could see just how happy her daughter was.

"You could go ahead and call Raylene tonight," Violet said, straightening up and turning away from the crib. "She might appreciate knowing that she's the one we want, and that we have already made our decision. You might even offer to drive over to Monroeville tomorrow and pick her up—that is, if you don't mind getting up just a little bit early."

"I don't mind getting up early," Myra May replied. "But why don't you call Joe Lee Manning and ask him for a list of houses for rent? The sooner she can find a place in Darling, the better." She wasn't crazy about driving back and forth to

Monroeville twice a day. Forty miles a day was a lot of miles, and Big Bertha wasn't cheap: gas was ten cents a gallon and tires were three fifty apiece.

"A rented house would be good in the long term," Violet said. "But for the short term, how about if she got a cottage out at the Marigold Motor Court? It wouldn't be fancy, but Pauline keeps the cottages clean and nice. She even puts vases of flowers on the dressers. And maybe we could ask if Raylene could get a discount if she's going to stay there for three or four nights."

The Marigold Motor Court had been built by Floyd DuBerry and his wife Pauline. It was on the Monroeville Highway, across from Jake Pritchard's Standard Oil filling station and just down from the intersection of Country Club Drive. In 1927, when things were still booming, Floyd built seven one-room frame cottages, spread some gravel over the mud in his yard for parking, and put up a sign right next to the highway. It was a big sign, so people driving in their automobiles could see it from a hundred yards away, announcing that each cottage had a flush toilet and a shower bath, electric lights, and CLEAN SHEETS AND TOWELS, all for only seventy-five cents a night, a dollar for two. This was substantially cheaper than the Old Alabama Hotel, which charged two dollars a night for a single and three for a double. The DuBerrys didn't serve food, but a couple of the cottages had what Pauline called a "kitchenette," with a hot plate for cooking and a sink for washing up. Or people could drive or walk into town to the Old Alabama or the Darling Diner to eat. Unfortunately, Floyd had died of a heat stroke a couple of years later, leaving Pauline all alone. But she was the type who could cope, and the Marigold filled a useful niche.

"The motor court is a very good idea, Violet," Myra May replied approvingly. "She could move in there right away."

"I'll give Pauline a call and ask if we can work out something about the rate," Violet said. She held out her hand. "Come on, Myra May. Let's finish that fudge cake."

As Myra May followed Violet into their parlor, however, she was frowning slightly. She was thrilled, of course, that they had found such a wonderful cook to replace Euphoria. It really did seem like magic, and she was grateful. But she kept coming back to the question: why would a person with Raylene's skills and experience want to come to Darling? Why did she want to work in a diner in such a small town? Was she simply looking for a new and different experience?

Or had she encountered some hard times, was running out of options, and this was the last place she'd tried?

Or was she simply . . . running?

EIGHT

A Louse, a Jerk, and a Two-Timing Heel

Over the past few months, Charlie Dickens had fallen into the habit of seeing Fannie Champaign on a regular basis, once a week at least, sometimes twice. He hadn't intended this to happen, of course. He was ashamed to admit it even to himself, but when he first began asking her to go out with him, he had persisted not so much because she was such an interesting person (she was a little too quiet to suit him), but because she was such an interesting *mystery*. Nobody knew anything about her—where she came from or why she had moved to Darling. And if that wasn't enough of an incentive to keep after her, Charlie had another. It was simply because she kept saying no.

Now, Charlie understood very well that "no" was not an adequate reason to pursue a woman. Still, he was intensely intrigued, for (like most newspaper reporters) he liked to know all the whys and wherefores and had the feeling that the whys that escaped him were the most *essential*. In this case, he was confronted with a puzzling—and challenging—enigma. He would ask Fannie to go to a movie or a picnic or some other Darling event, and she would say no, or sometimes just shake her head, never giving a reason. He would walk away with a laugh and tell himself it didn't matter—and then he would think about it and wonder.

Was she saying no because she didn't find him interesting or attractive? Or because she didn't like men in general?

Or because she liked doing whatever it was she did and didn't want to be interrupted?

Why, why, *why*?

Charlie was also aware that there were many other mysteries about Fannie, such as where she had come from and why she had decided on Darling, which seemed like a very strange place to try to establish a hat business. And where she was getting the money to live on, since it was clear (at least to Charlie) that making hats was a pretty poor way to support yourself, even for a woman of modest needs and desires. Perhaps she had a personal income—inherited money, a trust fund, or something of the sort—and didn't need to work. Perhaps she simply made hats because she wanted to make hats, and had come to Darling merely because she thought the countryside was pretty, the climate appealing, the people congenial. There were worse reasons to choose a town, Charlie supposed. But in order to get to the bottom of these mysteries, he would have to do some research. He would have to get acquainted with her. That is, he would have to take her out, and she wouldn't.

So it went for some months, Charlie asking (and getting more and more challenged and intrigued), and Fannie firmly saying no—until one day, not long after Christmas, she finally and surprisingly and even a little reluctantly said yes. Feeling as triumphant as a teenager, Charlie took her for a fine supper at the Old Alabama. Two weeks later, she said yes to his invitation to the Methodist Ladies January pie supper, and after that to the Dahlias Valentine party, and then to the Lions' Irish stew supper on St. Patrick's Day—all this, of course, in the way of research.

And then she began inviting him to her apartment for supper (chicken and dumplings or jambalaya or catfish) and an evening of dominoes or pinochle while they listened to the radio. They both liked "André Kostelanetz Presents," and Fannie adored George Burns and Gracie Allen. Charlie didn't like Burns and Allen (Gracie was such a dumb Dora), but he discovered that he did like to hear Fannie laugh.

He liked to look at her, too, for she had curly brown hair, expressive brown eyes, and trim ankles and slim hips and a beckoning softness about the rest of her. She was good company, as well, with a subtle wit that emerged as he got to know her better, and which proved a fine antidote to his irony and brittle skepticism. Charlie, who enjoyed an enduring reputation as a curmudgeon, actually started to enjoy being something else for a change, especially when their pleasant evenings together began to end with a few sweetly clinging kisses that promised even sweeter intimacies to come.

But while Fannie may have had some modern ideas about hats and women in business, she was very much a lady of the old school when it came to certain intimacies. She always knew where to draw the line and did it deftly and with grace and good humor—although it did seem to Charlie that the kisses got longer and the line got a little less clearly defined each time they approached it.

And so, by the time Charlie at last recognized that their pleasant evenings and sweetly promising kisses had become a habit (and a slyly, subtly dangerous one, at that, like cigarettes or alcohol, which could sneak up on you and *hook* you before you were aware that you were caught), it was already far too late. The Darling gossip mill had been turning industriously for weeks and folks had already pegged them as a couple.

Charlie should not have been shocked by this, but he was. And he was even more shocked—exactly as if he had unscrewed a light bulb and put his finger in the empty socket and turned on the switch—when he heard (at Bob's Barbershop) that Fannie had been overheard to say (at Beulah's Beauty Bower) that she was expecting a proposal of *marriage*. Whether she had actually said such a thing, he had no way of knowing. What he knew was that, as far as Darling was concerned, Miss Fannie Champaign and Mr. Charles Dickens were as good as engaged. All that remained was the formal announcement of their wedding plans, which would surely appear on the front page of the Darling *Dispatch* any day now. And everyone was looking forward to it. Darling loved a roses-and-romance wedding more than almost anything else in the world—except, perhaps, a divorce as juicy as a blood orange.

Poor Charlie. He was in an alarming predicament and he had no idea how to deal with it. He couldn't stop seeing Fannie without a good reason (he had none, for she was beyond reproach), and without breaking her heart. And even worse (oh, yes, much, much worse!) he couldn't break up with her without humiliating her in the eyes of the people of Darling. All he could do was berate himself for letting this happen. And of course, he was the one who was at fault here: he should have seen the cliff ahead. He should have stopped them before they got close enough to the edge to look over and see the rocks below.

But Charlie Dickens was not fool enough to be pushed into taking that ultimate step over the cliff, either by Fannie or anyone else. Oh, no! He reminded himself sternly that he had neither the temperament nor the means for marriage. He could barely support himself on what little money the *Dispatch* brought in over expenses. How in the Sam Hill could he support a wife? And since he had gotten along thus far in his life without one—and very handily, at that—he could see no special advantage to getting married at this late date.

But these arguments were generated by another, more powerful force that Charlie Dickens would not allow himself to recognize. It was *fear* that kept him from taking that ultimate step: fear of being confined—no, *trapped* was a better word—in a situation from which he could not escape. This subterranean fear had pushed him out of every relationship that had ever engaged his interest—including his brief and unsatisfying intimacy with Lily Dare (who was every bit as afraid of confinement as he was). It pushed him now to search for a way out of his relationship with Fannie Champaign, some kind of strategy that would deflect any blame from the blameless Fannie and cast it all on himself. Charlie was just enough aware of his feelings to recognize this as a noble impulse and to begin to think seriously about finding that strategy.

And that was where he was when the Texas Star agreed to bring her Dare Devil air show to Darling. This circumstance gave him an idea for a way to deal with what he now thought of as the "Fannie problem."

He didn't at all like this idea when it first occurred to him and he kept on not liking it as the idea grew into a plan. To tell the truth, the plan was pretty scummy and he wished he could think of something a little less hurtful for Fannie and not quite so damaging to his own reputation. But while it certainly was not a pretty plan, he told himself that it sprang from the right motive and was the best he could come up with under the circumstances. He didn't want to do it, but he had to. And the time to do it was *now*.

Charlie and Fannie usually had supper together on Wednesday nights. One week, they would walk over to the Old Alabama; the next week, Fannie would cook for them in her apartment, upstairs over her hat shop and the small rooms that housed the Darling library. That was the plan for this Wednesday night, and Charlie was glad, since it meant that he could say what he had to say in private, which seemed infinitely better to him than saying it in front of the other diners at the Old Alabama—although thinking about feeling glad only made him feel even worse.

The evening was quite warm and humid, and Fannie had put together a sandwich supper of cold meat, cheese, potato salad, and sliced tomatoes. To catch the breeze, she had moved a small table to the window overlooking the courthouse square, where people were still coming and going in the early evening quiet, most of them on their way to the Palace Theater to see the Marx Brothers in *Monkey Business*. The window was curtained in some sort of translucent white material that seemed to shimmer in the slight breeze, and the table was fresh and pretty, with a white tablecloth and flower-embroidered napkins and a bouquet of summer flowers from Fannie's garden.

Fannie wore flowers, too, a bouquet of tiny fresh white blossoms tucked into the lace-edged V-neck of her pretty blue dress. Seeing the trouble she had taken to make herself and the table attractive, Charlie felt like an even bigger heel. "Lower than a snake's belly," his father would have said, and his father would have been right.

Fannie was not quite as bright and lively as she usually was when they were together, and Charlie thought he detected a darker thread of melancholy beneath her banter. For his part, Charlie did his best to keep up his end of the conversation while they ate. But it was hard, because he kept thinking about the thing he was going to say after they had finished eating and wondering what was the easiest way to open an unpleasant subject.

The bright summer evening waned into a warm, dusky twilight, but Fannie did not turn on the light. Finally, when they had finished their dessert and were lingering over a cup of after-dinner coffee, she opened the subject for him.

"You haven't mentioned the Kilgores' party, Charlie. I don't usually go to country club parties—they're a little rich for my taste. But I'm planning to be there, since the Dahlias are presenting a potted plant to the guest of honor, Miss Dare—the Texas Star. It's a hibiscus." She looked at him with a half-smile that seemed to him hopeful, expectant, vulnerable. It struck at his heart. "You're going, too, aren't you? Perhaps we could . . ." The invitation hung in the air between them like an empty comic strip balloon.

"I'll be there." Charlie set his coffee cup into its saucer with a definitive click. "In fact, I'm escorting Miss Dare—if she's able to come, that is. There's a problem with one of the airplanes." He paused, steeling himself against hurting her but persuaded that cruelty was the only way. "Lily and I are old . . . *friends*," he said, putting a suggestive emphasis on "friends" and trusting that Fannie—who drew her own line with such deftness and grace—would hear it and understand.

She did. She stopped stirring cream into her coffee and sat quite still. A breeze lifted the curtain at her elbow, bringing the scent of fresh-popped popcorn into the room. Down on the street, in front of the Palace, somebody laughed.

"I see," she said, in a remarkably even voice. "It's good for old friends to spend some time together. I hope the two of you will enjoy your reunion." She spoke as if she had somehow prepared herself for his announcement, although he didn't see how that was possible. She lifted her eyes to his and pinned his gaze, holding it steadily.

There was a little leap in his stomach and a dull ker-plunk, like a rock dropping into a deep well. The feeling shook him. He wasn't a very good liar, but he replied with an attempt at nonchalance.

"Yeah. That's what it is, all right. A reunion. Lily and I have been talking on the telephone and it seems . . ." He stopped and glanced out the window at the darkening street, letting her imagine the conversation he might have had with Miss Dare. "I thought I'd better tell you before you saw us together at the party," he added deliberately. "Or at the movie tomorrow night. There's a special showing of *Hell's Angels.* I'm taking her."

She turned away to look out the window, too, and he slid quickly into the explanation he had rehearsed. "Lily and I, we go back quite a few years. We met when I was working for the Fort Worth *Star-Telegram.* At the time, she had a big ranch west of town where she liked to give parties. I'd spend weekends out there. We became quite good . . . friends."

Fannie seemed to draw back into herself, away from him, out of his reach. Still looking out the window, she said, "I suppose you're telling me that you mean to renew your friendship with Miss Dare in an important or permanent way." She turned to face him and added, quietly and evenly, "Is that it, Charlie?"

He nodded again, although this time, he found that he couldn't meet her eyes. "I'm sorry, Fannie. I mean, I'm really sorry. I didn't know it was going to be like this, or I would never have—"

He stopped, surprised and shaken by the pain he felt. It was as if he was putting a knife into her and feeling it slice through his own belly. The only thing that kept the thrust from being fatal was his knowledge that he was doing the right thing, the only thing, although with all his heart he wished it didn't have to be done.

He cleared his throat and tried again. "I shouldn't have pursued you the way I did, Fannie. I'm to blame, especially since I knew all along that I couldn't . . . that is—"

He fumbled for the words and couldn't find them. "I'm sorry," he said again. "Just . . . sorry."

"So am I," she murmured, and he thought she was. She sat silently for a moment, and he thought she must be weighing whether to leave the knife there or let him twist it one more time. He could see her holding her shoulders straight, hardening herself against the pain of another brutal thrust.

"I'm to understand that there was some sort of prior agreement between you and Miss Dare before you . . . before you and I started seeing one another." It wasn't a question.

He hesitated. "*Agreement* is too formal a word," he said, hedging against the outright lie. "But I guess it'll do. Yes. That's what I'm saying." He leaned forward, meeting her eyes, now speaking God's truth and willing her to believe him.

"Look, Fannie. I have been a cad of the worst sort. You have every right to call me that in front of this whole town, to tell everybody what I've done. I hope you will. I *want* you to. I've treated you very badly and I'm sorry for it. But I would feel even sorrier if I let you go on thinking that there's a chance that we could . . . That I—" He had rehearsed this part, too, but now he found that he couldn't remember the words.

"That you could love me even a little," Fannie said quietly, "when deep in your heart, all along, you have loved *her* instead. I suppose that's it."

"Something like that," he said, tasting the lie and feeling an abysmal self-hatred for what he was doing to her, unable now even to comfort himself with the knowledge that this was the right thing, the noble thing to do. And then, into the silence, crawled the ugly little worm of uncertainty. What if it wasn't the right thing to do? What if he had just broken something very beautiful and fragile, something not meant to be broken? What if—?

"Well, then." Fannie picked up her napkin and began to fold it, neatly and precisely, lining up the corners so that they were absolutely square. "Well, then," she repeated, her voice clipped and brisk, her shoulders still straight in her pretty blue dress. "I suppose we won't be seeing one another again—not *this* way, anyway."

"I guess that would be best," he said gruffly. Actually, he hadn't thought about what would happen between them after tonight, after he had said what he had to say to give her a reason to break it off. Now, having said it, he felt a sudden, surprising void—not a cliff, but a void—open up at his feet. It was wide and so deep he couldn't see the bottom.

Still in that brisk voice, she asked, "Will you be going off . . . with her?" She put down the napkin, adding quickly, "Forgive me for asking, but I think I should know. People might ask, and I would like to have something to tell them." She paused, waiting, and then said again, "Are you going off together?"

He hadn't thought of this question either, and found himself stumbling through a ham-fisted improvisation. "Actually, no. I mean, that's not . . . it isn't likely to happen. At least, it won't happen any time soon. Neither of us has the money. And I can't just walk away from the newspaper. There are debts." There weren't, luckily, but it was the best he could do on short notice.

"But if you love her," she pressed, "and she loves you— well, then, money shouldn't be an issue. And if you can't leave the newspaper, couldn't she come here, to be with you?"

The thought of Lily Dare staying in Darling was so

absurd that Charlie almost laughed out loud. "No," he said. "She couldn't. But I'll be seeing her, of course—as often as we can manage it." He managed to wrap a chuckle around his next lie. "Maybe she'll fly in for a weekend every so often."

"With that airplane, I suppose she gets around," Fannie said.

There was a long silence. Then she lifted her chin and he heard the hard, fierce honesty in her voice, truer than anything he had said to her.

"Well, then, Charlie Dickens, all I can say is that I'm sorry. I thought . . . that is, I had begun to feel that I loved you. And I thought you cared for me in the same way. I knew we couldn't expect to make a life together for a while, the way things are these days. But I let myself hope, very unwisely, that we might, when things got better." She clenched her small hands, the knuckles white and hard, her hard, fierce voice becoming even fiercer. "I can't believe I let you fool me this way, Charlie. I've been so foolish."

He wanted to say *No, I'm the fool, Fannie, the biggest fool in the world.* But of course he didn't. This was what he had wanted, wasn't it? It was better for her to be angry. Anger would dull the pain. Anger would shield her against the inevitable gossip.

He lowered his head against her fierceness and said, with a contriteness that was agonizingly genuine, "I'm a louse, Fannie. I'm a jerk. I'm a damned two-timing *heel*. It's better for you to know that now than to find it out later."

Outdoors, the last light was gone, and in the room there were only shadows between them. He shoved the rest of the words out roughly, as if he were pushing rocks uphill. "That's what I want you to tell anybody who asks. Tell them Charlie Dickens is a louse, a rat. Tell them how badly he's behaved."

She laughed then, a bleak laugh that was brittle with hurt. "What makes you think that people will have to be told? They have eyes, don't they, Charlie? When they see you with her, they'll know what kind of person you are. I won't have to say a word. Not one single word."

"I suppose so," he said, and the darkness grew darker. He had done what he set out to do. His plan had worked as he intended, although he wished that she were angrier, that she would lash out, would lay into him like a cat-o'-nine-tails, the way he deserved. That she would raise her hand and slap his face so hard that it would rock him down to the soles of his shoes.

"Well, then." She stood up, facing him in the dark, and he braced himself against her fury. But all she said was, "Well, then good-bye, Charlie."

Charlie looked into her face and she met his gaze quite steadily. He had expected that she might cry, and if she did, that he would feel sorry for her. But she hadn't cried, and feeling her steadiness, he suddenly felt sorry only for himself—sorry and very, very small. He had been so sure he was doing the right thing. But now he wasn't.

He looked down into the black void at his feet and wasn't sure at all.

NINE

"What the World Needs Is One or Two More Miss Marples"

On Thursday mornings, Mr. Moseley always reviewed the files for the upcoming cases and sent Lizzy over to Judge McHenry's office with any additional paperwork relating to a pending hearing. Lizzy enjoyed this little task, since she usually took the opportunity to drop in at the county treasurer's office and catch up on the latest news with her friend Verna.

Of all the Dahlias, Lizzy was closest to Verna, who——by virtue of the work she did in the probate clerk's office——had developed the mistrustful habit of listening between the lines for whatever disagreeable truths people were trying to conceal. Verna liked to say that whenever she stubbed her toe on a rock, she just had to stop and peer under it to see what was hiding there. Lizzy almost never looked under rocks unless she absolutely had to, but she was always interested in what Verna found.

This Thursday morning, Mr. Moseley had telephoned from Montgomery with instructions to take several folders to Donna Sue Pendergast, the clerk in Judge McHenry's office. After that, he said, she could take the rest of the day off. He paused.

"This is the Watermelon Festival weekend, isn't it? And you're in charge? Why don't you close up the office today—and take Friday off, too." With an apologetic chuckle, he added, "It's the least I can do after standing you up for the Kilgores' party."

Well, this threw a different light on the day, didn't it? Since there wasn't any office work to do, she could settle down to the garden club newspaper column, "The Garden Gate." For this week's column, she had chosen the topic "Summertime Beauty Ideas from the Darling Dahlias" and had collected tips from every club member. Working fast, she got everything typed up in a matter of thirty minutes. She would drop the pages off in the *Dispatch* office on her way to Judge McHenry's office.

The sky had looked threatening when Lizzy came to work that morning, so she had brought her umbrella. There was no sign of rain clouds now, however. So Lizzy put on her yellow straw hat (the color exactly matched her sunny yellow print dress), gathered her newspaper column pages and the folders, and went downstairs. Charlie Dickens wasn't there, but she left the pages with Ophelia, who took them to her Linotype machine at once.

As Lizzy turned to leave the newspaper office, she saw the stack of ready print pages that had just arrived on the Greyhound bus from the print shop in Mobile. These pages—which would be incorporated with the local news in Charlie's print run—were already made up with the latest national and world news, sports, comics, and women's news. The headline: *Roosevelt Promises New Deal*.

Curious, she paused and skimmed the article, but if the writer ever spelled out what a "new deal" was, she didn't see it. She hoped it wasn't going to be like the promises Hoover made when he was campaigning back in 1928, telling voters that presidents Harding and Coolidge (who also happened to be Republicans) had "put the proverbial 'chicken in every pot' and a car in every backyard." Hoover promised more of the same. "The slogan of progress is changing from the full dinner pail to the full garage," he had said, back in 1928.

A *full garage,* Lizzy thought a little wistfully—and she was still riding her bicycle. Not much progress, was there? As if to underscore that thought, as she went out the door, she glanced down Franklin Street and saw an old Keystone iron-wheeled farm wagon in front of Hancock's Grocery. It was hitched to a scarred brown mule, patiently flicking its ears and tail against the flies. A woman wearing a slat bonnet and a feed sack dress waited patiently on the wagon seat, a baby in her arms, a diaper over the tiny face to shield it from the sun. A small boy, towheaded, barefoot, shirtless and dressed in ragged overalls, sat in the back of the wagon with a black and white dog.

Parked beside the wagon was a rusty old Model T Ford. Mr. Betts, the Ford's owner, had made it into a truck by the simple expedient of taking out the backseat and the whole back end of the car and adding a big wooden box that stuck out over the back bumper like the bed of a truck. The box was filled today with a wooden crate of live chickens, a goat with its legs trussed, and a bushel of shelled corn.

And next to Mr. Betts' old Ford was Mr. Elias' older brown Packard, which lacked the passenger-side door, as well as both front and back bumpers. An old leather belt was slung across the missing door to keep Mrs. Elias from tumbling out when her husband turned a sharp corner.

Lizzy shook her head. There might be plenty of new cars in the garages in Mr. Hoover's neighborhood, but not here in

Darling—and not many full dinner pails, either. What would it take to get things moving forward again, even if Governor Roosevelt were elected? What could one man—even somebody as powerful as the president of the United States—do in the face of such a difficult situation? Mr. Hoover was a decent, good-hearted man who cared about people. Surely he would have changed things if he could—but he hadn't. Mr. Moseley said it was because members of his party wouldn't let him put any spending programs in place to boost the economy, but Lizzy didn't understand that. She had heard that the government was in debt to the tune of some sixteen billion dollars, an almost unimaginable sum. How could Mr. Hoover spend money the country didn't have?

Lizzy was still pondering this question as she walked down the dim courthouse corridor and into the clerk's office, where she put the folders on the desk. Donna Sue, the judge's clerk, turned around from a file cabinet and asked if Liz had heard that Myra May and Violet had hired a new cook.

"I knew they were holding auditions," Lizzy replied, "but I didn't know they had found somebody already. That was quick. Have you tried her food yet?"

"I stopped in there this morning," Donna Sue said. She was a hefty woman who ordered her dresses from the Montgomery Ward "stout ladies" pages and was obviously enthusiastic about food. She paused, an oddly puzzled expression on her round face.

"It was the strangest thing, actually," she went on. "Last night, I dreamed about my mama's grits and sausage casserole. She used to make it for Sunday breakfasts, and it was always so good. It's my favorite memory of her. When I woke up from the dream, I could almost taste that casserole." She closed her eyes and licked her lips.

Then her eyes flew wide open. "You are *not* going to

believe this, Liz. But lo and behold, when I went into the diner to get my usual doughnut for breakfast, Raylene—that's the name of the new cook—was just serving up a batch of—*guess what!*—grits and sausage casserole! And what's more, it tasted like my mama's, too—which is strange by itself, since there must be dozens of ways to cook up grits and sausage in a casserole."

"That *is* hard to believe," Lizzy replied, thinking that if anybody but Donna Sue had told her this, she would suspect that it was a made-up story. But Donna Sue was an unimaginative woman who did good work in the circuit court judge's office precisely because she was such a no-nonsense, nothing-but-the-facts-please kind of person. "You dreamed about it, and there it was," she mused. "You must have been surprised by the . . . coincidence."

"Surprised? Was I ever!" Donna Sue exclaimed. "But to tell the truth, it didn't feel like a coincidence. It felt like *magic.*" She added ruefully, "I'm afraid I made a pig of myself. That casserole was even better than my mama's, if you can believe that. I told Violet and Myra May that Raylene is a much better cook than Euphoria and I hoped that she would be cooking in their kitchen for*ever.*" She paused. "Really, Liz. You should go over there and give Raylene a try."

"I will," Lizzy said, and headed upstairs to the county treasurer's office to have a cup of coffee with Verna.

Verna was not the most cheerful person in the world, but this morning, her frown was even darker than usual. "I have bad news about the tents for the Watermelon Festival," she said, as she put Lizzy's coffee mug on the desk. "Two men from the Masonic Lodge brought a truck to the depot to pick them up, but the tents weren't on the train."

"Oh, dear!" Lizzy exclaimed, suddenly apprehensive. The sabotaged airplane and now this! She sat down in the chair next to Verna's desk. "Well, when *are* they coming?"

"No idea," Verna said shortly. "I called the rental agency in Mobile as soon as I got the word, but nobody answered the telephone. I called twice more this morning. I'll try again in a little while." She shook her head. "Sorry, Liz. I know that isn't what you wanted to hear. But I've got it under control."

Lizzy chuckled wryly, and Verna gave her a suspicious look. "What's so funny?" she demanded.

"I'm remembering what you said Monday night, at the Dahlias' clubhouse," Lizzy replied. " 'When everything seems to be under control, that's just the time when it isn't. When everything just plain goes to hell in a handbasket.' " She sighed. "Far as I'm concerned, this festival is jinxed. Everything is already going to hell."

"Uh-oh," Verna said, with evident interest. She liked it when someone confronted her with a problem she could put her mind to. Verna was a natural problem solver. "What else has gone wrong?"

"Too much," Lizzy said. Choosing her words carefully, she told Verna about the sabotage to Miss Dare's airplane, the possibility that the air show might be called off, and Charlie Dickens' concern for the physical safety of the Texas Star. Lizzy didn't say anything about the rest of it, of course: Charlie's relationship with Miss Dare (whatever it was) and the anonymous letters and photograph that had sparked Mildred Kilgore's fears about her straying husband. Those things had been told to her in confidence and were too deeply personal to share—unless she felt she absolutely *had* to.

"And that's the story," Lizzy concluded. "If the air show comes off as planned, Charlie plans to hang around the airfield and make sure nobody monkeys with the airplanes. And I agreed to stay at the Kilgores' while Miss Dare is there. I'm sleeping in the bedroom adjacent to hers, so I can keep an eye on her and make sure she's safe." *Or to keep her away from Roger,* she thought to herself. She laughed a little self-consciously. "I'm afraid this sounds a bit Miss Marple-ish, doesn't it? But it seems like the right thing to do."

Verna, a fan of true crime magazines and Agatha Christie's detective stories, had recently loaned Lizzy her well-thumbed hardcover copy of *The Murder at the Vicarage.* The book had reminded Lizzy that things were not always as they seemed, and that even small towns—like the quiet and innocent-appearing St. Mary Mead, where nothing important ever happened—could harbor some sinister secrets, secrets that nobody in the world could guess. Nobody, that is, except for a spinster lady of uncertain age with plenty of time on her hands.

Innocent little Darling had its dark corners, too, as Lizzy knew from her own experience over the past few years. There had been the dreadful murder of young, pretty Bunny Scott, which might have gone unsolved if she and Verna and Myra May hadn't gotten curious about a certain dentist in Monroeville. And that slick gangster from Chicago who had come to Darling looking for Al Capone's ex-girlfriend, who had moved in with her aunt right across the street from the Dahlias' clubhouse! And those sneaky shenanigans with the Cypress County bank accounts that had ended when the county treasurer drowned himself in a gallon of the local white lightning. You'd never in the world know that such ugly events could occur in such a lovely small town as Darling. But of course they could, and they had. And that was exactly the point. Bad things could happen anywhere.

"Personally, I think what this world needs is one or two more Miss Marples," Verna replied. "But I sincerely hope that Miss Dare hasn't collected as many enemies as Colonel Protheroe did. And that she doesn't end up the same way *he* did." She narrowed her eyes. "Stabbed to death."

Lizzy stared at her. It was the murder of Colonel Protheroe—a man who was hated by half the village of St. Mary Mead—that the astute Miss Marple had solved in *The Murder at the Vicarage*. Lizzy swallowed. And Lily Dare, like Colonel Protheroe, had a great many enemies. But it hadn't occurred to her that anyone might actually try to—

"You don't think there's a possibility of *that?*" Lizzy asked. She thought of the letters that Mildred had received and her mouth went suddenly dry.

"Obviously, somebody hated her enough to sabotage her plane. So yes, indeed, there's a possibility of that." Verna spoke with the grim assurance of someone who knows that when she turns over a rock she will find a snake or a scorpion under it—and the experience of someone who never expects anybody to act any better than anybody else (and usually a whole lot worse). "Oh, and if you need me to help you keep an eye on things at the Kilgores," she added casually, "you can count me in."

"Really?" Lizzy put down her coffee cup. She hadn't thought about asking someone else to help, but now that she did, it certainly made good sense to ask Verna, who was by nature a suspicious person.

"Really," Verna said emphatically, and Lizzy could tell that she would like nothing better.

Lizzy paused. "Actually, I don't know when Miss Dare is arriving—tonight or tomorrow, or perhaps not at all. And I have no idea what's going to happen. But I'm sure that two pairs of eyes would be better than one."

"And if nothing else, we can keep each other awake," Verna said with a chuckle. She flashed a wicked grin. "We could equip ourselves with whistles, so we can wake up the household if we spot somebody climbing the drainpipe with a rope over his shoulder and a knife in his teeth."

Lizzy had to laugh at this comical idea, which sounded

like something out of a silent-film melodrama. "I suppose I am taking this a bit too seriously," she said. "But Mildred said—"

She broke off abruptly. No, not Mildred. It was the anonymous letter writer who had said that Miss Dare was ruining innocent people's lives. That somebody had to stop the woman. Stop her how? By sabotaging her airplane? By following her to Darling and stabbing her with a knife, like poor Colonel Protheroe?

"What?" Verna regarded her curiously. "Mildred said what?"

Lizzy cleared her throat. "Nothing. Just . . . nothing."

She wanted to tell Verna about the letters, but if she did, she'd have to tell her about Roger Kilgore's relationship with Miss Dare, and about the money he was paying her. And what Charlie had said about Douglas Fairbanks and wedding rings. And she couldn't do that—at least, not yet.

"I'll check with Mildred," she added, "but I'll bet she'll be glad for you to stay. And I'm sure I'm just being a worrywart."

"Maybe, maybe not," Verna said darkly. "Bad things happen. Let me know when you need me, and I'll be available. We'll keep an eye on the drainpipes, just in case." She put down her coffee and reached for the telephone on her desk. "And I'll call the rental place about those tents right now. That way, you'll have the latest information."

This time, Verna was able to get through to the rental office, but the news she heard wasn't good. "The tents apparently went north," she reported gloomily, putting the phone down. "For some mysterious reason, the railroad shipped them to Indianapolis." She made a face. "They're not sure they can get them back here by tomorrow evening."

"Well, if we have to, we can manage without the tents, I

guess," Lizzy said slowly. "As long as it doesn't rain." Of course, if it rained, there would be more difficulties. If the flying circus got to Darling, could they fly in the rain? She paused. "Have you heard anything about the carnival?"

"I ran into Mr. Trice yesterday. He says it's on the way. Cross your fingers." She frowned. "There's nothing we can do about those tents, so I suppose there's no point in worrying. But I wonder how they happened to end up in Indianapolis, instead of here. Seems suspicious to me."

"Everything seems suspicious to you, Verna," Lizzy replied, rising from her chair. "But there might be something we can do. Mr. Moseley gave me the rest of the day off. I'll go back to the office and phone around and see if I can find another supplier. Just in case."

But Lizzy didn't get back to the office right away. After all, she had finished her "Garden Gate" column and she had the rest of the day off. As she came out of the courthouse, she paused on the steps for a moment, hearing a rumble of thunder and putting her hand up to settle her yellow straw hat against possible gusts. The air was sultry and heavy with heat and humidity, and to the northwest, the sky was beginning to fill with dark clouds. They could certainly use the rain, Lizzy thought, glancing at the annuals— marigolds, zinnias, strawflowers, and dusty millers—that the Dahlias had planted around the courthouse. They looked a little dry and wilted. And if it was going to rain, better that it rained on Thursday than on Friday, Saturday, or Sunday—especially if those tents didn't show up!

On this hot and muggy July morning, the streets around the courthouse square were busy, as usual. Deputy Buddy Norris, on his red Indian Ace motorcycle, swung around the corner and skidded to a stop in front of the Darling Diner, raising a fishtail of dust on the dusty street. He parked next to a string of cars in front of the diner. Lizzy spotted Toomy LeGrand's truck and the Newmans' Nash. Toomy and Hank Newman, who were brothers-in-law, were probably having lunch.

Lizzy glanced at her watch. Maybe she should go to lunch now, and see for herself whether the new cook that Donna Sue had told her about was really *that* good.

"Hey, Liz!"

Hearing her name, Lizzy looked across Franklin Street to see Charlie Dickens standing in front of the *Dispatch* office, his big leather camera bag slung over his shoulder. He was wearing a blue and white striped seersucker suit and a straw fedora tipped to the back of his head. He waved at her, and she crossed the street.

"Glad I saw you, Liz," he said. "I phoned upstairs to your office but didn't get any answer. I've got some good news. Lily Dare is on her way to Darling and is due to land in the next half hour. Looks like the air show is going to come off after all."

"That *is* a relief!" Lizzy exclaimed. "I'll go call Mildred Kilgore and let her know that her guest is arriving. What about the others? Rex Hart and that aerialist? Are they flying in today, too?"

"A little later in the day," Charlie replied. "The rest of the team is driving in. But I've already called the Kilgores— I figured they'd like to know right away." He hitched his camera bag higher on his shoulder. "I'm driving out to the airfield now. I want to get some pictures."

"Okay if I go with you?" Lizzy asked eagerly. "Mr. Moseley is out of town. He gave me the rest of the day off, so I'm free." She was dying to meet the fastest woman in the world, the beautiful, *sexy* woman who had tantalized Charlie Dickens and wormed her way into the heart (or at least the pocketbook) of Roger Kilgore.

Charlie eyed her. "Did you talk to Mildred Kilgore about . . . you know. What we discussed on Tuesday?"

"I told her what you said about the sabotage," Lizzy said. "And that there had been some sort of . . . well, threat. Mildred agreed that it might be a good idea if I stayed at her house. I'm to have the room next to Miss Dare's." She paused, wishing that she could tell Charlie about those letters—and the compromising photograph, and the checks Roger Kilgore had written to Lily Dare. But she had promised Mildred, so she couldn't.

"Oh, and Verna Tidwell has agreed to stay with me," she added. "Between the two of us, we ought to be able to keep an eye on the situation and make sure that nothing happens."

"Good," Charlie said. "Yeah. Come on out to the airfield with me, Liz. It's time you met Lily Dare."

TEN

The Fastest Woman in the World

Charlie owned an old green Pontiac four-door sedan. He was in the habit of driving fast with the windows open, and the wind and the engine noise made it impossible for Lizzy to ask the questions that were going through her mind. By the time they got where they were going, her hair was blown every which way. She'd even had to take off her yellow straw hat and hold it on her lap to keep it from blowing away. As they drove, she saw that the dark clouds that had been piling up to the northwest now covered a third of the sky, and flickers of lightning danced from one towering thunderhead to another. It was going to rain.

Darling's airfield was on the south side of town, past the Cypress Country Club and the Cypress County fairgrounds. It was a narrow, grassy strip about two hundred yards long with sycamore and pecan trees growing along the fence rows at either end. Off to one side stood a plywood shed, weathered gray by the sun and rain. It was roofed with corrugated sheet metal and large enough to house a couple of airplanes. The shed had been knocked together back in the mid twenties, when barnstormers came to town sometimes three or four times a summer. These days, though, there were fewer flying circuses, and since nobody in town owned an airplane, the airfield wasn't maintained. The grass and weeds grew hip-high around the unpainted shed and across the airstrip.

But today, the strip had been mowed, a wind sock was hung from a tall pole, and a row of wooden bleachers had been erected along one side of the field so that Darling's dignitaries could watch the show in comfort. The rest of the crowd would park their cars and trucks on both sides of the field and sit on the hoods and car roofs.

As Charlie drove up, Lizzy saw that the tall sliding doors on the shed were open and the building was empty. There were several cars parked around the back. Three men were standing in front, shading their eyes with their hands and looking southeastward, into the sky.

One of the men was Roger Kilgore, nattily dressed in a light tan summer suit with a red tie and brown and white shoes and looking very much like Clark Gable. Another was Amos Tombull, the county commissioner that everybody called Boss, in a Palm Beach suit with a vest that was buttoned tight across his bulging midriff, a flat-crown white straw hat on the back of his head. As usual, the Boss was smoking a large cigar. The third man was Darling's mayor and the owner of the feed store, Jed Snow. Jed was wearing his usual work clothes, a plaid shirt with the sleeves rolled up and wash pants. Young Sam Snow and his little sister Sarah were with their father. Sam was carrying a cardboard, hand-lettered sign: *Welcome to the Fastest Woman in the World!* Sarah, dressed in a starched pink cotton dress with ruffles around the hem, had a huge armful of lilies, almost more than she could carry.

"My, my. That's quite a welcoming committee," Charlie remarked dryly, getting out his camera equipment.

"Well, she's a celebrity," Lizzy said, although she couldn't help suspecting that it wasn't Miss Dare's fame or his official duties that had brought Roger Kilgore here. If that anonymous letter writer was telling the truth . . . But the photograph and the checks proved *that*, didn't they? She lowered her voice. "When you talked to Miss Dare on the phone, did she say anything more about the sabotage? Or about a threat?"

Charlie shook his head. "I'll ask her about that later, when—"

But before he could finish, there was an excited cry from the group, and the children began to dance up and down.

"There she is!" Jed Snow shouted. He put his hand on his son's shoulder and pointed toward the trees at the southern end of the field. "There's her plane, Sam. The Texas Star is coming in!"

As Lizzy and Charlie joined the group, the air was filled with the roar of an airplane engine, and a moment later, there it was, a small white biplane with a red, white, and blue star on the side, surrounded by the words *Lily Dare's Dare Devils*. The plane got bigger and bigger the closer it came until, no more than thirty feet above the ground, it raced the length of the field from south to north, its engine so loud that Lizzy had to put both hands over her ears. She saw Miss Dare in the open cockpit, wearing her white helmet and trademark red scarf, which streamed behind her like a bloody ribbon.

The airplane reached the northern end of the field, cleared the trees, then waggled its wings and began to climb sharply, up and up and up, hundreds of feet into the sky, where it was silhouetted against the angry storm clouds. Lizzy watched, openmouthed, as Miss Dare climbed past the vertical, the nose of the airplane falling back and over. A moment later, the Texas Star turned belly up. Miss Dare was flying upside down.

The Boss took his cigar out of his mouth. "My gawd a-mighty," he blurted out in his gravelly voice. "Just like they do it in the movies."

"The fastest woman in the world," Roger Kilgore said. He sounded almost reverent.

"What's she doing, Daddy?" Sarah whispered fearfully. "Why is she upside down?"

"She's looping the loop, Sarah," Jed Snow replied.

"She's doing an *inside* loop!" young Sam Snow shouted, hopping from one foot to the other. "An inside loop!"

"Is she going to crash?" Anxious, Sarah reached for her father's hand. "Daddy, is she going to *crash*?"

"Not a chance," Roger Kilgore put in. There was a note of pride in his voice. "You are watching the number one female stunt pilot in the country. In the *world*, by damn. She's done this maneuver a thousand times."

Lizzy watched, her heart in her mouth, as Miss Dare flew the Jenny upside down for what seemed an endless stretch of time, then pulled the nose down into a steep vertical dive, down and down and down until it seemed that she was aimed straight as an arrow at the earth.

The men gasped. Sarah turned and buried her eyes in her father's sleeve. "She's going to *crash*!" she cried. "She'll be *dead*!"

But she didn't crash. At the very last moment, Miss Dare pulled up from her dive, leveled out at the southern end of the field and brought the plane to a perfect landing as a great shout went up. While Lizzy had been keeping her eyes on the skies, a cheering, noisy crowd of fifteen or twenty men and boys had materialized as if out of nowhere—

actually, they had run over from the fairgrounds, where they were working.

As the plane taxied up and Miss Dare climbed out, they stampeded onto the airstrip and she was surrounded. There was so much commotion, it looked like Charles Lindbergh had just dropped down out of the sky, and that the crowd had mistaken Miss Dare for Lucky Lindy and the Mystery Ship Texas Star for the Spirit of St. Louis.

But that was not the case, for a chant went up as Miss Dare climbed out of her plane. "Lily Dare! Lily Dare!" some people cried, pushing forward, while others chanted "Texas Star! Texas Star!" A lesser woman might have been frightened, but the aviatrix was handling her adoring public with confident aplomb. Dressed in a sleek leather jacket and white jodhpurs, white helmet, and red scarf, she stripped off her gloves, signed a few autographs, allowed several snapshots, then made her way toward the small group waiting in front of the shed, the crowd parting to let her pass.

And then what did she do? She walked straight up to Roger Kilgore, put both hands on his lapels, and kissed him on the cheek. In a low, sultry voice she murmured, "Roger, my dear, it's oh, so good to see you again," as if the two of them were utterly alone.

Roger might look like Clark Gable, but he didn't *act* like Gable. Suddenly red-faced, he took a clumsy step backward, grasped Miss Dare's hands and pushed them away.

"On b-b-behalf of the Lions of Darling," he stuttered, "w-w-welcome to our little town."

"Yes, welcome to Darling," Sarah Snow cried, rushing up to her with the lilies. "These are for you, Miss Dare. And I'm so glad you didn't *crash!*"

"Why, thank you, my dear," Miss Dare said, smiling. She took the flowers. "Lilies—how very sweet of you. And no, I never crash. It's bad for business." She smiled at Sam, who squirmed and blushed to the roots of his hair. "And what a swell sign, young man. I am honored."

Then came the introduction to Mr. Tombull, who clutched his straw hat to his stomach and gazed soulfully at her, stumbling all over his short welcoming speech. The Boss was clearly and totally smitten. And Roger, too, Lizzy thought. The flush had ebbed from Roger's face and he was quite pale. But although he was standing well back from Miss Dare, he watched her hungrily, as if he couldn't get enough of looking at her. As if, Lizzy thought, he wanted to reach out and pull her to him and never let her go.

Then Miss Dare saw Charlie and turned eagerly toward him. "And here's my old friend Charlie Dickens," she cried, blowing him a kiss. "Hey, Charlie, it's swell to see you!" She pulled off her leather flying helmet and shook out her very dark hair. She stepped close to Roger, smiling and posing prettily. "Be a peach and take our picture, won't you, Charlie? I would just *love* to have a photo of Roger and me together."

Roger went even redder. He grabbed Jed Snow's sleeve and pulled him forward. "Come 'ere, Jed," he urged. "You have to be in the photo, too." He raised his voice. "Mr. Tombull, over here, sir. Charlie Dickens is gettin' some pictures for the paper and we want you in it." As Amos Tombull joined them, Roger stepped aside, so that Jed Snow and the Boss were on either side of Miss Dare and he was on the outside of the group. To Charlie, he said, "Hurry up, Dickens. It's fixin' to rain."

The rain held off long enough to take the photos and push the airplane into the shed and close the doors. As the first few drops began to spatter down, Jed Snow took Miss Dare's arm in a solicitous gesture. "The kids and I will drive you into town, Miss Dare."

"Oh, but I'm planning to ride with Roger," Miss Dare objected, pulling away. "After all, he's the one who arranged for the Dare Devils to come to Darling."

Lizzy thought that Roger looked as if he were torn in two. "Sorry," he said numbly. "I have to get back to the dealership. Mildred—my . . . my wife—is expecting you, at our house."

"Your wife." Miss Dare laughed lightly. "Of course. But do let's plan to get together. We have a great deal to catch up on, you know." With that equivocal remark (or at least it seemed so to Lizzy), she turned back to Jed Snow. "I have a bag in the back of the plane. Could you get it, Mr. Snow?"

But when Jed returned with the bag, there was another change of plans. Charlie had taken charge, introducing Lizzy and suggesting that Miss Dare ride back to town with the two of them. They would go to the newspaper office where Charlie would conduct the prearranged interview and take a few more photos. And then he would take her to get some lunch and show her around Darling before he drove her to the Kilgores'.

Miss Dare agreed to that, then leaned close and said to Charlie, in a low voice, "You said you'd get somebody to hang out here and keep an eye on the plane until Rex and the rest of the team show up. Have you—"

"All taken care of," Charlie said, and Lizzy saw him signal to Zipper Haydon, who was standing at the back of the crowd. Zipper was in his seventies and had a crippled foot, but he was known to be a reliable watchman. He stepped forward, clutching his brown felt hat in one hand. "Zipper will be on watch for the rest of today."

Miss Dare nodded and turned back to Roger. "I'm looking forward to meeting your wife. I want to thank her for inviting me to stay at your house." She smiled broadly. "And for the party, of course."

To Lizzy, the words seemed to have a significant emphasis—perhaps even a sinister one. Roger seemed to think so, too, for he seemed to flinch. Was he afraid that Miss Dare might tell Mildred about their relationship—and about the money he had given her? Lizzy looked quickly around to see if anybody else had noticed his reaction. But if they had, it wasn't apparent.

Amos Tombull put on his most ingratiating smile. "We are *all* lookin' forward to havin' the chance to get to know you, Miss Dare," he said cordially. "We are so honored to have you in our little town."

"Why, thank you, sir," Miss Dare said with a flirtatious smile. "I am just so *delighted* to be here in Darling. We're going to have a great show on Saturday."

And at that moment, there was a flash of lightning, a clap of thunder so loud that it seemed to rattle Lizzy's bones, and the skies opened. The rain began to pour down in a deluge and all discussion was halted as everyone scrambled for the cars.

ELEVEN

Who Is Lily Dare?

As Lizzy listened from the backseat to the conversation between Charlie and Miss Dare as they drove into town, it was clear that the two had once been friends—although she couldn't quite tell whether Charlie continued to harbor a romantic yearning for the woman. It almost seemed from his tone that he was angry at her. As for Miss Dare, she was so flirtatious with everybody that it was impossible to tell what her true feelings were toward Charlie.

When they got to the *Dispatch* office, Miss Dare slipped into the back room to change into street clothes. When she came out, she was wearing a lipstick-red silk crepe blouse that clung to her shapely curves and a pair of light-colored linen slacks, with red high heels. The words *Lily Dare's Dare Devils* was embroidered in white on the breast pocket of the blouse. She had combed her dark hair, renewed her lipstick and rouge, and added a dramatic blue eye shadow and mascara.

The woman was elegant and undeniably sexy, and Lizzy felt a sudden rush of sympathy for Mildred Kilgore, who—despite her expensive clothes—was plump and plain. Roger would probably mind his p's and q's this weekend, not wanting to be found out. But poor Mildred would forever afterward be plagued by the memory of Miss Dare's physical attraction, which was likely enhanced in most men's eyes by the dangerous work she did as a stunt pilot.

And now that Lizzy had met her, the idea that Miss Dare might have had an off-screen love affair with Douglas Fairbanks didn't strike her as at all far-fetched. By this time, she was deeply curious about this person. Who *was* Lily Dare, really?

Feeling that she had already been forgotten and that she might learn more if she didn't call attention to herself, Lizzy pulled a chair into a corner of the newspaper office and sat down to listen. On the other side of the plate-glass front window, the rain pounded down in a tropical torrent, while inside, it was hot and steamy. Charlie had taken off his seersucker jacket, rolled up his shirtsleeves, and turned on the small black electric fan, aiming it toward his desk. He opened the lower right-hand drawer and took out a bottle and two glasses.

Lizzy smiled a little. The bottle contained Mickey LeDoux's corn whiskey, manufactured in a still hidden on Shiner's Knob, in the wooded hills to the west of Darling and retailed by Archie Mann, Mickey's second cousin, from a secret shelf behind the horse harness and saddles in the back room at Mann's Mercantile. The stuff packed a wallop. Was Charlie aiming to get Miss Dare a little drunk?

"This place smells like the inside of an airplane hangar," Miss Dare said, wrinkling her nose.

"Printers ink and the gasoline I use to clean the press," Charlie replied. "Gets into the blood." He lifted the bottle.

"Join me in a little drink before lunch? It's no sippin' whiskey, but it'll do the trick."

Miss Dare seated herself across from Charlie, where she could get the breeze from the fan, and accepted the glass, which she tossed off with a quick swallow and a shudder. "That's the real thing," she said. From her bag, she took out a small brown cigar and an elegant gold lighter, and lit it, stretching her legs and sitting back with a sigh.

Lizzy blinked. It was considered risqué for women to smoke cigarettes, and Verna was the only one of her friends who dared to do it in public. But a *cigar*! Lizzy had never before seen such a thing.

"Still fond of those little Cubans, I see," Charlie said. He added wryly, "Nothing but the best for Lily Dare."

Miss Dare made a face. "Too true," she said in her low, sexy voice. "I may be dead broke but I still have one or two expensive habits."

"But you're flying a Jenny." Charlie gave her a sideways glance. "Not a real crackerjack of a plane, is it?"

"It'll do for these gigs in the boonies," Miss Dare replied shortly. "Another few months, I'll have the money for something better. I've got my eye on another Travel Air. Walter Beech is saving one for me, out there in Wichita."

Listening, Lizzy thought of Roger Kilgore's nine hundred dollars and wondered what other sources of money Miss Dare was tapping to finance another plane. Were there other men, like Roger, who were eager to help her out?

Charlie opened his reporter's notebook and picked up his pencil. "Well, Jenny or not, that was quite a show you put on at the airfield this morning. You impressed the natives."

"I wanted to give them a little taste of what they'll see over the weekend," she replied, slipping into what sounded to Lizzy like a practiced pitch, one she had developed for newspaper interviews. "Rex and I will do much more of that, of course, including a mock dogfight just like the one I flew in Howard Hughes' film *Hell's Angels*."

"Dogfight," Charlie said, writing fast. "That's good." He looked up. "Oh, before I forget—there's a special showing of *Hell's Angels* here in Darling tonight. It would be great if you would attend." He looked up, adding carelessly. "Roger's not available, so I'll take you."

Poor Fannie, Lizzy thought. Everyone would see Charlie with Miss Dare and wonder (as she was doing right now) how Fannie felt about it.

Miss Dare nodded and went on with her spiel, rattling off the number of airplanes they were flying (three, sometimes four), the number of people on the team (six, including herself), the number of shows they'd put on in the past month (eight), and the big crowds they'd entertained (thousands!). When she was finished, she peered across the desk at Charlie's notebook. "Did I go too fast, hon? You got all that?"

"Got it," Charlie said. "Sounds exciting."

Miss Dare made a face. "Yeah. Exciting. Thrilling. A chill a minute. But it's a helluva lotta work, I'll tell you, Charlie. The airplanes and crew have to be ferried from one town to another, whether the sky's lit up with lightning or the ground is blanked out with fog. And then there's the daily stuff that's got to be done to keep the planes in the air—repairing engines, grinding valves, replacing broken struts, mending fabric tears—all of it on a shoestring. If we don't get a good crowd, we come up short, when what we need is to bring in enough to buy fuel." She shook her head grimly. "It's a hard life, hand to mouth sometimes. But that's off the record. Nobody wants to know the real story. All they want is the thrills and chills." Her voice hardened. "All they want is to see somebody *die*."

Lizzy shivered. Hand to mouth? See somebody *die*? Her notion of Lily Dare was changing. She might envy the Texas

Star her beauty, her glamour, but she didn't envy that kind of life.

"Yeah," Charlie said. "The world is like that." There was a silence. The rain beat on the window. Not far away, the thunder rumbled, low. "Was it the Jenny that was sabotaged?" he asked at last.

Miss Dare puffed her cigar. She nodded, cautiously.

"What happened?"

She frowned. "I don't know if I ought to . . ."

"Off the record." Charlie put down his pencil and closed the notebook. "We go back a long way, Lily." He leaned back in his chair and lit a cigarette. "Odd as it may seem, considering our history, I'm worried about you. I'd hate to see anything happen to you—while you're here in Darling, anyway. Bad publicity for our little town."

Miss Dare chuckled throatily. "Charlie, sweetie, every time I get into an airplane, something's likely to happen to me. I could lose a wing, snap a strut, make a bad mistake." She paused. "But maybe you had something else in mind." Another pause. In a lower voice, she asked, "Something like a . . . threat, maybe?"

It didn't sound like a casual question, and Lizzy thought of the anonymous letters. The one she had read certainly seemed threatening—but was it a threat?

"None that I've heard about," Charlie said with a crooked grin. "But hey—I'm just a country reporter. What do I know?" His grin faded. "I'm not sure I'll go out of my way to help after you leave, Lily. You'd better take it while you can get it."

Miss Dare studied his face as if she suspected that he was making fun of her. She must have decided he wasn't, for her voice softened and she said, "It's nice to have somebody worry about me for a change, Charlie. Nobody else does." Her tone became bitter. "Nobody cares, not really."

That couldn't be true, Lizzy thought. Roger cared. She remembered the photo Mildred had shown her—and then his clumsy step backward, his efforts to keep his distance. But perhaps he no longer cared, or cared as much. Perhaps he was afraid she would compromise him.

But Charlie was thinking of someone else. He pulled on his cigarette. "What about Rex Hart? Doesn't he care? He may be 'King of the Air' but you're the Texas Star, the act that everybody comes to see." He chuckled cynically. "If anything happens to you, Hart's out of luck, isn't he?" He paused. "Or maybe it's the other way around. If you crash, he'll be the star of the show, won't he? He—"

"That's enough, Charlie," Miss Dare said sharply. She turned her head away, but not before Lizzy saw the pain on her face and guessed that Charlie had hit close to the truth—and it hurt. "Let's leave Rex out of it."

"Why?" Charlie prodded. "Because you know he's up to something and you want to handle it yourself?"

"Because I say so." She laughed under her breath, a jagged, grating laugh. "Like I said, Charlie. Most people come to the shows for thrills. They're hoping to see me crash. Or even better, to see Rex and me collide in midair while Angel is wingwalking and all three of us go down in flames. That would give you newspaper guys something sensational to write about, wouldn't it?"

Charlie sat back in his chair. He took a deep breath, then went back to his question. "What happened to the Jenny?" His tone was more neutral now.

"Well, since you've asked so nicely." Miss Dare put out her cigar in the ashtray on the desk. "It was tampered with. Twice. The first time, it was the old water-in-the-fuel-tank trick."

"Where?" Charlie asked. "When?"

"In Tampa, where we did a show several weeks ago, from

the airfield where Rex runs his flight school. I checked before I took off, of course, but something like that is pretty hard to catch. I was able to put the plane down in a plowed field. The wings were damaged but I walked away—which makes it a successful landing." She gave a short, dry cough. "When I told the little girl at your airfield that I've never crashed, I lied. I've had my share of hard landings. But as long as I can walk away from it, I don't consider it a crash. A crash is when you die."

Outside the window, the lightning flashed like a flash-bulb going off. Listening, Lizzy shivered. Miss Dare's voice was flat and uninflected, without a hint of fear. Were the woman's nerves really that steely? But she had probably been in many frightening situations during her flying career. She must have developed a certain indifference to danger, trusting to skill, or to luck, to get her through. Maybe she even courted danger, finding that it provided the excitement, the thrills and chills she needed to keep her going. And maybe she needed a big dose of excitement in her personal life, as well, so she took pleasure in risky rela-tionships. Lizzy shivered again.

Charlie frowned. "You said the plane was tampered with twice. Once in Tampa—and once in Pensacola?"

"Yes," Miss Dare said. "In retrospect, I'm glad that the Tampa thing happened. It wasn't fatal, luckily, and I knew it wasn't an accident. It put me on the alert. The second time—well, if I hadn't checked the propeller, I would have been a goner for sure." She tossed back the rest of her whis-key in a single swallow. "That would've been one crash I wouldn't have walked away from."

"The propeller?" Charlie picked up the bottle, offering a refill. Miss Dare shook her head to the offer, and Charlie helped himself.

"It's wood, you know," she replied. "Oak. The shank was

partially sawn through. Back to front, a couple of inches outside the hub. Could've been done with a hacksaw blade."

Charlie made a low, whistling noise through his teeth.

"Yeah, right." Miss Dare looked glum. "If I had managed to get off the ground and the blade had snapped off in the air, the plane would have immediately become unflyable. The end of the Texas Star." She laughed a low, throaty laugh, with no amusement. "A fitting end, some would say. Anyway, the attempt was really very clever. Devilish, you might say. It could have worked—if I hadn't gotten lucky."

Now, Lizzy thought, there was an undertone of something in her voice. Fear, was it, that she had almost been killed? Or excitement, at the near miss? She thought of the anonymous letter that Mildred had showed her. *A terrible person . . . she must be stopped.* She began to wish she had told Charlie about it. Maybe there was a connection between the sabotage and the letters.

"When did this happen?" Charlie asked.

"At some point after I parked the Jenny on Saturday, when the Pensacola show was over. I was planning to take a local photographer up on Sunday afternoon, to get some aerial photos for the local real estate barons. I spotted it then." She smiled ruefully. "If it had worked, it would have been a two-fer, I'm afraid. Me and my passenger both."

Charlie frowned. "The plane wasn't locked up?"

"You've gotta be kidding." Another laugh. "You know what those hangars are. They're like the shed where I parked the plane this morning. Open to the public. Danny Murphy was supposed to be on watch, but he didn't see it happen."

"Rex had access to the shed, of course," Charlie said.

"I *told* you," Miss Dare snapped. "Leave him out of it. He's not involved. Anyway, there are others on the team. Danny, Scooter, Clem. And Angel, of course." Half under her breath, she added, "Oh, yes, there's Angel. Little Miss Show-off. That girl does love the spotlight."

Charlie nodded. "Right. So how did you happen to notice it? Don't tell me you routinely check the backside of the propeller."

"Not hardly. I inspect for chips on the tips and cracks on the leading edge, yes, and I was looking pretty carefully, after that business with the water in the gas tank. But whoever played this particular dirty trick got careless." She chuckled. "Didn't bother to clean up the sawdust."

"Sawdust?" Charlie asked.

She nodded. "I happened to glance down and saw traces of it on the ground—not much, just enough to make me curious. Then it was a matter of looking up to see where it had come from."

"So you had to replace the prop."

She nodded. "It arrived yesterday morning, and Rex installed it. He'll be here in a few hours, with Angel. Danny and Scooter are driving the truck. Clem is flying his Stearman. He doesn't stunt with it, but if we get a decent crowd, we'll use it for rides."

Charlie gave her a narrow look. "Any idea who might have sawn that propeller, Lily?"

"Your guess is as good as mine." Miss Dare heaved an exaggerated sigh. "I push myself pretty hard. I push other people pretty hard, too. I don't exactly leave a string of friends behind me. It could be anybody."

"Oh, come on, now." Charlie's tone was light. "Let's name a few names. Your husband's two sons, for instance? Do they still think you cheated them out of their father's Texas ranch?"

Another sigh, even more exaggerated. "I'm sure they do. But I wasn't the one who did that to them. It was their daddy. He knew they didn't give a hoot about the land—unless it had oil on it, which it didn't. And if he left them money, they'd only use it to get themselves into even worse trouble. But yes, they still blame me, I'm afraid, especially after I lost the ranch." She chuckled wryly. "And there's the woman pilot who thought I cheated on the Los Angeles to Cincinnati race last year. She hung around for a while in Tampa, making a nuisance of herself."

Charlie nodded. "And Pete Rickerts' brother. Tom—wasn't that his name?"

Pete Rickerts, Lizzy thought. He was mentioned in the anonymous letter. *Pete Rickerts, who crashed his airplane because he was so crazy in love with her.*

"Yes." There was a small frown between her eyes. "Tom Rickerts occasionally sends me nasty little notes. But that's ancient history, Charlie. A long time ago."

"Maybe. But Tom is a pilot. Sawing a prop partway through sounds to me like something a pilot would come up with. And if he wasn't the one, I'm sure you could name a few dozen other men—and women—who have it in for you, for one reason or another." He paused, lighting another cigarette. "Rex Hart. Tell me more about him. How long have you been together?"

"Don't start that again," Miss Dare said, in a warning tone.

"I'm not starting anything. I'm just asking."

She hesitated. "Well, then, we've been together for three years—not consecutively, of course. We take the winter months off, then start flying again when the weather warms up. Winters, I go back to the West Coast and pick up stunt flying for the movies. Rex has the flight school in Tampa. That's where he hangs out in the off-season."

"Is he married?"

"Several times." She laughed lightly. "Not to me. And not now."

Charlie was persistent. "Are you two romantically involved?"

"Not anymore." Her mouth hardened. "Anyway, that's none of your business."

"Agreed. Do you have a mechanic?"

She shook her head. "Rex doesn't trust anybody else to work on the planes. He's better than anybody we could hire. And it means less expense, of course. Fuel isn't cheap. And there are parts to buy. The kind of flying we do—it's hard on the planes, you know."

"What about Angel Flame?" Charlie chuckled. "I don't suppose that's her real name."

"Of course not. Her name is Mabel. Mabel Hopkins."

"Has she been with you since the beginning?"

"No." Miss Dare's glance slid away. "No. Our other aerialist had an accident. Mabel—Angel was looking for a job. She'd been coming to our shows, so she knew all the tricks. It was just a matter of getting some experience. She's an exhibitionist at heart—loves to have people looking at her. And she's fearless."

She would have to be, Lizzy thought, to do stunts on an airplane in midair, with no safety net. Fearless . . . or crazy. Or both.

"And what about—"

But he didn't get to finish. "That's enough, Charlie." Miss Dare rolled her eyes impatiently. "I am sick and tired of this silly third degree."

"That's too bad," Charlie said. "You may not take your situation seriously, but I do. Sabotage isn't the only thing that could happen, you know."

"Oh, yeah?" Miss Dare rolled her eyes. "Like what else?"

"Like kidnapping," Charlie replied. "You read the papers, don't you? The Lindbergh baby isn't the only victim. The *New York Times* says there's a kidnapping wave sweeping the nation—some 400 kidnappings in two years in Illinois alone. A long shot, maybe. But criminals obviously think it's a good way to get easy money."

Lizzy frowned. Kidnapping? It might sound far-fetched, but Charlie was right. Times were hard, and people would do almost anything for money. According to the newspapers, Colonel Lindbergh had paid a $50,000 ransom to get his little Charles back, although the baby was already dead. But not all ransom demands were that high. An Atlanta woman had been kidnapped recently and released—unharmed—when her husband paid five hundred dollars. (He said he was glad that they didn't think she was worth any more than that, because five hundred was all he had.)

Miss Dare's laugh was short and sharp. "They wouldn't get much of a ransom for me. There's no money."

"Oh, yeah?" Charlie raised a skeptical eyebrow. "Hell, Lily, you're the famous Texas Star. To somebody on the outside, especially somebody who knew you from the old days at the ranch, it looks like there's *plenty* of money. You're the perfect target."

"Plenty of money. That's a laugh!" Miss Dare's face darkened. "You want to know the *real* story, Charlie? The money's all gone, every cent of it. The Dare Devils Flying Circus is flat broke. Rex and me, we're in hock up to our eyeballs to family, friends, sweethearts—anybody we can squeeze for a little cash to keep the planes in the air. We live hand to mouth. Every dollar we earn goes into fuel and repairs. The new propeller? The money came from Angel—no idea where in the hell she got it. Most nights, we're so broke we can't even afford a room in a fleabag hotel. We sleep with the airplanes. You better believe I'm looking forward to sleeping in a bed tonight—haven't slept in one for a couple of weeks. And maybe, if I'm lucky, I'll get a bath in a real bathtub, and I can actually wash my hair." She laughed harshly. "The idea that somebody would try to squeeze a ransom out of us—it's just crazy, that's all. You're a lunatic."

Lizzy was listening with amazement. The famous Lily Dare was *broke*? The woman who flew stunts for the movies? The fastest woman in the world? But maybe that's where Roger Kilgore's nine hundred dollars had gone—to keep the Flying Circus in the air.

"Well, if you're broke, you manage to hide it pretty well," Charlie said wryly. "Nobody would guess. And crazy or not, here's what's happening. I'm taking you to the movie tonight. I've also arranged for a couple of ladies—Liz Lacy and Verna Tidwell—to keep an eye on you. They'll be staying at the Kilgores' while you're here. But don't worry, they won't get in your way. You won't even know they're there."

"Keep an eye on me?" Miss Dare gave an unpleasant laugh. "That's sweet, but really, Charlie. I may be down and out, but I can take care of myself. I always have, you know."

"And I'll be out at the airfield overnight, with the planes," Charlie went on, as if she hadn't spoken. "If that dirty trickster follows you to Darling, he's not going to get a chance at a repeat performance."

Lizzy remembered that Rex Hart planned to stay at the airfield, too, and understood that Charlie would be watching him, as well as the planes.

Miss Dare shook her head. "I really don't think this is necessary, Charlie. I—"

But Charlie was firm. "You can risk your life in the air all you want, Lily. That's your business. But regardless of what happened between us—or maybe *because* of it—when you're on the ground here in Darling, I'm making you my responsibility. You and your airplane. And that's all there is to it." He grinned. "If you want to, you can chalk it up to my being crazy."

Miss Dare gave in, grudgingly. "Well, if you put it that

way, I suppose I'll have to accept. You're sweet, Charlie. Regardless of the past, you'll always have a special spot in my heart."

She leaned forward and kissed him lightly, and then again, her arms around his neck, her lips against his. Charlie pulled back, which seemed to surprise her.

"What's the matter, Charlie?" she teased. "You've found yourself another girl? One of your local pretties, I suppose. Is she letting you off your leash for the weekend?"

With a sinking feeling, Lizzy thought again of Fannie Champaign. How was she going to feel when she saw Charlie squiring Miss Dare around town?

Charlie chuckled without amusement. "Now, now, Lily, don't be catty. It's not becoming." He glanced up at the clock, then out the window. "Hey, it's time we got you something to eat. Anything special you have in mind? We don't have a lot of options, though," he added. "Darling is pretty small."

Miss Dare had a ready answer. "Well, to tell the truth, it's been a while since I've had a decent meal. Do you suppose I could get a pulled pork sandwich? I used to know a hotel chef who made that, with some sort of white sauce, and it was delicious."

Charlie put the whiskey bottle and empty glasses back in the drawer, and stood up. "I like pulled pork, too, but we'd have to drive over to Buzz's Barbeque in Monroeville to get it. It's not on the menu at the diner, and anyway, their regular cook quit. Dunno who's cooking there today— probably won't be much good." He glanced toward the window. "Looks like the rain has let up. We could walk across the square to the Old Alabama Hotel. I'm sure we can get something decent there."

Lizzy stood, too, glad to take a lunch break. Breakfast seemed like a long time ago and she was hungry. "The diner has a new cook," she offered, stepping forward. "I'm told she's very good. Even better than Euphoria."

Charlie and Miss Dare both looked startled, and Lizzy knew that they had indeed forgotten that she was there.

"Better than Euphoria?" Charlie repeated with a skeptical lift of his eyebrow. "I'll have to see that for myself."

"I'll eat anything," Miss Dare said hungrily. "Just so I get some food."

And a change of subject, Lizzy thought. It was obvious that the Texas Star didn't want to talk about the people who might have a serious grudge against her—might even be angry enough to try to kill her. And from what she had heard, the list could be a long one.

Usually, a hard rain settled Darling's dust, washed and cooled the air, and brought relief from the summer heat. But this rain seemed to have been poured out of a teakettle that had been sitting on the back of the stove all day, keeping warm. The puddles steamed, the sun peered resentfully through a sweltering haze, and the air was so oppressively hot that Lizzy could scarcely get her breath. The flag on the courthouse pole across the street hung limply as a wet dishrag.

The diner was nearly empty when the three of them walked in. The Dr Pepper clock on the wall under the neon Coca-Cola sign announced that it was one fifteen. Earlynne Biddle's boy Bennie was still clearing the tables, Myra May was straightening up after what looked to have been a very busy noon meal, and in the kitchen, Lizzy could hear the murmur of voices and the clatter of china plates being washed in the sink. There was a delectable smell of roasting meat in the air.

While Charlie and Miss Dare sat down at the table in

front of the window, Lizzy went to the counter. "I hear that you and Violet have found a new cook already," she said to Myra May. "What's she serving today?"

Myra May wiped the sweat off her forehead with the back of her hand. She looked frazzled. "I don't know what we've got left back there, Liz, but I'm sure we can come up with something. Seems like everybody in town turned out to give Raylene—that's our new cook—a trial run. Every table was full and all the counter stools, too." She grinned. "For a while there, it was almost more than we could handle. It was *wonderful*."

"How'd your new cook do?" Lizzy asked, thinking of Donna Sue's praise for the grits and sausage casserole she'd had for breakfast.

"She's a big hit. I think we're all going to love her." Myra May leaned forward. In a low whisper, she said, "Who's that sexy dish with Charlie Dickens?"

"Miss Lily Dare, the Texas Star," Lizzy replied. "The fastest woman in the world."

"Some broad," Myra May said, straightening up. "That fast, huh?"

"You'd be amazed." Lizzy grinned. "Bring a menu and come over to the table. Charlie will introduce her."

"I'm afraid we're all out of everything on the menu. How about grilled cheese sandwiches with fried green tomatoes?" At the disappointed look on Lizzy's face, she grinned. "Just kidding. I think Raylene has already started supper. Let me check and see what she has on the stove."

Lizzy went back to the table. A moment later, Myra May followed with three glasses of water on a tray. Charlie introduced her to Miss Dare. "Sorry we're late," he said. "I guess we missed out on the fried chicken, huh?"

Myra May nodded briskly. "As I was telling Liz, the noon crowd pretty much picked us clean. We're out of fried chicken and the meat loaf is gone, too. All we have is what Raylene is working on for tonight's supper." She grinned hospitably. "Or grilled cheese sandwiches with fried green tomatoes. If you want, I can whip those up in a jiffy."

Miss Dare shrugged one shoulder, looking displeased. "I don't like fried green tomatoes. Or grilled cheese. I guess I'll have whatever you've got for supper. I'm hungry."

"I'll have whatever Miss Dare is getting," Charlie said.

"Me, too," added Lizzy, who felt that she was hungry enough to eat almost anything, except grilled cheese.

"Thanks for understanding," Myra May said apologetically. "I saved back some lemon meringue pie. You can have that, no charge." She turned away from the table and raised her voice. "Violet, we'll have three pulled pork on buns out here, quick as you can."

"Pulled pork?" Charlie asked, both eyebrows going up. "You don't mean—"

"Yeah," Myra May said. "Seems to be a specialty of our new cook. She stirred up some of that good white barbeque sauce, too—lots of pepper. You folks want that, I reckon."

Miss Dare let out her breath. Lizzy shook her head in disbelief.

"Well, I'll be damned," Charlie said.

The food was delicious, and they lingered over it. When they finally finished, Myra May brought the coffeepot and poured another cup of coffee for everyone. "I hope you enjoyed your food," she said.

"It was wonderful," Lizzy said with a heartfelt sigh.

"Just terrific," Charlie said, leaning back in his chair with an expansive expression. "I predict that Euphoria will never be missed."

Miss Dare smiled up at Myra May. "You have a treasure of a cook," she said. "I hope you appreciate her."

"You have no idea," Myra May said fervently. "Would

you like to meet her? She's been so busy that she hasn't had a chance to get out of the kitchen since she came in this morning. But I'm sure she'd like to hear what you think of her food."

A moment later, the diner's new cook was standing beside their table and Myra May was introducing her. Raylene Riggs—that was her name—wore a gray print cotton dress and a large white apron. Quite attractive without being pretty, she had a decided mouth, dark brows, and graying auburn hair, cut short. Her eyes were fixed, with some surprise, on Miss Dare.

"Lily! Lily Dare!" she exclaimed. "My goodness, this *is* a surprise!"

"Raylene!" Miss Dare cried. "Why, I never in the world would have guessed I'd meet *you* here! What a coincidence! So it's *your* pulled pork. It was so good—I should have guessed."

"You two know each other, it seems," Charlie said.

Miss Dare nodded, smiling. "Raylene—but I don't think you were Riggs, then, were you? You went by the name—"

"By my married name," Raylene broke in quickly. "I'm using a . . . a different name now. Are you and Mr. Hart doing a show here?"

"You haven't seen the fliers and advertising?" Lizzy asked. "The Dare Devils will be performing at the Watermelon Festival this weekend. The whole town has been looking forward to it for months."

"Raylene has been staying over in Monroeville," Myra May explained. "This is her first day on the job."

"And how do you two know one another, Lily?" Charlie asked curiously. "Texas? The West Coast?"

"Florida." Miss Dare smiled. "We met in Tampa, where Raylene was the chef at one of the local hotels. In fact, she's the one who introduced me to pulled pork. When was that, Raylene? Two years ago? Three?"

"About that," Raylene said. To Charlie, she added, "My . . . husband was taking flying lessons from Mr. Hart, and I spent a lot of time at the airfield, watching. Miss Dare and I struck up an acquaintance. She used to tell me about her flying adventures—she's led quite a life, it turns out. Once, we went to see a movie where she'd done some stunt flying, and she told me how the scenes were filmed. Why, she even took me up in her airplane."

Miss Dare laughed. "I was trying to entice you into taking flying lessons, too. You seemed like such a natural. And you knew a lot about airplanes, too. Even Mr. Hart said so."

"I knew about airplanes because of my husband," Raylene replied. "Me, I'm a natural *cook*. The only wings I know anything about are chicken wings."

"Well, we're glad you're cooking here," Lizzy said diplomatically. "And I'm sure that Myra May and Violet are thrilled."

"Oh, you bet," Myra May said, with emphasis. Under her breath, she added, "Eat your heart out, Euphoria." Lizzy laughed, glad to see that Myra May was feeling good again.

But Charlie was wearing a puzzled look. "What I want to know," he put in, "is how Miz Riggs knew that Miss Dare was asking about pulled pork *before* she knew it was on the menu here at the diner."

"She did?" Raylene's dark eyebrows went up and her mouth quirked with amusement. "Oh, for heaven's sake. Now, isn't that just the *funniest* coincidence? It's grand when it works out that way, isn't it?"

Lizzy blinked, remembering what Donna Sue had said about dreaming of her mother's grits and sausage casserole and finding it at the diner for breakfast. She could imagine a coincidence like that once. But twice? Still, what else could it be?

Charlie got up. "Excuse me, ladies. I saw the latest Mobile *Register* on the newspaper rack out front. I'm going to get a copy." He stepped away from the table.

Miss Dare leaned forward, frowning as if she had just thought of something. "Raylene, I'll be here in Darling for a couple of days. I'd sure like it if we could get together. You know, catch up on what's been going on. Could we maybe do that?"

"That would be swell," Raylene said. "I'm here at the diner during the day. I haven't located a house yet, but Violet found me a little cottage at the Marigold Motor Court, out on the Monroeville Highway. I'm in Number Four. It's not fancy, but it's clean and the price is right."

Miss Dare nodded. "Sure. I saw that place when Charlie drove me into town this morning. I could give you a call and see if you're there before I come out."

"There's no phone," Raylene replied. "But I'll likely be there when I'm not here." She smiled. "I'd better get back in that kitchen, or there won't be any supper." She turned and went back to the kitchen just as Charlie came back with the *Register* under his arm.

Lizzy, Charlie, and Miss Dare were leaving the diner when they heard the roar of a motorcycle and Deputy Buddy Norris brought his Indian Ace to a stop at the curb. Behind him on the motorcycle was an athletic-looking girl, tanned and freckled, her brown hair cut in a boyish bob. She wore tight denim pants and a red short-sleeved shirt with the words *Lily Dare's Dare Devils* in white printed on the back.

"Oh, there you are, Lily!" she cried, jumping off the motorcycle. "Say, when I get a little more money, I'm going to buy one of these motorcycles for myself. It's almost as much fun as flying!" She gave Buddy a comradely poke in the arm. "It was nice of Deputy Norris to give me a ride from the airfield. He really knows how to fly a motorcycle."

"Hello, Mabel," Miss Dare said coolly. "So you and Rex got in okay? No problems with the plane?"

"Mabel?" Buddy Norris glanced at the girl, obviously confused.

"Why, didn't she tell you her *real* name?" Miss Dare asked sweetly. "It's Mabel. Mabel Hopkins."

Lizzy wondered if Mabel herself had chosen her exotic new name, and what it revealed about her personality. She also remembered what Miss Dare had said about Angel being an exhibitionist. Stood to reason—you'd have to want to show off if you were going to do what Angel did for a living.

"Miss Dare?" Buddy asked in an awed tone. *"Miss Dare?"* He snatched off his goggles and helmet, pulled himself up to his full height, and introduced himself. His eyes, Lizzy noticed, were fixed on Miss Dare's clinging red blouse. "I sure am glad to see you, Miss Dare," he blurted. "On behalf of the Sheriff's Department, let me welcome you to Darling. We are just plumb delighted to have you here. Plumb delighted."

"Thank you, Deputy Norris." Miss Dare gave him an enticing smile. "It's very sweet of you to say so."

Angel narrowed her eyes. "Come on, Deputy Norris. I'm hungry."

But Buddy acted like he didn't hear her. "Oh, but it's *true*," he said, clutching his helmet in his hands. "Why, the fastest woman in the world, faster than Amelia Earhart, and she's right here in Darling!"

Lizzy had to smile. If there was anything on this earth that Buddy loved more than *speed*, she didn't know what it was. He drove his motorcycle, as Grady put it admiringly, like a bat out of hell. No wonder he was dazzled by the Texas Star.

"Tell you what, Deputy Norris." Miss Dare reached into her pocket and pulled out a little white card. She wrote something on it and handed it to Buddy. "That's a ticket for an airplane ride. Just give it to the ticket-taker and you'll be the next guy to go up." Her smile was dazzling. "The ride's on me."

"Holy cow," Buddy breathed. He looked up and his eyes met hers. "Golly, thanks! I mean . . . well, just holy *cow*!"

Angel Flame poked Buddy again. This time, it wasn't a comradely poke. "Deputy, I am going to get some lunch. I swear, I am hungry enough to eat a *pig*." She opened the diner door to go in.

"Oh, sure thing," Buddy said, although he looked as if he was having a hard time tearing himself away from the divine Miss Dare. Reluctantly, still looking back over his shoulder, he turned to follow the girl.

"Oh, Mabel," Miss Dare called. "You be sure to tell them you want the grilled cheese sandwich and fried tomatoes." She gave a teasing laugh. "Don't let them talk you into ordering anything else. You hear?"

That laugh, Lizzy thought with some surprise, held a malicious barb. Watching Lily Dare's flirtatious little drama, she could understand what Angel Flame might have against the Texas Star, who had just upstaged her with Buddy Norris.

But what did the Star have against the Flame?

TWELVE

The Trouble with Passion

When they left the diner, Charlie drove Miss Dare and Lizzy to the Kilgores' house. He made arrangements to take Miss Dare to supper and then to the special showing of *Hell's Angels* and went back to the newspaper office. Miss Dare announced that since she was going out for the evening, she would take a bath and a long nap and would appreciate not being disturbed. She disappeared into her room—the yellow room at the top of the stairs. Lizzy and Mildred sat down in the kitchen over a cup of tea.

Looking at Mildred, Lizzy thought that she had not slept for several nights. Her eyes were like dark holes in white paper. "Are you all right?" Lizzy asked, concerned.

Mildred looked away. "She's even more beautiful than her pictures, Liz," she said bitterly, "and much more sexy. If I had known about her and Roger, I wouldn't have planned the party. And I would *never* have invited her to stay under my roof!"

Lizzy opened her mouth to say something, but Mildred

was going on. She clenched her hand into a fist. "I could scarcely keep myself from telling her off, right there in front of Mr. Dickens! I don't know how in the world I can stand it, having to be polite to her until she leaves. Just looking at her makes me want to throw up."

"You can do it, Mildred," Lizzy said comfortingly. She reached across the table and patted her friend's hand. "I know you can. Anyway, if you told her off, what would you say?"

Mildred leaned forward. "What would I say?" Her face was suddenly twisted and ugly and her voice was full of disgust and revulsion. "I would scare her little lacy panties right off her, that's what I would do. I would make her read that anonymous letter out loud, word by word. I would show her that photograph and those checks. I would threaten to drag her name through the mud if she didn't stop foolin' around with my husband. And if she gave me so much as one word of sassy backtalk, I would slap her, hard. Or maybe I'd take a fireplace poker to her." Mildred's eyes blazed with an almost volcanic anger. "That pretty face wouldn't be so pretty when I got through with her."

Shocked, Lizzy sucked in her breath. "I . . . I really don't think you would do that," she said inadequately. Of all the women she knew, Mildred was the most self-contained, always behaving with the calm, unruffled decorum of a Southern lady who never acknowledged such a thing as a hard feeling. "Butter wouldn't melt in Mildred's mouth," Aunt Hetty Little had once said. It had always been true—until now.

Mildred held herself rigid for a moment, then slumped back in her chair, sighing like a deflating balloon, all the energy going out of her. After a moment she spoke in a low, shaky voice.

"You're right, Liz. Of course I wouldn't. My mother

taught me never to cause a ruckus, *never*. She would be hor-rified if she knew what I just said. I take it all back, every word." She leaned forward again and put her cold hand over Lizzy's. "Please," she said urgently. "Forget what I said. Just forget it."

Lizzy was stunned into silence. Mildred might want to take back her words, but she had said them with a ferocity that made them difficult to forget. And saying a thing and doing it were not all that far apart. If Mildred felt that her marriage and her home and the family business were all in jeopardy, wouldn't she actually *do* what she had just said? Lizzy shivered. She didn't like to feel that her friend would resort to violence, but she had to admit the possibility.

The silence dragged out until at last Lizzy disengaged her hand. She heard herself say, "Well, it probably wouldn't do any good to threaten Miss Dare, Mildred. Judging from what I heard her tell Charlie Dickens earlier today, I don't think you can frighten her into doing something—or into *not* doing something. She is scare-proof."

And that, Lizzy told herself, is what made Miss Dare such a dangerous person. She did exactly what she chose, without regard for anyone else—or for the consequences. It was no wonder that Mildred was angry, after what she had learned. How many other people were just as angry as Mil-dred, or even angrier? And even more eager to translate their anger into action? Miss Dare was playing with fire.

Mildred picked up her teacup with a sigh. "I'm sure you're right, Liz. It wouldn't do one single ounce of good." She paused, pushing her mouth into a smile and trying to speak in something resembling her normal voice. "Well, then. Do you know what the plans are for the evening? I'm wondering about supper."

Lizzy tried to match her tone. "Charlie Dickens is taking Miss Dare to supper and to the special showing of *Hell's*

Angels at the Palace. That seems to be the plan, anyway. While everybody's out for the evening, I need to go to my house and pack a suitcase. Verna and I will come back here later and stay the night. But this afternoon, while Miss Dare is sleeping, I have to make some phone calls about the festival. May I use your phone to do that?"

"Verna?" Mildred asked.

"I hope that's okay," Lizzy said tentatively. "If it isn't, I can cancel. I just thought that two of us might be better than—"

"Of course." Mildred got up. "I'm glad that Mr. Dickens thought of suggesting that you do this, and that Verna will be here, too. That woman has already caused enough trouble. I wouldn't want anything to happen to her while she is a guest in *my* house." She took their tea cups to the sink and rinsed them. "I have some work to do in the garden. Help yourself to the telephone."

Lizzy spent the next hour on the telephone, checking up on the arrangements for the weekend festival and making sure that everything was going according to plan. The carnival was due to arrive that evening to start setting up at the fairgrounds. Verna reported that the tents hadn't gone all the way to Indianapolis after all. They had been spotted at Montgomery, put on the next southbound freight, and arrived safely at the depot. The Masons had already picked them up—so that was one problem solved. And Aunt Hetty reported that the watermelon roundup was going even better than expected. "We're not going to run out *this* year," she said triumphantly. "Now, if all the Dahlias will just show up to do the picking for the farmers market booth, we'll be in great shape."

Later, when Lizzy was preparing to leave, she asked about Roger. He wouldn't be home until late, Mildred said in an offhand way. He had to attend a city council meeting, and he and Jed Snow and a couple of the other council members would probably stay behind for a game of poker.

Remembering Roger's clumsy attempt to get out of Miss Dare's reach when she had landed a kiss on his cheek, Lizzy wondered whether he might be trying to avoid her—and trying to stay out of his wife's way, as well. Even though he didn't know about the anonymous letters and wasn't aware that Mildred knew about his transgressions, he couldn't be very comfortable.

Whatever Roger's motive for staying away, he hadn't yet returned by the time Lizzy and Verna arrived at the Kilgores' house in the sporty 1928 red LaSalle two-seater Verna had bought, used, to celebrate her promotion to acting county treasurer. Lizzy had lashed her bicycle behind the rumble seat so she would have a way to get around the next day, and they had both brought clothes for the weekend. Riding in the LaSalle was an adventure, because Verna had only recently learned to drive and Lizzy had to hang on for dear life as Verna rounded corners and dashed down straightaways at frightening speeds. As they raced down the last three blocks to the Kilgores' house, Lizzy dared a glance at the speedometer and shuddered to see that it registered 35 miles per hour. (Of course, she reminded herself, Grady drove fast—but *he* knew how to drive!)

It had rained again that evening, and the music of the summer cicadas was loud in the velvety darkness as Lizzy and Verna got their bags out of the car, walked up the path to the house, and knocked at the door. Mildred, looking pale and tense but composed, showed them upstairs to their bedroom, which was adjacent to Miss Dare's and across the hall from Miss Flame's. She turned on the overhead light.

"The ladies aren't back yet," she said, "but I imagine

they'll be along shortly." She opened a door. "This is your closet. That other door"—she pointed—"opens into Miss Dare's room. You can bolt it on this side, and she can bolt it on her side, as well. The master bedroom is at the far end of the hall. Melody's bedroom is next to ours, but she's staying with one of her cousins this weekend. The bathroom is on the other side of the hall, next to Miss Flame's room. There are fresh towels on your beds."

"A very pretty room," Verna said approvingly. There was cream-colored wainscot and pink wallpaper on the walls, twin beds covered in ruffled pink coverlets, and a pink and cream braided rug on the floor. A small cream-colored rocking chair sat beside the open window, which was dressed up in crisscross curtains of pink marquisette and pink window blinds. "Isn't it, Liz?"

"It's lovely," Lizzy said, although to her way of thinking, there was a bit too much pink. "We'll try our best not to put you to any trouble, Mildred. Verna has to work tomorrow, of course. But Mr. Moseley gave me the day off, so I'm available to help with the party preparations—until the afternoon, anyway, when I'll be working in the Dahlias' garden and taking care of last-minute festival stuff."

Mildred nodded. "And Miss Dare's plans?" Her voice was carefully neutral.

"She said she would spend the day at the airfield," Lizzy said. "They're giving rides—well, selling rides." She smiled. "A penny a pound, according to the fliers."

Mildred seemed relieved, and Lizzy knew why. If Miss Dare was working, she wouldn't be with Roger. She said nothing at all about the reason for Liz's and Verna's overnight surveillance, if that's what it could be called. Lizzy didn't either.

"Well, then, I'll see you at breakfast," Mildred said. "It's been a long day and I'm very tired. I'm going to bed as soon as the ladies get back from the movie." As if on cue, there were voices downstairs, and a woman's laughter. "Oh, there they are," she said, sounding relieved. "Well, I'll say good night."

She left, closing the door behind her. Lizzy watched her go, feeling distinctly uncomfortable. Mildred's manner seemed strained and oddly disconcerting, with an unusual tension that was unlike her usual self-possessed calm. It reminded her uncomfortably of their conversation that afternoon, and she felt a ripple of apprehension.

Verna did not appear to have noticed anything out of the ordinary. She turned on the lamp between the beds and turned off the overhead light. "Now that we're here, I feel a little silly," she remarked, sitting down on one of the beds. She took out a package of Pall Malls and lit one, dropping the match into the ceramic ashtray—in the shape of a pink donkey—beside the lamp. "All this seems so . . . normal." She gestured around the room. "You don't really think there's any serious threat against Miss Dare, do you?"

"I'm afraid I do," Lizzy said ruefully, thinking about the woman's many enemies—including their hostess. "And as Miss Marple might say, there's a difference between what seems and what *is*."

She pulled the window shade down, then opened her bag and took out the red print blouse and slacks she planned to wear the next day, as well as the gray silk dress for the party. She carried them to the closet and hung them up, then put her underthings and stockings in the top drawer of the bureau beside the window, taking special care with the chiffon-weight silk stockings with the French heels that she had bought especially for the party, for the unreasonable price of a dollar forty-nine a pair. The stockings were folded in tissue paper, to protect them from snags.

"But I don't think anything is likely to happen *here*," she added, over her shoulder. "If there's trouble, it will probably be out at the airfield, with the airplanes. That's why Charlie is staying out there tonight, with Mr. Hart." She paused, frowning. "Although—"

There were footsteps and women's voices outside in the hallway, and the sound of doors closing, first one, then another. In a moment, Lizzy heard a window being raised in the adjoining room.

"Although what?" Verna asked. She picked up the ashtray and swung her stockinged feet onto the bed, propping herself up against the headboard with a pillow. "Don't keep things to yourself, Liz. If there's something important, I ought to know it—oughtn't I?"

It was a good question. Verna already knew about the airplane sabotage, but Lizzy had actually been thinking that perhaps she ought to tell her about the other things— the anonymous letters, the checks, the uncomfortable and perhaps perilous triangle involving Roger, Mildred, and Miss Dare. Yes, she had promised Mildred she would keep those things confidential. But Mildred's comments that afternoon, as well as her manner just now, were definitely disturbing. And there was that odd business between Angel Flame and Miss Dare after lunch at the diner. It wasn't likely that something was going to happen here, tonight. But if it did, and if Verna understood what was going on, she would know better how to respond.

Verna listened intently to Lizzy's complicated story, smoking in silence. When she had finished, Verna let out her breath, and a stream of blue smoke. "I had no idea," she said softly. "Miss Dare certainly has her share of enemies, doesn't she? Sabotage is one thing. But *kidnapping?*"

"I think Charlie went a little overboard on that," Lizzie said. "But I heard on the radio tonight that there was a kidnapping in Mobile yesterday—the wife of a local grocery store owner. The crooks were asking three thousand dollars, but she tricked them and got away." She sighed. "It seems to be happening everywhere."

Verna was thinking about something else. "I wonder what's going on between Miss Dare and Angel Flame—jealousy, maybe? Could be personal, could be professional. And we don't know much about Rex Hart. How do you think he fits into this?"

Lizzy frowned. "Charlie thinks he may have had something to do with the sabotage, especially since both attempts seem to have been made by someone who knows something about airplanes. But Miss Dare refused to answer any questions about him. She told Charlie to leave him out of it."

"Mmm," Verna said thoughtfully, and stubbed out her cigarette. "Do you suppose Rex Hart wrote those anonymous letters?"

Lizzy hadn't thought of that possibility. She cocked her head on one side, considering. "The letter I saw was written in purple ink on pink paper. Mildred said that the handwriting was a woman's, but now that I think about it, I'm not sure. It could have been a man's—and I suppose a man could have used that paper and ink, especially if he wanted to make the letter look as if it were written by a woman." She frowned. "But what motive would Rex Hart have?"

Verna shrugged. "Maybe he's jealous of Roger Kilgore and hoped that Mildred would tell her husband to drop Miss Dare or else. Or maybe he was trying to push Mildred to the point where *she* would make serious trouble for Miss Dare. And then of course, there's the blackmail. Maybe—"

"Blackmail?" Lizzy asked blankly. "What blackmail?"

Verna frowned at her. "Really, Lizzy. Haven't you thought through this at *all*? Those checks Roger wrote. It sounds to me as if Miss Dare has been blackmailing him. Threatening to reveal their relationship if he didn't pay up."

Lizzy blinked. "Really, Verna, I don't think I—"

"Come on, Liz, *think*," Verna broke in urgently. "Why else would he be paying her? I've had several dealings with Roger Kilgore in the probate clerk's office. The man is by no means a pushover. I seriously doubt that he would fork over nine hundred bucks out of the goodness of his heart."

"Not even for love?" Lizzy ventured, feeling that she had not looked deeply enough into this complicated situation. It was a good thing Verna was here to set her straight.

"Not even for love," Verna replied firmly. "Roger is not that kind of guy." She gazed up at the ceiling, tapping a fingernail against her teeth, thinking. After a moment, she said, "But of course there are other possibilities. It could be that our anonymous letter writer is the one who is doing the blackmailing. After all, we don't know for sure *who* got the three checks that were written to Lily Star."

"But I don't understand," Lizzy said, puzzled. And then she did. Of course: Lily Star might be, or might *not* be, Lily Dare. And they had no idea to whom the checks were mailed, or who actually received and cashed them.

"Yes," she said, slowly. "I think I see." She looked gratefully at Verna, glad that she had told her everything, even though it meant breaking a confidence. Verna was clever. Like Miss Marple, she saw things that other people failed to see—perhaps because (like Miss Marple) she did not expect the best of everyone.

"Well, good," Verna said. "So let's see where we are. We know that Roger Kilgore is sending money to somebody— it could be Miss Dare but it might just as well be somebody else—to keep mum about something. The odds are good that it is his relationship with Miss Dare, which he doesn't want his wife to know about. She controls the money."

"She does?" Lizzy asked. "Oh, yes, of course she does. She told me so just yesterday." It was true. Roger Kilgore might have built up the dealership into the successful business it was—or that it had been before the Crash. But the money to start it had come from Mildred's father's cotton fortune. And Mildred was afraid, very afraid, that her money might all be gone soon.

"Of course, Roger could be trying to hide something else altogether." Verna frowned. "In any case, I wouldn't be surprised if he's already stopped loving that woman, or lusting after her, or whatever his feelings were when he got himself into this tricky situation. He's no dimwit. He may have already broken it off."

Lizzy nodded. "He has to know that their relationship is dangerous in a lot of ways. Maybe he's trying to extricate himself." On the other hand, maybe Roger was like Miss Dare, who seemed to thrive on danger. Maybe that was what had brought them together in the first place.

She shivered. She couldn't love someone—*truly* love him—if she had to worry about the risk involved. Maybe that was why she felt more comfortable with Grady than with Mr. Moseley. Grady was safe, and Mr. Moseley was . . . well, not so safe. Mr. Moseley himself was *not* a dangerous man, of course—in fact, he was rather conservative and sometimes even stodgy. But there were certainly potential dangers in a relationship with him.

Verna thought for a moment. "And Roger seems not to be the only one dangling from Lily Dare's string. There are those *other* men you mentioned."

"Yes," Lizzy mused. "The men who 'support her expensive habits,' was the way the letter put it."

Verna stood up and stretched. "I've had enough mysteries for one night. I'm going to brush my teeth. Do you want to take the first watch, or shall I?"

"The first watch?" Lizzy asked, still thinking about those other men.

"Two hours, don't you think? Whoever's on watch can sit in the rocker beside the window. Miss Dare has her window open, too, so we're sure to hear if she screams or anything. Why don't I go first?" She looked at her wristwatch. "It's ten o'clock. You get some sleep and I'll wake you at twelve. Then you can be on watch until two. Okay?"

Lizzy began to unbutton her blouse. She was glad that Verna was there to think things through for them and make a plan, since she herself usually just took things as they came.

"But I think we ought to leave our clothes on," Verna went on. "Just in case we hear something and have to investigate, I mean." She walked to the window, let up the shade, and looked out. "And for whatever it's worth, there's another way out than the stairs," she remarked, over her shoulder. "We're only about ten feet off the ground, and there's a trellis under this window—and the one next door. We could climb down easily."

Lizzy went to look. "I'm pretty sure Miss Marple would draw the line at climbing down a trellis from a second-story window."

Verna grinned and pulled down the shade again. "Maybe. But Nancy Drew would be just fine going down, don't you think? And somebody could certainly climb *up*. Heigh-ho. I'm off to brush my teeth. Back in a flash and then it's your turn."

A little later, back from her turn in the bathroom, Lizzy pulled off her shoes and stretched out, still wearing her clothes, on the pink chenille coverlet on one of the beds. She was dozing off when Verna spoke into the shadowy darkness.

"Grady Alexander came into the office today on some property business. He said you're going to the party tomorrow night with Mr. Moseley. True?"

"Not true," Lizzy said. "I mean, it *was* true when I told Grady. But Mr. Moseley had to go out of town. So I don't have a date." As an afterthought, she added carelessly, "Which is fine with me."

"It's definitely not fine with Grady," Verna remarked. "He thinks he's lost you and he doesn't know what to do about it."

"Did he say that?" Lizzy asked, surprised.

"Not in so many words," Verna admitted. "But I could hear it in his voice. You're not going to see him again? You two have broken up?"

"Not exactly," Lizzy said, and told Verna what had happened. She didn't often talk about her feelings, even with Verna, who was a close friend—her best friend, actually. But the dark made the words come a little easier, somehow. And made it easier for her to admit that she'd been wrong.

"I wish I hadn't agreed to go with Mr. Moseley," she said. "That was where I made my mistake."

"Mistake?"

"Well, yes." Lizzy hesitated. "For one thing, I'm not sure how easy it would be to work with him afterward."

"After what?"

Lizzy frowned. "After—well, you know." She wished that Verna would be satisfied with one answer instead of always pushing for more. It was very irritating.

"After a few kisses—or something else?"

"Nothing else!" Lizzy said indignantly, and then subsided. "But a few kisses would be bad enough, wouldn't they? Bad as in dangerous, I mean."

It might be easy for Verna to work with a man she had kissed. But not for Lizzy. Grady had kissed her often enough—and passionately enough—and she knew how she felt afterward. If Mr. Moseley kissed her the way Grady did, it might be hard for her to sit on the other side of the desk while he dictated letters to her the next morning—no, not hard; impossible! She could never in the world pretend that nothing important had happened between them when it *had.* Just thinking about it, she could feel her insides softening and her cheeks burning.

"Liz, sweet Liz," Verna said pityingly. "You do have a *lot* to learn. Not that I'm an expert when it comes to romance," she added. "But if you've decided that it's too dangerous to go out with Mr. Moseley, I think you should do something about Grady. He's pretty unhappy."

"He's unhappy because he's been taking me for granted," Lizzy said, not very logically. "And now he knows he can't. Or shouldn't." She slid back down on the bed. "Or won't. Or . . . something," she added, and pulled the pillow over her face.

"You don't sound very happy, either," Verna remarked.

"I'm not," Lizzy confessed. "Not when it comes to Grady. I just wish he—" She stopped. She couldn't finish the sentence because she had no idea *what* she wished. She was utterly confused and she hated it. Hated being confused, that is.

Verna laughed shortly. "Well, I'm afraid you're going to be even unhappier when I tell you who Grady has asked to the party tomorrow night. I'm sorry to be the bearer of bad news, but somebody has to tell you so you can be prepared."

Lizzy pushed the pillow aside and sat bolt upright. "Grady is bringing somebody? To the party?" She swallowed. "He's got a date with somebody *else?*"

"Yes, yes, and yes," Verna replied. "He said he's asked the former Miss Cotton of Monroeville. DeeDee Davis. Fourth runner-up in the 1930 Miss Alabama contest. And voted Miss Congeniality, too."

The news burst on Lizzy like a bombshell. "Oh, no, not *her*!" she moaned. "Not DeeDee Davis!"

She buried her face in the pillow. Everybody knew that blond, curvaceous DeeDee Davis was the most beautiful girl in three counties. She was nice, too. And young—no more than twenty-five, if that. She worked as a secretary in the Monroe County Ag office. As agriculture agent for both counties, Grady no doubt saw her whenever he went over to the Monroeville office.

"Jealous?" Verna inquired gently.

"Absolutely *not*," Lizzy snapped, dropping the pillow. "What makes you think I'm jealous?"

"Sounds like you're jealous."

"Well, I'm not." Grady's mother might think they were going to get married. *Her* mother might think so, too. But they were both wrong. Lizzy knew for a fact that she and Grady were not committed to one another, so there was no reason to be jealous. No reason at all.

"That's good," Verna said. "That way, you won't be the least bit upset when you see them together tomorrow night."

"Oooh," Lizzy groaned, and rolled over to face the wall. Why did life have to be so *complicated*?

"Two hours," Verna said. "I'll wake you."

The day had been a long one and Lizzy was bone-weary. Despite fretting over Verna's bombshell (and no, she was definitely *not* jealous), she was soon asleep. How long she slept, she didn't know. She was dreaming that she was driving a bumper car in a carnival ride, dressed in her gray silk party dress and wearing her silver earrings and bracelet. Mr. Moseley and Grady, driving separate cars, were bumping her car, very hard, each one shouting that he had come to take her to the party because she had promised to go with *him.* To make matters worse, she knew she had promised one of them but she couldn't for the life of her remember which one, and she felt terribly guilty for forgetting such an important commitment—almost as important, it seemed in her dream, as a promise to marry.

And the minute she thought of that, Lizzy remembered that she definitely *had* promised to marry one of them. Which one? Was it Grady or Mr. Moseley? Or maybe she had promised to marry *both* of them! Oh, dear! She must love *one* of them, mustn't she, or she would never have promised to marry him. Or maybe she loved them *both*?

But that was impossible—wasn't it? And anyway, she couldn't marry either one of them because she was wearing her gray dress (*married in black you'll wish yourself back; married in gray you'll die far away*) and she loved living in her little doll's house all alone, with only Daffy for company. Which of course was entirely and unforgivably selfish, just as her mother said, but there was nothing she could do about that.

And then, to make matters worse, DeeDee Davis, decked out in her Miss Cotton gown and crown, suddenly appeared in Grady's car. Grady pulled over to the side and the two of them began necking passionately. To escape the sight, Lizzy drove her car out a door and down a dark, winding alley into an empty field. She was sitting there, wondering what she should do next, when she felt someone gently shaking her shoulder. It was Mr. Moseley. "Wake up," he said. "Wake up, Liz, it's time to go to the party. Wake up!"

Startled out of the confusion of her dream, Lizzy opened her eyes into the shadows of Mildred's pink guestroom. Verna was leaning over her, still shaking her shoulder, not so gently now.

"Wake up," she repeated urgently. "Wake up, Liz!"

"What time is it?" Lizzy asked blurrily. Since she'd fallen

asleep, the moon had risen and was casting silver tree shadows across the floor so that the room was in half-twilight.

"Eleven fifty-five," Verna said in a whisper. "Wake up, Liz. Mildred is in Miss Dare's room."

Lizzy struggled to sit up. "*Mildred*? What's she doing there?"

"Shh!" Verna put a finger to her lips. "They're talking—in whispers, since they obviously don't want to be overheard. But you can hear—sort of—if you put your ear to the door."

Lizzy got up and went to the door. Crouching with her ear against it, she could hear two women's voices, so low that only fragments of sentences were audible, and just barely. But she recognized Mildred's voice—a Mildred who was even angrier than she had been that afternoon. And who definitely didn't want Lizzy and Verna to overhear. Or did she? She might feel safer, knowing that somebody was listening.

". . . telling you to leave my husband alone!" she said fiercely.

". . . don't know . . . talking about, my dear," Miss Dare said. "I'm not—"

"You see this photograph?" Mildred demanded. "And . . . two letters, detailing. . . . I am no fool. I know . . . going on, and I'm telling you . . . leave him alone!"

Miss Dare's laugh was like breaking glass. The floor creaked, as though she were moving around the room, and when she spoke, her voice was a little louder.

"I hate anonymous letters," she said in a caustic tone. "They are so *cowardly*. But you've found us out, so I might as well admit it. I'm not the one you should be talking to, though. It was Roger's idea in the first place, you know. He came after me. You should talk to him."

The floor creaked again. Mildred's voice was a little

louder now, too. "I don't believe that for a second," she hissed. "You're the one who tempted him. You're a seductress. And I'm telling you, you have to stop. I won't have you wrecking my marriage and destroying my husband's business!"

"Destroying—"

"I know about those checks he wrote you. I don't know what you were threatening to do if you didn't get it, but you're a blackmailer. You—"

"What checks?" Miss Dare broke in. "I don't know anything about any checks."

"Did you hear that?" Verna whispered, elbowing Lizzy. "Blackmail. Like I said!"

"We may look rich," Mildred said, "but we're not made of money. We can't afford—"

Verna pushed Lizzy a little aside so she could get closer to the door. But by now, the women in the other room had forgotten all about keeping their voices down.

"I don't have any idea what you're talking about." Miss Dare's voice was ominously flat. "I have never asked Roger for one cent."

"You're lying!" Mildred cried. "You're a liar. You're a damned *liar*!"

"Oh, my," Lizzy breathed, eyes wide.

"That's crazy," Miss Dare said rudely. "You should see yourself, Mrs. Kilgore. You look like a crazy woman." Her laugh was a taunt. "You *are* a crazy woman!"

"I have *every* right to be crazy! You are making me crazy, trying to steal my husband, blackmailing him—"

"Blackmailing? *Blackmailing?*" Miss Dare shrilled. "What are you talking about? I am *not* blackmailing him! I have no idea what—"

"Liar!" Mildred cried furiously. "You are a *liar*! I've seen the check register myself! Three checks, nine hundred dollars. He paid you *nine hundred dollars*!"

"You tell her, Mildred," Lizzy said under her breath.

"But maybe she *isn't* the blackmailer, Liz," Verna whispered in her ear. "All Mildred knows is that Roger was mailing those checks to *someone*, but she doesn't know for sure who. Why, Roger himself might not even know."

Listening to Verna, Lizzy missed whatever Miss Dare replied. Mildred was even angrier now, but she had lowered her voice, so that Lizzy could hear only broken snatches once more. ". . .You'll be sorry. . . I'll make you *pay* for this . . . I'll drag your name in the . . ."

Miss Dare's response was much more audible. Her voice was flint-like. "You can try, of course, but I must warn you that better women than you have—"

"Better women!" Mildred shrieked. "I'll show you who's *better*!"

There was the sound of a sharp slap. And then a second. "We ought to break this up," Verna said, "before somebody gets hurt." She shot the bolt back and tried to open the door. But it wouldn't move—it was bolted on the other side.

"You struck me!" Miss Dare said, low and ominous. "All right—you want to fight, sister? I'll snatch you bald!" There was the sound of scuffling and a muffled cry, then another, and more scuffling.

"My eye!" Mildred cried. "Oh, my eye!"

"We have to do *something*," Lizzy said urgently, and started for the door of their room. But by the time she reached it, Miss Dare had shoved Mildred into the hall with a rough "Get *out*!" Her door slammed, and Mildred retreated with hasty, stumbling steps in the direction of the master bedroom. Across the hall, Lizzy saw Angel Flame's door silently close. She had been listening, too.

Lizzy shut the door and leaned her back against it. "Mercy," she said weakly. "That was just like in the movies!"

"I wonder who won," Verna said ironically. "Or more to

the point, who will be wearing a black eye for tomorrow's party. And how she will explain it when people ask."

"Maybe they both will," Lizzy said. "Wear a black eye, I mean. And then they won't have to explain it—it'll be obvious. But I shouldn't joke about it. It's not funny. I wonder how they're going to face each other at breakfast tomorrow." Facing somebody you've punched might be almost as hard as facing somebody you've kissed, she thought. She glanced at the clock on the bureau and corrected herself. "Not tomorrow, *today*. It's after midnight."

"So it is," Verna said with a yawn. "Your watch, Liz. My turn to get some sleep."

"Good," Lizzy said, and sat down in the rocking chair. "I hope nothing more happens."

"Oh, I don't know," Verna said, pulling off her shoes and flopping down on the bed. "That was interesting, don't you think? And revealing. I never suspected that Mildred could be so passionate about anything."

"If you say so," Lizzy replied. "But personally, I prefer a little less passion, thank you." The trouble with passion was that it could get you into trouble, and Lizzy, a cautious person, liked to avoid trouble whenever she could. "And I definitely didn't want to know all those things about Mildred—or Miss Dare, either," she added. Passionate people could be dangerous, or at the very least, disturbing.

"Not me," Verna said emphatically. "The more I know about people, the better I like it. And a little passion never hurt anybody, Liz."

Verna was about to get what she wanted—and then some.

THIRTEEN

"Gone? Gone Where?"

Lizzy was keyed up and on edge, so she didn't find it hard to stay awake, and she found herself puzzling over what they had heard. Verna was right when she said that the argument was revealing. Mildred had always seemed so placidly smug, so comfortable and contented in the midst of all her possessions. Her argument with Miss Dare had definitely disclosed a side of Mildred that Lizzy had never suspected—and which was definitely unsettling. She had never imagined mild-mannered, sweet-as-cream Mildred getting up the energy to strike a blow.

Lizzy shivered, thinking of the questions that had been raised by the argument they had just overheard and not liking any of them. How far would Mildred go to protect her home, her husband, the business, their way of life? And what about Miss Dare? How far would she go to get what she wanted? If she wanted Roger Kilgore, what would she do to get—and keep—him?

But there were no easy answers, so Lizzy gave up. She

raised the window shade and passed the time watching the moon rise higher in the sky, tracing the outlines of the trees as they slipped across the silvered floor and into the shadowy corners of the room. Outside, the mysterious darkness was scented with honeysuckle and roses. Somewhere in the distance a dog barked, out and about on a nocturnal excursion. Nearer at hand, the summer cicadas and katydids sang in the trees. Nearer still, Verna snored gently and shifted in her sleep. There were no sounds from Miss Dare's room.

But the drone of the insects was hypnotic and staying alert got harder and harder. Lizzy felt herself drowsing, then jerking awake as her shoulders slumped and her chin dropped onto her chest. After alternately dozing and waking for a time, she finally pushed herself out of the chair and tiptoed across the hall to the bathroom. As she did, she saw a light at the far end of the hall and the rise and fall of voices. Roger must be home, and he and Mildred were talking.

Lizzy felt apprehensive. Would Mildred tell her husband about her argument with Miss Dare? Would she tell him the truth? How *much* would she tell him?

In the bathroom, she got a glass of water and brought it back to the room. She sat, sipping the water slowly, looking up at the starlit, moonstruck sky and trying not to think about anything—especially not about Grady and DeeDee Davis, the most beautiful girl in three counties. After a while, she was distracted from her efforts not to think about Grady and DeeDee by the surreptitious sound of a door opening, then closing again.

Was it the door to Miss Dare's room, or the bathroom door, or the door to Angel Flame's room, across the hall?

She got up and went to the hallway door and opened it cautiously, but the hall was much darker than their bedroom and she couldn't see any movement. So she went back and knelt beside the door to Miss Dare's room. She didn't even have to press her ear against it, for she could now clearly hear the sound of voices. Miss Dare's voice—and a man's.

Roger Kilgore! And from the sound of it, he had been drinking pretty heavily at that poker game. Miss Dare was trying to shush him, without success.

"I want to know why you told Mildred," Roger was saying in a gruff, slurred voice. "What'cha do it for?"

"I didn't tell her!" Miss Dare protested. "I *didn't*!"

Lizzy turned away to the bed to wake Verna, but she was a light sleeper. She had heard the voices and was instantly awake.

"Grand Central Station over there," she whispered, joining Lizzy at the door. "Roger, isn't it? Sounds like he's fully loaded."

Lizzy nodded, trying to imagine the scene. "I wonder what she's wearing." Something soft and clingy, probably. And sheer.

"Or not, as the case may be," Verna added dryly. "Maybe she sleeps in the raw."

"Well, wasn't me who told her," Roger growled. "So it must've been you."

"He's been talking to Mildred," Lizzy whispered. "I saw the light on in their bedroom and heard their voices. He knows that she knows about the affair, although maybe she didn't tell him quite everything. Or he was too drunk to get the whole story."

"Probably too drunk," Verna said. There was a sharp sound, like a chair falling over. "Uh-oh. Here we go, fight fans. Round two."

But Roger must just have stumbled.

"You clumsy dolt." Miss Dare laughed lightly—the same brittle laugh they had heard before. There was no amusement in it. "Come over here and sit down beside me."

The bed creaked. "Why are you so sore at me, sweetie?" she crooned. "Did you leave your brains at the poker table? Telling your wife about us is the *last* thing I'd do."

"Then how did she—" Roger was obviously confused. "I can't figure out how she—"

"Somebody sent her an anonymous letter. Didn't she tell you that?" Miss Dare's voice tightened, becoming fiercely sarcastic. "She was eager enough to tell *me*."

"An anon . . . nonymous—" He stumbled over the word and gave it up. "Who wrote it?"

Lizzy could picture Miss Dare rolling her eyes. "How the hell should I know who wrote it? The damn thing wasn't signed. She said there were two of them, but she got rid of the first one. She also had a photograph of you and me together—a compromising photograph, I should add. It was taken when we were eating at that café in the French Quarter. She was delighted to shove my nose in it. She didn't show it to you?"

"She's bawling her head off," Roger said thickly. "Got a washcloth over her face. Won't talk to me. Keeps saying I have to talk to *you*, that you know all about it."

"Well, maybe we'd better talk in the morning when you're sober," Miss Dare said. "And when your wife has stopped crying. There's some business the three of us have to settle."

"The three of us?" Roger asked warily. "I don't think so. Whatever it is, let's leave Mildred out of it. But first—" His voice dropped. "Com'ere, sweetheart. We've got other fish to fry." The bed creaked. Clark Gable was making his move. "Gimme a kiss, babe."

There was a silence, a long silence.

Lizzy pressed her ear to the door. It wasn't hard to imagine what was happening on the other side. She had seen Miss Dare in action twice before: kissing Roger and kissing

Charlie. Only this time, the woman was wearing . . . what? A filmy negligee? Lizzy closed her eyes, but the image stayed with her. Miss Dare in a clingy nightgown that concealed none of her personal assets, Roger Kilgore kissing her, his hands all over her body, his mouth on hers. For some odd reason, Lizzy thought of Grady and her own mouth went dry. And then she thought of Grady and DeeDee Davis and—

"Cut it out, Roger," Miss Dare said firmly. "I'm not in the mood." The bed creaked again, as if she had pushed him away and gotten up. "If you want to settle our business now, you can start by telling me about the blackmail. Nine hundred dollars was what she said."

"Can it, Lily," Roger snapped. "You want more? Forget it. You've got every nickel you're going to get from me. There's nothing left. Nothing." He didn't sound drunk now. He sounded angry.

There was a silence. Then, "What *are* you talking about, Roger?" Miss Dare asked, sounding genuinely baffled. "I don't understand. What is all this crap about money?"

"You damn well know what it is," Roger said roughly. "It's about those telegrams you sent me. You said you were desperate for cash and I was the only one you could turn to, and I believed you. You said you loved me and I was fool enough to—"

"By golly," Verna whispered. "He *did* do it for love! What an idiot."

Roger was going on. "Mildred says it was blackmail, but I don't agree. I didn't think you were threatening me. I just thought you needed money."

"But I didn't!" Miss Dare said hotly. "I mean, I always need money. But I didn't ask *you* for any. And I didn't say I loved you and wanted—" She stopped. "I mean, I *do* love you, sweetie, heart and soul, honest Injun, cross my heart and hope to die. But I never sent you any telegrams asking for money. And I never got a cent from you. Not one red cent!"

"But if she didn't ask for it," Lizzy whispered, puzzled, "who *did*?"

"Yes," Verna said. "That's the question, isn't it? And if it wasn't blackmail, it was extortion. Somebody was using her name—fraudulently." Then, true to her habit of looking under every rock, she added, "But maybe she's lying. I wouldn't put it past her."

Roger seemed to think so, too. "You're lying, Lily. And I've got your signature on those checks to prove it."

"I don't know who the hell signed those checks," Miss Dare said grimly, "but it sure wasn't *me*. I didn't know the first thing about them until your precious little wifey started waving that letter under my nose and screaming like a banshee."

"You could at least be respectful," Roger replied in an ominous tone. "Mildred hasn't done anything to you."

"Oh, she hasn't, has she?" Miss Dare hooted. "Be respectful—after that little witch popped me in the eye? See this? If you think it looks bad now, just you wait until tomorrow. I'm going to have a pretty purple shiner. And when people ask me where I got it, I'll tell them that your battle-ax—"

"Don't you call Mildred names," Roger said, low and hard. "She's twice the woman you are. You took my money and—"

"But I *didn't* take your money!" Miss Dare cried petulantly. "You big sap! You don't have the sense God gave a billy goat! You've been played for a sucker. Somebody rolled you for a wad of dough and you think you can blame me for it. Well, I'll show you. I'll—"

"Shut up," Roger snarled. "You just shut your mouth!"

The bed creaked again as if he had gotten up. Lizzy heard a scuffling noise, then heavy breathing and more scuffling.

"Ouch!" Miss Dare gave an injured whimper. "Stop twisting my arm, you big bully. If you don't lay off, I'm going to—"

There was the loud sound of a fist striking flesh.

Verna straightened up. "He's beating on her! Liz, we have to—" She started for the door, Liz at her heels. But once again, they were too late.

"Damn!" Roger exclaimed, flabbergasted. "You slugged me, Lily! Right in the eye!"

"You bet I slugged you!" Miss Dare cried. "And I'll do it again. Get out of my room or I'll start screaming. *That'll* bring your sweet little wifey running."

Roger apparently took her at her word, for the door opened and shut and heavy footsteps stomped down the hall.

After a moment, the silence in the other room was broken by a frenzied sobbing.

"Do you think we'd better go and see if she's okay?" Lizzy asked worriedly. "I promised Charlie that we'd make sure—"

"Maybe just one of us," Verna said. "You go, Liz. I haven't even been introduced to her. In fact, I've never even laid eyes on the woman."

At Miss Dare's room, Lizzy didn't bother to knock; she just pushed the door open and went in. In the shadowy darkness, she could see that the lady, wearing a glamorous lace-trimmed peach nightgown, had thrown herself across the bed, face down. She was weeping noisily.

Lizzy leaned over the woman and put a hand on her shoulder. "It's Liz," she said. "Liz Lacy. We had lunch together—remember? I'm in the room next door and I couldn't help overhearing. Are you alright? You're not hurt, are you? Is there anything I can do?"

Miss Dare gulped back a sob and struggled to sit up. "Oh, yeah. Liz. You're my babysitter, aren't you? My protector." Her dark hair was disheveled, her face was splotched and puffy, and there was a purple-green bruise under her left eye. "Well, there's nothing you can do unless you know a sure cure for a shiner." She looked down at her right arm, where three finger marks were an ugly red against the pale skin. "And a twisted arm," she added bitterly. "I'm just lucky that stupid lug didn't break it. He certainly tried hard enough. I thought he was going to pull it right out of the socket."

Lizzy persisted. "You're sure you're okay? You wouldn't like a glass of water?" She looked at Miss Dare's eye. "Or a cold washcloth for that eye or—"

"Whiskey," Miss Dare said optimistically. She touched her eye with a tender finger. "If you haven't got that, brandy will do. Or rum."

"Sorry," Lizzy replied. "I don't have any booze. And I don't know where Roger keeps it."

"Well, then, you're not much good, are you, honey?" Sniffling, Miss Dare got up and went to the dresser, where she opened her brown leather handbag, took out a small brown cigar, and came back to the bed and sat down, crossing her bare legs.

"But maybe you know something about those checks Roger and his missus keep talking about," she went on, swinging one foot, shod in a peach-colored satin mule with a fluffy peach pompom. She added darkly, "I'd sure like to find out whose big pockets that nine hundred smackeroos went into—especially since somebody got that cash by using my name."

Lizzy shook her head. "I heard, yes," she admitted. "But I don't know any more than you do, I'm afraid." Then, timidly, she ventured a question. "Do you have any idea who might have sent those telegrams? Or written the letters?"

Miss Dare reached for a matchbook on the nightstand. "Actually, I have a pretty good idea who did it," she said, in a low, angry voice. "In fact, I'm about ninety-nine percent sure. And I've had just about all I can take from—"

She struck a match and held it to the cigar, but her hand was shaking so hard that the match went out. She tried again, with another match.

"I intend to settle some hash over this," she added savagely, blowing out a stream of smoke.

Settle some hash. Who did Miss Dare suspect? Was it Rex Hart? If she thought he sent the telegrams, did she suspect him of writing the anonymous letters and sending the photograph? And sabotaging her airplane, too? But Lizzy didn't feel that she could ask those important questions. Lamely, she said, "Well, if you need me in the night, just yell. I'm right next door. I can be here in a few seconds—faster, if you'll unbolt the door between our rooms."

"I am *not* unbolting any doors, baby doll." Miss Dare looked straight at her, her eyes hard. "Go back to bed and go to sleep. And don't bother me again, no matter what you think you hear in this room. You got that?"

"But I promised Charlie—" Lizzy began.

"I don't care what the hell you promised Charlie," Miss Dare said icily. "And you can tell him I said so. I resent being looked after. And I don't like knowing that there's a spy in the room next door, eavesdropping on my private conversations. Get out. *Now.*"

"I'm sorry," Lizzy said, feeling like a little girl who'd been caught doing something she shouldn't. Miss Dare was making a very valid point. She backed toward the door. "Good night. I'll see you tomorrow, I guess."

Miss Dare didn't reply. Lizzy left her, sitting on the bed, smoking and swinging that peach satin mule. As she went into the hall, she saw Angel Flame's door close and wondered uncomfortably how much she had heard.

Back in their bedroom, Verna was waiting. "I guess that wasn't such a good idea, huh?" she said quietly. "How is she?"

"She's in pretty bad shape," Lizzy replied. "Black eye, bruised arm. She was so shaky that she could barely light that cigar of hers."

"Cigar?" Verna frowned.

"Cigar," Lizzy said. "And I think she's right, Verna. Regardless of why we were doing it, we shouldn't be eavesdropping on her private conversations. I'm turning in now. And I don't care what happens next door—even if somebody gets *shot*—I am *not* getting out of this bed." She pulled her green cotton nightgown out of the dresser drawer. "And I am sleeping in my nightgown," she said pointedly, beginning to undress.

Verna considered this for a moment, then nodded. "Our hearts were in the right place, but I guess you're right." Her grin was lopsided. "Just out of curiosity, though, tell me what she wears to sleep in."

"A see-through peach negligee trimmed with lace," Lizzy said. "And peach-colored satin mules on her feet. Like a Hollywood starlet. She may be broke, but she sleeps in style." She turned back the pink coverlet and crawled into bed. "Whatever happens can happen without me. Good night."

As she fell asleep, she wondered if Miss Marple ever regretted snooping into the private affairs of anyone in St. Mary Mead—and whether she'd gotten into serious trouble when she was doing it. Maybe she should write to Miss Agatha Christie and ask.

* * *

Lizzy was wakened from a sound sleep by the insistent hammering of a woodpecker in the sycamore tree outside the window. The sun was brightening the room and the inviting smell of bacon and coffee wafted through the early morning air. As she opened her eyes, she saw that Verna was already up and dressed.

"It's seven o'clock on a Friday," Verna announced briskly, "and I'm a working girl. I have to get to the courthouse, so I'll just skip breakfast here. I can pick up something quick at the diner."

Lizzy sat up and rubbed the sleep out of her eyes. "You're skipping breakfast here because you don't want to face the awkwardness," she said accusingly, thinking of what was ahead. "Mildred, Roger, and Miss Dare across the breakfast table. Oh, and Angel Flame, too."

"Doesn't sound like much fun," Verna agreed soberly. "Maybe we shouldn't have listened in last night, but that doesn't change the fact that there are three pretty unhappy people in this house this morning."

"Make that four." Lizzy swung her feet onto the floor. "I'm going to tell Charlie that Miss Dare doesn't need a Miss Marple—or a nanny, either. She can take care of herself. Which means I won't be sleeping over here after the party tonight." The party, she thought forlornly, to which Grady was bringing the beautiful DeeDee Davis. But at least she hadn't dreamed about her again.

Verna nodded slowly. "I won't either, then. Shall I let Mildred know, or will you?"

"I will," Lizzy said. "I'm sure it will be okay if we leave our clothes, though. We can dress here for the party."

"Good idea," Verna said, picking up her handbag. "Thank

Mildred for the hospitality, will you? I'll see you later today." At the door, she paused. "Oh, and I'll leave your bicycle out front. You'll want it today, I'm sure."

Lizzy combed her hair, dressed in slacks and her red print blouse, and added a touch of red lipstick. Then she went downstairs to the breakfast room, where a table was spread with a snowy white damask cloth and centered with a crystal bowl of pink roses. It was set for five.

But Mildred, wearing a lilac-colored sundress, was the only person there. Her eye was puffed and purpled, although it wasn't nearly as bad as Miss Dare's had been last night.

"Oh, dear," Lizzy said quietly. "Oh, Mildred, your poor *eye.* I'm so sorry."

"Well, I'm not," Mildred replied staunchly. "I gave as good as I got—and maybe some better, too. You overheard the whole thing, I suppose."

Ollie Rose, wearing her starched black uniform and white cap, brought in a plate of scrambled eggs, bacon, and biscuits and set it down on the table.

"Thank you, Ollie Rose," Mildred said. She picked up the silver coffeepot. "Coffee, Liz?"

"Thank you." Lizzy held out her cup as Mildred poured. "Yes, I overheard," she confessed somewhat guiltily.

"And you overheard Roger's conversation with her?" Mildred giggled. "I don't think it went quite the way he expected. You should see *his* eye."

Lizzy flinched. "Verna and I both wish we hadn't put all of us into that situation," she said contritely. "If I had thought the whole thing through, I might have realized that it wasn't the best idea in the world. I feel terribly awkward about it, Mildred. I apologized to Miss Dare, and I'm apologizing to you. I *am* sorry."

"Oh, I don't know," Mildred said thoughtfully, and put

down the pot. She smiled. "To tell the truth, Liz, I actually felt better knowing that you were on the other side of that door, in case . . ." She shrugged one shoulder. "Well, just in case. And I'm glad I told you about the letters and the money. Talking about it made me see things a little more clearly. I didn't have a chance to discuss anything with Roger this morning—he got up and went to work very early, while I was still asleep. But we said enough last night to make me hope that we'll get things straightened out— once Miss Dare is gone." She frowned. "Of course, my opinion of her is still the same. She is a *tramp.*"

"I think you and Roger will get things straightened out," Lizzy said warmly, "and I'm glad. Just the same, Verna and I feel it would be better if we went home after the party tonight." She helped herself to the scrambled eggs and bacon. "Oh, and Verna asked me to thank you for your hospitality," she added, taking a biscuit. "She thought she'd better skip breakfast and go on to the courthouse."

"You all are welcome any time," Mildred said. "We rattle around in this big house." She glanced at the clock on the sideboard. The hands stood at eight o'clock. "I wonder where Angel and Miss Dare are. Last night, Mr. Dickens said he'd be here at eight fifteen to pick them up and take them out to the airfield, so they asked for breakfast early. I'll ask Ollie Rose to go upstairs and knock."

But just as Mildred was reaching for the small gold bell beside her plate, Lizzy heard the sound of hurrying footsteps on the stairs.

"Mrs. Kilgore!" Angel Flame, dressed in khaki trousers and a navy blue blouse, burst into the dining room. Her hair was sticking out in every direction and the sandy freckles were popping out all over her face. "Mrs. Kilgore, oh, come quick! Quick! Lily is—" She gulped. "Miss Dare is *gone!*"

"Gone?" Lizzy echoed. "Gone where?"

"I have no idea," Angel replied breathlessly. "I went to wake her up just now and her room is empty. And there's been some sort of . . . of trouble. In her room."

"Trouble?" Mildred asked sharply. She pushed back her chair and stood up. "What kind of trouble?"

"Come and see," Angel said, and turned to run back up the stairs.

A moment later, they were standing at the door of Lily Dare's bedroom. "You see?" Angel said excitedly. "It looks like there's been a struggle of some sort!"

She was right. The lamp from the nightstand lay on its side, the light bulb shattered and the lampshade broken. The ashtray had spilled and cigar ashes were scattered across the floor. Bedding was twisted and pulled from the bed. A straight chair lay on its side. A vase of flowers had been knocked over and the water spilled. The window shade was askew. Lily Dare was nowhere to be seen.

"The window!" Lizzy exclaimed, and rushed toward the open window, which was pushed up as high as it would go. The screen was missing, and a torn scrap of sheer peach fabric was snagged on a corner of the sill. She put her head out and looked down. There was a bare wooden trellis on the wall beneath the window. On the ground beneath the window, about ten feet below, lay the window screen—and one peach-colored satin mule.

"Her slipper," Lizzy said to Mildred. "It's down there, on the ground." She pointed to the scrap of fabric. "And that's her nightgown."

"You mean, she's out there somewhere in her negligee and just one slipper?" Mildred asked incredulously.

"She would never go out dressed like that!" Angel Flame cried, clapping her hands to her mouth. "She's been kidnapped. Somebody forced her out that window!"

"Kidnapped!" Mildred wailed. "Oh, no! This can't be happening. Not in *my house*!" She swiveled to face Lizzy. "This mess, the breakage—surely there would have been some noise. What did you hear?"

"Not a thing," Lizzy said disconsolately. "Not after—"

She stopped. She had been about to say that she hadn't heard any signs of an altercation after Roger left Miss Dare's room, but she didn't want to discuss it in front of Angel Flame. Angel had been at her door, listening, and Lizzy didn't know what she had overheard.

"Not after—" Angel prompted, watching her. "Not after what? What do you mean?"

But Lizzy was saved by the bell—the doorbell, pealing sharply downstairs.

"Thank heavens," Mildred said, hurrying to the door. "It must be Mr. Dickens. He'll know what to do."

"I think you should call the cops," Angel said loudly, to Mildred's back. "Call 'em right now! Don't wait another minute." She looked around the room, shuddering. "Something *bad* has happened to Lily," she muttered. "Something really, *really* bad. I can feel it in my bones!"

Lizzy sighed, thinking of Sheriff Roy Burns, who would go clumping through the house like Mr. Norris' clumsy old horse. The sheriff could handle Old Zeke when he got drunk and disorderly, and he could manage the rowdies out at the Dance Barn out on Briarwood Road. But he had neither finesse nor imagination, and she was sure he would have no more idea of what to do than they did.

And what was worse, if the sheriff came, he would likely start asking questions, and she would end up having to tell about the confrontations of the night before. And *that* could cause all kinds of unwarranted embarrassment and trouble for Mildred and Roger.

Then Lizzy pulled in her breath, reminding herself of a

question that Mr. Moseley would most certainly ask. Was it *really* unwarranted? What if one or the other of the Kilgores—or both—had a hand in Miss Dare's disappearance?

But that wasn't likely.

Was it?

FOURTEEN

"And She Only Paid for One!"

Verna usually walked to work, from the small frame house at the corner of Larkspur and Robert E. Lee, where she lived with her black Scottie, Clyde. But Clyde had spent the night with Verna's neighbor. And since she was already in the car, she just drove on into the middle of town and parked her LaSalle against the nearly empty curb in front of the courthouse, where old Mr. Tucker was just raising the flags, the U.S. flag on one pole, the flag of the Confederate States of America on the other. Out of respect for the fallen, he always raised the Confederate flag first and stepped back to salute it.

Getting out of the car, Verna glanced up at the clock on the tower. It was only seven thirty. She hated to admit it, but Liz had been right—she had skipped breakfast at the Kilgores' because she wanted to avoid the unpleasantness. She felt like a heel, leaving Liz to cope with Mildred and Roger and Miss Dare, but she promised herself that she'd make it up to her.

Meanwhile, she needed some breakfast. Donna Sue, the clerk in Judge McHenry's office, had raved about the sausage and grits casserole that she'd gotten at the diner the morning before, which (according to Donna Sue) tasted exactly like her mama's casserole and maybe even a bit better. This was saying a *lot,* Verna knew, since Donna Sue had always claimed that nobody in the world could hold a candle to her mama's cooking.

Grits and sausage casserole sounded good to Verna, along with a cup of Myra May's strong, black coffee, Violet's cheerful morning greeting, and the chortles of little Cupcake. She crossed the street, feeling the warm summer sunshine on her shoulders and smiling with anticipation. The night had been awkward (to say the least!), and she was sorry that she had volunteered to snoop into something that was really none of her business. That's what came of indulging her regrettable habit of poking around under rocks. A satisfying breakfast with her good friends at the Darling Diner would go a long way to restoring her balance—and her self-confidence.

But when Verna opened the door and went in, the diner was such a scene of noisy chaos that she simply stopped and stared. The stools at the counter were almost all taken, the tables were full of chatting patrons, and Myra May, Violet, and Earlynne Biddle's boy, Bennie, were running back and forth with plates of food and pots of coffee, all three wearing anxious and harried expressions. Obviously, word about the new cook had gotten around. Myra May was going to have to hire additional help.

Verna took the nearest available seat at the counter, sliding in next to Mr. Greer, the owner of the Palace Theater. Over a full plate of eggs and ham, he was telling Mr. Musgrove about the large and enthusiastic crowd they'd had at the showing of *Hell's Angels* the night before. The film had featured several aerial dogfights, with one of the planes flown by Miss Lily Dare, the Texas Star—who would be flying at the air show that weekend.

"And the Texas Star herself came to the movie," he announced, speaking over the morning farm market report (corn was up, beans and pork bellies were down) on the white Philco radio behind the counter. He spoke loud enough to be heard three stools down by Archie Mann, from Mann's Mercantile.

Archie Mann leaned forward to reply to Mr. Greer past Lester Lima (the owner of Lima's Drugstore) and Jake Pritchard (who owned the Standard Oil filling station out on the Monroeville Highway).

"That pilot lady's a real looker, too, by damn," he said with a sly chuckle. "Ol' Charlie Dickens, he's landed hisself a stunner this time. That Miss Dare, she can fly my plane any day of the week," he added, and broke into a raucous guffaw that was echoed along the counter by all the men who were listening—and all of them were.

Lester Lima, a thin, stoop-shouldered, fussy man with gold eyeglasses, frowned down at his eggs and bacon. "It is my understanding," he said prissily, "that Mr. Dickens is engaged to Miss Champaign, the little lady who makes the hats."

"Yeah, that's what I thought, too," Jake Pritchard put in, slathering grape jelly on a biscuit. "My missus heard Miss Champaign say so at the beauty salon."

"Well, if they was engaged, they ain't engaged no more," Mr. Greer replied in a knowing tone. "At least, ol' Charlie ain't. Lily Dare was hangin' on to him like a tick on a hound dog, and I didn't see him objectin' none."

Mr. Greer, who operated the movie projector at the back of the theater, kept a running score of the developing romances of the Palace patrons, especially among the younger crowd. He could be counted on to know who was courting who and whether the courting looked like it was going to lead somewhere it shouldn't, at least in his theater. When things got too steamy, he'd been known to take a flashlight and roam the aisles, throwing a little light on the offending couples.

Jake Pritchard laughed. "Well, I reckon ol' Charlie's found out why it's good to stay a bachelor, although the missus is gonna be plumb disappointed. She was figurin' on a new hat for the weddin'."

Verna listened, at first with a frown and then with a growing dismay. She had heard about Fannie and Charlie from several different sources, although (in her usual skeptical fashion) she hadn't quite believed the part about the engagement. Still, she knew that Fannie and Charlie were an item, and that Fannie (a fellow Dahlia) probably cared more than she should for Charlie. Poor Fannie was much too sweet for her own good, while Charlie had always struck Verna as the footloose-and-fancy-free type. When Fannie found out that Charlie had been seen at the movie house with Lily Dare, it would be a blow.

Verna shook her head disgustedly. This was exactly why she had decided, after her husband Walter stepped out in front of that Greyhound bus, that she didn't need another man in her life, thank you very much. You couldn't trust a one of them any farther than you could throw him.

Myra May rushed around the end of the counter and skidded to a stop in front of Verna. "Mornin', Verna," she said, brushing the hair out of her eyes. "Sorry it took so long to get to you. We're a little rushed this morning." She picked up the coffeepot and slopped coffee into a mug, pushing it across the counter. "What'll you have, hon?"

"Donna Sue Pendergast raved about your new cook's

grits and sausage casserole," Verna said with happy anticipation. "That's what I'll have."

"Oops, sorry," Myra May said regretfully. "Raylene didn't come in this morning. You can have eggs any way with bacon or ham, plus grits, and gravy. That's all we've got. Oh, and biscuits, of course. Violet just made another panful."

"She didn't come in?" Verna asked, surprised. She took a couple of sips of her coffee. "But I thought—"

"So did we," Myra May said glumly. "We thought our problems were solved. Raylene is a swell cook, great with the customers, seems to be able to come up with exactly what they want, like it's by magic. Really, Verna. You gotta see it to believe it. Magic."

"What happened?" Verna asked. "Did she quit?"

"I wish I knew," Myra May said. "Maybe she just over-slept. Or maybe she's sick, although she seemed okay when we closed up last night. If I could get away, I'd drive out to the motor court and see what's wrong. She's staying out there until she can find a cheap place to live in town." Myra May wiped the counter with a rag. "We can get by here for today, but she's supposed to help us with the catering for Mildred's party. If she's skipped, Violet and I will have to figure out something." She wiped the sweat off her forehead with the back of her hand. "What, I don't know," she said wearily, "but *something*."

Verna took another drink of coffee. "She's staying at the Marigold? Why don't you call out there and see what's happened?"

"There's no phone in any of the cottages," Myra May replied. "I called the office to ask Pauline to skip over and knock on Raylene's door, but nobody answers. Pauline's probably cleaning or doing the laundry. I'll just have to keep on trying."

"Myra May!" Violet yelled from the kitchen. "Myra May, I *need* you!" At the same time, little Cupcake, corralled in her playpen at the back of the dining room, began to wail, adding to the general cacophony.

Verna looked at her watch. "Tell you what," she said. "I've got my car this morning. I'll run across the street to the office and get Melba Jean and Ruthie started for the day." She gulped the last of her coffee and slid off the stool. "Then I'll drive out to the Marigold and find out what's what. If she's just overslept, I can drive her back. Her name is Raylene, you said? Which cottage is she in?"

"Oh, *would* you, Verna?" Myra May asked happily. "You'll earn our undying gratitude. Right—Raylene Riggs. She's in Number Four." She grabbed a paper napkin and two biscuits off a plate, wrapped them up, and thrust them at Verna. "Here. Take these with you so you won't starve. And when we get ourselves organized again, you've got a couple of free breakfasts coming."

"I'll let you know as soon as I find out anything," Verna said.

From the kitchen came the ominous sound of grease crackling. "Myra *May!*" Violet yelled, louder this time. *"Help!"*

Verna had been working late recently to reorganize the county bank accounts, so she felt justified in taking a little time off this morning. She got Ruthie and Melba Jean—her two employees—settled on the day's work, signed a couple of documents, and returned a telephone phone call. Twenty minutes later, she was back in her LaSalle, heading out to the Marigold Motor Court.

Pauline and Floyd DuBerry had built the motor court back when people were upbeat and hopeful and could spend a little extra money to put gas in their tanks and new tires on their cars and drive somewhere for a vacation. They had lost their only child, Herman, in the Great War, and they had nothing except the motor court cottages, their house, a few chickens, and a garden. And then Pauline had lost Floyd to heat stroke, one hot July afternoon two years before, when he shouldn't have been out mowing but was anyway, because it needed doing. That was Floyd, she said sadly, out there in the noon sun without a hat. Stubborn as an old mule. You couldn't tell that man a blessed thing.

With Floyd gone, Pauline had to hire Jake Pritchard's boy to come over from the Standard Oil station across the road and cut the weeds and fix the plumbing and do whatever had to be done to keep the motor court looking attractive. The Marigold income was all she had to keep her going in her old age, which she had already reached, since Pauline was sixty-two and wishing she could slow down.

Unfortunately, things weren't working out that way. When she stopped by the courthouse to pay the property tax, Pauline (a chatty little old lady) told Verna that she was lucky to have more than two guests on any one night and there were lots of nights when all the cottages were vacant and she was out there by herself. What little she made was barely enough to keep the electric lights on and the toilets flushing, let alone pay down the mortgage Floyd got from Mr. Johnson at the Darling Savings and Trust to build the cottages.

"A measly seventy-five cents a night is all I charge for one, plus a quarter for two," Pauline said, but folks still couldn't afford it. They'd sleep in their cars, sometimes right there in the parking lot beside the CLEAN SHEETS AND TOWELS sign.

"I'd give just about anything if Senator Huey P. Long would run for president instead of that rich man Roosevelt," Pauline had added wistfully. Many Southerners favored Long over Roosevelt, who was not only wealthy but had an aristocratic look and talked like a college man and a Northerner, to boot. Long, on the other hand, was a down-home good ol' boy. He talked just like everybody else and looked out for the people's good.

As she counted out ten ones and twenty-six cents for her property tax payment, Pauline had said, "Did you know that Senator Long is in favor of old age pensions for everybody over sixty? If I had one of *them*, I could sit back and put my feet up." She had sighed heavily. "Of course, I'd still have my swolled-up ankles, but my money troubles would be over."

Verna pulled into the motor court, parked her car, and looked around. The seven one-room frame cottages were arranged in a half-circle around the sides and back of the DuBerry house—each cottage painted a different color because Floyd had bought the paint in a closeout sale at Musgrove's Hardware. A red neon VACANCY sign blinked hopefully in Pauline's parlor window, which was also the motor court office. There was only one car in sight, a dilapidated black Model A Ford, missing both its front and back bumpers, parked in front of Cottage Two.

Verna got out of the car and hesitated a moment, wondering if she should go and look for Pauline, then decided to try the cottage first. Number Four was painted a bright lemon yellow, with orange window frames and a blue door. Pauline had carried out the color motif at the front window with yellow print curtains edged with several rows of bright orange rickrack. A battered tin water bucket planted with red and gold marigolds stood beside the door.

Verna rapped, listened intently, and rapped again, louder. There wasn't so much as a footstep inside, at least one that she could hear. She rapped a third time, much more loudly. Still no response.

Verna frowned. If Raylene Riggs was inside, she was

either asleep or sick. If she was just sleeping late, she would surely be glad to be awakened so she could get to work. If she was sick, she might need help. It was time to take some action, and Pauline would have a key. Verna turned away to go to the house, and as she did, she saw the corner of the yellow curtain twitch.

She hesitated, watching to see if the door would open after all. But it didn't. The curtain twitched again, this time decidedly, and Verna frowned. Maybe Raylene was neither asleep *nor* sick. Maybe she had decided that she didn't want to work at the diner after all and was getting ready to skip town. But Myra May was counting on Raylene and she needed to know one way or another. It wasn't fair for Raylene to simply hide out and refuse to answer the door.

Verna turned and went in search of Pauline, whom she found gathering eggs in the small chicken coop directly behind the main house. She was a plump little lady with a face as round as a melon, dressed in a faded lavender print wash dress and muslin apron, her gray hair tidied up in a hair net. She wore a pair of Floyd's old shoes. After Verna told her what was going on, she agreed, a little reluctantly, that they ought to check out the situation.

Trailed by two Barred Rock hens and a bedraggled red rooster, they went to the parlor-office, where Pauline took a ring of keys from a hook beside the front window.

"I hope there hasn't been trouble," she said, as they went down the front steps. "I had to call the sheriff a couple of days ago, y'know. There was some rowdies in Cabin Seven, liquored up and shootin' off a gun and scarin' the chickens— three of 'em, when they had only paid for two. Buddy Norris rode his motorcycle out from town and shushed 'em up good, though. And made 'em pay for the extra." She set her mouth. "What I hate is when somebody comes in and pays for one in the cabin and then he starts unloadin' the car and

I look out there and see three or four sneakin' in. Shame on 'em, is what I say. Cheatin' an old woman!"

"Are you ever afraid, out here by yourself?" Verna asked. Most older Darlingians relied on their family for help when they got to the point where they couldn't do for themselves, which was natural, because families stuck together. But Pauline didn't have a family. She was vulnerable, especially at night, with strangers in the cottages and who-knows-what-kind-of-people drinking and shooting guns around the place.

And as times got harder, people got more dangerous, it seemed, and not just in the big cities, either. In Oklahoma, a couple of tourist camps and motor courts had been robbed and people shot to death. In rural Ohio and Kentucky, Pretty Boy Floyd and his gang were shooting things up. And in little Sherman, Texas, Machine Gun Kelly's boys robbed the Central State Bank to the tune of $40,000; later, his girlfriend handed out spent shell casings as souvenirs. Even in Darling, folks were on edge, and more so in outlying areas, where the law could be miles away.

Pauline nodded, jingling the keys. "Well, yes, I'm afraid sometimes, especially with business so slow, the way it's been and me here all alone." She brightened. "But with the festival this weekend, I'm hoping for more business. And Miz Riggs, well, she's booked herself for a full week, which is good, since it means less laundry. I even gave her a free night, just four dollars and fifty cents for the week instead of five and a quarter, seein' as how she paid in advance. She seemed like a nice lady. I surely hope she's not sick or been boozin' it up all night so she can't work this mornin'." She shook her head sadly. "As I told the preacher man last Sunday, prohibition is all well and good but it don't mean a blessed thing when a person is bound, bent, and determined to drink."

Boozing. Verna frowned. She hadn't considered that possibility. Myra May's cook might be new to town, but anybody would be glad to tell her that she could get a bottle of good corn liquor from Archie Mann, at Mann's Mercantile. If Raylene Riggs had got herself so soused after her first day on the job that she couldn't get up and go to work, it didn't bode well for her future at the diner. Myra May was not a teetotaler, Verna knew. But she wouldn't put up with a cook who drank, especially with little Cupcake around.

By that time, they had reached the cottage. Pauline banged with her fist on the door and called out, "Miz Riggs! Miz Riggs, you got a friend here lookin' for you."

Nothing. Pauline banged and called again, and again.

Still nothing.

"Well, I don't usually do this," Pauline said with a sigh, "but I guess I need to find out if she's sick or drinkin'." She located the key and stuck it in the lock. "We're comin' in, Miz Riggs," she called cheerily. "Hope you're decent."

"No!" a voice cried. "I'm *not* decent! Don't come in. I—"

But it was too late. Pauline pushed the door open and went in, Verna on her heels. Pauline stopped a few paces inside the door and put her hands on her hips.

"Who the dickens are *you*?" she demanded brusquely. "You ain't Miz Riggs. And she only paid for one!"

FIFTEEN

Texas Star Kidnapped
on Eve of Air Show!

Lizzy was looking around Miss Dare's room, pondering the question of whether Mildred or Roger could have had a hand in her disappearance, when Mildred, still wearing a stunned and disbelieving expression, brought Charlie Dickens upstairs.

He stood in the open doorway, glancing around, frowning. He was dressed casually, in an open-necked blue shirt—no tie—and slacks. He looked tired and rumpled, as if he hadn't slept much, and there was a coffee stain on his shirt.

"What's going on here?" he asked. He looked at Angel Flame. "I thought you and Miss Dare wanted to get out to the airstrip early."

"We do!" Angel's voice dropped. "That is, we did. Until—" She gestured dramatically. "You can see for yourself, Mr. Dickens. She's not here. She's . . . gone!"

"Gone where?" Charlie asked, his frown deepening.

"We wish we knew!" Mildred cried, clenching her fists.

"Mr. Dickens, I promise you that the front door was locked all night long, until I unlocked it myself, first thing this morning. We're hoping you can figure it out. Please, please help us!"

Lizzy pointed to the scrap of sheer material caught on the sill. "That's her nightgown," she said. "If you'll look out the window, you can see her mule, down there on the ground."

Charlie leaned on the sill, looking out. "Her *mule*?"

"Her high-heeled slipper," Mildred explained.

"That proves it, as far as I'm concerned." Angel Flame's voice was thin and high. "She's been kidnapped! I *know* it!"

Charlie turned to Lizzy. "I thought you and Verna were supposed to keep an eye on her," he said accusingly.

"We did," Lizzy said. "Sort of, that is. Until—" She glanced at Angel Flame, then at Mildred.

Mildred got the point. "Miss Flame," she said, "let's go downstairs and get some coffee. Mr. Dickens and Miss Lacy want to talk."

"But I want to *hear*," Angel objected. She stamped her foot. "I think we ought to call the cops. We have to find out what's happened to Lily!"

"We will," Charlie replied grimly. "Just give us a few minutes to sort things out. We'll join you shortly."

Mildred led Angel, still protesting, out the door and closed it behind her.

"Now," Charlie said, scowling. "What's happened here, Liz?"

"I don't have the foggiest," Lizzy confessed. "But it was a very eventful night, believe me." Mr. Moseley had trained her to remember and report conversations in detail, since information from a client could be very important. So she told Charlie everything she could remember about the two angry encounters—Mildred and Roger, with Miss Dare—that she and Verna had overheard. She had to tell him about Roger's relationship with Miss Dare, as well as the anonymous letters and the telegrams asking for money. But at this point, breaking a confidence seemed irrelevant. She also told him about her conversation, afterward, with Miss Dare.

"She told me to get out and not to bother her again," she said, "no matter what. So even if Verna and I had heard something—an argument or noises or something like that—we probably wouldn't have rushed in here. By that time," she added, "we were feeling pretty foolish about the whole thing. And this morning, we decided we wouldn't sleep over here tonight. I'm sorry, but that's the way it is."

"I guess I can understand that," Charlie said, shaking his head over all she had told him. "But you didn't hear anything? After you talked to her for the last time, I mean. Or outside—you didn't hear a vehicle?"

"No, not a sound," Lizzy said. "Outdoors or in." She glanced around. "I know it looks like there's been a struggle, and I don't see how we missed hearing it. It should have woken us up, don't you think?"

"*If* there was a struggle," Charlie said in a skeptical tone. "But maybe there wasn't." Under his breath, he muttered, "Damn the woman, anyway."

"No struggle? What about all this?" Lizzy gestured helplessly. "Somebody knocked over all this stuff. But who? And why? I can't believe that Roger . . . or Mildred—" She stopped. "It could have been somebody from the outside, I suppose. But how did he get into the house without being heard? Did he climb up the trellis and come in through the window?"

Charlie threw out his hands. "Look, Liz, if this was anybody else but Lily Dare, I might see it differently, and I'd be the first to call in the law. But Lily—" His eyes were narrow, his voice gruff. "Do you remember what I said yester-day? She's a schemer."

Lizzy stared at him. "I don't understand." She went to the window and looked out. "Are you suggesting that she . . . she *staged* this? But why? What possible reason could she have?"

Charlie countered with his own question. "If you were sleeping in this room and somebody came in and pulled you out of bed and dragged you toward that window, you'd *yell*, wouldn't you? Especially if you knew that there were two women in the adjacent room and another right across the hall? You'd scream at the top of your lungs, wouldn't you?"

"Oh, definitely," Lizzy said hotly. "I'd not only scream, I would scratch his eyes out!"

"And if you couldn't scream—if you were gagged, say, or somebody had his hand over your mouth—you'd kick the floor. You'd make enough noise to wake the dead. Wouldn't you?"

Lizzy nodded. "Of course I would. But maybe . . ." She thought of something she had read in one of the true crime magazines Verna was always loaning her. "Maybe the kid-napper hit her over the head and knocked her out, or used chloroform or something."

"Maybe. But if she was unconscious, there wouldn't have been a struggle. We wouldn't see the furniture knocked over." Charlie went to the window. "But more important, Liz, just how do you think a kidnapper is going to get an unconscious woman out of this window? Is he going to *throw* her out? Let's reconstruct this—hypothetically, that is."

Doubtfully, Lizzy looked out the window. It was only a ten-foot drop. "Maybe he lowered her?" she suggested. "By her arms, I mean. She's not a very big woman. Around 120 pounds, maybe."

"Possible, I grant you. But if she's unconscious, she's a

dead weight. The kidnapper would have to be strong enough, which lets out quite a few candidates. Angel Flame couldn't have done it, for instance."

"Angel?" Lizzy asked, puzzled. "Why would she—"

But Charlie was going on with his hypothetical reconstruction. "So this muscular kidnapper has lowered an unconscious Lily to the ground. And then what? Does he drag her into a waiting vehicle which is parked out front—and which nobody heard? I don't think so, Liz." He paused. "And who would have done this, anyway? Not Roger, although he might be strong enough. This is *his* house. He'd be at the top of the suspect list. And if he were going to kidnap her, there'd be none of this window nonsense. He'd take her out the front door."

"The same goes for Mildred," Lizzy said thoughtfully. "She would never have wanted Miss Dare to disappear from *her* house. If nothing else, it's a huge embarrassment." She considered for a moment. "How about Rex Hart? I know that you've been suspicious of him."

Charlie chuckled shortly. "Where do you think I've been all night? I was in the shed at the airstrip, keeping an eye on those planes—and on Hart. I wanted to make sure he didn't have a chance to try any dirty tricks with Lily's plane. He could have been behind the earlier sabotage, but I can swear that he didn't leave the shed all night long. Same with the rest of the crew—the three guys who drove in yesterday afternoon in an old rattletrap truck."

"I see," Lizzy said.

"Right. So who are we looking for? Some mystery man—a strong guy—who has never shown his hand until now?" He shook his head. "Uh-uh, Liz. I don't think anybody else was in this room after you left it last night. I think this is one of Lily Dare's damned cockamamie schemes."

"I see what you're saying," Lizzy said. She looked around

the room. "Which means that she did all this herself. She turned the furniture over—"

"Quietly," Charlie put in, "so you and Verna wouldn't come running over here and stop her."

"Turned the furniture over quietly," Lizzy continued. "She had to get dressed, because she wouldn't want to go wandering around Darling in her nightgown. She ripped a piece off her nightgown and snagged it on the windowsill. And tossed her mule onto the ground and then climbed out the window and down the trellis. And she took her handbag."

"Her handbag?" Charlie asked.

"Yes." Lizzy went to the dresser. "It was right *here*, Charlie. A big leather handbag. I saw her take a cigar out of it. A woman would never go anywhere without her handbag—it has her wallet in it, her identification, her money, her smokes, everything. But a kidnapper likely wouldn't think about such a thing. He wouldn't *need* it, so he wouldn't bother with it. He'd be too busy trying to handle her."

"Ah," Charlie said, nodding. "Of course, Liz. You're right. It's something a man wouldn't even think of."

"But that doesn't answer the central question," Lizzy replied. "Where did she go in the middle of the night? And *why*?"

"I have no idea," Charlie replied. "You said that both of the arguments last night were pretty awful. Some harsh words were said, punches thrown. Maybe she just couldn't face Mildred or Roger this morning. Couldn't look them in the eye—especially if theirs were as black as hers." He shook his head. "So she skipped. Classic Lily Dare behavior."

"Maybe, but . . . Hang on a minute, Charlie." Lizzy frowned, concentrating, trying to remember. "Miss Dare said something last night, as I was leaving the room. I asked her if she had any idea who might have written the letters to

Mildred or sent those telegrams asking for money. She said she was ninety-nine percent sure that she knew who did it. Then she said she intended to 'settle some hash' over it. She sounded pretty angry, too."

Charlie nodded approvingly. "Sounds like Lily. She's got some sort of plan."

"Maybe," Lizzy replied. "But that doesn't explain the faked struggle."

"Right." Charlie pushed his lips in and out. "If you ask me, she's playing for attention. Lily likes to be the star of the show. Something as dramatic as this—" He shrugged. "It would suit her. She's always playing for attention, you know, with that airplane and those aerial stunts. A promoter. A *self*-promoter. She can probably read the headlines in her mind: *Texas Star Kidnapped on Eve of Air Show!*"

"You've convinced me," Lizzy said. "But you have to convince Angel Flame. She's ready to phone the sheriff's office. Now that we've come to this conclusion, it doesn't seem like a very good idea—to me, anyway. I don't want to answer questions about Roger Kilgore and Miss Dare. There are some things that are better kept private."

"Well, maybe," Charlie said. "But blackmail is a crime, you know, and so is extortion. And it may have escalated into something else—like that sabotage."

Lizzy crinkled her nose. "You're thinking that the same person—"

"I am. But I agree that we don't want the sheriff asking questions." Charlie started for the door. "Come on. We'd better get downstairs and make sure that nobody makes that phone call."

But they were too late. As they came down the stairs, Deputy Buddy Norris was knocking at the front door in response to a telephone call from Angel Flame, which she'd made over Mildred's strenuous objections.

"It's Miss Dare!" Angel informed him excitedly. "She's been kidnapped!"

"The Texas Star, kidnapped?" Buddy was incredulous. "Here in little ol' *Darlin'*?"

"Yes, oh, yes!" Angel grabbed Buddy's arm. The freckles were standing out all over her pale face. "Please, Buddy! You've *got* to find Lily—before something terrible happens to her!"

SIXTEEN

"Hearts Full of Passion..."

Verna looked over Pauline DuBerry's shoulder. The motor court cottage was dim, since the cotton curtain was drawn across the only window. But enough daylight filtered into the small, low-ceilinged room to see that the walls were painted a dirty gray and the floor was covered with green linoleum. The furnishings were spartan: a pine chest of drawers with a wall mirror over it, a wooden straight chair, and two narrow single beds with a lamp table and a lamp between them. Both beds were unmade, and a dark-haired, good-looking woman was sitting on one of them, wearing a peach-colored, lace-trimmed nightgown with a raggedly torn hem. Her hair was mussed from sleep and her left eye was purpled and puffy. She was smoking a small cigar.

"I said, 'I'm not decent,'" the woman said in a testy voice. "I'm not dressed for company."

"And I'm askin', who the dickens are you?" Pauline

DuBerry repeated sternly, hands on hips. "Miz Riggs paid for one. If there's goin' to be two of you sleepin' in this cottage, she's goin' to have to pay for two. Means more laundry, you know. Bed sheets and towels gotta be washed."

"Don't nag, I'll pay," the woman said, reaching for her leather handbag. "And Raylene didn't invite me, so don't be mad at her. I knocked on her door in the middle of the night, looking for a place to stay, and she was sweet enough to let me in. How much do I owe you?" She put her cigar in the ashtray and took out her wallet. "And while we're at it, could I book a cottage for myself? I'd like it for tonight and Saturday night."

"Oh, well," Pauline said, mollified. "If you're bookin' for you, we'll just forget last night. A dollar fifty. Seventy-five cents a night for two nights."

"Here's two dollars," the woman said, and handed over the bills. "Keep the change."

"Why, thank you." Pauline smiled as she tucked the money into her apron pocket. "Stop by the office and get a key. I'll put you in Number Five. The one with the red door." She opened the door, then turned back. "If you want something for that shiner, I can brew up some sage tea and make you a compress. That's what my mama did for us kids when we was little. Works, too."

"Thanks," the woman said, and put her handbag on the floor beside her. "Maybe later. I have some things to do this morning."

"Later will be too late," Pauline cautioned. "Black eyes— you gotta get to 'em quick, or they'll be around for a while."

"I'll risk it," the woman said.

Pauline shrugged and left but Verna stayed behind, now very puzzled. "Miss Lily Dare?" she asked tentatively. The cigar, the black eye, the sheer peach negligee—it had to be her, although as far as she knew, Miss Dare was either still asleep in Mildred Kilgore's guest bedroom or sitting at Mildred's breakfast table. So what was she doing *here?*

"I don't think we've met," the woman said coolly. She picked up her cigar, saw that it had gone out, and laid it back in the ashtray. "Yeah, I'm Lily Dare. How'd you know? And just who the devil are *you?*"

"Er, ah . . ." Verna was almost never at a loss for words, but she was now. She didn't want to confess that she had been playing amateur detective the night before and had intentionally eavesdropped on the unpleasant conversations in Miss Dare's room. She doubted that Agatha Christie had ever let Miss Marple get cornered in such a sticky wicket.

"I . . . I was at the movie last night and somebody pointed you out," she lied. "*Hell's Angels.* That was a *really* good flick—loved that air combat. I heard you were staying at the Kilgores', so I'm a little surprised to see you here."

"I *was* staying at the Kilgores'," Miss Dare said. "In fact, I was invited to spend the weekend. But I changed my mind. I'm staying here." She gave Verna a pointed look. "Just what did you say your name was?"

Verna stared at the woman, thinking that she had to have left the Kilgores' *after* Liz talked to her—and how did she get all the way out to the Marigold Motor Court in the middle of the night? It must be at least a mile. Had she *walked?* In that see-through negligee she was wearing?

"Your *name?*" Miss Dare asked again.

"Oh, sorry," Verna replied hastily. "I'm Verna Tidwell. Actually, I came here looking for Raylene Riggs. She didn't show up at work this morning, and Miss Mosswell, her boss at the diner, is worried about her."

Miss Dare got up and went to the mirror over the dresser,

touching her eye tenderly. "Raylene is on her way to work. We were up kind of late talking and we both overslept. But she got a lift into town. She should be at work by now." She leaned toward the mirror, peering at her reflection. "Does this eye look very bad to you?"

"Not too bad," Verna said diplomatically. She paused. "How did it happen?"

"I walked into a door," Miss Dare said in a bored voice.

Oh, right, Verna thought sarcastically. More like Mildred's fist.

Miss Dare opened her handbag and took out a little jar, deftly applying something to her face. She regarded herself in the mirror, added a few touchups, then turned around. "There. Does that look better?"

"Oh, much," Verna said, although the black eye was still quite noticeable. She was dying to ask Miss Dare how in the world she got here, to the motor court, and *why.* But she couldn't think of a way to do it.

"Good." Miss Dare took a comb out of her bag and began to work on her hair. "I've got a party to go to tonight, and I don't want to look like I've been trading punches with the local heavyweight. Say, Verna, I need to get out to the airstrip this morning. Does this burg have a taxi?"

"Not really," Verna said, suppressing a smile. "That is, it does . . . I mean, we do. But Mr. Clinton mostly goes between Darling and Monroeville, and the airstrip is out of his way." She added, deferentially, "I could drive you out to the airstrip, Miss Dare. I have my car here."

"Oh, would you, dear?" Miss Dare asked warmly. "Please call me Lily." She picked up a small canvas bag. "I'll get dressed—it'll just take a jiffy—and then go pick up my key at the office. I'm glad I came," she added confidentially, as she headed for the bathroom. "This place may not be fancy, but it's clean and private. And I can lock the door and keep folks from barging in on me."

I can lock the door. Verna flinched, remembering her own role in the invasion of Lily Dare's privacy. Did she leave because she knew that people could overhear every word that was said in her room? Or was there some other reason? If so, could she get Lily to tell her what it was?

Maybe, maybe not. But Verna vowed to give it her best shot.

It was over an hour later when Verna pulled her LaSalle into a parking place in front of the courthouse, next to Judge McHenry's old gray Buick. The judge's bluetick coonhound, Buck, was sitting erect behind the steering wheel. He barked cheerfully at Verna when he recognized her—Buck was a frequent visitor to the courthouse and remembered Verna, who always scratched his ears.

She knew she ought to run up to the office and check on Melba Jean and Ruthie. But she had something else on her mind, so she went straight across the street to the diner, where she found Myra May wrapping silverware in paper napkins for the noon rush. It looked as if peace and sanity had finally been restored. The morning crowd was gone, the tables were empty, and Rudy Vallee was crooning (on the Philco) "As Time Goes By," one of Verna's favorite songs. "Hearts full of passion, jealousy and hate . . ." Somehow, it seemed apropos to what she had just heard from Lily Dare.

"Did Raylene make it to work okay?" Verna asked. "She had already left by the time I got out to the Marigold. Her roommate told me she got a lift into town."

"Yes, she got here," Myra May said, "and we were plenty relieved. She's back there in the kitchen right now, working on the food for the noon crowd. After lunch, we're going out to the Kilgores' and get started on the party stuff." She picked up the coffeepot. "Coffee? You got out of here earlier without a full cup. We owe you."

"Just what I need," Verna said gratefully, sliding onto a counter stool.

Myra May filled a mug and pushed it across the counter. "Raylene's got a roommate?" she asked with a curious, sidelong look. "She didn't mention it to me."

"It was a one-night thing," Verna said, and then, when both of Myra May's eyebrows went up, added, "A woman she's known for several years. An old friend."

Myra May's eyebrows went back down. "Ah," she said.

Verna added sugar to her coffee and stirred. "Myra May, would it be okay if I had a talk with Raylene? Something . . . well, puzzling has come up. Disturbing, actually. I think she may be able to shed some light."

"She's pretty busy right now," Myra May said doubtfully. "Could you maybe do it after the party?"

"That could be too late," Verna said. "Or maybe not. The thing is, I just don't know. Maybe it can wait, or maybe not. It all depends on—"

The diner door popped open and Liz rushed in. "Verna!" she cried excitedly. "I went up to your office and Melba Jean told me you were out this morning. And then I saw your car and I thought you might be here. I'm *so* glad I found you!" She gulped a breath. "You will never guess what's happened!"

"Oh, I think I can," Verna said. "Lily Dare disappeared from her room sometime after you left her last night. You don't know where she is and everybody's looking all over for her. You want me to help."

Liz stared at her, uncomprehending. "Yes, but how did you know? How *could* you know, Verna? You left the

Kilgores' before Mildred and Angel Flame and I discovered that she was gone!"

"I'm psychic," Verna said with a smug chuckle. She sipped her coffee.

"Ha!" Myra May hooted. "Verna, you are the most un-psychic person I know." She leaned her elbows on the counter and turned serious. "Raylene Riggs, on the other hand, is *really* psychic. She knows what people want to eat, she knows things that are going to happen, she even knows—"

"Excuse me, Myra May," Liz said impatiently. "I'm sorry for interrupting, but this is important." She sat down on a counter stool beside Verna. "Verna, you are *not* psychic, and if you were, you would never in the world admit to it. Now you tell me. How did you know Miss Dare has disappeared?"

Verna picked up her coffee cup and took a sip. "Because I found her," she said calmly.

"You *found* her?" Liz leaned forward, her eyes widening. "Is she okay? Where *is* she? How did she get there? Why did she—"

Verna held up her hand, damming the flow of Liz's words. "Yes, she's okay. Right now, she's out at the airstrip. I drove her out there just a little while ago. As to why, that's a long story." She put her cup down. "Oh, by the way, Liz. I stopped at the fairgrounds on my way back to town. You'll be glad to know that the carnival got in last night. They're setting up this morning. The rides look as if they're in pretty good repair and the sideshows actually look decent for a change. The Masons are putting up the tents for the exhibits. I think we're in pretty good shape for the festival weekend." She paused. "As for the air show, well, that's something else. We need to talk about that."

"But I want to talk about Miss Dare!" Liz exclaimed. "I want to know why she—"

Myra May picked up the coffeepot again. "Liz, you sound like you could use a cup of coffee, on the house. How about it?"

"Yes, thanks. But I want—" Liz broke off. "*Where*, Verna?" she asked urgently. "Where did you find her?"

But before Verna could answer her question, there was another interruption.

"Hi," a voice said, and a woman came out of the kitchen, drying her hands on a towel. She was Myra May's height, and her auburn hair, gray-streaked, was cut short and curled around her ears. She was wearing a white cook's apron over a red print dress.

"Somebody's wanting to talk to me?" she asked in her soft Southern voice. To Myra May, she added, "I just finished putting three pecan pies and two pans of meat loaf in the oven. The potatoes and eggs are cooked for potato salad, so all we have to do is chop the celery, onions, and pickles and put it together." She hung up the towel. "I'm ready to take a little break."

"There," Myra May said with satisfaction, and poured Liz's coffee. "You see? Violet and I have decided that Raylene is positively psychic. Nobody told her that you two were out here, wanting to talk to her. She just *knew*. Same way she knew that Donna Sue was dreaming of her mother's grits and sausage casserole and that J.D. wanted some sweet potato meringue pie. It's a gift she has."

"Well, now that she's here and ready to take a break," Verna said, "is it okay if we talk to her?"

Myra May rolled her eyes. "Who am I to say no?" She muttered an answer to her own question. "Just the boss, that's all." She picked up a mug and poured coffee for

Raylene. "Sure. Go ahead and take a break. And take those leftover doughnuts with you. But maybe you'd better go over to that back table, in case somebody comes in." She turned away. "You want me, I'm in the kitchen."

Raylene put three doughnuts on a plate and led them, coffee mugs in hand, to the back table. They took seats under the Ferguson Tractor Company calendar from the feed store. As they sat down, Verna introduced herself to Raylene.

"I came in here for breakfast this morning," she went on. "I happened to have my car, so when Myra May said you were late for work, I volunteered to drive out to the motor court and check on you. I didn't get an answer when I knocked on the door of your cottage, but I saw the curtain twitch so I knew someone was inside. I got Pauline DuBerry to bring the key and—"

"And you found Lily." Raylene smiled. "You must have been surprised. Did you wake her? We stayed up and talked pretty late. She said she was going to sleep late this morning."

"Lily? Lily Dare?" Liz exclaimed excitedly, and the questions began to spill out. "She's at the Marigold? So *that's* where she went! But why? And how did she get there? The motor court is a good mile from the Kilgores'. She's never been to Darling, and it was dark. How come she didn't get lost?"

"She walked," Raylene replied. "Walking a mile isn't any big challenge for Lily. She's always liked to stay in shape— says she couldn't fly if she didn't have plenty of physical stamina. And when she's up in the air, she often has to find her way by flying along roads and railroads in marginal conditions, so she's always mentally storing away information. She knew where the motor court was because she noticed it when Mr. Dickens drove her into town. And I happened to mention it to her when she was here for lunch yesterday. It wasn't hard for her to figure out how to get there."

As Raylene talked, Verna thought that there was something familiar about the strong set of her jaw—or maybe it was her penetrating gaze, the way she held your eyes and didn't let you look away. Had she met this woman somewhere before? But the impression was fleeting, and the question was gone almost as soon as it occurred to her.

"Oh, and the moon was out last night, you know," Raylene added, picking up a doughnut. "Lily said it was almost as bright as day."

"I take it that she didn't walk that mile in her negligee, barefoot," Verna remarked dryly. "Especially with the moon as bright as it was." She reached into her handbag and took out a pack of cigarettes, offering one to Raylene.

Raylene shook her head. "No, thanks. No, Lily was fully dressed—pants, shirt, the clothes she wears when she's working around the airplanes. She brought her nightie in her bag." She turned to Liz. "You'll remember that I saw you and Lily here yesterday, after lunch, Liz. That's when I invited her to drop in and see me at the motor court while she was here in Darling."

"Yes, but in the middle of the night?" Liz asked, taking a doughnut.

Raylene laughed. "It was a bit of a surprise when she knocked on the door and woke me up, I'll admit. But Lily has always been . . . well, impulsive." She tilted her head to one side. "And unpredictable. She's like a kid that way. There's no daylight between her idea and her doing. She gets herself in trouble sometimes, not thinking things through." She said the last sentence regretfully and in a lower voice, almost as if she were talking to herself. "I'm not being critical," she added, biting into her doughnut. "That's just Lily. It's the way she is."

"But I still don't understand why she felt she had to leave the Kilgores'," Liz protested, looking from one of them to the other. "Especially the way she did it."

"I can answer part of that." Verna flicked a match to her cigarette. "We talked when we were driving out to the airfield. She told me she didn't want to face Roger and Mildred across the breakfast table. She knew they would all three have matching black eyes and it would be just too embarrassing. And she was very upset at the idea that somebody— I'm afraid she was talking about you, Liz—was in the next room. She's going to be staying at the motor court, where she can have some privacy."

"You were there, too," Liz said accusingly. "You were listening right along with me."

"I know." Verna sighed, feeling guilty. "But she didn't know about *me*. I was trying to get her to talk to me and I didn't think she'd want to if I told her that part of it. So I let you take the blame. Sorry about that."

"Thanks," Liz muttered dryly, and sipped her coffee.

Raylene sat forward on the edge of her chair. "How much of the rest of it did Lily tell you, Verna? Did she say anything about her . . . suspicions?"

"Well, some," Verna said. "But I have no way of knowing if she told me everything." She tapped her cigarette into the Darling Savings and Trust Bank ashtray on the table. "And of course, I can't guarantee that what she was telling me was the truth." She glanced at Raylene. "That's what I hoped you could help with. Figuring out how much of what she says is true."

"Yeah." Raylene finished her doughnut, licked powdered sugar off her fingers, and leaned back in her chair. "With Lily, it's hard to sort the truth from . . . well, the stories. She loves drama. She loves anything exciting—which is why she loves flying. She invents. And sometimes she gets carried away with her invention, to the point where she's not sure about the difference between it and the truth."

"Well, I for one would sure like to know why she invented an *abduction*," Liz said testily. "She could have sneaked down the stairs and gone out the front door without overturning the furniture and snagging her nightgown on the sill and throwing her slipper out the second-story window, all of which made us think that somebody carried her off." She crossed her arms on the table and looked at Verna. "Did she tell you about that?"

Verna nodded. "I'm not sure she was thinking straight when she was doing all that. She said that by the time she got to the motor court, she wished she'd just walked out and left a note. But she was scared."

"Scared?" Liz asked, frowning. "Scared of what?"

"Scared of *who* is more like it," Verna replied. She turned to Raylene, who was listening intently. "But you probably know more about that than either of us, Raylene. That was *really* why she came to your place, wasn't it?"

"Yes," Raylene acknowledged. "She came to me because the more she thought about it, the more afraid she got. She thought she needed a friend. Somebody she could talk to—and trust. And she didn't trust anybody in the Kilgores' house." She looked at Verna with that penetrating gaze. "She told you that?"

"Some of it," Verna said slowly. "It was the anonymous letters and the photograph that scared her. And Mildred's charge that she—Lily, I mean—was blackmailing Roger. Finding out about that stuff really frightened her. It made her feel vulnerable."

Raylene looked from Verna to Liz. "So both of you know about the letters and the telegrams?"

"Yes," Liz said. She picked up her coffee cup. "Mildred told me a couple of days ago—in fact, she showed me the second letter and the incriminating photograph. And I told Verna."

"And we both overheard Mildred accusing Miss Dare of sending the telegrams," Verna said. "Of blackmail."

"*Extortion* would be a better way to describe it," Liz added, sipping coffee.

"Extortion, yes," Raylene said, shaking her head. "An ugly word. She swears she had nothing to do with that and hates it that Roger Kilgore thought those telegrams came from her—that she was asking for money. She's sorry she let herself get into a relationship with him and she says she's going to break it off permanently. But the letters and those telegrams—together with the sabotage—have convinced her that somebody's out to get her."

Verna nodded. They were getting to the heart of it now. "But if you ask me," she said, "it was when she figured out *who* sent those letters and the telegram and connected it to the sabotage of her airplane—that was when she got scared." She looked at Raylene. "Did she tell you who she suspects?"

"Yes," Raylene said slowly. "But I . . ." She stopped.

"Well, who?" Liz demanded eagerly. "Come on, Verna, *who*?"

"Rex Hart," Verna replied.

"Rex Hart?" Liz frowned. "But Charlie Dickens said that he couldn't have been involved. He was at the airstrip all night." Her frown deepened. "No, wait. That's not right. Charlie was talking about the abduction, not the letters or the telegrams. Or the sabotage."

Verna looked at Raylene. When she didn't say anything, she said, "Lily has decided that it's Rex Hart who sent the letters. He was in New Orleans when the photograph was taken. He wasn't with them at the café—Lily and Roger, that is—but she knew that he was nearby. She believes that he took the photo and wrote the letters to Mildred. *And* sent the telegrams to Roger."

"Why?" Liz asked, puzzled. "I mean, why did he do it? What was his motivation?"

"She thinks it's because he's jealous," Verna replied. "Because he's in love with her himself. He figured he could convince Roger that the relationship with Lily was too costly— and too dangerous—to pursue. That it could wreck his marriage, and maybe his business. She says Hart wrote the letters to Roger's wife so she would pressure Roger to break it off."

"It makes sense, I guess," Liz said slowly. "But what about the sabotage? Is that his work, too?"

"That's what Lily says." Verna frowned. "I could understand the letters and telegrams, but that's where I lose it. I mean, if Rex Hart loves Lily enough to be jealous of her other relationships, why would he sabotage her aircraft? If he loves her, he wouldn't try to *kill* her, would he? And there's the damage to the show, in which he has a financial investment." She turned to Raylene. "That was what I wanted to ask you, Raylene. Lily said that you and she met in Tampa several years ago, when your husband was taking flying lessons from Rex Hart. You know both Lily and Hart. Is she right about him?"

For a long moment, Raylene didn't answer. At last, she countered with her own question. "Let me ask you this. If Rex Hart is in love with Lily, why doesn't he just tell her so? He's a grown-up and so is she. Nothing is standing in their way."

Verna raised a surprised eyebrow at her. "You mean, he *hasn't*? From the way Lily talked, I thought he'd told her he loved her—maybe even asked her to marry him—and she turned him down. I got the impression that he's a disappointed lover trying to get even."

Raylene shook her head emphatically. "He isn't. In fact, I happen to know that Rex is seriously involved with somebody else."

Verna was surprised. "Oh, really? Who?"

"A young woman in Tampa, named Sarah. She and Rex have known one another for several years, although they only got together about six months ago. The two of them have kept it secret because of Sarah's mother, who's terminally ill. And because Lily is . . . well, possessive about the members of her team. If she knew about Rex and Sarah, she might—" She shrugged. "Who knows?"

"Ah," Verna said.

Raylene nodded. "Anyway, they're keeping it to themselves, which is one reason why Lily can persuade herself that Rex is in love with *her*. Although she can persuade herself of that sort of thing pretty easily," she added with a small smile.

Liz leaned forward. "But if this love affair is such a big secret, how do *you* know about it, Raylene? Did Sarah or Rex tell you?"

Raylene bit her lip and her glance slid away. There was an uncomfortable silence.

"They didn't tell you," Liz said at last. She looked squarely at Raylene. Myra May is right, isn't she? You know because you're psychic. Isn't that right?"

Raylene sighed. "I don't like to make a big point of it," she said at last. "It's relatively easy when it comes to knowing what people want—like Lily's pulled pork sandwich, or your friend's sausage and grits casserole. When somebody wants something, there's always a great deal of . . . well, energy around the wanting. So it's easy to get the message— sort of like turning on a radio, to a station that comes through loud and clear."

"I suppose it works better with a Ouija board," Verna remarked ironically.

"Yes, sometimes." Raylene smiled. "It's okay to be skeptical about it, Verna." She spoke as if she understood Verna's feelings. "Lots of people don't understand how it works. Lots more don't believe—or don't want to, which amounts to the same thing. And even psychics themselves aren't always very happy with it."

Liz cleared her throat. "But if you know what somebody like Donna Sue wants to eat for breakfast, surely you know who wrote the letters and sent the telegrams." She paused, then added, "And who sabotaged Lily's airplane."

"Yeah." Verna chuckled dryly. "Why are we sitting around wondering who's behind all of this? Why don't you just tell us, Raylene? Let us in on the secret?"

"Verna, please." Liz put her hand on Verna's arm. "Let's just . . . listen. Okay?" To Raylene, she said, "Please, tell us whatever you think we ought to know so we can help to get this all cleared up."

Raylene hesitated. "Well, it's complicated," she said, after a moment. "There are some things I know for sure. The easy things that people want you to know, or have no special reason to hide. But other things . . . well, they're not so easy. This business we're talking about, the letters and the telegrams and the sabotage—somebody is trying to hide what's going on. There's a lot of conflict, even guilt. The energies are all confused and contradictory. It's like static on a radio. And remember that I heard about all this for the first time last night, from Lily—who is blaming Rex Hart for everything."

Verna stared at Raylene, wanting to flatly refuse to give any credence to such out-and-out nonsense but at the same time, feeling an odd desire to hear more.

Liz was nodding. "Yes, I can see that," she said. "It's all very complex. Lots of layers. It would take a while to get to the truth."

Raylene leaned forward. "But I am sure of what I know about Rex Hart and Sarah. I know why they haven't told Lily. And since I know that much, I have to question what Lily says. If Rex isn't in love with her, he has no reason to be jealous. No motive for writing anonymous letters or sending telegrams asking for money."

Hearts full of passion, jealousy and hate, Verna thought. If there was no passion, then there'd be no jealousy—or hate. Right?

Liz sighed. "Which leaves us with the big question, doesn't it?"

"Yes," Verna said. "If Rex Hart didn't do it, who did? Who cares enough to do things like that?"

With a thoughtful expression, Raylene turned her coffee mug in her fingers. "Let me tell you a little story. Before Mabel Hopkins joined the flying team—"

"Mabel Hopkins?" Verna interrupted.

"That's Angel Flame's real name," Liz told her. "I guess she thought she needed a more exotic name, as a performer."

"I can understand that," Verna muttered. "'Mabel Hopkins' Dive of Death' sounds like a joke, not an aerial stunt."

"Before Mabel joined the team," Raylene went on, "Lily and Rex worked with another aerialist, a young woman named Bess. She was very good, one of the best, Rex used to say. She was strong, with excellent coordination, and she'd trained as a trapeze artist in the circus. She had no fear, so wingwalking was easy for her."

"I heard Miss Dare telling Charlie Dickens about her," Liz said. "But she had an accident and had to quit, didn't she?"

"She had an accident and *died*," Raylene said gravely. "They were doing an air show in Tampa. Bess was hanging from a trapeze under Lily's plane during one of the stunts. One side of the trapeze broke loose from the plane and she fell to the ground. She was killed instantly."

"Oh, dear," Liz said. Her hand went to her mouth.

"It's a hazardous profession," Verna said. "The fatality rate must be pretty high. But I don't see—"

"Bess was Mabel's sister," Raylene said. "Mabel was in the crowd, watching, when the trapeze let go and Bess fell."

There was a silence. After a moment, Liz said, very slowly, "Are you suggesting that Angel Flame—Mabel—could be responsible for the letters and the telegrams?"

"She certainly has a motive," Raylene said. "When the accident first happened, Mabel was distraught, understandably. I was in the crowd, too. I heard her say that Lily was responsible for what happened—that she didn't maintain the equipment the way she should. That's why I was surprised when I heard, a couple of months later, that Mabel had taken her sister's place as an aerialist for the team." She smiled. "You see? Even psychics don't know everything."

"She could do the work?" Verna asked in surprise. "Wingwalking seems . . . specialized."

"Mabel and Bess had worked together as trapeze artists in a Florida-based circus," Raylene said. "And she was always out at the airfield when her sister was practicing. I don't suppose that part of it was hard for her. But flying with Lily—"

"That must have been hard," Liz said, shaking her head. "I wonder how she could do it."

Raylene nodded. "Anyway, as Lily was telling me about the letters and telegrams, I got the feeling—" She broke off, glancing almost apologetically at Verna. "I got the very strong feeling that Mabel was behind it. I didn't want to say anything to Lily—and anyway, she wouldn't believe me. She was focused on Rex Hart." She turned to Liz. "Is there anything you and Verna can do to help straighten this out?"

"I don't know what we could do," Liz said helplessly. "We don't know everyone involved and we—"

But Verna's mind was already racing through the possibilities. "Wait, Liz," she said. "Let's think about this for a minute. There might be a way."

Raylene pushed back her chair. "If you can help, I'd be grateful," she said. "I don't blame Lily for being afraid. If I were in her shoes, I'd feel that way, too." She stood up and smiled down at them. "Myra May is going to start yelling at me any minute now. I'd better get back to work."

She had walked no more than a few paces when Myra May stuck her head out of the kitchen and called "Raylene! Hey, Raylene, we need you back here."

Liz nudged Verna. "See?" she whispered. "Psychic." Verna rolled her eyes and Liz laughed. "Okay, Verna," she said. "Let's hear it."

In a low voice, Verna told Liz what she had in mind.

Liz listened, frowning a little. "I don't know," she said slowly. "Do you really think she'll go for it?"

"Have you got a better idea?" Verna countered.

"I'm fresh out," Liz confessed. "I'm not sure yours will work, Verna, but we don't have a lot of choices. I guess we ought to give it a try. Where do we start? And when?"

"We have to start with Mildred," Verna said. "And the sooner, the better." She pushed her chair back and stood up. "Come on. Let's go."

They took their cups to the counter and said good-bye to Myra May, who was filling catsup bottles. As they went out the door, Verna found herself humming, *"Hearts full of passion, jealousy and hate . . ."*

As they went out on the square, they heard the clattering,

metallic thunder of an airplane engine. They looked up and instinctively ducked, for the plane seemed to be coming straight at them along Robert E. Lee, not a hundred feet above the buildings and trees. As it came closer, Darling citizens spilled out of their houses, offices, and shops onto the street. Men stamped and whistled, women gasped, girls shrieked, boys shouted, dogs barked, pigeons and blackbirds squawked and fluttered, horns blared. Down the street, hitched to the rail in front of Hancock's Grocery, Leroy Whittle's old white mare Dolly reared up, whinnying and pawing the air with her forelegs more wildly than she ever had in her filly days. Mr. Whittle barreled out of the store and grabbed Dolly's bridle to calm her down. He raised his fist at the sky and yelled, "Dad-blasted airplanes! You got the sense of a goose, flyin' into town and scarin' the horses! Whoa there, Dolly. *Whoa, you old nag!*"

The airplane was towing a large red and white advertising banner that screamed: *Sky Rides TODAY.* And perched on the top wing of the bi-plane, in a red bathing suit that bared her long legs and revealed other attention-getting attributes, was Angel Flame. As Verna and Lizzy watched, she began throwing handfuls of white cards into the air. They fluttered down like small white birds. One fell at Verna's feet and she stooped to pick it up.

"*Write your name on this card,*" she read aloud, "*and deposit it in the basket at Kilgore's Motors for the drawing, 3:30 p.m. Sunday. Winner receives one free airplane ride after the show.*"

"Clever advertising," Liz remarked admiringly, still following the flight of the plane as it swooped overhead. "A good way to get people to pay to come to the show."

Behind them, Mr. Musgrove had come out of the hardware store and was peering nearsightedly into the sky. "I'll be dad-blamed," he muttered, under his breath. "That woman up there, she's near naked! She better watch out. She'll get sunburnt."

At that moment, the airplane made a sweeping turn and began another earsplitting pass over the street. On the ground, there was more stamping, whistling, gasping, shrieking, shouting, barking, squawking, honking, and whinnying.

And high in the air, on the wing of the airplane, Angel Flame did a handstand.

SEVENTEEN

Who Is Raylene Riggs?

During the past few days, Myra May and Violet had gone over the party menu several times, with Mildred's caution in mind: "Please be thrifty. I've got to cut every corner I can."

In the end, they had agreed on a light buffet supper: sausage puffs; slivers of ham with slices of fresh cucumber on buttermilk-cheese biscuits the size of silver dollars; finger sandwiches in three shapes, made with a variety of fillings; small tomatoes stuffed with chicken salad and topped with sprigs of mint; deviled eggs; Southern banana pudding with whipped cream; and watermelon and cantaloupe cubes. When Raylene looked at the menu, she suggested that they add a cheese custard pie with onions and sausage.

"Custard pie with . . . *cheese?*" Violet had asked dubiously. "Never heard of it."

"I saw it in a cookbook called *The Joy of Cooking,* by Irma Rombauer," Raylene said. "It's a book she published herself, a couple of years ago. The recipe uses lots of eggs, which are cheap, and you can scrimp a bit on the cheese if you add more eggs. My version includes onions and sausage and a few herbs. Oh, and you can make it ahead and serve it warm or cold."

"Well, I guess we can give it a try," Myra May said. Armed with the shopping list, she went down the block to consult with Mrs. Hancock, who had ordered what she didn't already have in stock—for example, two boxes of vanilla wafers for the banana pudding and extra bread and fresh buttermilk.

On Thursday night, after the diner closed, Myra May and Violet stayed up late, boiling eggs, slicing ham, baking cheese biscuits, and making sandwich fillings. On Friday, as soon as the noon lunch crowd left, Myra May and Violet put all the prepared food and groceries into big baskets, which they loaded into Myra May's Chevy touring car, Big Bertha. Bertha was a genuine antique but was still bravely running. (Just in case, Myra May always said a fervent "Bless your heart, Bertha," every time she turned the key in the ignition and patted the dashboard affectionately when Bertha coughed into life.) Violet was staying behind at the diner with a cook who was coming in to try out for part-time work.

Myra May and Raylene drove Bertha, fully loaded, out to the Kilgores' house. They planned to assemble and prepare everything in Mildred's kitchen, add the finishing touches, and be ready to serve to the guests around eight o'clock that night.

At the Kilgores', Myra May pulled around the back and parked near the kitchen door so they could start unloading. When Mildred came out to give them a hand, Myra May was a little startled to see that her friend's eye was purple and puffy. She thought about making a joke out of it

("What does the other person look like?") but she didn't want to hurt Mildred's feelings, so she didn't.

"I'm glad to see you two," Mildred said, taking the small basket Myra May handed her. "Things were a little chaotic this morning, but we're back to normal now, more or less. I think everything is all set for tonight—except for the food, of course." She called to the two neatly uniformed colored girls from the Darling Academy that she had hired for the day and evening. "Girls, come and help carry this stuff to the kitchen."

With everyone's help, they made quick work of unloading the car. In the spacious, fully modern kitchen, Myra May and Raylene put on their aprons and began organizing their team of helpers for the greatest efficiency. As they worked, Myra May was delighted with Raylene's proficiency in handling a large party prep, which she chalked up to her experience in a hotel kitchen. She wondered once again why a woman with Raylene's skill and talent would want to bury herself in the small town of Darling. Surely there was a mystery here.

Myra May was also mystified by the obviously serious conversation that Raylene had had with Verna and Liz at the diner that morning. But she couldn't think of a way to open the subject and Raylene didn't volunteer any information. Raylene seemed unusually quiet and thoughtful, though, as she organized the making of the dozens of party sandwiches Mildred had ordered. She set out loaves of fresh bread and bowls of the sandwich fillings that Myra May and Violet had made and put the helpers to work at the long table in the dining room, where there was plenty of clear workspace.

"Okay, girls, here's how you do it," she said, speaking as she worked. "You lay out eight slices of bread and butter them, which keeps the filling from soaking through. Then spread the filling evenly on four of the slices and top each with another slice. Then you trim off the crust on each side, like so." She deftly demonstrated. "Then slice each sandwich into four fingers. Stack the fingers over here on this cookie sheet and cover them with a damp towel. Then start over again with eight more slices, except this time, cut the sandwich into four triangles and put them on the other cookie sheet. The third time, cut your sandwiches into four squares. That way, we'll end up with a variety of fillings and shapes. Got it?"

The sandwich preparation underway, Raylene began browning the sausage for the sausage puffs that they would mix and bake later, while Myra May started peeling the cold hard-boiled eggs. Myra May had just finished the first dozen eggs when the kitchen door opened and Aunt Hetty Little—a neighbor of Mildred's—came in. She was carrying two large, ripe melons, fresh from her garden. Her white hair was twisted into a bun at the back of her neck and she was wearing the shapeless old green print dress that she wore in the garden.

"Hi, Myra May," she said as she put the melons on the kitchen counter. "I'm getting ready to meet the Dahlias over at the clubhouse garden and wanted to deliver these first. I promised them to Mildred for her party tonight."

"Oh, these look good," Myra May said, pausing in her egg-peeling to have a look at the melons. "We'll let Mildred know they're here—and put one of the girls to work cubing them."

Over the tops of her gold-rimmed eyeglasses, Aunt Hetty peered curiously at Raylene. "And who's this?" With her customary bluntness, the old lady added, "I don't think I know you."

"I guess you haven't met Raylene Riggs yet," Myra May said. "Maybe you heard that Euphoria is now cooking over in Maysville at the Red Dog? Well, I'm happy to say that Raylene is her replacement, as of a couple of days ago. Raylene, this is Aunt Hetty Little. She's a member of our Dahlias' garden club."

Raylene turned from the skillet, a spoon in one hand. When she saw Aunt Hetty, her eyes widened, startled, and she ducked her head and turned away again. For a moment, there was a silence.

Then Aunt Hetty said, very quietly. "I'm sorry—what did you say your name was, hon?"

When Raylene didn't immediately answer, Myra May repeated, a little louder, "This is Raylene Riggs, Aunt Hetty. She's been working in Tampa as a hotel chef and has had lots of experience as a cook. Violet and I think we're downright lucky to have her."

"Raylene, is it?" Aunt Hetty said. She went to Raylene, then put up her hand and gently turned Raylene's face toward her. "I know you, don't I?"

Raylene pulled back, shaking her head, her lips pressed tightly together. But Aunt Hetty was not deterred. She put her hand on Raylene's arm.

"I *do* know you, Raylene—or I used to, a long time ago. Put down that spoon and come over here by the window, child. I want to see you up close, in the light."

Raylene cast an anxious glance at Myra May, who shook her head slightly and continued to peel the boiled egg she had in her hand. She knew better than to interfere when Aunt Hetty had her mind set on something. As one of the oldest women in Darling—certainly the oldest Dahlia—she was a law unto herself. Reluctantly, Raylene followed the old lady.

"Now, you just let me have a good look," Aunt Hetty said, as they stood in front of the window. She lifted her hand and traced the outline of Raylene's face and mouth.

"Yes, I know you, my dear," she said softly. There was a tremor in her scratchy old voice. "And you know me."

"No. No, I don't think so," Raylene said, and tried to turn away.

But Aunt Hetty took her by the arm and turned her back. "Well, I do," she said. "I know I do. And while I may not be a spring chicken any longer, there's nothing wrong with my memory. I never forget a face." She turned to look at Myra May. "Don't you, Myra May?"

Myra May put her peeled egg down on the plate and sliced it down the middle. "Don't I what, Aunt Hetty?" she asked casually. With a spoon, she scooped out the cooked yolk and dropped it into a bowl. She picked up another egg.

"Know this lady," Aunt Hetty said. "Why, I'm sure you *must*, Myra May. You don't recognize her?" She gave a long sigh. "No, I don't expect you do, and no surprise. You were too young, I reckon. You were just a little 'un, not two years old, not even talking yet. You wouldn't remember."

"Really," Raylene said, and tried to turn away again. "I have so much to do for this party tonight, Miz Little. I can't stand around talking about—"

"You're Ina Ray, aren't you?" Aunt Hetty said, still clutching Raylene's arm. "Miss Ina Ray Sparks." She paused, while the silence lengthened. "Mrs. Ina Ray Sparks Mosswell."

Myra May dropped the boiled egg she held in her hand. It smashed onto the floor and rolled under the table. Her knees felt suddenly weak and she groped for the nearest chair.

"Myra May," Raylene said, in a choked voice. "Please—"

Myra May was staring at Aunt Hetty. "Ina Ray?" she whispered. "But she . . . she *can't* be! My mother is dead, Aunt Hetty. Don't you remember? She died when I was a little baby. She went on a visit to Savannah, to see her parents, and she got sick. She died and she was buried there. My father told me. He said she was dead. He said—"

And then Myra May stopped and looked at Raylene. But she was also seeing the gold-framed photograph on her dresser, her striking young mother dressed in a lacy white shirtwaist and long dark skirt, in a photograph taken when Myra May was the baby girl in her mother's arms. Her mother's face—and Raylene's face, thirty years younger. The same firm jaw, the determined mouth, the wide-spaced eyes. Raylene and Ina Ray. They were the same, weren't they? *Weren't they?*

"He said you were dead," Myra May repeated. She bent over, clutching herself, and began to cry. "Why did he say you were *dead?*"

Raylene was at her side in two strides, gathering her into her arms. "There, baby girl," she whispered, holding Myra May tightly against her, both of them crying now. "There, there, baby girl."

After a few moments, Aunt Hetty coughed. "I understand why Dr. Mosswell sent you away, Ina Ray. But I never understood why he and his sister told ever'body you were dead. Didn't seem right then. Doesn't seem right now."

"They did it because I was dead to them," Raylene said in a choked voice. "To both of them. They wanted me to be dead to my daughter." She was still holding Myra May to her, crushing her, as if she would never let her go. "He warned me. He said if I ever came back, he would tell Myra May how *evil* her mother had been. He would destroy me forever in her eyes, in her heart."

"Not evil, just foolish," Aunt Hetty amended quietly. "It was a mistake, you and that young man—but we all make 'em." She paused. "That young man. I misremember his name."

"Roscoe," Raylene whispered. "Roscoe Bennett."

"Ah, yes. Preacher Bennett's middle boy. You were so young. And Jeremiah Mosswell was—what? Twenty years older? Twenty-five? And proper. All them Mosswells was stiff and proper as deacons. Never had an hour of fun in their lives."

"Mama?" Myra May whispered incredulously. She lifted her eyes, the tears blurring her vision so that all she could see was the shape of the pale face, the smiling face in the photograph. *"Mama?"*

"Yes," Raylene said. kissed her forehead tenderly. "I am so sorry, Myra May. So, so, *so* sorry. I don't know how I could ever have gone away and left you behind. How could I have done that?"

Aunt Hetty sighed. "We do what we have to, Ina Ray. And you were so young. I said at the time, I don't know what your daddy and mama could ever have thought, marrying you off to a stuffed-shirt Mosswell. Sixteen, were you?"

"Seventeen, just barely," Raylene replied. "I was rebellious. They thought I needed to be taken in hand, and that Dr. Mosswell was the one to do it," Raylene said. Myra May heard the note of bitterness in her voice. "He and my daddy were old friends, you know. Daddy trusted him to settle me down. Well, he was bound to do that, body and soul. Settle me down."

"Jeremiah would do that, and more," Aunt Hetty said darkly.

Myra May couldn't take her eyes off Raylene—off her mother. "Mama?" she whispered again. "Is it really *you*? Really?" Her vision was beginning to clear. The remembered photograph faded and all she could see now was the face of the woman. Raylene's face.

"Really. Yes, really." Raylene knelt down beside Myra May. "You're too young to remember, sweetheart, but the first time I left your daddy, I bundled up all your little dresses and toys and took you with me. We didn't get far, only to Pensacola. That's where the police caught up with us and made us go back to the Mosswells, to your daddy and his sister." She smiled shakily. "You were so sweet, Myra May, such beautiful dimples and little fat hands and a glorious laugh that went straight to my heart. I meant . . . I thought . . . I was *sure* I'd be able to come back to Darling and get you. I even tried, twice."

"You did?" Myra May gulped, still incredulous. She put out a hand to touch Raylene's face. "You really . . . came back for me?"

Raylene nodded. "Once when you were six and again when you were eight." A smile played across her mouth—a mouth, Myra May thought, that was very like her own. "The first time, I just stayed out of sight and watched. The second time, I got a room at the Old Alabama and walked past your house several times, watching you playing outdoors. When you ran off with one of your friends, I went into your daddy's office to talk to him. I wanted to take you with me for a visit."

"But you didn't talk to me?" Myra May whispered. "You were that close and you didn't talk to *me?*"

Raylene shook her head. "I couldn't, Myra May. He had already told you I was dead." Her muscles of her jaw tightened. "I can't tell you how much that hurt. But I had to agree with him that it would be too confusing, too difficult for you to handle. And it looked like your Aunt Belle was taking good care of you—"

"Auntie Bellum," Myra May said, and managed a tearful laugh. "Oh, she took good care of me, all right."

Raylene threw back her head and laughed. "Yes. Antebellum. She was a Mosswell, that's for sure—stiff and unbending and old-fashioned as all get-out. I am sure that woman wore a steel-boned corset until the day she died, bless her heart. But I stayed around for a while after I talked with your father, and watched you with Belle. You were such a beautiful little girl, and so strong and lively—a handful. Too much, I suspected, for your aunt. And too much, certainly, for your daddy. But they were taking good care of you. I was sure of that."

"That might be true," Myra May said somberly. "But I almost never saw him, you know. Not then. Not when I was a little girl. He was always away, taking care of other people's kids. Auntie Bellum said it was because I reminded him of you, which I thought ought to make him happy, since he always said he loved you. It didn't, though."

"I'm sure it didn't," Raylene murmured, touching Myra May's cheek. "But as I was watching you, it seemed to me that *you* looked happy. And I knew I couldn't give you all the things your father could give you—a comfortable home, nice clothes, an education. Especially an education. What kind of an education would you have if you came with me? So I went away feeling sorry for myself and thinking I'd come back when you were older and independent. But things happened in my life and the years went by and—"

She broke off, frowning a little. "You *were*, weren't you, Myra May? You *were* happy, growing up? You seem so happy now that I think you must have been happy then."

"Most of the time, yes, I suppose," Myra May said, "except for missing you. All I had was your photograph, and a big empty hole where *you* were supposed to be." She knew that her voice sounded petulant and whiney, a little girl's voice, but she couldn't help it. Yes, she was happy now. But there had been long stretches of her girlhood when she was pinned under the thumb of strict Aunt Belle and all she could do was squirm. Those years would have been much happier if she'd had her mother. Wouldn't they?

"Don't look so sour, Myra May," Aunt Hetty said in a

kindly tone. "You neither, Ina Ray. Doesn't help to hold a grudge, y'know. Life's too short for that."

Raylene wiped her eyes with the back of her hand. "I remember something I heard you say once, Aunt Hetty. Something about keeping our faces to the sun so we can't see the shadows."

"And planting sunflowers and marigolds amongst the collards and sweet potatoes and okra," Aunt Hetty added. "It's true, too. Life's too short to be bitter. Look on the bright side, is what I say."

Raylene chuckled. "How could I be bitter," she said, "when I have everything that's wonderful and sweet, right here." She bent over and cupped Myra May's face in her hands. "Right here, right in front of me."

Myra May caught at her hands. "You'll stay this time, though? You'll *stay*?"

"That's why I'm here." The tears were running down Raylene's cheeks. "That's why I'm here, my precious, my beautiful daughter."

EIGHTEEN

Closed Until Further Notice

Charlie Dickens usually ran off the weekly *Dispatch* on Thursday evening, so he could take the papers to the post office for mailing on Friday morning. But this week, he had postponed the press run in order to escort Lily Dare to the special showing of *Hell's Angels*, and then he had spent the night at the airstrip in the company of Rex Hart. Having shared a companionable bottle of Mickey LeDoux's white lightning with the fellow, Charlie was about ninety-nine percent certain that Hart had had nothing whatever to do with the sabotage of Lily's airplane. He seemed to be concerned about the safety of the planes—as well he might be, since his job depended on it.

And as for the Texas Star herself—well, after that ridiculous little abduction stunt at the Kilgores' house, Charlie was entirely disgusted with her. It didn't matter what kind of a run-in she had had with Roger and Mildred, she wasn't justified in doing what she did. Climbing out of the window was utterly stupid, and it was even stupider to make it look like she'd been kidnapped. Charlie had lost all patience with her—and she had lost any attraction she ever held for him. He'd be just as glad if he didn't see Lily Dare ever again. He didn't owe her so much as a second thought.

But Charlie couldn't hold back the swarm of second thoughts that had continued to plague him since he had left Fannie Champaign on Wednesday night. The echo of her sad little sigh, the memory of her disappointment in him—these stung him now even more piercingly than they had when he had left her, wearing the noble righteousness of his lie like a badge of honor. Then, he had thought it was better to convince Fannie that he wasn't suitable husband material and that he intended never to marry—and that the best way to do this was to get her to see him as a two-timing jerk. Lily Dare had happened along at exactly the right time to assist in this deception.

Now, giving the matter the second thoughts he should have bestowed on it in the first place, Charlie was beginning to think that he might have taken the wrong approach. He had shown himself to be a complete and utter cad with absolutely no redeeming qualities—and that, surely, was not the case. He certainly wasn't an angel, but he wasn't the devil with horns that Fannie now must think him. Maybe he shouldn't have painted himself as an unregenerate louse who would two-time her with Lily Dare and humiliate her in front of her friends. After all, he hadn't *really* two-timed her, had he? He'd just pretended to. To put it bluntly, he had told her a lie for the sake of the truth, but it was nevertheless a lie.

Now, giving it some second thought, he decided that instead of lying, he should have come straight out and told her that he wasn't interested in matrimony—at least, not just now, at the moment when it seemed that everybody in town already had them standing at the altar. He should probably have added that he very much enjoyed being with her (which was true) and would miss their evenings together if they stopped seeing one another (also true) and as a matter of fact did not *want* to stop seeing her (most definitely true).

So, having given the matter due consideration, he decided that it would be best if he dropped in at Fannie's hat shop today and cleared up any misapprehension she might have about the true nature of his character. That would allow them to continue seeing one another, but without any inconvenient expectations on her part.

This vigorous back-and-forth debate was going through Charlie's mind on Friday morning as he put on his heavy canvas apron and a pressman's hat made of folded newsprint, to keep the ink out of his hair. At the makeup table, he took one last, careful look at the type forms that made up the four pages of home print—the local news and advertisements that occupied half of the newspaper. The pages looked pretty good, he thought, considering. There was plenty of news, anyway, although he could have wished for a few more ads.

Headlining the local page was an article Charlie had written about Gene Ralston, a Darling veteran who had gone to Washington, D.C., to join the Bonus Army. Earlier in the spring, some 43,000 veterans of the Great War began to gather at the Capitol to demand the cash bonuses that had been promised to them back in 1924. Their hopes were fired up in June when the House passed a bill authored by Texas Representative Wright Patman, allowing them to collect their bonuses immediately, in cash—then dashed when the Senate defeated it a couple of days later. But the vets were still in Washington, still trying to pressure President Hoover to act on their behalf—a wasted effort, in Charlie's estimation. Hoover had to hold on to his political base, the Republican loyalists who didn't approve of any government-backed relief efforts. The president couldn't afford to do anything that would make them angry enough to stay home come Election Day next November. Roosevelt's promises of a "new deal" (whatever that was) appealed to a great many people, more than enough, Charlie thought, to elect him. Hoover was facing an uphill battle.

There were several other page one stories: the arrest of a couple of local moonshiners by the Revenuers; the monthly meeting of the American Legion; an article on a better way of feeding chickens that resulted in higher egg production, written by County Ag Agent Grady Alexander. Page four featured Elizabeth Lacy's regular Garden Gate column and the article Ophelia Snow had written about the cooking auditions being held at the Darling Diner, although Charlie was pretty sure they were going to hire that woman who had just popped up—Raylene, her name was. He hoped so, anyway. He'd love to see pulled pork added to the diner's regular menu. By golly, he'd eat every meal there, if that happened.

Charlie locked the type into the form, picked up the heavy forms, and carried them one at a time to the old Babcock flatbed cylinder press in the back of the room, where he set them in place. Then he inked the rollers, loaded the paper, and began running the home print pages—two and seven, four and five—on the backs of the ready print pages: one and eight, three and six. These came in on Thursdays on the Greyhound bus from a print shop in Mobile, already made up with the latest national and world news, a sports page, the comics, and the women's page.

While the pages came off the press and went into the folding machine, Charlie took a short break to read the front page. One of the lead articles was about Roosevelt's "new deal," although the writer seemed to be as much in the dark about what that meant as everyone else was.

The other article was headed by a photo of men waiting in line for a bowl of soup in New York, where more than 750,000 unemployed men, women, and children were dependent upon city relief, with an additional 160,000 on a waiting list. For each person on relief, the city spent about $8.20 a month.

Below the fold, there was a follow-up story on the suicide of Violet Sharpe, one of the servants in the rural New Jersey home of Charles and Anne Lindbergh. The woman had killed herself after being repeatedly questioned by the police about the kidnapping and murder of little Charles Jr., whose body had been discovered in May, some two and a half months after the crime. According to the article, she had nothing to do with it; she was the victim of police bullying. The cops had no other suspects, and while some of the ransom money had turned up, they hadn't been able to track down the rest.

From that depressing news, Charlie turned to page six and the lighter side: "Out Our Way" and "Our Boarding House," with the comically big-headed Major Amos Hoople, two comic strips that always gave him a chuckle. But even though things weren't as bad in Darling as they were on the east coast, there wasn't a whole lot to smile about. Charlie was practically giving the newspaper away (twelve cents a week, including two cents for postage), but the circulation kept on going down as people cut back on their expenses—only 427 subscribers as of this month. Ophelia was working hard to bring in more advertising and print jobs, but both the ad revenue and the printing business were declining as well. The local merchants couldn't afford to put money into advertising when they could barely pay their other bills.

Charlie didn't like to think about what was likely to happen when the cost of the paper and ink and ready print and

Ophelia Snow's twelve bucks a week amounted to more than the little bit he took in every week. Maybe he'd just lock the door and hang a big *CLOSED* sign on it. If people wanted newspapers, they could subscribe to the *Monroe Journal*, over in Monroeville. Yes, he had lied to Fannie Champaign when he told her that the newspaper was in debt. (Why had he done that? He couldn't remember.) But there wasn't any money, either. Not one extra red cent, and Charlie was still fighting his way up a steep mountain of personal resentment for having been saddled with his father's business in the first place. It wasn't what he had expected or wanted and he still hadn't reconciled himself to it.

His father, Randolph Dickens, had been owner, publisher, and editor of the Darling *Dispatch* for four decades, along with running a small job printing business on the side. Charlie had taken the newspaper over when the old man died of lung cancer several years before—not so much because he wanted to, but because he couldn't think of anything else he wanted to do instead.

That was the way Charlie had lived most of his adult life, floating from here to there as possibilities and opportunities presented themselves, doing first one thing, then another. Some people were driven by desire, but Charlie wasn't one of them. He was driven by nothing at all. He drifted along with whatever current pulled him, and Darling was just another backwater he'd gotten stuck in— temporarily. As soon as the spirit moved, finances improved, and he could unload the *Dispatch*, he'd be on his way again. In the meantime, the ordinary tasks of putting out the weekly paper were a kind of crutch to get through the days and weeks and months, limping along, managing to keep himself and the business going, with the help of liberal doses of Mickey LeDoux's bootleg medicine.

Printing 427 newspapers plus a couple of dozen extra for

the boxes in front of the hotel and the diner didn't take long. The press run finished, Charlie stopped the Babcock, shut off the motor, and raised the ink rollers. He pulled off the forms and carried them to the makeup table, where he washed the ink off the type with a gasoline soaked rag, then went back to the press and cleaned it off, as well. He carried the folded papers to another table, where he took out the long galleys that held the names of the dwindling numbers of his subscribers. He inked each galley, placed it into the mailing machine, then fed the folded newspapers into the mailer. Each one came out with the name and address of a subscriber printed at the top and went into a large cardboard box.

The last paper labeled, Charlie cleaned the mailing machine and then took off his canvas apron and his printer's cap and washed his hands at the sink in the back corner of the room. He glanced at the old octagon Regulator clock on the wall—nearly noon, he saw. It was time for lunch, and he thought hungrily of the possibility of a pulled pork sandwich on the noon menu at the diner. But he had two things to do, and decided that he'd better take care of the first— getting the papers to the post office—before Mr. Stevens closed for lunch.

He picked up the box of newspapers, hefted it onto his shoulder, and took his straw boater off the peg. Jamming it on his head and kicking the door shut behind him, he headed for the small frame building that housed the post office. It was just down the block on Franklin Street, past Hancock's Grocery and the Palace Theater, then a right turn onto Rosemont.

But in front of the Palace, he ran into Don Greer, the owner and operator of the theater, who was sweeping the dust off the sidewalk with a straw broom. He paused in his work, leaned on his broom, and gave Charlie a knowing wink.

"Hello, you sly old dog, you," he said, and chuckled. "Saw you last night with that Texas Star. Quite some gal, ain't she? Looked like you two was havin' yourselves a high ol' time, back there in the next to the last row, in the dark."

Charlie paused, frowning. "Don't know what you mean, Greer," he said stiffly.

"Oh, yeah?" Greer's chuckle became a broad leer. "Just remember that folks are lookin' over your shoulder, and one or two of 'em might carry tales."

"Carry tales?" Charlie asked, and immediately regretted his question.

Greer lifted both eyebrows. "To that other lady you're sweet on. The one that makes hats. The missus told me she heard that you and her are figurin' on gettin' hitched sometime soon."

Charlie, who was normally pretty swift with a comeback, found that he had no ready answer to this. The best he could do was a muttered "Don't believe everything you hear, Greer."

"I'm just repeatin' what folks're sayin'," Greer replied cheerfully. As Charlie walked away, he began pushing his broom with a greater energy, whistling the tune to "Falling in Love Again."

Gritting his teeth, Charlie rounded the corner and went into the post office. "Here's this week's batch of newspapers," he said to old Mr. Stevens, the post master, and slid the box over the counter.

"A little late, ain'cha, Charlie?" Mr. Stevens had bushy white chin whiskers and wore sleeve garters and suspenders and a green eyeshade. "Y' missed the morning mail run. Guess you stayed up too late last night with your out-of-town ladyfriend, huh?" He snickered. "I seen you and her, comin' out of the picture show."

Charlie bit his tongue. It didn't pay to talk back to Mr. Stevens. "I'm a little late," he acknowledged stiffly. "But no matter, so long as the papers go out tomorrow."

"Oh, they'll go out all right," Mr. Stevens said. "But it may not be tomorrow. Tom Wheeler's old car broke down halfway through his deliveries this mornin' and had to be towed. May be next week before he gets it fixed. In the meantime, he's puttin' Old Fred to work." Old Fred was Tom Wheeler's horse, which he hitched to his buggy when his car wasn't running. "The post office ain't made of money, you know," he added sternly. "The best we can do is the best we can do. And the best we got right now is Old Fred."

Charlie nodded. There was never any point in arguing with Mr. Stevens. He had, once, and regretted it, when he learned that after their argument only half of the press run had reached his subscribers. Not that Mr. Stevens was nasty. He was just inclined to be irritable, and it was better to stay on his good side if you could, so he wouldn't misplace your mailings—temporarily, of course. The missing papers had arrived two weeks late. The post office always delivers, Mr. Stevens had told him knowingly.

The newspapers taken care of (and their final delivery date resting on the weary shoulders of old, slow Fred), Charlie thought once again about lunch, but felt that he would rather accomplish his second objective without any further delay. He went out onto Rosemont, crossed Franklin, and walked past the Darling Savings and Trust to the second building on the block, Fannie Champaign's Darling Chapeaux.

As he walked, Charlie's heart grew lighter and his steps swifter, for he planned to correct the regrettable impression about his character that he had left with Fannie on Wednesday night. He wasn't quite sure how he was going to do this—that is, exactly what he was going to say. But he was confident that the right words would come when he saw Fannie's sweet, tremulous smile and felt the encouraging touch of her hand.

Now feeling a sudden rush of surprised eagerness and the unexpected warmth of actually *wanting* something, he took the wooden steps two at a time and grasped the brass handle to push open the front door.

But the door was locked. And in the window, there was a hand-lettered sign:

Miss Champaign Is Out of Town
Closed Until Further Notice

NINETEEN

Purple Ink, Pink Paper, and Two More Black Eyes

When the airplane topped with a half-naked Angel had disappeared back in the direction of the airstrip, Lizzy and Verna climbed into Verna's LaSalle and headed for the Kilgores' house.

Lizzy wasn't very enthusiastic about the plan Verna had suggested. For one thing, they might be barking up the entirely wrong tree. After all, the main thing they had to go on was Raylene's intuition, although it had already proved fairly powerful and was supported by a fact or two, such as the death of Mabel's sister, Bess. But basically, they were operating on Raylene's say-so, which might or might not be accurate.

Still, as Lizzy and Verna both knew, they didn't have a whole lot of choices, so they agreed they should give it a try. And since Mildred Kilgore had the documents that were the key to the plan's success, they would begin with her.

When they arrived, Lizzy was startled to see that Mildred's eye looked a lot worse. It was turning purple, with green streaks and shadows, and was almost swelled shut. But neither she nor Verna were so impolite as to call attention to it.

Mildred was overseeing the boys who were setting up the tables in the garden and the girls who were working in the kitchen, but she was ready to take a few moments out to talk. They took glasses of iced tea to the back veranda, where Mildred could keep an eye on the boys. When they were settled at a table, Verna said, "We've got news, Mildred," and told her about finding Lily Dare in Raylene Riggs cottage at the Marigold Motor Court.

Mildred shook her head as she listened, then gave a disgusted little *hmph*. "I'll have somebody take her things over there," she said. She stiffened her shoulders and raised her chin. "I may have to be civil to that woman tonight," she said thinly, "but she's not going to be sleeping here."

"We can take her things," Verna offered. "We're driving past the Marigold on our way out to the airstrip. That way, you won't have to bother."

"Thank you," Mildred said, slightly mollified. "I'll be glad to have them gone."

Then Lizzy told Mildred about the conversation she and Verna had had with Raylene at the diner that morning— most importantly, Raylene's surprising story about Bess and Mabel Hopkins (aka Angel Flame), and Raylene's hunch. And then Verna told her about their plan.

"We don't know if it'll work," Lizzy said when Verna was finished. "But we think it's worth a try. Of course, we'll have to apologize if it turns out that we're wrong. But that's a small price to pay for the possibility of getting to the bottom of that nasty business of the letters and the checks. Don't you agree, Mildred?"

Mildred wore a doubtful look at first, but she listened with a growing interest and when Verna and Lizzy had finished, she agreed that it was worth a chance. She went indoors, got the items they asked for, and came back down.

"I hope you won't show these to anybody else," she said, handing them over. "I'd hate for them to fall into the wrong hands. Darling is such a horrible place for gossip. Everybody would be talking about it." She sighed and touched her eye. "As it is, I don't see how I can face people tonight. What will I tell them?"

"If you want to tell them that you walked into a door," Lizzy said sympathetically, "we'll be glad to back you up."

"Roger's got a black eye, too," Mildred said.

"And so does Lily Dare," Verna put in.

Lizzy tried to think of something snappy, but all she could come up with was "I don't think anybody will believe *three* doors."

"I don't think so either," Mildred replied gloomily. She looked from one to the other of them, pushing her mouth in and out. "But I wonder," she said. "What if each of you had a black eye? That way, none of us would stand out."

Verna blinked. "You want *us* to whap one another in the eye just to—"

"No," Lizzy said firmly. "We'll do what we can to help, but that is *not* a good idea, Mildred."

Mildred threw up her hands. "Well, it's the only idea I have." She stood. "I need to get back to work now. Black eyes or not, I have a reputation to uphold." She sighed. "And from the looks of the bank account, this will be the last big party I'll give."

Back again in the LaSalle, Verna drove first to Lizzy's house, where Lizzy went inside and got one of the fliers they'd printed up to publicize the air show and the Watermelon Festival. They made another stop in town, where they talked for a few moments to Buddy Norris, letting him know what they were up to and why—without spilling more of the private details than they could help. And then they drove out to the Marigold Motor Court and dropped off Lily Dare's bag.

By this time, it was nearly noon, and the morning had turned into one of those glorious days that sometimes bloom in the middle of a hot summer. The air was cool (well, cooler than it had been, anyway), the sun was cheerful but not overbearing, and the trees and grass were the color of polished emeralds. A pattern of birds wheeled overhead, their wings flashing silver against the serene blue sky.

"Perfect weather for the Watermelon Festival," Lizzy said happily. As they drove past the fairgrounds, she was glad to see that the ticket booth was in operation and decorated with a flock of tethered red, white, and blue balloons left over from Darling's Fourth of July parade. The tents were all erected and the carnival rides were up. The merry-go-round was playing a cheerful hurdy-gurdy tune, the Ferris wheel was turning, and threaded through the hubbub Lizzy could hear the shouts of the carnies going about their work. The odor of fresh hot buttered popcorn filled the open car.

"I love the smell of popcorn," Lizzy said. "Before we go back to Darling, let's stop at the fairgrounds so I can have a look around. I want to be sure that the tent where Aunt Hetty will put our Dahlias' garden stuff is set up and ready to go."

"Yeah, we can do that," Verna said grimly. "But we need to get this other business settled before we do anything else."

She was staring straight ahead and driving more carefully than usual. Clearly, she was already concentrating on what they were planning to do. In Lizzy's estimation, though, their scheme depended way too much on luck. It was a gamble, and Lizzy wasn't optimistic. Raylene's hunch could be completely wrong, and then what?

When they got to the airstrip, they saw that the airplane

with its advertising banner had done its job, and then some. There was already a sizeable crowd, with cars, wagons, and bicycles parked along both sides of the grassy landing area and more arriving all the time. Dozens of onlookers—mostly men and boys, in farm overalls, work clothes, and battered old hats—were wandering across the grass or sitting on the hoods of their vehicles, the men smoking cigarettes, chewing tobacco, and occasionally pulling a surreptitious flask out of a back pocket.

Rex Hart's yellow Stearman, with a passenger, was already taxiing out to the end of the grassy runway, like an eager bird maneuvering to get airborne. Lily Dare was seated in the cockpit of the Jenny, and a young man wearing the team's distinctive red shirt was helping Jed Snow climb into the plane for a ride. When Jed was securely buckled in, the young man ran around the front of the plane and pulled the propeller, then pulled it again. The engine caught, the propeller began to spin, and as the watching crowd cheered, Lily revved the motor and turned the plane to taxi for a takeoff, scattering onlookers from the field. A third plane, blue, with an American flag painted on its nose, waited on the grass to take on the next passenger.

Angel Flame had abandoned her red bathing suit and was dressed in tight-fitting white pants, the team's red shirt, a blue spangled scarf, and lightweight canvas shoes—her aerialist outfit, Lizzy guessed. She was standing just inside the big sliding doors to the shed, next to a scale with a big sign on it. *Ride High for Only a Penny a Pound!* Angel weighed each passenger, noted his weight, took his money, wrote his name on a list, and handed him a ticket. From the length of the line, Lizzy guessed that people would be waiting their turns for airplane rides for the rest of the day—a good thing, as far as the Dare Devils were concerned. With three planes in the air, they ought to turn that profit Lily was hoping for.

Lizzy did a quick mental calculation. If the flights lasted twenty minutes, a plane could do maybe three flights in a little over an hour, if they turned the passengers around very fast. If there were three planes in the air, that would be nine flights an hour times—what? An average of a dollar fifty or sixty per flight? That would be thirteen, fourteen dollars an hour. If they could keep it up for six or seven hours, they could maybe earn a hundred dollars for a day's flying. And if a hundred automobiles showed up tomorrow, that would be another hundred. Two hundred dollars.

She frowned. It sounded like a lot of money. But was it enough to buy fuel and parts and repairs—not to mention food for the flying team and ground crew and beds for the night, and for all the nights until the next air show? She thought of her comfortable little house, with her garden in the back, Daffy on the front porch, and plenty of food in her big G.E. Monitor refrigerator, and she shook her head. She had imagined that Lily Dare—the fastest woman in the world, a stunt pilot for Hollywood films—led a glamorous life. Now, she knew that wasn't true. Once, she had envied the Texas Star. Now, no more.

Verna parked her LaSalle in the shade of a large oak tree behind the shed and waited beside the car. They had already decided what they were going to do, so when the line of eager airplane passengers had dwindled to a few, Lizzy went up to Angel, who was tucking a wad of dollar bills and a handful of coins into a purse that was fastened to a belt around her waist.

"Hey, Angel," she said with a cheerful smile. "How about taking a break for a few minutes? I'd like to introduce you to somebody." It was their good luck, Lizzy thought, that Verna had stayed in their room the previous night and left that morning before Angel got up, so Angel hadn't met her yet. "She has a request for you, from one of your fans."

Angel started to reply but was interrupted by the metallic roar of Rex Hart's plane, coming in for a landing. A young man in a red shirt came up to her and yelled something into her ear. She pointed to a name on a list and the young man hurried off, in search of the next passenger.

"From a fan?" Angel asked in pleased surprise, when she could make herself heard. "Well, sure, Liz, I'd be glad do that. Let me just finish up these last few guys in line, and I'll be right with you."

Lizzy went back to join Verna under the tree. Overhead, they could hear the drone of Lily's airplane. At the fairgrounds behind them, the music of the Ferris wheel joined the hurdy-gurdy of the merry-go-round in a pleasant circusy cacophony. "Do you think it will work?" she asked uncertainly.

"No way to tell until we try," Verna answered, leaning against the car. "Anyway, we have nothing to lose."

A few moments later, Angel sauntered toward them. Her bobbed brown hair was wind-tossed, and her tight white pants emphasized her lithe, athletic figure. She was no doubt quite athletic and brave, Lizzy thought. Very brave—or very foolhardy. She'd have to be, to perform on the wing of an airplane or on a trapeze slung underneath, hundreds of feet above the unforgiving ground, especially after she had seen her sister die in a fatal fall from Lily Dare's airplane.

Lizzy introduced the two women. "I'm glad to meet you," Verna said easily. "I've heard a lot about you from my cousin, Annie. She's a real fan." Verna, Lizzy knew, had no cousins named Annie.

"That's nice," Angel said with a chipper smile. "Is she the one Liz told me about?"

"She sure is," Verna replied. She reached into the car and picked up Lizzy's flier from the seat. "Annie lives in Florida. She's watched you do your aerial stunts and would dearly love to have your autograph." Verna held out the paper. "This is one of the fliers we had put up around town to publicize the air show. Maybe you could sign it for her?"

The flier in Verna's hand featured photos of Lily Dare and Rex Hart and a blurred photograph of Angel, doing a handstand on the wing of Hart's airplane, just as she had done earlier that day, in the air above the courthouse square. Verna added, "Could you sign it 'To Annie, with all best wishes from your friend, Angel'? I know she'd love that." She made a little face. "It's a lot to write. I hope you don't mind."

"Oh, golly, no," Angel said gallantly. "People are always begging Lily and Rex for their autographs. It's swell whenever somebody asks for mine. And just in case, I always bring my favorite pen."

She fished in the purse on her belt and pulled out a silver fountain pen. Seeing it, Lizzy's eyes widened and she held her breath. Could it possibly be? If it was, it was certainly lucky—more than they'd had any right to hope for!

Angel uncapped the pen and scribbled swiftly across the flier, *To Annie, with all best wishes from your friend, Angel Flame.*

Lizzy let out her breath in a long puff. "Oh, my," she said, admiring the inscription—and blessing Angel Flame's desire to show off. "Purple ink!"

"Yeah, I like to use it for letters and stuff," Angel said carelessly. "I have some pink paper, too, which I use for letters sometimes." She handed the flier back to Verna. "Kinda gives it a personal touch, you know?" she added. "A little bit of individual flair. Not too many people use purple ink and pink paper."

"You're right about that," Verna said emphatically. "It is certainly distinctive." And with that, she reached into the car and took out the anonymous letter Mildred had given them a little while before. "But here's something interesting, Angel. A friend of ours got a couple of letters in the past few months from someone she didn't know. This is one of them. And it's written in the same purple ink you're using—on pink paper, of all things!"

Watching Angel's face, Lizzy saw her eyes widen.

But Verna was going on. "And look—isn't this strange? The way you've written 'with all best wishes from your friend' on the flier? It's exactly the same as the same phrase in this letter! And it's written in exactly same way. See how the *t* is crossed with a little flourish? And the *f*s have those funny little short tails? The similarities are so amazing—why, I think *you* must have written it!"

Angel's mouth tightened and a muscle in her jaw was working. "Where'd you get that?" she demanded. "Give it to me!" She tried to snatch the letter away.

"Not so fast, Angel," Lizzy said, pulling at Angel's arm as Verna stepped back, out of reach. "You can't have that letter. It belongs to Mildred Kilgore. Roger Kilgore's wife—the woman you sent it to."

Angel sucked in her breath. Under her freckles, her face had gone ashen, with blotches of ugly red high on her cheeks. She looked uncertain and afraid, as if she were struggling to keep her balance on a shifting airplane wing.

"And there's more," Verna went on calmly. "These three canceled checks, made out by Roger Kilgore to someone named Lily Star—to Lily Dare, he thought." She held them up. "But Lily Dare never got the money, did she, Angel? And what's so interesting about these checks is that they've been endorsed with that same distinctive purple ink you used in the letters—and in the inscription just now." She shook her head pityingly. "You weren't so clever after all, Angel. You've left a trail a mile wide."

Angel's eyes narrowed and her anger overwhelmed her uncertainty. "Give me those!" she snapped menacingly. "Do you think I'm going to let you pull a cheap trick like that on me?" She lunged free of Lizzy and grabbed for the checks in Verna's hand. When Verna held on to them, Angel punched her in the face, then slammed her, hard, against the wall of the shed, pinning her with a strong forearm across her throat. "Give me those checks," she growled, "or I'll break your stupid neck!"

Verna gasped futilely for air, trying to wrench Angel's arm from her throat, but the wingwalker, athletic and years younger, was too strong for her.

"Lay *off*!" Lizzy cried. Frantic, she grabbed Angel's hair and jerked her sharply back. "Verna can't breathe! You're hurting—"

She was stopped with a fist in the eye, as Angel swung sharply around and hit her, hard, with all the force of her swinging body. Stunned, Lizzy saw an explosion of stars against a canopy of velvety black. The next thing she knew, she was sprawled flat on the ground.

"Hey!" Buddy Norris yelled, suddenly appearing out of nowhere. His deputy's badge was pinned conspicuously on his khaki shirt. "That's enough of that!" He knelt beside Lizzy. "Are you okay, Liz?" he asked and helped her sit up.

"I . . . I think so," Lizzy gulped, trying not to cry. She put a hand to her eye, which hurt fiercely. When she pulled it away, her fingers were smeared with bright red blood. Her cheek was bleeding.

"You've got a little cut," Buddy said sympathetically, and pulled out his handkerchief, dabbing it gently to her face. "Sorry to be delayed," he said. "I got tied up on a long-distance telephone call." He handed her the handkerchief.

"You okay now?" When she nodded, he helped her to her feet.

Angel's menace had abruptly disappeared. "Oh, Buddy," she cried, going to him and putting her hand on his arm. She smiled sweetly up at him. "Gosh, Buddy, you've got great timing! These two women have something that belongs to me and I've been trying to convince them to give it back." Her smile became flirtatious. "I'm sure they'll do whatever you say. Please tell them to hand over my stuff!"

"What kind of stuff?" Buddy asked.

"Oh, just—" She stopped, seeing the dilemma. "Just some . . . papers."

"What kind of papers?" Buddy smiled in a helpful way. "I can't make these women hand them over unless I know they belong to you—now can I?"

Desperate now, Angel said the only thing she could say. "It's . . . it's a letter I wrote, and some canceled checks. Come on, Buddy—they're *mine!*"

"There!" Lizzy crowed. "Did you hear that? She's just *confessed!*"

Buddy nodded. "I heard that. But first things first. Miss Flame, I saw what happened a few minutes ago, and it looked to me like you were using your fists to get what you wanted. Here in Darling, we call that assault and battery." He paused and looked from Verna to Lizzy. "Hate to say it, but you two look like this woman landed a few pretty good punches—she got you both right in the eye. What about it? Do you want to press charges?"

"Maybe," Lizzy said. Her left eye was throbbing and the cheek below it was still bleeding. She held Buddy's handkerchief to it and looked at Verna. "You've got a shiner, too, Verna."

"I'm in favor of charging her with assault," Verna said

grimly. She rubbed her throat, where the bruise was already beginning to show. "She's strong as an ox. I'm lucky she didn't break my neck."

"Assault?" Angel rolled her eyes, as if their complaints were just plain silly. "That's nonsense. I was only trying to persuade them—"

"Shut up, Miss Flame," Buddy said. He held out his hand to Verna. "Okay, now that we've got that settled, let's see these papers that Miss Flame insists are hers."

"Oh, but it's not necessary for you to *look* at them," Angel said hastily. "They're just a few pieces of paper, with no importance to anybody but me." She pointed to Verna. "If she'll give them to me, I'll forget all about charging her with theft."

"Theft?" Lizzy hooted. "Talk about *nonsense!*"

But Buddy was paying no attention. Verna had handed him the letter, the canceled checks, and the flier that Angel had signed. He was studying them carefully, chewing on one corner of his lip. Of course, he had already seen the letter and the checks when Lizzy and Verna had stopped at the sheriff's office on their way out to the airstrip and asked his help with their plan. Now, all he had to do was compare the handwriting.

After a minute, he said, "Well, it looks to me like you and Liz got it right, Verna." He folded the papers together and put them into his shirt pocket. "I'll make sure that these documents get back to Mrs. Kilgore when we're finished with them in the sheriff's office." He turned to Angel with a frown. "We don't much like extortionists here, Miss Flame—or Miss Hopkins, or whoever you are."

"Extortion?" Angel's mouth worked. Her face was splotchy. "No! You've got it all wrong," she said. "All of you."

Lizzy took a deep breath and stepped forward. "We have

it right," she said firmly. "*You* wrote the letters and the telegrams. You endorsed the checks. And on one of the checks, you wrote 'For deposit only' under your signature."

"So when that check is traced back to its deposit in your bank account," Verna put in, "that will take care of any possible question. Your problem is that you just didn't think things through. You didn't cover your tracks. You thought you were so far out of the picture that nobody could trace you." She chuckled shortly. "But you left a trail a yard wide and a mile long. Pink paper and purple ink. Dumb, dumber, *dumbest.*"

Angel's chin trembled. "But why . . . why would I do such things?" she asked plaintively, trying to defend herself. "What possible motive could I—"

"Well, for starters," Verna said, "there's revenge. Bess Hopkins died in a fall from Lily Dare's plane. You could be trying to get even with her for your sister's death. You could be—"

Verna stopped. Angel's face had crumpled at the mention of her sister. She squeezed her eyes shut and made a fist of her right hand and brought it to her mouth, as if to hold back a sob.

"Bess," she said, very low. "Bess . . ." Her shoulders began to shake. "Lily was using second-rate equipment on that plane. She cuts corners. People die because of her—like Pete Rickerts. He's dead, like Bess." Her voice grew shrill. "She needs to pay for what she's done."

"That's for the justice system to decide," Verna said. "Not you. Anyway, you weren't trying to get even with Lily when you defrauded Roger Kilgore out of nearly a thousand dollars. Why, for all we know, you've been pulling the same dirty tricks on other men—impersonating Miss Dare in order to solicit money."

"And on top of assault and extortion, there's the airplane

sabotage," Buddy Norris put in. "Could amount to attempted murder."

"Attempted *murder*?" Angel's eyes flew open. "Oh, no! I didn't mean—that is, I was just . . ." She shook her head, now sounding desperate. "It was just a . . . a joke, that's all. I figured the prop would break when the ground crewman turned it, before she took off. I only wanted to cause a little trouble, make her a little more careful. I wasn't trying to *kill* her!"

"The Pensacola police have a different idea," Buddy said, unclipping the handcuffs from his belt. "I was on the phone with them just before I came out here. It turns out that they've located a witness who saw you take a hacksaw to that propeller. They're going to want you to star in a police lineup down there." Deftly, ignoring her protests, he turned Angel around and cuffed her hands behind her back, then turned to Verna.

"I've got a favor to ask, Verna. I can't transport the prisoner into town on the back of my motorcycle. Can you and Liz take her in, in your car? I'll give you a police escort, to make sure there's no trouble."

"Oh, you bet," Verna said. Gently, she touched her swollen eye. "It will be a pleasure. A *pleasure*."

TWENTY

"A Happy Ending,
Don't You Think?"

Wednesday, July 20, 1932

It was, all the Dahlias agreed, the most exciting and best-managed Watermelon Festival ever. The air show was a spectacular success, attracting almost two hundred cars to the air strip on Sunday for a program of (as promised) thrills and chills and some really top-notch aerobatics, including both flying and wingwalking. The show culminated in an aerial dogfight so amazingly realistic that many spectators were convinced that the Texas Star and the King of the Air would collide and come crashing to the ground in blazing balls of fire—and some of them no doubt secretly hoped so. When all the excitement was over, Lily Dare and the Dare Devils packed up their gear and flew off to the next airshow, in Paducah, Kentucky. Unfortunately, one of the wing struts on Rex Hart's Stearman broke and the King of the Air was grounded until Monday, when he, too, flew off to Paducah.

Everything else went remarkably smoothly. The Ferris wheel did not get stuck (to the disappointment of the junior

Darlingians, who hoped to get stranded at the top for at least an hour or two). Mr. Burley's goats stayed in their pen, sulking; the best they could do was a red ribbon. (Muddy Waters' goats took the blue.) The Ladies Club tent did not collapse. The Chamber of Commerce popcorn machine did not catch fire. The Eastern Star's hot dogs held out until the last bun, just before closing time, and there were exactly enough watermelons for everybody to have exactly as many pieces as they wanted. The 1932 Darling Baby award went to Violet and Myra May's little Cupcake (all of Darling applauded this choice). Mrs. Peabody watched her step; she did *not* fall off the stage and break her nose again.

And best of all, when Aunt Hetty turned in the nickels and dimes and quarters the Dahlias had earned from the sale of their fresh garden vegetables, it was enough to buy *two* pressure cookers and *three* cases of Mason jars and lids. Lizzy and the other officers were already making arrangements for their first canning party in the kitchen of the Dahlias' clubhouse (the Kentucky Wonder green beans would need picking again next week) and planning for the Dahlias' contributions to the Darling Family Food Pantry.

Wednesday morning was a hot one, with the temperature already nudging ninety and the air heavy with humidity. At Beulah Trivette's Beauty Bower, the screen door and all the windows were open and the fans were turning. Several of the Dahlias were gathered to catch up on the latest Darling news and gossip and enjoy tea and cookies while Beulah and Bettina made them beautiful.

And there was a very great deal to catch up on. Lizzy, who was getting a shampoo and trim, had to tell everybody about the excitement of her very first airplane ride. She had gone up after the air show in the Texas Star, piloted by Miss Lily Dare. She had expected to pay $1.26 (a penny a pound). But Miss Dare gave her and Verna free rides, to thank them for their help in identifying Mabel Hopkins as the person who had sabotaged her plane, not just once but twice.

"Was it *fun*?" Beulah asked doubtfully, when Lizzy finished her story.

"It was so noisy and there was so much vibration that I thought the top of my head was going to fly off," Lizzy said. She sat up and let Beulah wrap a dry towel around her head. "But it was incredibly gorgeous up there, the sky all around us, open and free, and the plane turning and wheeling just like a bird. The trees and fields were all spread out below like a rumpled-up green chenille bedspread. And there was Darling itself, with all the toy houses with their flower gardens and the town square and the courthouse with its bell tower and the neat streets and the trees." She followed Beulah to one of the barber chairs and took her seat, while Beulah fastened a pink cape around her neck. "I looked right down on my roof, and my backyard, with my own garden like a tiny jewel, and it was all just perfect and perfectly beautiful."

"I'd get perfectly dizzy," Beulah said, getting out the tray of metal curlers she kept at her station. "I believe I'd keep my eyes closed the whole entire time I was in the air." She poured some of her homemade setting lotion out of a bottle and into a jar. Dipping a comb into it, she began combing it through Lizzy's hair.

"You and Verna are *brave*," Bessie Bloodworth said, from her place under the permanent wave machine, where she was getting her graying hair electrically curled. Another Dahlia, she had been a big help in getting the garden vegetables picked and carted out to the festival grounds. She went on: "Honest to Pete, Liz, I'd chew my nails down to the wrists if I had to go up in one of those machines. It might fall right down out of the sky with me in it!"

"The only thing that fell out of the sky was that

wingwalker," Aunt Hetty said. Completely covered by a pink cape, she was settled in the other barber chair, where Bettina, wearing an embroidered pink smock, was combing out her white hair after a shampoo and set.

Bettina gasped and her eyes opened wide. "She really did *fall?*" Bettina had gone to her mother's over the weekend and missed the air show. "She was *killed?*"

"It wasn't a she," Aunt Hetty replied crisply. "It was a he, and he didn't really fall, at least not all the way, because he was wearing a parachute."

"Oh, of course," Bettina said, teasing out a fluff of white hair and patting it delicately into place. "This must be somebody who took Angel Flame's place after she got arrested." She picked up the scissors and snipped off a stray strand.

"That's right," Verna said, leafing through a magazine while she waited for her turn in Bettina's barber chair. "The new wingwalker was a guy named Wiley Tuttle."

Lizzy was watching in the mirror as Beulah deftly wound her hair around a fat metal roller and fastened the clip. "Wiley Tuttle is one of the members of the ground crew," she said, handing Beulah another clip out of the bowl in her lap. "Neither Miss Dare nor Mr. Hart guessed that he had any experience as a wingwalker or a parachute jumper. But it turns out that he had been wingwalking with a flying circus that went broke a couple of months ago. He signed on with the Dare Devils, hoping to get a chance to strut his stuff."

"He had plenty of stuff to strut," Aunt Hetty said admiringly. "One minute that young fella is way up there in the sky, dancing around on the airplane wing like it's a ballroom floor. And then the next minute he flies off that wing like a bird with his arms out." She raised her arms to demonstrate and Bettina put a hasty hand on her shoulder.

"There now, Miz Little, you don't want me to snip a bit off your ear, do you?"

Aunt Hetty dropped her arms. "And he's falling like a rock, falling and falling and *falling*." She took a deep breath. "And then just when I think he is going to crash into the ground right in front of my very eyes, he pulls a cord and *whomp!* like a lily blooming, that big white parachute opens up. And he lands—*splat!*—right in the middle of Archie Mann's mattress!" She shook her head, disbelieving. "How that young fella could pick out that little tiny mattress to land on is completely beyond me."

"Miss Dare says he's a better wingwalker than Angel Flame," Verna said. She looked up from her magazine. "Of course, his legs aren't as pretty as hers, but he's a lot stronger. He rode the wing through a loop and a spin. Imagine, hanging onto a wing while the plane is flying *upside down*! She said that Angel Flame could never have done that."

Beulah wound a curler over Liz's left ear. "Upside down," she murmured. "I just can't believe these modern marvels. Why, next thing you know, folks'll be wanting to fly to the moon."

"That'll be the day!" Bessie Bloodworth hooted.

"What I want to know," Bettina said, "is what's going to happen to Miss Flame. Is it true that she's in jail in Pensacola?" Peering into the mirror, she patted Aunt Hetty's white hair. "What do you think, Miz Little? Does it look all right to you?" She brushed the back of Aunt Hetty's neck and took off the cape with a flourish. "Here. Tell me what you think." She handed Aunt Hetty a mirror.

"Looks just beautiful, child," Aunt Hetty said, turning so that she could see the back of her head. "Real professional."

"Professional." Bettina beamed. "Thank you, Miz Little. I just love to hear that word. I try so hard to be a professional!"

Verna took Aunt Hetty's place in the barber chair and Aunt Hetty went to sit where Verna had been sitting. "To answer your· question, Bettina, Buddy Norris took Angel Flame—Mabel Hopkins, her real name is—down to Pensacola on the Greyhound. They put her through the lineup and she's been charged. And yes, she's in the jail, for now."

"Mr. Moseley says that Angel will probably hire a lawyer who will try to get her some sort of plea deal," Lizzy added, as Beulah wound another curler. "Whatever happens, she won't be performing with the Dare Devils again. And Miss Dare said that if she has anything to do with it, Angel won't be wingwalking with any of the other flying circuses. She's going to spread the word that Angel can't be trusted."

Roger and Mildred had already talked to Mr. Moseley about pressing extortion charges, but they hadn't yet decided what to do. If Mr. Moseley could get Angel to give back the nine hundred dollars she got under false pretenses, they would probably let the matter drop. But of course, Lizzy didn't say any of this out loud, since it was a legal matter and she never talked about what went on in Mr. Moseley's office.

"I thought Mildred's party was a great success," Bessie Bloodworth remarked, from her place under the electric permanent wave machine.

"Yes, it was," Verna agreed. "A complete success. The weather, the food, everything."

Beulah started on the hair at the back of Lizzy's head. "You looked just beautiful in that gray dress, Liz. And your hair—well, it was just gorgeous, if I do say so myself. I got a really good do on you that time." She smiled at Lizzy in the mirror. "It was a dang shame that Grady Alexander wasn't there to see you."

Lizzy returned the smile. "Poor Grady. I can't believe

that DeeDee Davis did that to him—and she was Miss Congeniality, too!"

"What did DeeDee Davis do to Mr. Alexander?" Bettina asked curiously. She unwound the pink towel from Verna's head. "I don't think I heard about that."

"Why, she stood him up for her old boyfriend, Tookie Turner," Aunt Hetty said. She was leafing through Verna's magazine while she waited for Bettina to do her manicure. "Grady showed up all decked out in his black tie to take her to the party and DeeDee's mother told him that she had eloped with Tookie Tucker just that afternoon."

"Eloped!" Bessie Bloodworth exclaimed. "With Tookie Tucker?" She rolled her eyes. "She'll rue the day she said yes to that young man, you all mark my words."

"Eloped," Bettina murmured. "Poor Mr. Alexander. Must have spoiled his evening."

"Spoiled it so much that he decided not to come to the party," Verna said with an ironic laugh. "Went home and took off his dinner jacket and sulked, was the way I heard it. Doctored himself with a big dose of Mickey LeDoux's medicine." Melba Jean, one of the women who worked in Verna's office, lived next door to the house where Grady lived with his mother, and she and Mrs. Alexander were back-fence buddies.

"A nice piece of humble pie won't do Grady Alexander one bit of harm," Aunt Hetty said firmly. "Don't mean to be hard on him, but that young man thinks he's God's gift to women."

Lizzy wouldn't have admitted it, but she was glad that Grady hadn't shown up at the party with Miss Cotton of Monroeville. It would have completely spoiled what was an otherwise very nice get-together, with great food (the ladies from the Darling Diner had come up with an amazing assortment of tasty dishes), and pleasant company. There was even dancing, to the tune of the Kilgores' Victrola rather than the band Mildred had originally planned to hire. (The cost of the party had begun to worry her, apparently.)

And those five shiners? By Friday afternoon, all five—Mildred's, Lizzy's, Verna's, Miss Dare's, and Roger's—were quite spectacular and sure to raise questions. But just before the party, Mildred had come up with a scheme. She cut up a piece of black cloth and made five eye patches, giving them the rakish look of pirates.

She also made five extras and persuaded Myra May, Raylene Riggs, Aunt Hetty, and Ophelia and Jed Snow to wear them. So there were ten people walking around with black eye patches, none of whom would offer a word of explanation (other than the expected "You should see the other guy"). The eye patches were a big mystery, and the other party guests seemed to be amused by it.

Halfway through the evening, Mildred announced the presentation of the beautiful Texas Star (*Hibiscus coccineus*, as Miss Rodgers' would say), decorated with a big green bow. Lizzy did the honors, Miss Dare gave a polite acceptance speech, and everybody clapped. The next morning, the Texas Star was kind enough to go with a group of the Dahlias to the garden behind their clubhouse, where they planted the *Hibiscus coccineus* and put up a wooden sign, handpainted by Beulah herself, commemorating the grand occasion.

Charlie Dickens came to the ceremony to snap a couple of photographs for the newspaper, but he left as soon as he finished. He seemed silent and unusually out of sorts. He hadn't come to the party, either. Lizzy privately wondered whether his mood had anything to do with the CLOSED sign on Fannie Champaign's hat shop and the blinds that were drawn at Fannie's windows in the flat above the store.

Aunt Hetty turned a page of her magazine. As if she had read Lizzie's mind, she remarked, "Charlie Dickens could do with a slice of humble pie, too."

"Why do you say that, Aunt Hetty?" Beulah asked. She dipped a fluff of cotton into the setting gel and began patting it along each curler, saturating Lizzy's hair. She held the bowl close to Lizzy's head to catch the drips.

"It's because of the way Mr. Dickens behaved at the picture show with Miss Dare," Bettina said severely. She tchtched with her tongue. "Scandalous, if you ask me. And poor Miss Champaign sitting home all alone."

"Does anybody know where she's gone?" Lizzy asked. She closed her eyes as Beulah worked around her forehead with the setting lotion and the cotton. "I'm worried about her."

"She has a sister in Miami and a cousin in Atlanta," Bessie Bloodworth said. "She might have gone there." She sighed. "I can't believe that Charlie Dickens would act like such a louse. Why, he and Fannie were as good as engaged, from what I heard. Why did he do it?"

Nobody knew the answer. But that mystery was eclipsed by a much greater one, which had stunned everyone when they heard about it. It was Myra May Mosswell's introduction of her mother, whose cooking was such a huge hit at the diner: Raylene Riggs, aka Ina Ray Mosswell.

"When I heard that," Bettina said, combing Verna's hair down in the back and trimming with her scissors, "you could have knocked me over with a feather. Imagine finding out that the cook you've just hired is *really* your long-lost mother!"

"Long *dead* mother," Verna corrected her. "That's what Myra May thought, anyway. That's what her father told her—and the aunt who raised her."

"What I don't understand," Lizzy said, "is why some of the older folks around town didn't recognize her."

"Charlie Dickens' sister Edna Fay thought she looked familiar," Verna said. "Myra May told me that. But she didn't recognize her."

Beulah set the lotion on the counter. "Of course," she said, considering, "Ina Ray left Darling thirty-some years ago. It's hard to remember what a person looks like if you haven't seen her for thirty years."

"Especially if your memory isn't very good." Bessie Bloodworth laughed a little. "Like mine."

"Especially," Bettina said, "if you think she's been dead all that time."

"Especially if her husband and her sister-in-law have both *insisted* that she's dead," Verna said. "Not once but dozens of times."

"But you saw through all that, didn't you, Aunt Hetty?" Lizzy said, catching Aunt Hetty's glance in the mirror. "You recognized Ina Ray right off."

"Not right off," Aunt Hetty admitted, closing the magazine on her finger. "It took a minute. But the more I looked at that lady, the more like Myra May she looked, and then I had it. But of course, I had the advantage of knowing that Ina Ray wasn't actually dead. Belle Mosswell confessed that to me years ago and made me swear never to let on. Poor Belle. She felt guilty about that lie right up to the day she died, but of course her brother made her do it." Aunt Hetty narrowed her eyes. "Belle Mosswell never could stand up to that man—she let him walk all over her from the time they were children. I don't blame Ina Ray for leaving. A pity she didn't take her baby with her, but I understand. Times were hard back then, almost as bad as they are now."

"I hear that Myra May's mother is a real good cook,"

Bettina said, fluffing her fingers through Verna's hair. "Is she going to stay in Darling and help out at the diner?"

"She says she's going to settle down here," Aunt Hetty replied. "She and Myra May are getting acquainted. She loves Violet. And she downright adores little Cupcake. Says it's like having a grandbaby."

Beulah put the rest of the curlers in a drawer. "But where's she going to live? I've been in Myra May's flat. It's pretty small, especially with the baby. They couldn't put a mouse in there."

"You haven't heard?" Lizzy asked. "Raylene and Pauline DuBerry have struck up a friendship, and Pauline has asked her if she'd like to live upstairs in the DuBerry house. Raylene is going to pay rent, which will give Pauline enough extra money so she can hire somebody to help her clean the cabins and do the laundry. Pauline's getting on, you know. She doesn't have any children and with Floyd gone, it'll be good for her to have somebody living in the house. She's even agreed to let Raylene use her car to drive to work."

"Raylene," Verna said thoughtfully. "So we're not going to call her Ina Ray?"

"Raylene says that Ina Ray's dead," Aunt Hetty said flatly. "She doesn't want to be Ina Ray anymore. Everybody's supposed to call her Raylene—except for Myra May, who can call her Mama any time she wants. Violet, too. And Cupcake is already calling her Grandma."

Beulah unbuttoned Liz's pink cape and took it off. "There, Liz—you're all done. Let's put you under the hair dryer." Lizzy followed her to the chair and sat down, while Beulah adjusted the big metal bonnet over her head and flicked the switch. The machine began to hum and warm air swished down around Lizzy's ears. "And I just made something I want all you ladies to try out," Beulah added. She disappeared in the direction of the kitchen.

"I think it's so sweet about Myra May and her mother," Bettina said softly. "Such a lovely reunion—especially after so many years apart. A happy ending, don't you think?" She swiped at one eye with the back of her hand. "Makes me tear up just to think of it."

Verna clucked her tongue. "Bettina, you are just so sentimental."

Bettina's forehead puckered in a puzzled frown. "Well, what's so bad about being sentimental? I mean, if you've got feelings in your heart, you should show them, isn't that right?"

"But you can't *know* if this is an ending," Verna said in a practical tone. "I mean, as far as Myra May and Raylene are concerned, maybe it's a beginning. Or somewhere in the middle. And maybe it won't be so happy. Maybe they won't like each other as much as they think. Maybe—"

"Verna, Verna," Aunt Hetty said, shaking her head darkly. "You are the most distrustful person the good lord ever allowed to walk on this green earth. Isn't she, Lizzy?"

"What?" Lizzy smiled at Aunt Hetty. "I can't hear a thing with this hair dryer going."

Beulah came out of the kitchen with a spoon and a small crockery bowl of a fluffy white mixture. "All right, ladies," she said. "I want you to hold out your hands. I'll give you each a spoonful of my new magic hand cream. I want you to rub it in and tell me how it feels." She went around to each of them with the bowl and the spoon.

It was cool, Lizzy thought as she rubbed the mixture into her skin. "It feels smooth," she said. "And rich."

"Good on these old hands," Aunt Hetty agreed, rubbing.

"Not at all sticky," Verna said in an approving tone. "So many of the hand creams I've tried feel sticky."

Bessie sniffed her hands. "Smells good, too. Smells like Blue Waltz."

"You guessed it, Bessie," Beulah said happily. "I added just a couple of drops of Blue Waltz, from the five-and-dime, to make it smell pretty. But before you leave, you'll want to rinse it off."

"Rinse it off?" Verna wanted to know. "But why?"

"Because you might attract flies," Beulah said. "It's mostly mashed potatoes."

"Mashed potatoes!" the Dahlias cried in unison.

Beulah nodded smiling. "Well, you know my motto, ladies. We may not have much, but we get beautiful when we use what we've got."

The Garden Gate

GETTING BEAUTIFUL FOR PENNIES

BY MISS ELIZABETH LACY
DARLING *DISPATCH* FRIDAY, JULY 22, 1932

Every woman wants to be beautiful, but in these hard times, most women don't have a lot of money to spend on their appearance. If nickels and dimes are scarce at your house (and the dollars even scarcer), try these tips and tricks, contributed by the friendly ladies of the Darling Dahlias, who know a thing or two about staying beautiful.

Cucumber and Mint Cleanser

Bessie Bloodworth grows cucumber and mint in her garden and aloe on her back porch. She buys the glycerin at Lima's Drugstore.

3 tablespoons fresh mint leaves, chopped
1 cup water
3 tablespoons fresh cucumber juice
2 tablespoons aloe vera gel, scraped from a fresh leaf
1 tablespoon glycerin

In a nonreactive pan over medium heat, brew the mint leaves in the water for 5 to 8 minutes, to make a strong tea. When it's cool, strain out the leaves, add the cucumber juice, the aloe vera gel, and the glycerin and mix well. To use, wet a clean cloth with the cleanser and rub lightly over your skin. Store the leftovers in the icebox to keep from spoiling.

Honey Facial Cleanser

Alice Walker's husband Arnold keeps bees, and Alice makes a facial cleanser with their honey.

½ cup honey
2 tablespoons mild shampoo (such as Rexall's or Palmolive, from Lima's Drugstore)
1 cup glycerin

Put everything in a bowl and mix it up together. You don't have to keep this one in the icebox.

Rose Skin Toner

Earlynne Biddle has lots of roses. She saves the petals and hips and uses them in the old recipes handed down from her mother and grandmother. This is one of her grandmother's recipes. Earlynne says you don't have to keep this in the icebox but it will be nice and cool if you do.

3 tablespoons fresh rose petals
4 tablespoons fresh sage leaves

2 tablespoons rosemary
1 cup white wine vinegar

Put your clean plant material in a quart jar. Heat the vinegar and pour it over the leaves. Put a lid on the jar and let it sit for about ten days, shaking every day. Strain out the leaves. Apply to your skin with your fingertips or cotton.

Bessie's Bath Powder

Bessie Bloodworth has been making her own bath powder ever since Mr. Lima raised the price on her favorite brand. She keeps this in a jar with a lid on it and shakes it up every couple of days to keep it from getting lumpy. But if it does, she says you can just mash the lumps with a fork.

1 cup cornstarch
½ cup baking soda

Mix it up in a bowl. If you want a little scent, add a tablespoon of ground cloves and a tablespoon of mace. Or get some dried rose petals from Earlynne, grind them up fine, and add them. Bessie says to dust a little into your shoes, as a foot deodorant.

Beeswax and Honey Lip Balm

Lucy Murphy reports that this lip balm is better even than Tangee, because it stays on longer. She gets her beeswax and honey from Alice Ann Walker, who will be glad to save you some, too—*all you have to do is ask. The baby oil is fifteen cents a bottle but it's good for lots of other things: on squeaky hinges, as a furniture polish (mix with a little lemon), and as a cuticle softener. But if that's too pricey, Lucy says just melt a couple spoonfuls of Vaseline with the beeswax. It won't smell as good but it will work just fine.*

4 tablespoons grated beeswax
2 tablespoons Johnson's baby oil
1 tablespoon honey

Melt the beeswax in a double boiler. Add the baby oil and stir well. Line a little box with wax paper (like the little box of wooden matches that Mrs. Hancock sells for a nickel). Pour the mixture into it and let it cool. Then you can take it out and leave it on your dressing table.

Banana Hair Conditioner

Myra May Mosswell, at the diner, usually has a banana or two that's past its prime. If it's too far gone for banana pudding, she uses it to make a hair and scalp conditioner.

1 ripe banana, mashed
1 tablespoon honey
1 egg

Mix everything together until it's nice and creamy. Before you shampoo, wet your hair and massage the conditioner into your hair and scalp. Wrap a warm towel around your head and leave it on for about 20 minutes. Rinse well and shampoo as usual. This makes enough for one treatment. Don't try to save any leftovers.

Beulah's Setting Lotions

Beulah Trivette has been using her own homemade setting lotions at the Beauty Bower. She has two recipes she's willing to share with you, but she says her best Beauty Bower Secret Formula Setting Lotion is still a secret. We're working on that.

Quince Seed Setting Lotion

Seeds from 1 fresh quince (that will usually be 20 to 25)
¼ cup water

In a bowl, cover the seeds with water. Let them soak for 2 to 3 hours. The longer they soak, the thicker the lotion. Strain out the seeds.

Flaxseed Setting Lotion

1 cup flaxseed
3 cups water

Simmer flaxseed and water together for a few minutes until it's about as thick as you want it. Put through a strainer and throw the seeds away. If the mixture thickens too much, thin it with a little water.

Whipped Cream Body Mask

Ophelia Snow admits that she's never tried this but it sounds like it would be just wonderful, if you happen to have an extra cup of heavy cream that you're not putting to some other use, such as strawberry shortcake. (Ophelia says her kids would rather have the cream on their shortcake, rather than on their mama, and anyway, she never has fifteen minutes to loll around with whipped cream all over her.)

1 cup fresh heavy cream

Whip until soft peaks form. Cover your body with the cream, rubbing it into the dry, scaly spots. Leave it on for 15 minutes. Rinse off in a warm bath and pat dry.

Fig Facial Mask

Elizabeth Lacy's mother has a fig tree in her back yard. If there are any figs left over after making fig jam, Mrs. Lacy uses them for a facial.

One ripe fig
1 tablespoon honey

Cut the fig in two and scrape out the soft fruit into a bowl.

Mash with a spoon until smooth. Add the honey and mix well. Spread it on your skin and go sit on the front porch for five or ten minutes. Rinse.

Mashed Potato Hand Cream

This formula for beautiful hands also comes from Beulah Trivette, who has tested it on her clients at the Beauty Bower. They give the recipe a big thumbs-up!

2 potatoes, cooked and mashed
1 tablespoon of cream or top milk
1 tablespoon glycerin
1 tablespoon aloe vera gel

Blend everything together into a smooth, thick paste. Massage into your hands. After ten minutes, rinse. May be stored in your icebox for several days. Be sure to label the bowl so the late-night snackers in your family don't get into it. Aloe vera is a little bit . . . well, laxative.

Clove Mouthwash

Miss Dorothy Rogers says that she has used this mouthwash for decades and recommends it highly. It will sweeten your breath. She also recommends Syzygium aromaticum *(clove) oil for a toothache. (Ask Mr. Lima for this—he keeps it behind the counter so he can tell people they are not supposed to eat it or get it on their skin. But the whole ones are okay.)*

    2 tablespoons whole *Syzygium aromaticum* (cloves)
    2 cups boiling water

Cover the *Syzgium aromaticum* with the boiling water. Cool. Strain into a clean jar and store in the icebox. Rinse your mouth morning and evening.

Dry Feet Remedy

Verna Tidwell says that if you suffer from dry skin on your feet, she has the perfect solution.

Before you go to bed, rub Vaseline on your toes and soles and put on a pair of socks. Tomorrow's toes will be a whole lot softer. You can also use it to scrub the dry skin off: add a couple of spoonfuls of cornmeal or sugar to the Vaseline and rub hard with a washcloth.

Carrot-and-Egg Facial Mask

Fannie Champaign suggests a carrot facial mask to keep the skin young looking.

    3 large carrots, cooked and mashed
    1 egg
    1 teaspoon cider vinegar
    4 tablespoons honey

Mix together and apply to the skin. Fannie says that since this mixture is bright orange, you might want to stay out of sight while you're wearing it. Rinse with cool water after 10 minutes.

Molasses Nail Soak

For gardeners, Mildred Kilgore recommends a molasses nail soak to prevent dryness, soften cuticles, and promote nail health.

2 tablespoons molasses
1 tablespoon cider vinegar
¼ cup warm water

Mix together as a soak for fingernails. Ten minutes a day will make a big difference, Mildred says. But she adds that you really ought to wear gloves when you are working in the garden. She does.

Recipes

*Any Southerner will tell you that the miracle of the loaves
and fishes was the only church supper in history that
didn't include fried chicken.*
—RICK MCDANIEL, *AN IRRESISTIBLE
HISTORY OF SOUTHERN FOOD*

The foods and recipes featured in this book illustrate the range
of foods—traditional dishes and dishes that use more modern
ingredients—that appeared on Southern tables during the
early 1930s. You will notice (or perhaps you will remember)
that cooks of the era used plenty of animal fat (pork was cheap
and plentiful, so the fat was usually bacon grease or lard),
sugar, and salt. I haven't made any effort to substitute, but you
can experiment with your own low-fat, low-sugar, low-salt sub-
stitutes. Or maybe you'll just want to read the recipes and
reflect on the way we cooked and ate before we became health-
conscious. Recipes for other foods mentioned in this series may
be found at www.darlingdahlias.com.

Aunt Hetty Little's Pecan Jumbles

*According to the Oxford English Dictionary, the word "jum-
bles" goes back to the word "gimbal," a doubled or twisted*

ring—*a kind of double pretzel. The first published occurrence of it is in a recipe flavored with aniseed, published in* The English Housewife, *by Gervase Markham in 1615. An 1857 version includes cinnamon, nutmeg, and caraway seeds. By the late 1800s, cooks stopped going to the trouble of rolling the dough and pretzeling it, but the name stuck. This version uses evaporated milk, which was widely promoted in the 1920s and 30s as better-than-breast milk for baby. It appears in many recipes from the era.*

½ cup soft shortening
1 cup brown sugar
½ cup white sugar
2 eggs
1 cup undiluted evaporated milk
1 teaspoon vanilla
2 ¾ cup flour
½ teaspoon soda
1 teaspoon salt
1 cup chopped pecans

Mix shortening, sugars, and eggs until blended and creamy. Mix milk and vanilla, and gradually stir into shortening-sugar-egg mixture. Stir in flour, soda, salt, and nuts. Drop by teaspoon on ungreased cookie sheet. Bake until set and browned.

Raylene Riggs' Sweet Potato Meringue Pie

Meringue pies—the meringue piled high and deep, swooped and sculpted and topped with tiny brown curls—are the

*dessert stars of the Southern dinner table. This one features
sweet potatoes* (Ipomoea batatas), *an important staple,
grown in every Southern garden and making an appearance
in everything from soup to dessert. The pie can be made with
or without coconut, which was available in the 1930s both
in canned and packaged form.*

2 cups cooked, mashed sweet potatoes
3 egg yolks, well-beaten
3 tablespoons melted butter
½ cup sugar
1 teaspoon salt
½ teaspoon ground nutmeg
½ teaspoon vanilla extract
⅓ cup shredded coconut, toasted
1 cup evaporated milk
1 unbaked 9-inch pie shell

Preheat oven to 325°F. Mix together the mashed sweet
potatoes and egg yolks. Add the butter, sugar, salt, nutmeg,
vanilla, coconut, and milk. Pour mixture into pie shell and
bake at 325°F about 35 to 40 minutes, until the filling
is set.

Meringue

3 egg whites
6 tablespoons sugar

Beat egg whites until soft peaks form. Add sugar, a tablespoon at a time, and beat until stiff peaks form. Spread
meringue on hot filling, sealing to edges. Return pie to

oven and bake an additional 12 to 15 minutes or until golden brown.

Grits and Sausage Casserole

Grits (also called hominy) was likely introduced to the colonists at Jamestown around 1607 by the Algonquin Indians, who called it rockahominy, meaning hulled corn—hence hominy. The word grits comes from the Old English grytt (bran) or greot (ground) and is usually treated as a singular noun. The colonists made it by soaking corn in lye made from wood ash until the hulls floated off, then pounding and drying it. Stone-ground grits is usually preferred to instant or quick-cook grits because the germ is still intact, but it has a shorter shelf life and is best used quickly after it is ground.

3 cups water
1 cup uncooked grits
3 tablespoons butter
1 cup shredded Cheddar cheese
½ pound ground pork sausage
¼ cup chopped green onion tops
¼ cup chopped red pepper
6 eggs
¼ cup milk
salt and pepper to taste
2 tablespoons butter
½ cup shredded Cheddar cheese

Preheat oven to 350°F. In a large saucepan, bring the water to a boil. Stir in grits. Reduce heat, cover, and simmer about

5 minutes, until liquid has been absorbed. Add butter and cheese, stirring until melted. Set aside.

In a skillet over medium-high heat, cook the sausage, onions, and pepper until the sausage is browned. Drain off all but two tablespoons of the fat. Stir the sausage mixture into the grits. Set aside.

In a bowl, beat together the eggs and milk and pour into the skillet. Lightly scramble, then mix into the grits. Season with salt and pepper to taste.

Pour the grits mixture into a prepared baking dish. Dot with butter and top with cheese. Bake 30 minutes in the preheated oven, until lightly browned. Serves 6.

Slow-Cooked Pulled Pork with White Sauce

In the South, the meat of choice has always been pork and there isn't much of the pig that hasn't made its way onto the breakfast and dinner tables. Pigs were easy to keep and cheap to feed, and piglets born in spring were fair-sized porkers by the first freeze, when butchering usually occurred. The animal produced roasts, hams, bacon, chops, and ribs, as well as fatback, headcheese (from the head, feet, and ears), and liver—not to mention sausage from the leftover bits, lard from the fat, and chitterlings from the . . . well, intestines. Brains were fried with eggs, the tail was cooked with rice. Everything that wasn't eaten fresh was dried, pickled, salt-cured, and/or smoked.

Pulled pork was usually made with fresh pork, cooked (barbequed or simmered) long and slowly enough so that it "pulls to pieces" and is easily shredded. It may be served over rice or noodles or in a bun, as a sandwich. In some regions, the meat is topped with a tomato-based sauce. In

Alabama, the sauce most often used is a tangy mayonnaise-horseradish-vinegar sauce. This recipe uses a slow cooker.

2 pounds pork shoulder (also called pork butt, Boston butt, shoulder roast)
¾ cup apple cider vinegar
½ cup water
3 tablespoons brown sugar
2 teaspoons salt
1 teaspoon freshly ground black pepper
1 teaspoon onion powder
½ teaspoon dry mustard
½ teaspoon ground red pepper
½ teaspoon chili powder
½ teaspoon garlic powder

Place the meat in a slow cooker. Mix the remaining ingredients in a nonreactive saucepan and bring to a boil. Pour over the pork, cover, and cook on low for 4 to 5 hours, or until the meat is tender. Remove and shred, pulling apart with two forks. Return to the slow cooker and keep warm until serving. To serve with rice or noodles, place pork in a serving dish and pour cooking liquid over it. Alternatively, serve with a dish of white sauce. To serve as a sandwich, pile meat on a lightly toasted bun, topped with white sauce (not too much—you don't want to drown it).

White Sauce

½ cup mayonnaise
2 tablespoons white vinegar
1 teaspoon fresh lemon juice
1–2 teaspoons grated horseradish

½ teaspoon pepper
Dash salt

Combine ingredients. Refrigerate unused sauce.

Cheese Custard Pie, Served at Mildred Kilgore's Party

In 1931, Mrs. Irma von Starkloff Rombauer was newly widowed and in need of money. The celebrated St. Louis hostess struck on the idea of turning her personal recipes and cooking techniques into a book and self-published The Joy of Cooking: A Compilation of Reliable Recipes with a Casual Culinary Chat. *The rest, as they say, is history.*

Rombauer's recipe for Cheese Custard Pie (p. 60 in the 1931 edition) may be the first published recipe for a quiche to appear in an American cookbook. The recipe, she writes in a note, comes from a "vile-tempered cook named Marguerite" that the family employed in Switzerland. The Cheese Custard Pie was "always served in solitary state," its flavors varying with "Marguerite's moods and her supply of cheese." This is Raylene Riggs' heartier version, which will be more familiar to us.

1 deep-dish pie crust
½ pound ground pork sausage
½ cup chopped onion
¼ cup chopped red bell pepper
1 ½ cup grated sharp Cheddar cheese
1 tablespoon flour
3 eggs, beaten
1 cup evaporated milk

1 tablespoon minced parsley
¾ teaspoon salt
¼ teaspoon garlic
¼ teaspoon pepper
Paprika

Heat oven to 350°F. Pre-bake the pie shell for about 10 to
12 minutes. Cool. Reduce oven to 325°F. In a skillet, brown
the sausage, breaking it up into small pieces. Drain, except
for 1 tablespoon fat. In the same skillet, in the reserved fat,
sauté onion and pepper. Drain. Combine cheese and flour.
Stir in sausage, onion, and pepper. Spread on the bottom of
the pre-baked crust. Combine remaining ingredients and
pour over sausage mixture. Bake 45 minutes. Let cool about
10 minutes before slicing.

Resources

Here are a few of the many books I have found useful in my research for the Darling Dahlias series:

Around the Southern Table, by Sarah Belk. The recipes are modern; the book is valuable for its historical notes.

Biscuits, Spoonbread, and Sweet Potato Pie, by Bill Neal. The Southern heritage of breads and sweets, with historical commentary.

Daily Life in the United States 1920–1940, by David E. Kyvig. How Americans lived in the Roaring Twenties, the Depression era.

Dry Goods, Butler Brothers 1934 general merchandise catalog. What people were wearing and using during the early thirties.

Everyday Fashions of the Thirties, As Pictured in Sears Catalogs, edited by Stella Blum. Helpful period descriptions of clothing styles, fabrics, materials.

The Happy Bottom Riding Club: The Life and Times of Pancho Barnes, by Lauren Kessler. Barnes was a barnstormer, racer, cross-country flier, Hollywood stunt pilot, and the "fastest woman on earth." She was a model for Lily Dare.

Month-by-Month Gardening in Alabama, by Bob Polomski. What Alabama gardeners might be doing at different seasons of the year.

On the Wing: Jessie Woods and the Flying Aces Air Circus, by Ann L. Cooper. The real-life account of a woman wingwalker and owner of a flying circus in the 1930s.